About the Author

Peter Theoharis is an expatriate of Imvros (Gökçeada) Turkey, who, like all his fellow Turko-Greeks, was compelled to leave country and home and seek a future elsewhere.

He attended Zografion High School and the University of Istanbul. He is a retired hospitality executive and lives in Kanas City.

Spanning more than two decades, this tumultuous epic is centered on the quadrangle of Imvros (Gökçēada), ancient Troy, Istanbul and USA.

This is a novel of historical animosity, ethnic persecution, socio-political struggle and religious conflict. Caught in a web of an interracial and interreligious romance, the protagonists seek to ameliorate the shortcomings of human frailty, through love, compassion, love of country, love of wisdom and love of freedom.

This story is also about the shortcomings of religion, with all its petty, dogmatic differences that lead to war, injustice, discrimination and rapacious behavior. If Jehovah, God and Allah are one and the same, humanity's failure to grasp the Divine is the truest form of insanity.

Dedication

To my departed parents,

my family

and

to my fellow Imvrians,

who have dispersed to the four corners of the world;

and

to the peoples of

Greece and Turkey,

who I implore to bury their past and embrace

reconciliation and coexistence.

Theoharis

Prologue

Süheylā, the Muslim Madonna, the Turkish princess, has wrapped herself around Costa like an octopus. Her aroma of mint, basil and Ottoman roses has invaded his senses with a narcotic effect. "Nothing will ever separate us" she vows. "We are blood-brother and sister."

A little girl, Nilüfer—no more than two, dazed and bleeding—is crying for her mom. Their rescue helicopter had been shot down over the mountains of Kurdistan; she is the only survivor. A family of fleeing nomads scoops her up, and she disappears into their Kurdish refugee camps for three years.

Table of Contents

Chapter 1: The Minarets of Santa Sophia

With Süheylā's farewell letter weighing heavily on his mind, Costa arrived at the bus station, feeling lost. The love of his life had disappeared into the thin air, and his world had turned ugly. It was only a few months ago that they promised to marry each other and spend their honeymoon in Austria waltzing through the halls of Vienna.

Finally the bus rolled out of the station, taking Costa along. Istanbul was fading away, fast. The thought that he might never see his beloved city again choked him to tears. He did not even want to contemplate such a possibility with Süheylā. As the bus made its way through the heavy traffic, he had the strangest of visions. The four minarets of Santa Sophia looked like giant scimitars ready to cut the glorious building to pieces, while the great mosques shadowed the city's skyline like ghosts on parade.

I am not feeling any remorse for leaving this country. It treats its minority citizens like dogs. How can anyone have any love for a place like this? As the bus made its way along the narrow road, he watched the ground go by and became sick. Yes, he had planned to leave Turkey sooner rather than later, but never under such conditions and never without Süheylā. He leaned back in his seat and unfolded the newspaper he'd bought at a kiosk. *This might be the last time I will ever read anything in Turkish.* Immediately, his eyes caught the main headline:

Chapter 1: The Minarets of Santa Sophia

"Two Policemen are dead"

In a gun battle with terrorists at "the Meyhane[1] Diyarbakir," one of whom is presumed to be the ringleader, Zelal Hanum[2].

According to the article, this café was a hashish house and revolutionary pesthole at which unsavory characters dealt in clandestine activities. The two brave police officers died in a gun battle with the occupants of the café during a raid. When other police forces rushed to assist, a fire broke out, and Zelal Hanum and her accomplices burned to death.

Praise and accolades to the security forces for their service to the motherland Turkey . . .

With hands trembling, he read the rest of the article, all the while with the desire to scream. Zelal was one of the most caring people he'd ever met. She and her friends gave him food and shelter and nursed him back to health from his injuries he'd suffered when student radicals had attacked him. She had also assisted him financially to bribe his way out of the country. Zelal's death was a terrible loss, and if he ever hoped to find Süheylā, she was his only reliable contact in Turkey. The article reeked of suspicion. In all probability, it was all a setup by the Secret Turkish Police.

An elderly woman sitting next to him noticed his tears and asked him if he was all right. He touched her hand and closed his eyes, promising himself to throw a stone behind[3] him the minute he stepped on foreign soil.

Sounds of shuffling feet caused Costa to jump in his seat—he must have slept. The border guards were herding his fellow passengers into the Customs house as if it were

---

1. A typical Turkish entertainment establishment.

2. "Mrs. Zelal" or "Madam Zelal."

3. The symbolic act of revulsion for a place that does not merit love.

a pen for cattle. Gingerly he stepped out of the bus. With his eyes diverted, he was hoping to avoid another confrontation with a Turk.

"Hey you!" barked one of the guards. "Don't look so dumb. Pick up your shit box and stand over there."

He did as instructed and carried his suitcase to the forming line. He was last, behind the old woman who'd sat next to him on the bus, and a young mom with two little girls; she seemed tense and worried. The older girl was clutching a pillow with a crocheted face of a tiger. The other one was holding onto her mom's dress as if it were a lifeline. Slowly they inched their way into the Customs building.

"Move it! Move it!" the guards kept shouting. It was almost twilight, and they were in a hurry.

The group neared the building, the border in full view. *The Promised Land* was just across the bridge. "Hellas[4]," they whispered. The old woman crossed herself and thanked the Almighty for bringing her close to freedom; the gesture did not escape the eyes of the vengeful guards.

One of them nudged her with the butt of his machine gun. "Wait until you get over there to pray to your stupid god. This is Turkey, understand?"

The frail woman cowered in fright. With tears streaming down her cheeks, she stared into the void.

Soon after, it was her turn to face the burly inspector. With a huge mustache and two enormous eyes bulging from their sockets, the chief inspector glared. "Common woman, open your suitcase," his dissonant voice like a laser.

This is an ugly human being. Costa turned toward the old woman and placed her suitcase on the inspection table.

---

4. Greece.

The inspector tried to open the latch. "The key! The key!" he barked. "Don't you know to leave it unlocked?!"

The old woman searched her pocketbook, but her hands shook uncontrollably.

The inspector lost patience. With a forceful sigh, he took out a set of pliers from his desk and twisted the latch off. "Now let's see what you got here." He stuck his hand into the middle of the suitcase. "What is this?" he shouted at the old woman, waving a small icon in her face. "Don't you know that the exportation of artwork is prohibited? This item belongs to Turkey; now go," he hissed.

Momentarily speechless, the old woman gaped. The icon of the Virgin Mary was her protector, to whom she prayed every night before bedtime. With agonized words, she pleaded, "please, sir—oh, please—let me have my icon."

"No!"

Costa raised his voice and glared. "That is a five lira[5] icon at the bazaar, Inspector. Be a charitable Muslim and give it back to the lady."

The inspector scowled at Costa and flung the icon into the woman's suitcase. "Get out of my sight," he growled, "and don't come back."

Costa helped the old woman close her suitcase. She gave Costa a bitter smile and slowly dragged her suitcase out the door.

Next in line was the young mom with her two little girls. The border guards took her suitcases apart, flinging the children's clothes onto the inspection tables, much of them falling onto the floor. The inspector questioned the young woman as if she were some major smuggler. Not satisfied with her answers, he pointed at her two little girls and asked if she had hidden anything in their clothing.

---

5. Equivalent to 50 cents.

"I have not," she whispered. "Why would I do a thing like that?"

"I don't believe you," he snarled. Looking at the older girl, he commanded her to walk toward him. "Let me have your pillow," he ordered acidly.

Costa sidestepped from his spot, asked the little girl for her pillow, and handed it to the inspector.

"I know you giaours[6]," mumbled the inspector. "You hide property that you stole from the Turkish nation in your pillows." He took a box cutter from his desk drawer and sliced across the crocheted tiger's face, nearly cutting the small pillow in half. Impassively, he flipped the pillow upside down and shook it, letting the goose feathers fall out onto the floor until not a single one was left in it.

The little girl screeched hysterically; that was likely her favorite pillow, and it was now destroyed.

Costa shook his head and grimaced; this inspector had the heart of a stone.

Satisfied with his brilliance, the inspector flung the empty pillow at the little girl. "You and your mother can go on now. You've caused us enough trouble already." He ordered the mother to pick up her strewn belongings and shove off.

She obeyed immediately, moving frantically about the floor to collect her articles while the little girls tugged at her, crying. Having herded everyone through the door, the inspector sat and lit a cigarette.

It was Costa's turn.

"Your passport," he demanded, puffing away.

Costa handed it to him.

"Why do you have a two-week sailing permit?"

"That is all the military would grant me."

---

6. Infidels, pigs, monkeys, slaves, second-class citizens—a term used by most Turks at that time against all minorities of Turkey, such as Armenians, Jews and mostly Greeks. It approximates "nigger."

"How much foreign exchange do you have?"

"Six hundred German Marks."

"Why German marks? The rule is two-hundred dollars."

"There were no dollars available at the banks."

"You have to carry two-hundred dollars to leave the country. It is state policy."

"The six-hundred marks are an equivalent exchange."

"I know that, giaour. Why do you think I am in this position? Open your shit box." The inspector did not seem to have much interest in it, but he noticed Costa's university report cards.

"Why are you taking these report cards with you?"

"In case I enroll into a foreign university."

"But you only have two-week permission. You are lying. You are not planning to come back, are you?"

Costa got angry; this was adding insult to injury. "Turkey does not want any of us giaours back, does she, inspector?"

The inspector jumped from his chair. "How dare you insult Turkey?! Do you want to go back to your stupid Imvros[7] right now? Watch your mouth or I will send you back to your fucking mother in your shit box. Take off the jacket—and your shirt, too."

"What for?"

"Because I said so."

"I have nothing to hide."

"Take them off, wise guy," he barked with eyes ready to pop.

As Costa took off his jacket and started unbuttoning his shirt, the inspector yelled louder, "come on, hurry up, you are keeping your giaour relatives waiting."

Noticing the medallion hanging from his neck, the inspector moved closer and yanked it away with its chain.

---

7. A large island located in front of the straits of Dardanelles. It has been renamed Gökçeada.

It was the medallion Süheylā had given him in Kilyos Beach, their most memorable night.

"Please, sir, that is my most cherished thing in the world. Here, take my six-hundred German marks; just give me my medallion back."

"You are not allowed to take any gold out of our country, giaour. This is state property," howled the inspector, while studying the medallion. When he saw the etching of Santa Sophia, he frowned. "You are like all other giaours. You worship Aya Sofya[8] but you don't give a damn about the Sultan Ahmet[9]." He tried to read the inscription in the back, but when he saw the Greek lettering, he gave up. "Giaour crap," he mumbled and threw it in his drawer. "Scram," he shouted, tossing the jacket back at Costa's face.

Costa's mind went numb; getting that medallion back was the only thing that mattered. He eyed the inspector's gun. He wanted to shoot the bastard and as many guards as he could, but he would surely be killed in the bargain. Surprising himself, he lunged at the drawer and grabbed the medallion. Immediately, the guards wrestled him to the floor. When they could not pry the medallion from his clenched fist, one of them took out his club and slammed it across Costa's hand. Costa winced in pain—resistance was futile; there were too many. Trembling with rage, he stood up and retrieved his suitcase.

"Get the fuck out of Turkey, giaour," yelled the inspector after Costa.

Giaour, giaour, giaour. How many times would a Greek like Costa have to endure this gross insult from so many ignorant Turks? He glared back at the inspector. Rubbing the bastard's face into rock salt slowly until he bled to death would have given him great pleasure. *Walk*

---

8. Turkish for Hagia Sphia

9. The Blue Mosque.

forward, he mumbled to himself, *and never look back at this dreg of a country.*

Just as he sat down in his seat on the bus, the gorilla inspector, followed by a couple of his lackeys, charged into the bus looking for Costa.

"You, over there, you are under arrest. Get out."

He grabbed Costa by the collar of his shirt, pushed him through the bus walkway, and shoved him out the door. One of his lackeys ordered the driver to open the baggage compartment of the bus and pull out Costa's suitcase. They marched him back into the Customs building and pushed him into a steel cage. It was a holding cell without a toilet or windows—the stench of urine was overpowering. A flickering light bulb dangling from the center of the ceiling and a filthy cot in the corner with blotches of dried bloodstains were the only things in the room. *This was going to be ugly.* He would rather sit on the floor, but dozens of roaches scurried about it in protest. Filthy or not, he lay on the cot and laced his fingers behind his head. With Süheylā, his Turkish princess gone, his *Muslim Madonna*, he couldn't care less what happens to himself now.

Chapter 2: Close But No Freedom

Costa woke up on the filthy cot thirsty and in need of a bathroom. There was no one around so he hollered as loud as he could. Finally a guard appeared.

"I need to go to the bathroom right now," he pleaded.

"Calm down," said the guard kindly as he unlocked the cage. By force of habit, the guard walked behind Costa, keeping his hand on his gun holster. He pointed with his finger. "Walk," he ordered.

The bathroom was at the end of the hallway. It was even smellier than his cage.

When Costa came out of the bathroom, the guard asked, "What are you in for?"

"I have no idea," replied Costa, scratching his head "Can I have a bottle of water, please?"

The guard locked him back in his cage, saying he would return. Costa sat on the cot and stared at the floor. His only thoughts were of Süheylā.

The guard's voice startled him. "Here is your water," he said and handed Costa two bottles of water through the door's iron ribs.

"Thank you," said Costa, sensing a touch of kindness.

"You have been arrested for conspiracy," said the guard. "According to the warrant, you have been plotting against the state."

"That is a lie!" Costa shrieked. "Your government is making things up!"

The guard shrugged. "You are complaining to the wrong man," he said compassionately as he walked away.

Costa called the guard back. "I have six-hundred marks in my pocket. You can have half if you let me make a phone call."

"Are you crazy? I can't let you do that."

"Why not? I saw a telephone at the end of that hallway."

"Okay. Give me the money first."

Costa counted out three-hundred marks and handed them to the guard. The guard opened the door and let Costa walk to the phone. Hoping for the best, he dialed. He was calling the chief of the secret police of Istanbul, whom Costa had befriended by sheer luck. His heart leaped when Mr. Akduman answered.

"Mr. Akduman, this is Costa Rigas. I am in deep trouble."

"What kind of trouble, Costa?" asked Mr. Akduman.

"I have been arrested for conspiracy. They have locked me up in Edirne at the Customs house."

"That should never have happened. Are you all right?"

"As well as I can be under the circumstances."

"Stay calm and don't do anything foolish."

Before Costa could say anything else, Mr. Akduman hung up. The guard marched him back to his cage and locked the door.

"Are you really a Kurdish co-conspirator?" he guard asked.

"Where did you hear that?"

The guard reached into his pocket and pulled out a folded piece of paper. "Read it," he said and handed it to him.

By the order of the Turkish State, Costa Rigas is to be arrested for the following charges:

A: Conspiring with Kurdish terrorists

B: Engaging in Anti-State Propaganda

The Department of Interior

Chief of Investigations / Mustafa Beylerbey.

Costa read the warrant and looked at the guard with incredulity. "Do I look that stupid?"

"No, but you are brave."

"Brave for what?"

The guard ignored Costa's question. "How many Kurdish people did you know?"

"I knew a few."

"That is why they locked you up."

"How the hell do you know?"

"Because I am a Kurd," he whispered.

"So!" protested Costa politely, folding the warrant in his hand. Suddenly a Custom's official appeared through the hallway, and the guard turned around to chat. Quickly Costa shoved the warrant in his back pocket. For some reason, the guard forgot to ask him for it back. The guard turned to look and, Costa, hoping to distract the guard from asking for the warrant back, thanked him repeatedly until the guard stopped him.

"Okay, okay, you thanked me enough. I am going to let you walk out of here. Can you swim?"

"Oh no, I know that trick," mocked Costa. "Swim across the river so that the guards can shoot me in the back, is that it?"

"No, it is not. I am going to give you your money back."

Costa was surprised. "First you were going to let me swim the river, and now you will give me my money back! Is this a joke?"

The guard reached into his pocket, took out the three-hundred German marks, and handed them back to Costa. "I could have used it," he mused, "but Kurds do not take a friend's money. Let me know if you still want to swim to your freedom," he said, and he disappeared down the hallway.

Costa sat back on the cot trying to figure out if he should take the guard up on his offer. He had no idea how long he lay there thinking. When two guards suddenly opened his cage, he stood up.

"Follow us," one of them ordered. "We are taking you to the müdür[10]."

I am a coward. I chickened out from swimming across that short river to my freedom.

They brought him into an office and pushed him into a chair in front of a large desk, behind which sat the ugly inspector looking over some papers. Finally, he looked up at Costa. "You must have powerful friends, giaour. Here is your passport. My guards will show you the way to Yunanistan[11]."

The guards marched him toward the bridge and stood him up against the barrier. One of them reached into Costa's pocket and took out the six-hundred marks.

"Now fuck off, giaour," they laughed and shoved him away.

Costa turned around and glared. "Why don't you shoot me?" he challenged, ripping his shirt open. When he saw their bewildered expression, he pointed at his chest. "Common cowards, do what you do best. One less giaour won't matter."

Abruptly one of the guards swung the butt of his machine gun into Costa's face. Costa ducked, but the blow caught him on the shoulder and knocked him over the barrier and into the neutral zone between the two borders.

Costa staggered to his feet. Although he'd had nothing to eat during the last twelve hours, he leaned over the bridge railing and vomited.

The Greek border was about two-hundred yards away, but the taste of freedom no longer seemed appealing. He wanted to go back. Every step across the bridge was a reminder of his last two years with Süheylā. His biggest

---

10. The Custom's director.

11. Greece.

regret was that he'd never gotten around to telling Süheylā that she was his 'Muslim Madonna.'

Will I ever see her again?

Chapter 3: Süheylā

It was as if Paris of Troy had just met Helen of Sparta. Süheylā's volcanic smile sent Costa soaring above the ramparts of the ancient citadel and set his heart on fire. Tall and languid, with puffy lips, blonde hair and cerulean eyes, Süheylā was the prettiest girl he had ever seen.

They met in the ancient city of Troy during a tour with their high-school graduation class—Costa from the island of Imvros and Süheylā from the city of Çanakkale. As a rule, in an Islamic country like Turkey, Christian men never intermingled with Muslim women, but Costa knew Major Ersoy, Süheylā's class chaperone. Aware of Costa's knowledge of ancient Troy, Major Ersoy had asked Costa if his group could tag along. By the end of the tour, Costa and Süheylā had set a date in two weeks for Istanbul.

For Costa, waiting two weeks felt like an eternity. He remembered the books about classical Greece she had asked him to lend her, and put them on the coffee table before he went to bed as a reminder not to leave them behind. He tossed in his bed all night—Süheylā's Eurasian face would not leave his thoughts.

"Allah u Ekber! Allah u Ekber![12]*"* It was the Muezzin[13] from the minaret next door calling the faithful to prayer. The melodious voice—more soothing to Costa's ears than his hometown's church bells—woke him up. Today was his date with Süheylā, but 4:30 p.m. seemed a long way off. With so much time to kill, he put on his running shorts and went out for a long run at the

---

12. "Allah is Great, Allah is great," the Turkish version of "Allah U Akbar."

13. Islamic religious leader.

Gezi Park[14]. Running was his only way to calm his nerves. He inherited this affliction from his father.

When it was time, he dressed up and took the trolley to the Emek Theater[15], the spot where he and Sūheylā had agreed to meet. He arrived several minutes early and, not seeing anybody, killed time by gawking at movie posters.

He felt a tug on his arm and turned around.

"Have you been waiting long?"

There, a girl—no more than twelve—stood staring at him. "Who are you, Miss?"

"I am Gūlēngūl, Sūheylā's sister."

"What happened to Sūheylā?"

"She is waiting at that pastry shop," she pointed, winking her eye.

"And you must be the chaperone," Costa mused, glinting in response.

"That is right," said Gūlēngūl tempestuously. "My sister never goes anywhere without me!"

"All right, Gūlēngūl, you lead the way."

She pulled Costa by the hand as if *he* were the child and *she* the adult, led him across the avenue and guided him through the door.

His heart skipped. Sitting at a table across the room, she was looking straight at him, smiling. When Gūlēngūl finally ushered him to the table, Sūheylā stood up and extended her hand.

"Hello, Costa."

"Hello, Sūheylā; how are you?"

"I am fine," she replied, fixing her eyes on his face. Gūlēngūl, who was still holding Costa by the hand, tugged on him to sit.

---

14. The only large green space of Istanbul's European section—by the Taksim square, the city center.

15. The Melek Cinema opened in 1924 and was renamed Emek in 1958. It was one of the greatest cinemas in Turkey . . . perhaps even in all of Europe.

"Thank you, Gülēngül, I will."

She was tall and slender, light skin and with gleaming, almond-shaped eyes—with a mischievous tempestuosity about her, something Costa had never seen in a girl before. Colorful maxi-skirt over black pantaloons, cream-color jacket over an embroidered pink chemisette, she was the most sophisticated girl Costa had ever seen. Her younger sister looked just like her. In spite of their ornate head covers[16], their blonde hair still fell over their shoulders like myriad strands of gold. Immediately his nose again caught the distinctive smell of basil. He remembered the aroma from the time they had first met in Troy. He blinked his eyes and inhaled deeply. In as much as he wanted to compliment her that she smelled divine, he stayed silent.

"My mom will not let me out unless I take my little sister along," explained Süheylā, fluttering her eyelashes. "I apologize for not being by the theater."

"No problem," blurted Costa.

"As much as I love this city, I find the men rude and aggressive. When they see young women without male escorts, they hassle them constantly. We spotted this pastry shop, and Gülēngül agreed to be my emissary!"

"It was a good idea. I would like to invite you for a light supper. Will you accept?"

"Gladly, but we have just ordered tea. Why don't we enjoy that first?"

The server brought the tea along with a tray of sweets. When, unintentionally, Süheylā brushed his arm while extending the tray toward him, her electrical discharge raced through his veins. Her charm was irresistible. Trying to keep his composure, he struggled for something to say. "You look so different!"

She smiled again, showing off her perfect teeth.

---

16. Yashmak in Turkish.

"I think you look fantastic, especially in that outfit," he added.

"I knew you would be surprised. It is fun to dress in this city."

"I think you would look good in anything," he added, feeling more relaxed.

"Oh, thank you. You look different, too. What happened to your long hair?"

"I took my mother's advice and cut it. She didn't think I would look good at the university."

"I thought you looked so original."

"I agree," cut in Gülēngül. "Anybody can wear short hair."

"Speaking of the university, are you studying for the entrance exam, Süheylā?"

"Yes, every day, how about you?"

"I spend two to three hours a day."

"As I remember, you are planning to major in Business, is that correct?"

"Yes, and you?"

"I will major in Law, although I am planning to take a few credit hours of Ethnology."

"Why Ethnology?"

"Different cultures have always fascinated me."

"That should be an interesting subject."

"What interests do you have, Costa?"

"Jogging and playing my guitar, but now I must look for a job."

"Could that be the main reason you cut your hair?"

Girl, are you quick! "Yes; nobody hires anyone who looks like a Spartan."

"What is that?"

"Sparta was one of the ancient Greek city states. Its soldiers wore their hair long."

"What about the Spartan women?"

"They wore their hair short; they practically shaved their heads!"

Süheylā rolled her yes. "I wonder how people would react if I shaved my head," she commented coyly.

"They would throw stones at you!" he joked, letting the echo of her cascading voice melt into his mind.

"When did you arrive?" she continued, jolting him from his revelry.

"A few days ago," he replied, still spellbound. "And you?"

"We got here a week ago."

"Do you like Istanbul?"

"Of what I hear and see there is no city like it."

"Historians call it 'the Queen City.' "

"What a fitting name!" she commented approvingly.

"Before Istanbul, its name was Constantinopolis."

She looked perplexed. "Can you repeat that?"

"For about a thousand years its name was Constantinopolis. It means the 'City of Constantine', named after its first Roman emperor; it is a Greco-Roman name."

"Our teachers never mentioned anything about that."

Costa shrugged his shoulders. "It is Istanbul[17] now."

"Who changed it?"

"It was a gradual change over the last century or so. During the reign of the Ottoman Empire it was called 'Kostantiniye.'"

"What does 'Istanbul' mean?" she asked shyly as if apologizing for her lack of knowledge of the city.

"It means 'to the city'; it is a composite Greek name."

This time she really looked surprised. "I had no idea."

"No big deal; that is the name of the city now."

"Some day you must tell me the true history of this city."

Some day? Wow! "Speaking of names, what does 'Süheylā' mean?"

---

17. The word "Istanbul" is a mispronunciation of three Greek words: "ees teen poleen."

She looked at Costa with a smirk. "It means 'beautiful, charming.' Since you speak perfect Turkish, I thought you knew."

"I didn't. It fits you."

"My name means 'smiling rose' " butted in Gūlēngūl. "And some day I am going to be a famous singer!"

Sūheylā chuckled. "She says that all the time; I am beginning to believe it!"

"She already knows what she wants!"

"Before I forget, what does the name 'Costa' mean?"

" 'Steady and faithful'. It is a Latin name, short for 'Constantine'."

"Now I get it. You have the same name as this city."

"No," corrected Costa politely. "It was the city's previous name, but don't tell anybody. They might try to change my name to 'Istanbul.' "

The girls thought his joke was funny and giggled heartily. Sūheylā in particular let out a Lauren-Bacall-after-one-too-many-cigarettes laugh. Her tendency to lift her head skyward when she laughed was the sexiest nuance he had ever seen.

Gradually the three of them began to feel more at ease. They drank more tea, all the while making small talk. Costa wondered whether anyone in the world looked as beautiful as Sūheylā, or like her younger sister, Gūlēngūl.

"By the way," asked Sūheylā, "did you remember to bring those books?"

Costa became distressed. "I am very sorry, Sūheylā," he apologized. "I forgot them on my coffee table. I promise to bring them at the next opportunity."

"No problem, Costa."

"Great!" *I could not have planned this any better.*

They left the pastry shop to walk the Avenue of Beyoĝlu, the famous artery of Istanbul; fashion stores, boutique shops, kiosks, pastry shops, leather shops and restaurants—the best the city has to offer.

"I love it here" whispered Sūheylā, squeezing his arm.

He could not get over her ease of manners. Her poise astounded him. He never expected a provincial girl to act in this fashion. In their matching maxi-skirts and ornate headscarves, the two sisters looked as if they had just popped out of a fashion magazine. Süheylā's most striking feature was her way of walking. He could not tell whether she fluttered like a butterfly or glided like a ballerina. With each step her blonde hair, dangling below the head cover, cascaded over her shoulders like an undulating wheat field.

She must be walking on air. He never expected to meet such a girl—a Muslim girl.

"Where is your high school?"

"I spent three years in that building over there" he replied, pointing. My friends and I walked this avenue at least twice a day six days a week. Its curriculum is Greek, Turkish and English."

"As I recall when we met in Troy, you told us about *The Iliad*. Is that where you studied it?"

"No. I learned *The Iliad* from my father."

"I'd never heard of it until I met you in Troy," she lamented. "By the way," I did not get to thank you for letting us join your group that day. You were a most knowledgeable tour guide."

"I had a lot of practice. My father was a fanatic of the classics, and he took me to Troy several times."

"I see. By the way, how do you know Major Ersoy?"

"He is a long-distance relative. His mother is from my village." Now I have the same question for you. How do you know him?"

"He is a friend of my father."

"Is your father in the military?"

"No. He is a judge in Çanakkale. He also deals in some military matters."

"I see. Your father works with Major Ersoy."

"Yes. That is how our group got to do that daily excursion to Troy with him as the chaperone."

"Lucky for us," smiled Costa.

"No, it was our luck that you knew Major Ersoy. As you know, the guide assigned to us for the day had to leave because of illness."

"Yes. I know," Costa smiled, feeling lost in her enormous eyes.

"I must confess, Costa, my friends and I thought you were Turks. We never imagined that Greeks would speak such perfect Turkish!"

"We are Turkish citizens. Turkish is our primary language. Greek is a secondary and optional language of all Turko-Greeks like me."

"It wouldn't have mattered anyway. My friends and I had never seen such a group of great-looking guys," squeezing his arm again.

Adrenaline raced through Costa. This was the third time that she had initiated some sort of physical contact.

They strolled down the avenue window-shopping and making small talk. The constant traffic, the people and the overall bustle were all very exciting. After a while, it was time for a quick bite.

"Let's go into this place" said Costa, pointing. "It is called 'The Atlantic.' "

Süheylā and Costa ordered grilled sausage. Gülēngül preferred something called a 'hamburger.'

"Why did you order that?" asked Süheylā.

"I heard Mom talk about the city of Hamburg, Germany. I am curious to see how it tastes."

Costa and Süheylā both laughed.

"Where did your parents meet?" asked Costa.

"They met at the University of Vienna. My mother is Austrian."

"That explains your blonde hair and blue eyes." You have the combined features of Austrian and Turkish."

"Not quite," she replied.

"Did I make the wrong assumption?"

"I will explain—some day."

Some day? "Okay" said Costa, smiling. "What is your mothers' name?"

"Her Austrian name is Regina; her Turkish name is Perihan. My father's name is Mehmet."

"My mom's name is Anna, and my dad's name is Phillip," responded Costa.

"Are they Christian names?"

"Phillip is Greek; Anna is biblical. Are you ready for some dessert?"

"That would be very nice," she said, smiling.

"Let's go to that pastry shop across the street. They make the best ekmek kadayif[18] in Istanbul."

They ordered ekmek kadayif and savored it together. When it was time to leave, Süheylā said, "thank you so much, Costa. We have been in the city for a week. This has been our best day so far. Will you promise to bring us here again?" she asked.

"How can I refuse?" Costa replied as his heart leaped in his chest.

She looked at her watch. "We have to get back soon. Mom will be upset if we are late."

"I will escort you to your apartment. Will that be okay?"

"That will be great. This way we won't have to put up with any unruly men."

"There is still plenty of time for you to get home. Would you like to stop by the Cumhuriyet Anıtı[19]?"

"What a great idea" voiced Süheylā enthusiastically. "I brought my camera with me. Let's go."

They arrived after a five-minute walk. Süheylā reached into her pocketbook. "Here is my camera, Costa. Will you take our picture?"

---

18. Turkish bread pudding.

19. The Monument of the Republic, crafted by the Italian sculptor Pietro Canonica in 1928. The monument commemorates the fifth anniversary of the foundation of the Republic of Turkey.

To his surprise, both sisters took off their head covers and tilted their heads, letting their blonde hair fly about their faces. For Costa this was an opportunity to hide behind the camera and take a good look at their features. Süheylā's eyes in particular were enormous. Their color of deep blue reminded him of the waters of the Aegean. She had the angelic face of the Madonna, but a closer look gave him the feeling that he was staring into the eyes of a tigress. *I have never seen a more interesting face,* Costa wanted to tell her, but he bit his lip and snapped away with the camera. After quite a few shots, he gave the camera back to Süheylā.

The trolley was packed. Süheylā and Costa had no choice but to squeeze closer. From time to time Süheylā glanced at Costa wearing a slight smile and then look away. A sudden brake by the trolley pushed her into him. When Costa snuck his fingers around her hand, she squeezed in response and locked eyes with him; they were now so close their hips were brushing. Feeling lost in each other's eyes, they were suddenly aware of Gülēngül talking.

"Come on, Süheylā, we are home."

"Okay, Gülēngül, don't be so impatient," protested Süheylā. She reached in her pocketbook and handed Costa a piece of paper. "Here is our phone number, Costa. Will you call me?"

"Of course I will," squeezing her hand one more time. She looked at him and exhaled straight into his nostrils. Her minty breath and the smell of basil hit him with the effect of a narcotic. Wishing he could hold in her breath forever he closed his eyes, but the sudden stop of the trolley stirred him from his imaginings. He escorted the two sisters to their apartment building about two blocks away. They shook hands and said good night.

Costa was too excited to ride the trolley home. He walked back to his apartment and sat on the couch, still dazzled by Süheylā's captivating charm.

Chapter 4: The Prince of the City

Obsessed with racial purity, post-Kemalist Turkey had no work for Greeks like Costa—not even for Turks for that matter, but the Greek minority was expendable.

This was not the vision of the great Kemal Atatürk.[20], the founder of modern Turkey. His successors were hell-bent to revenge the demise of the Ottoman Empire; the minorities—the Greeks, the Jews and the Armenians—were the scapegoats; they had no right to exist, and Costa was one of them. Turkey was for Turks only.

For Costa, finding a job was a matter of survival, although his chances were next to zero. He did however have one thing going for him that most Turks did not: he was fluent in English and even spoke some French.

He dressed up and headed for the city. The food kiosks along Istiklal Avenue were a great place for a quick bite. Fresh breakgfst rolls, Bogaça[21], bőrek[22], along with a bottle of buttermilk, was a cheap breakfast. Along the way, he stopped by several airline offices to inquire, with no luck. Uncle John, his father's friend, was the *maître d'* at the Park Hotel, and he decided to pay him a visit. He walked through the lobby and asked for his office.

---

20. Kemal Atatürk is the founder of modern Turkey and its most revered leader. The name means 'the father of all Turks.' By his sheer personality and charismatic leadership, he created new Turkey out of the ashes of the Ottoman Empire by organizing a fierce resistance against the invaders. In spite of his great vision, his successors, pretending to wear the mantle of Atatürk, created economic disasters, trampled on the rights of the citizens, and used the minorities as a scapegoat for all of Turkey's ills.

21. Turkish breakfast rolls.

22. Turkish-style lasagna.

"Hello, Uncle John."

"What are you doing here, Costa?"

"I am looking for a job."

"There are no jobs for young people like you in this city."

"I know the English language well; there must be a place I can use it."

"There is a travel agency next door. I know the owners. Would you like to meet them?"

"I would be grateful."

He followed his uncle. Off to the side of the hotel was Hermes Travel, a large space lined with several desks manned by travel agents. An attractive brunette receptionist greeted them.

His uncle introduced himself. "I am John Rigas, and this is my nephew Costa. We are here to see Mr. Gregory."

At the far end was a private office separated by glass where a distinguished man in his mid-forties sat behind a desk. When he caught sight of Uncle John talking to the receptionist, he got up and opened the door.

"Come in, John" he said kindly, inviting them in. "Would you like something to drink, gentlemen?" he asked before they'd had a chance to sit.

"No thank you, Thomas," replied Costa's uncle politely. "My nephew here, Costa, is looking for a job. Can you help him?"

The man looked Costa over. "Are you trained in anything, young man?" he asked.

"I have worked part-time in the correspondence department of the Mobil Oil Corporation. I also drove a taxicab."

"Are you a student?"

"I am preparing for the university entrance exam."

"Do you know the city well?"

"Like my own village."

"Do you speak any languages?"

"I speak English fluently and some French."

"How good is your English?"

"I think it is pretty good."

"Would you be willing to take a test?"

"Gladly."

"The test is a few pages of written questions. It should not take you more than forty-five minutes." He opened a side door and escorted Costa into an impressive interior office where a distinguished-looking woman was sitting behind a large desk. "This is my wife Martha, our personnel manager," said Mr. Gregory, giving his wife a kiss. She will administer the test."

Mrs. Gregory shook Costa's hand and invited him to sit at a large conference table. She took out a folder from a drawer and placed it in front of Costa. "This is it, young man. Take your time. Let me know when you are done."

Costa opened the folder and took a quick look. Although the test was several pages long, he finished it in less than thirty minutes.

"You are done already?" exclaimed Mrs. Gregory. "There is also an oral session with Mr. Gregory and me. Are you up to it?"

"Yes, Mrs. Gregory."

She asked her husband into her office, and the two of them engaged Costa in conversational English. Their main interest was his knowledge of Greco-Roman and Ottoman history. When the oral test was over, Mr. Gregory asked him to wait by the hotel's courtyard café, while he and Mrs. Gregory looked over his written test.

With his heart racing, Costa sat down at a table, trying to catch his breath. The last hour or so was a blur. He ordered a bottle of sparkling water and pondered his chances. He would love to have a job, any job, even cleaning floors. Mr. and Mrs. Gregory were an impressive couple; their tailored suits and impeccable manners bespoke of an aristocratic background. Mr. Gregory was a handsome man and Mrs. Gregory was a classy woman.

With pitch-black hair tucked in a bun, raised cheekbones, black eyes and a disarming smile, she exuded confidence. He had never met such a couple.

Within fifteen minutes, they joined him at his table. "Your English is excellent," complimented Mr. Gregory. "We are impressed. Are you a good driver?"

"I've never had an accident, sir."

"Do you have any references?"

Costa reached into his pocket and took out his letter of recommendationfrom the Mobil Oil Corporation. "Here it is, Mr. Gregory."

Thomas Gregory glanced over the letter and put it in his pocket. He looked at his wife, and they both smiled. "My partner and I need a driver," said Mr. Gregory. "He will have to meet you personally."

"Certainly, sir, any time."

"I like your attitude, young man," commented Mr. Gregory. "Do you see that Mercedes parked over there? Here are the keys. Go inside the car, familiarize yourself with the controls, and pull up by the hotel's entry in ten minutes. He gave his wife a kiss and walked into the hotel's lobby. "

Costa took the keys and got into the car. He had never set foot in such a machine: mahogany dashboard, leather interior, power windows and many other extras. The engine purred like a kitten. Within ten minutes he pulled up to the hotel's entry to wait.

When he saw Mr. Gregory walking out with an imposing looking man, he rushed out and opened the doors.

"Costa, drive to Abdullah's for lunch," instructed Mr. Gregory. The other man took his seat without saying a word.

Costa drove the two men to the famous restaurant, prepared to wait, but Mr. Gregory instructed Costa to join them. Never in his life did he expect to see the inside of this establishment, let alone sit in the company of a very important Turk. He found a spot, parked the car and went in. The *maître d'* led him to their table.

"Costa, this is Mr. Sariyer," said Mr. Gregory, "my partner in the travel business."

Intimidated by this imposing Turk, Costa extended his hand. This man was dressed impeccably in a gray flannel suit. Tall and handsome, he had a square face, perfectly combed hair with a touch of grey, starched white shirt, and a grey tie to match; he looked like a movie star. His demeanor spoke of a very important citizen. *Who was this impressive Turk.* Powerful Turks always scared him.

"Sit down," said the Turk kindly, pointing at a chair.

Costa took his seat with much anxiety.

"Costa," said Mr. Gregory. "Mr. Sariyer would like to ask you a few questions."

Costa tensed up. *Now what?*

"Relax, young man," smiled Mr. Sariyer and patted him on the shoulder. "How old are you?"

"Nineteen, sir."

"Before I ask you a few things, order what you like."

Costa looked over the menu and ordered a Turkish-style mixed grill.

"Have you ever committed a crime?" asked Mr. Sariyer the minute Costa completed his order.

"No, sir," replied Costa with assurance.

"Mr. Gregory tells me your English is excellent."

"It could be better, Mr. Sariyer."

"So could my Turkish! By the way, I also think your Turkish is excellent."

"Thank you, sir."

"How would you like to work for me and Mr. Gregory?" asked Mr. Sariyer, training his dark eyes straight at Costa.

Costa's heart fluttered. "It will be a dream come true, Mr. Sariyer. I need a job, any job."

"Good man," commented Mr. Sariyer. My partner and I need an English-speaking driver-guide for our English and American VIPs—someone who knows the history of our country, its monuments, *and keeps his mouth shut.* Can you handle a job like that?"

"Yes, sir, I can," replied Costa with a tad of bravado.

"Good," said Mr. Sariyer. "Your pay will be four-hundred liras a week. Officially you work for Hermes Travel. Is that understood?"

Costa swallowed hard. "Perfectly, sir" he replied, trying to avoid looking apprehensive.

"The car you just drove is leased under Hermes Travel. You will have sole possession of it. You are to be available at all times. By the way, do you have a telephone?"

"No, Mr. Sariyer."

"Leave your apartment unlocked tomorrow. My office will instruct the phone company to install one for you. Either Mr. Gregory or I will be in touch with you often. Is all that clear?"

"I will not let you down, Mr. Sariyer," replied Costa, feeling the enormity of the task.

"Good. Now drive us back to Park Hotel. Mr. Gregory will fill in the rest."

During the drive back the two men engaged in deep conversation. Costa shuddered at the thought of screwing up on this job. One thing was certain: either Mr. Sariyer was staying at the Park Hotel, or he was the owner of the property. Costa parked the car and walked into the agency's office for any further instructions.

"Congratulations, Costa," exclaimed Mrs. Gregory. "You will be working for one of the most important men of Istanbul."

He wanted to ask who this 'Mr. Sariyer' was, but he did not want to appear nosy.

"Costa, you need to go with Mrs. Gregory to the men's store," added Mr. Gregory. "We want you to look a lot more presentable."

"Mr. Gregory, what do I do with the car during the down times? Where do I park it?"

"Right here in the hotel's courtyard. Its spot has been arranged."

"I don't really know what to say. I hope I can live up to your expectations."

He followed Mrs. Gregory to the clothing store. *Maybe a jacket and a shirt,* Costa thought, but Mrs. Gregory picked out an entire wardrobe. *What was he going to do with all this?* He was even more surprised when the shop owner asked him for his address; one of the employees was going to deliver everything to his apartment.

"You are done for the day," said Mrs. Gregory. Be here tomorrow morning by seven. You are driving Mr. Gregory and Mr. Sariyer to the airport."

"Thank you, Mrs. Gregory. I will be forever grateful."

Costa went back to the car to do some cleaning and polish the interior. When he saw Mrs. Gregory walking toward the car with an envelope in her hand, he got out.

"Here is an advance for you, Costa. I am sure you can use the money. Drive carefully and take good care of Mr. Sariyer."

Costa was speechless. He shook her hand once more with much enthusiasm. He followed Mrs. Gregory into the office to thank Mr. Gregory. Then he walked into the hotel to thank Uncle John.

His next stop was the post office. He sent a telex to his parents telling them the good news, then rushed to the nearest phone. He had to call Süheylā! With his heart pounding, he dialed her number.

"Hello" answered a female. "Who is calling?"

Loud music was blaring in the background, and Costa had difficulty distinguishing the voice. He knew it was not Mrs. Gülpinar.

"Hello" he blurted out.

"Is that you, Costa?" It was Süheylā!

"Yes, it is me, Costa. I was calling to invite you to a movie this Saturday afternoon."

"I would, but you know the rule. My sister must come along; otherwise, my mother will not let me out . . . and we must be back on time."

"Of course," replied Costa, feeling excited. Shall we say four-thirty?"

"Yes, four-thirty is great, replied Süheylā enthusiastically.

"I will pick you up by the trolley stop, the one closest to your apartment?"

"We will be there."

Costa stared at the receiver, still reeling from the echo of her voice. Its tenderness bore through his heart like a soft arrow. He could listen to it all day long.

Chapter 5: Kissing in Public is a "No-No"

The anticipation of seeing Süheylā again was driving Costa beyond anxious. He'd never before felt like this; her Eurasian face followed him everywhere. To keep calm, he went out jogging twice. The thought of picking up the two sisters with the Mercedes crossed his mind, but he dismissed it as pretentious. After a shower, he dressed and then boarded the trolley. Within a few minutes, Süheylā and her sister arrived.

"Have you been waiting long, Costa?" greeted Süheylā.

"Not at all" he replied, elated to see her again.

"What have you planned for us?" chimed in Gülēngül.

Costa smiled at her precociousness. "A movie of course," he answered. "What else?"

"Just checking" she replied teasingly.

"What is the name of the movie?" asked Süheylā as they took their seats in the trolley.

" 'Antony and Cleopatra'; I hope you like it."

"This will be our first movie in Istanbul."

"I feel honored."

Like their first date, the two sisters were dressed in perfectly matching outfits: long black skirts, white summer jackets and ornate headscarves. Costa was impressed with their *penchant* for fashion. Their mother's European influence was obvious.

The movie theater was only a block away from the trolley stop. They took their seats in the last row, with their backs against the wall. Costa sat between the two sisters. The commercials came on, and Gülēngül became engrossed.

"What is this movie all about?" asked Süheylā.

"It is the story of Antony, the Roman general, and Cleopatra, the queen of Egypt."

"How do you know all that?"

"Greco-Roman history was part of my high-school curriculum."

"Another subject my high school did not broach. All they teach us about is the glory of the Ottoman Empire."

"Well, they should. That is your heritage!"

She smiled kindly. "What is your heritage?"

"My parents told me it was Hellenic, but I am not sure where my heritage lies. In school, I learned more about the Ottoman Empire than any other."

"Can we talk about this subject another time, Costa? I really want to know more about this movie."

"According to the reviews, the movie was filmed in the Cine Cita, Italy. It almost bankrupted Twentieth Century Fox, the movie company. It also resulted in the divorce of Richard Burton from his wife Sybil."

"Who is Richard Burton?"

"The protagonist—he plays Antony. He was seduced by that actress, Elizabeth Taylor—she plays Cleopatra."

She hesitated. "I heard you use that term in Troy— something like Paris seducing Helen of Sparta—but I was too timid to ask you then. What does 'seduce' mean?"

This was a *faux pas*. Within the Islamic culture, terms of sexuality are immodest. He attempted to stall, but Süheylā was quick.

"Aren't you going to explain?"

"It means that an individual uses his or her charms to attract someone of the opposite sex," he scrambled.

She lifted her eyebrows. "Where did you learn this term?"

"In psychology class."

She shook her head. "You surprise me every time."

Her face was only a few inches away from his. His nostrils caught her breath. Her smell of mint and basil was intoxicating. As the lights dimmed he leaned over and gave her a quick kiss.

He thought she might at any moment bolt from her seat, but to his surprise she turned around.

"Was that a kiss?" she whispered and without waiting for his response, she planted her lips on his mouth. Gülengül, who never missed anything, elbowed him in the ribs.

He took Süheylā's hand. At first, she remained unresponsive, as if she were having second thoughts about the kiss. The movie came on, and it piqued her interest. As time wore on, she leaned ever closer, squeezing his hand tighter. He could feel her hand's perspiration and sensed her anxiety. She seemed unsure, probably wondering whether holding hands with a man of a different race and religion was the right thing to do. This was taboo for Muslim women. He had a sense that she might be feeling its crushing weight, but to his surprise, she snuggled even closer. When ran his palm across her cheek, she squeezed it against her face. Behind her Madonna-like persona, Costa had the sense he was dealing with a volcano.

The movie was finally ending. As the lights slowly come on, Süheylā turned around and planted a quick kiss on his cheek.

"Thank you, Costa. This was a great movie."

The minute they found themselves in the main artery, Gülengül shook her finger at Süheylā. "I saw it" she teased. "At least you don't have to keep talking to me about when Costa will be kissing you."

Süheylā could not believe her sister's audacity. "Are you happy now, Gülengül?" She looked at Costa and as usual, she lifted her head skyward and started to laugh, as Costa did the same. Gülengül's remark had caught both of them off guard. "I am sorry about my little sister; she is such a pest." Then she leaned over and gave her sister a hug.

There was plenty of time until curfew so they walked to the fish market. With its many food kiosks and much variety of fast food, it was a moving feast. Deep-fried muscles, grilled kebabs, sardines, and the cheese and meat bőreks were outstanding. The baklavaria offered more than twenty kinds. Süheylā looked relaxed, commenting several times that she had never expected to have so much fun. Gülēngül, who was always up to something, challenged Costa to kiss her sister.

"Kissing in public in our country is a 'no-no,' " Costa pretended to scold her.

"It is a silly rule. If you like my sister, you must kiss her now" she demanded, putting her hands on her hips.

"I like your sister," replied Costa hastily, trying to shake her off. No sooner had he spoken than Süheylā gave him a quick kiss on his cheek. Costa winked. "I think your sister likes me."

"Are you happy now?" Süheylā teased her sister.

Gülēngül scoffed. "That wasn't a kiss, Süheylā. You must kiss him on the lips!"

"Didn't you hear Costa? Kissing in public is a 'no-no' here."

"I guess I'll have to wait until another time," she grumbled. Just then, a trio of strolling musicians came by their table and asked them if there was a song they could play. Costa looked at Süheylā for her approval, but Gülēngül was already on her feet.

"My sister likes "I heard that you forgor the color of my eyes[23]" she said, clapping her hands. It was one of those classical, unforgettable, Ottoman songs. By the middle of the song, Gülēngül was singing. Her incredible voice invited everybody's attention. The musicians and patrons alike were astounded.

Costa tipped the musicians for one more song. After that it was time to go. He suggested a taxi. Gülēngül took the passenger's seat as Süheylā slipped into the back with

---

23. "Duydum ki unutmuşsun gőzlerimin rengini."

Costa. The taxi was infinitely more comfortable than the trolley. Gülēngül kept her eyes trained on the passing scene, and Süheylā was now alone with Costa. He had expected her to be fidgety and even nervous, but she was the opposite.

"I really enjoyed the movie, Costa. That Cleopatra woman is a fascinating character. And that Elizabeth Taylor is a beautiful actress."

"Well in the movie Antony fell in love with Cleopatra, and in real life Richard Burton fell in love with Elizabeth Taylor."

"I thought you said that she seduced him. Tell me again. What does it mean?'

"The use of physical and mental charms to attract a person of the opposite sex."

"Have you ever been seduced?"

You are seducing me right now. He coughed to camouflage his surprise. "Not really; I have not met anyone who was attracted to me that much."

"I doubt that," she smiled, fixing her enormous eyes on his face. "I find you very handsome."

Costa reached out and took her hand. "I am glad. I find you very attractive, too."

"Does this mean we can seduce each other?" she inquired innocently.

Costa did not know how to reply. "I think you misunderstood the word 'seduction'."

"How so?"

He was still trying to find the right words.

She stared at him. "Aren't you going to tell me?"

"If you insist. 'Seduction' means . . . 'sexual engagement'."

She blushed. "I am sorry. I really misunderstood."

"There is nothing to be sorry about. Thank you for coming to the movie with me."

"Thank you for taking us!" She again fixed her eyes on his face. "I think you like me, don't you?" She put her palm on Costa's cheek and gave him a quick kiss, on the lips this time. "I love that Cleopatra woman. She knew what she wanted."

"I think you have the same potential," joked Costa.

"You mean it?"

"I do."

"I'll remember that."

"Can I ask you a personal question?"

"Of course."

"You and your sister always smell so nice. What are you wearing?"

She gave him a smile. "It is a special soap my mom makes; it is one of her hobbies. She mixes it with distilled basil and mint. Would you like a couple of bars?"

"I would love it."

"I will bring them the next time I see you."

Costa searched his pocket and took out a business card from the travel company. He also scribbled his phone number.

"You can call me on these phones if you like. It will be hit and miss. Most of the time I will be out on the road."

She looked at the card. " 'Hermes Travel.' What do you do there?"

"I work."

"You have a job?"

"I do."

Just that moment the taxi driver stopped in front of their apartment. "Here we are, folks. I can only stop for a few seconds."

Süheylā looked at Costa, placed her palm on his cheek, and gave him another quick kiss. "Thank you again for taking us to the movie, Costa!" she smiled and bolted out of the cab before Costa had time to react.

He paid the taxi and watched the two sisters disappear behind the door. His extreme euphoria made him want to scream. Süheylā was more than beautiful; she was intoxicating.

Chapter 6: Treading on Taboo Ground

The village where Costa came from had no running water, no electricity, no indoor plumbing, and but a single phone—in the mayor's office. Yet here in Istanbul his simple apartment had all those luxuries—and more. The contrasts between his island and the city were unfathomable. Like most Imvrians his family was poor and always on the edge of destitution. Education was important, maybe the only way out, but he had no idea how he could get one. Like all his compatriots, his only hope out of poverty was to seek a better opportunity elsewhere. Calculating such odds was impossible, and yet he never thought about any odds, not even of being poor or helpless. Now that he had met Süheylā, his male ego took a giant leap forward. He picked up the receiver and dialed. Thankfully it was Süheylā and not her mother. She sounded worried.

"Are you all right?"

"I am fine."

"Is there anything I can do?"

"I wish you could. My father is coming to spend time with us. We are not happy about it."

"Why?"

"He's been making my mom's life miserable lately."

"I thought your parents were happy together."

"Not since my father developed a fascination with Islam."

"He is a believer. What is wrong with that?"

"He is more than a believer. He has become a fanatic."

"How so?"

"He demands that my mom attend mosque services every Friday. What's worse is, he wants her to dress in conservative black clothing; she hates it."

"But hasn't your mom converted to Islam?"

"Yes; she did it to please my father, but Islam has become too restrictive."

"All religions have their rules."

"The rules of Islam are suffocating. My mom refuses to go to the mosque."

"She is not alone. My father will not go to church with my mother either."

"I am sure your mother does not force him to go."

"She tried, but he is a nonbeliever."

"Your father does not believe in God?"

"He doesn't."

"What about you?"

"I am not sure."

"Do you attend church services?"

"Not lately; what about you and your sister?"

"We go whenever my father asks us to."

"Have patience. He'll only be with you for a week or so."

"He will probably invite the imam and his wife to dinner."

"You don't like the imam?"

"The Imam is a kind man, although I shy away from men in robes; but I do not like his wife. She dresses up like the Black Death. You can only see her eyeballs. I don't even know how the poor thing breathes," Süheylā joked.

"I hope you do not discuss this with your friends."

"No, I don't."

"Keep it that way. Discussions like that will get you in trouble."

"I know."

"Does your mother know anything about us?"

"I told her I met a student. As long as I take my little sister along, she has no problem."

"Have you told her who?"

"Not yet."

"Seeing me might not be a good thing."

Chapter 6: Treading on Taboo Ground

"What do you mean?"

"We come from very different cultures. I would hate to see you get hurt."

"But I would like to continue our friendship. I dreamed about you last night."

Costa felt a joyous lump form in his throat. No girl had ever been so direct with him. He pretended he did not hear. "If your father knew you are seeing a Greek, he would go to extremes to stop it."

"Costa, did you hear me. I said I dreamed about you last night," ignoring his comment.

He hesitated. "I've been thinking about you since the day I met you."

"I am glad to hear that; now what about my father?"

"He will have no tolerance for our friendship."

"You are probably right."

"Promise me that you will keep our friendship secret."

"Okay, I promise."

"Let's talk more about this another time."

"When?"

"I will look at my work schedule and call you tomorrow."

"I can hardly wait for our next date!"

"Me too. I have a suggestion. It will always be better if *you* call *me*. I don't like calling you at your apartment. I don't want your mom picking up the phone."

"Okay, Costa. I look forward to seeing you. Good night!"

While this Turko-Greek relationship was exciting, it also felt uncomfortable. Costa was treading on taboo turf. She was a judge's daughter, and he was a lowly Greek from an island of sponge divers. He thought of ending it before it progressed any further, but Süheylā was once-in-a-lifetime girl. When she'd told him that she'd dreamed about him, he'd been thrilled beyond measure. He never thought that he would ever meet anyone like her. She was a real rarity, and with all the ramifications of an Islamo-Christian relationship, this was going to be complicated.

Chapter 7: Religious Modesty

With another date with Süheylā fast approaching, Costa's mind raced in all directions. His young life was suddenly and quite unexpectedly full of hope. His youthful anxieties had turned to euphoria, something that he had never experienced before.

For the third time in two weeks, he and the girls were meeting in front of the Emek movie theater. The two sisters arrived in a jovial mood.

"I thought your father was in town. What happened, Süheylā?" inquired Costa, elated to see her.

"He had to leave sooner than he'd planned," she replied, smiling widely back at him.

"I am so glad you called me. I will be gone next week."

"Where?"

"I am driving this American couple to Ephesus."

"Is that what you do with Hermes Travel?"

"Yes. I mostly drive English-speaking people to tourist attractions and provide translation. I also do deliveries, errands, and ferry VIPs to and from the airport; things like that."

"I had no idea your English was that good!"

"It is okay. Anyway, would you like to see the car?"

"You have a car?"

"No. I just drive one. "

"Where is it?" she asked as if Costa were playing a game.

"It is around the corner. We can go for a short ride."

"You are joking, right?"

"No, I am not."

She pretended to go along with Costa's farce. "All right," she smiled coyly, "as long as we do not go too far!"

Park Hotel was a few blocks away. Costa waved to the gate attendant and pointed at the glistening black Mercedes. "There she is."

She searched his face, still convinced he was joking. When Costa took out the keys to open the rear door for Gülēngül, Süheylā was speechless. He opened the passenger door and invited her in. She slid in, still convinced that it was all a prank.

"You will have to wear seat belts," instructed Costa. "It is company policy."

Süheylā looked helpless. "We have no idea how these things work. Can you show us?"

"Gladly." First he secured Gülēngül's seat belt in the back seat. Then it was Süheylā's turn. He pulled the seat belt out as far as he could and carefully started to loop it around her when he lost his balance and landed on her. He apologized hastily, feeling embarrassed. He closed her door, walked around the car and slipped behind the wheel.

He started the engine. "Where to?" he asked, trying to recover from his carelessness.

"Anywhere you want, Costa."

"How about Bosporus[24]?" he offered. "You will love the shore line."

Finally she realized it was not a joke and by the time she settled into her seat, the Saray of Dolmabhaçe[25] and Bosporus were in full view.

"What a sight," commented Süheylā enthusiastically. She turned toward Costa and smiled. "I like the seat belt

---

24. The name comes from Greek Bosporos (Βόσπορος), analyzed as bous βοῦς 'ox' + poros πόρος 'means of passing a river, a reference to Io from Greek mythology who was transformed into a cow and condemned to wander the earth until she crossed the Bosporus where she met Prometheus. Between the limits, the strait is 31 km (17 miles) long.

25. The palace of the Ottoman Empire's Sultan Abdülmecid 1, 1843-1856. The cost of the construction was 35 tons of gold, the equivalent of three billion dollars today.

around me, Costa," she said, running her palm across her chest. She saw Costa blush and smiled. "I appreciate your concern for our safety."

Get hold of yourself, Costa. This is no ordinary girl. She is a dynamo, a volcano. "Costa, can you turn on the radio, please?" It was Gülēngül from the back seat.

Costa turned on the radio, eased the car out of the hotel's courtyard, and headed to Bosporus, following the coastline.

"My next opportunity, I promise to take you to the beach," he said probingly. "Have you ever been to the beach?"

"Oh my God," Süheylā gasped. "Muslim girls do not go to the beach."

"I assume you do not have a bathing suit?"

"Muslim girls do not wear things like that," she smiled, looking apologetic.

"Why not?" Costa asked, although he knew the reason.

She looked at Costa sideways. "You know why. Don't be a tease!"

"Religious modesty?"

"Of course; if my father ever saw me in a bathing suit, he would kill me."

"Not unless you invite him to the beach!"

"Ha, ha! Maybe we can sneak out to the Tea Garden of Taksim. Forget the beach."

"That sounds great."

Süheylā began to look more relaxed and tapped him on the shoulder. "I like this ride, Costa."

"I like cars," he replied with assurance. "They make you independent."

"You took the words right out of my mouth. Could you teach me how to drive?"

"You want to learn to drive?"

"Why not?"

"Do you have you any idea how many women drivers are in Turkey?"

"Not really."

"Not that many," he said, wishing to discourage her.

"Who cares? I am not like any of the other women."

This was a new one. "If you want to learn to drive, we have to go to the driving park. That is the only place you can learn."

"It is far better than learning in the streets of Istanbul!"

"There might not be any other women at that place."

"So what," she protested. "I really want to learn to drive."

"Okay," he replied reflectively. "We will have to find a way."

"Oh thank you, Costa." She inched closer. "I am really excited."

Costa spotted a small café. He parked the car and invited the two sisters for a quick snack. Remembering the packet of books he had put in the trunk of the car, he retrieved it and carried it with him into the café, placing it on the table without saying a word.

"What is in the package, Costa?"

"The books you asked me about."

"Can I see them?"

"Of course."

She opened the package. When she saw the picture of the Parthenon on the cover, her eyes grew wide. "What is this building?" she asked. "It looks very old."

"It is the Parthenon of the Acropolis. It is in the city of Athens, Greece."

"How old is it?"

"About twenty-five-hundred years."

"My God, I have never seen anything so beautiful." She flipped the cover page. The statue of the naked Zeus holding the thunderbolt startled her. "Who is that?"

"It is the God Zeus."

"I never thought God would look so beautiful."

"Süheylā, let me see it," cut in Gülēngül.

"I will let you see if you promise not to tell Dad. I am taking them home with us."

"I never thought God was naked," giggled Gülēngül.

"Me neither," echoed Süheylā, smiling at Costa.

"For your information, Zeus is one of the twelve gods of ancient Greece."

The sisters looked surprised. "Are they all here?" asked Süheylā as she flipped rapidly through the pages.

"Yes they are."

"Where did you get these books?"

"My cousin Demos, who is an artist, bought them at the Archeological Museum of Athens."

"These gods look so human."

"According to the Bible, God made Man to look like Him."

"They are giving me goose bumps. Look at this one; he is gorgeous. Which god is he?"

"That is Kouros, the statue of a youth."

She scrutinized his face and gave him a smile. "Had you not cut your long hair, you would have looked like this Kouros, Costa—except you have your clothes on."

Costa smiled. "You make me blush, Süheylā."

"I meant it. Who made these things anyway?" she followed quickly, trying to make light of what she had just said.

"Various sculptors of stone and marble."

"Does Christianity have these kinds of art books?"

"Only since the last few centuries."

"I know Islam doesn't. It prohibits the exhibition of nudity and holy images."

"Yes I know. Christianity has an obsession with icons."

"What are icons?"

"Hand-painted images of saints—Jesus Christ, the Madonna and others."

"Are they naked, too?"

"That would be against religious modesty."

"Thank you for lending me these books, but I cannot read Greek."

"We can search in the American library. They might be available in Turkish."

"Just at the American Library?"

"I suspect so."

"Why? What is wrong with books like that?"

"You know why. Turkey is an Islamic country. These books are considered immodest, even for Greece."

"Has Greece given up on the twelve gods?"

"It has. It has no tolerance for nude statues and things like that. As a matter fact, Christians and Muslims have been destroying these statues and other works of art whenever they can."

She looked befuddled. "That really makes me mad. Now I don't know what to think about Islam or Christianity." She closed the books and rewrapped them tightly. "Next time we meet, will you pencil their names in Turkish? I want to draw this Kouros—or you," she said, forming her lips into a sly smile.

"I didn't know you drew."

"I meant to say sketch. It is a hobby I picked up from my mom."

"Your mom is an artist?"

"It is her passion."

"What kind of subjects does she draw?"

"Landscapes, animals, even some nudes."

"I am impressed."

"About your cousin—what kind of artist is he?"

"He is an aspiring painter studying at the University of Sorbonne."

"What art period?"

"The Romantic Period[26], I think."

"Does your cousin have any art books of that era?"

---

26. The Romantic Art Period—1800 to 1860.

"He promised to drop off a couple of them on his way to Paris. They are a collection of Eugene Delacroix's works."

"Can you lend them to me also?"

"Gladly."

When he'd given her the art books, he was certain she would be intimidated and even offended. To his delight, she embraced them like an art lover. Even though she might have told him in jest that she would like to sketch him . . . his mind wandered off.

"Where did your mother study art?"

"My mother studied art at the University of Vienna."

"That is impressive. Your mom and my cousin have a lot in common."

"Where is your cousin now, Costa?"

"He is in Imvros for the summer."

"Do you draw?"

"A little."

"Maybe some day we can draw together."

"That would be nice, Süheylā. I'll look forward to that."

Pursing her lips into a seductive frown, she reached into her pocketbook, took out a small box and handed it to him.

"What is it?"

"Open it when you get home, Costa."

"Thank you, I will."

When they were a block away from their apartment, Costa pulled to the curbside. "I hope you liked the ride," he said, staring straight into her eyes.

"We loved it, Costa." She moved closer, grabbed his face and gave him a long, hot kiss.

Costa again felt adrenaline surge through his body. This girl was beyond hot.

Gülēngül, who never missed anything, clapped her hands. "Bravo, big sister; *that* is what I call a kiss."

Costa returned to his apartment eager to open Süheylā's gift. He knew what it was—her mother's handmade soap. It had that divine smell of fresh basil and mint, and even more so it reminded him of Ottoman roses. He pulled out the note.

Dear Costa:

Please accept this small gift as a token of our friendship.

I dream about you every night.

See you soon.

Süheylā.

He read her card many times over. He placed one of the bars in the bathroom and the other under his pillow. He would sleep better tonight.

Chapter 8: The Andersons

At seven-thirty that evening Costa drove by the entrance of Istanbul Hilton. He got out of the Mercedes and introduced himself to the door attendant. "I am Costa Rigas. I am here to pick up the Andersons."

The door attendant looked at Costa and smirked. "Seriously?"

"Yes, seriously"

"You are in for a challenge buddy. Do you see all these photographers?"

"What is that all about?"

"They are here to pick up the Andersons, too," he joked.

"I don't understand."

"Of course you don't. Do you know who Mrs. Anderson is?"

"I have no idea."

"Have you ever heard of Erika Schmidt?"

"I can't say I have. Who is she?"

"She is the new Mrs. Anderson, a famous European model."

Just at that moment, he saw a marvelous creature hanging on the arm of a very tall man; they were making their way out of the revolving door. The photographers were snapping away with total disregard for the couple's privacy.

Costa rushed through the photographers, introduced himself to the Andersons, and guided them to the car while the door attendant opened the doors. Quickly, Costa got behind the wheel and stepped on the gas. He looked in the rear view mirror, introduced himself one more time, and apologized for the intrusion of the photographers.

"We are glad to meet you, Costa," said Mr. Anderson. "Mr. Sariyer told us all about you."

"Welcome to Turkey, Mr. and Mrs. Anderson. I will be at your service."

He saw Mrs. Anderson smile and he took a deep breath. When she crossed her legs her miniskirt hiked far up her upper thigh. She had a square face, pronounced, high cheekbones, ruby-red lips, long blonde hair, and eyes that could kill. Her white silk shirt hugged her chest so tightly that if it were not for that heavy diamond necklace holding her breasts down, they would have popped out.

"We are looking forward to exploring Istanbul," said Mr. Anderson. "And we want to go to Troy and Ephesus."

"Mr. Sariyer has already told me. You will love the sights," replied Costa politely, mindful to keep his eyes on the road. *Look what I have to deal with. First, it was Süheylā, then the Gregorys and Hermes Travel, then Mr. Sariyer, the Mercedes, and now Erika Schmidt.*

Mr. Anderson appeared to be in his mid-forties, but Mrs. Anderson could not have been more than thirty; she was stunning. After half an hour's ride, Costa pulled into the Sariyer's courtyard; it was a magnificent villa.

The Sariyers welcomed the Andersons and invited them to sit by the veranda. Mr. Sariyer introduced Costa to his wife, Cihan[27], and asked Costa to sit next to her.

"Mrs. Sariyer needs your interpretive skills more than I do," he joked. He was a charmer, too. He boasted that he knew English well—phrases like "how are you" and "I love you." As far as he was concerned, that is all a man needed to know about English.

Two servants immediately began passing out *hors d'oeuvres*. Costa knew the routine and was careful. Translating was his full-time job, eating was not. Erika had sat close to her husband, nodding politely and smiling constantly. Apparently, they had married only a few months before and this was her first time in Istanbul.

---

27. Pronounced "Geehun."

Before they left for the restaurant, Mrs. Sariyer took Costa into the kitchen, where she introduced him to their chef, a Frenchman named Pierre, and to the butler, Mustafa. She then presented him to "the governess of the house," she called her. "Mademoiselle Neriman is a very special person in our lives. When Mademoiselle Neriman calls, Costa, you run," suggested Mrs. Sariyer half seriously.

"It will be my pleasure, Mademoiselle Neriman," bowed Costa politely.

Hors d'oeuvres at the villa and dinner at the Kőrfez restaurant was an incredible experience. Costa had never before dreamed of such an evening. Tea at Emiryan Palace was very special. It seemed as though everybody jumped at the sight of the Sariyers. Mrs. Cihan Sariyer, in her long evening dress and with her aristocratic air, was the grand dame of Istanbul. If Erika was beautiful, Mrs. Cihan Sariyer was regal. The *maître d'* rushed to kiss Mrs. Sariyer's hand while others catered to her every wish. For Costa, it was non-stop translation all evening. It was obvious that the Sariyers and the Andersons were wealthy and powerful people.

Costa had sat between Mr. Sariyer and Erika the entire evening, struggling in the company of such famous and important people. On the other hand, Erika was a rolling seduction. Her every move was an expression of sensuality and sex. The way she laughed, moved, held her fork and puckered her lips all night long at James Anderson was enough to drive all the service staff to distraction. Mrs. Sariyer on the other hand was a model of composure, a princess.

Costa remembered his father's words: "Son, there are three things one cannot hide—beauty, money, and class." These people had it all.

On a couple of occasions, Costa felt Erika's leg brush by his and he shuddered. Reflexively, both times he moved his leg away. At the end of the evening, Erika was halfway drunk, and when Costa felt her hand slither over his thigh, he rose from his chair quickly with the excuse to go to the bathroom. This could not be happening.

Mercifully, by two a.m., he dropped off the Andersons at the Hilton and drove the Mercedes back to its parking spot. Although he was exhausted, he was happy and troubled at the same time. Working for Hermes Travel, and now for the Sariyers, was a dream job, but Erika Anderson was another matter. He dismissed the entire episode with Erika as a byproduct of too much champagne and went to bed dreaming about his coming date with Süheylā.

Chapter 9: Santa Sophia

Santa Sophia was Costa's favorite museum. This basilica, the greatest legacy of the Greco-Roman Empire, gave him a sense of connection to his Greek ethnicity. Within an Islamic country like Turkey, where Christians were treated like lepers, Santa Sophia was a place where Costa could feel the spirit of his ancestral roots and hold his head high, even though he no longer subscribed to Christianity. There was no building like it in Istanbul or anywhere in Turkey, except the Blue Mosque, which was built a thousand years later. Today, more than any of his previous visits, he was excited to be visiting the museum with Süheylā, his Muslim girlfriend. Christianity and Islam were opposing religions, which often clashed violently and with tragic consequences. Santa Sophia was a church first, a mosque later, and now a museum. Unwittingly, the two youths were about to fuse their budding friendship at one of the greatest epicenters of Christianity and Islam.

Furthermore, Costa would be driving Süheylā and her sister Gülēngül in the Mercedes, a luxury that only the very rich could afford. Feeling like royalty, Costa parked the car and waited. When he saw them approach, he got out and opened the doors.

"You will like the museums," Costa greeted them cheerfully. He reached into his glove compartment and took out two small boxes. "I got these chocolates for you," he offered.

Süheylā, looking pleased, said "how did you know we liked chocolates, Costa?"

"I took a wild guess," he replied, smiling. He was surprised when she moved closer.

"You smell so good, Costa," she smiled, winking.

"Thanks to youm Süheylā; I love your mom's soap."

"Great! I will bring you more, unless we find something better," she teased.

Something better?

"First we visit Hagia Sophia[28] and then Sultan Ahmet," he said, trying to keep calm. He was riding with the sexiest girl he had ever met. Everything about Süheylā was a temptation. Her eyes, her face, her dress, her head cover, her gestures, her mouth and those puffy lips—*what he could do with them!*

"What does 'Hagia Sophia' mean?" asked Süheylā.

"It means the 'Church of Holy Wisdom'. It is the greatest work of Byzantine architecture."

"Byzantine? What is that?"

"It refers to the empire of Byzantium, otherwise known as the Eastern Greco-Roman Empire. It was conquered by the Ottoman Turks in 1453."

"Where does the name 'Byzantium' come from?"

"It comes from the name Byzas, the Greek colonizer of the city of Megara, Greece. He founded the original colony about seven-hundred BC and named it Byzantium. It is now the city of Istanbul."

"Now I get it; Constantine the Great renamed the city Constantinopolis."

"You have a great memory. By the way, did I tell you that my middle name is Byzantius?"

Süheylā was surprised. "You have more than one name?"

"A few of us Greeks have two names."

"I didn't know. What happened to all the Byzantines?" she asked, suddenly looking serious.

"Well, I am one of them."

"Don't tell me. The Ottoman Empire drove them away."

"No, modern Turkey did."

---

28. Aya Sofya in Turkish, Santa Sophia in Latin, Hagia Sophia in Greek.

"I am sorry to hear that, Costa."

"What is done is done, Süheylā. We cannot undo history."

When they arrived at Hagia Sophia, Süheylā was amazed at the sight of the impressive building surrounded by the four minarets. "I have seen photos of this building in my high-school texts. I think these minarets are spoiling its look."

"This basilica was converted into a mosque by the Ottomans after they conquered the city. Its most magnificent part was its golden dome and the huge golden cross on top."

"What happened to it?"

"I assume it was removed some time after the conquest of Constantinopolis."

"Wouldn't that look magnificent?"

"Yes it would, but the Ottoman Turks preserved the basilica, unlike the barbaric Christians, who did not respect any ancient monuments."

"How so?"

"In their fanaticism, the Christians destroyed all ancient temples from the foundations up. Whatever they could not burn or trample down they took apart stone by stone. They even burned the library of Alexandria."

"That is the worst barbarity I ever heard."

"Fatih[29] Sultan Mehmet let this magnificent building stand as it was. He did what he thought was right by Islam by converting it into a mosque."

"Now I understand."

"There is an anecdote about this building. When Sultan Mehmet entered the Hagia Sophia to thank Allah for his conquest of Costantinopolis, he saw one of his Yenitsars[30]

---

29 "The conqueror" in Turkish.

30. The household troops of the Ottoman Sultans, a force created by Sultan Murat from the recruitment of Christian boys who were converted to Islam.

destroying a piece of art or some part of the building. When he asked him what he was doing, the Yenitsar replied, 'I am destroying the giaour's monument.' Sultan Mehmet had him executed on the spot."

"Costa, I am so impressed with your knowledge of things."

"Thank you. Let's go in; you will love this museum."

The minute they were inside the building, Süheylā moved closer and took his hand. Costa was elated.

"There are too many people around here, Costa; I don't want to lose you." She motioned Gülēngül to go to his other side and take him by the hand as well.

Clever girl! She knew how to cover all the angles.

Costa gave the girls a tour of the building, its meaning, history and architecture. Süheylā was thrilled with Santa Sophia; she asked more questions than Costa had answers.

"Who built this building, Costa?"

"It was commissioned by Emperor Justinian and inaugurated on December 27th, 537 AD."

"He must have been a great Emperor."

Costa thought for a second or two. "History has named him "Justinian the Great.""

"I detect a note of apprehension."

"Well let's say, unlike his predecessors, he was a benevolent Christian."

"What do you mean by that?"

"The previous Greco-Roman emperors used all sort of violent tactics to force-convert all Greeks and other pagans into Christianity. If anyone refused, their limbs were cut off."

Süheylā placed her palm on her lips. "That is horrible. What did Justinian do to be so benevolent?"

"He issued an edict forbidding the severing of both limbs, upper or lower."

"Should we be staying here? I don't like what I just heard."

"Well those were different times, but in most things, Justinian was a great emperor. All those things are in the past. We cannot change history."

"Did the Ottomans practice Islamization by violence?"

"Maybe selectively, but not *en masse*. Unlike the Byzantines, the Ottomans gave their conquered peoples two choices: Convert to Islam and become a full participant of the empire, or remain as you are and become a raya."

"What is a raya?"

Costa was not surprised that Süheylā was not familiar with this word, a derogatory term applied to all Christians. Between her Austrian mother and her highly educated father, Costa deduced that their family was an exception, unlike most Turkish and Greek families who raised their children with hate and prejudice. "The status of a second-class citizen—a slave more or less—paying heavy taxes to the Ottoman treasury," he replied.

"I feel much better knowing that the Ottomans were more humane than the Byzantines."

"We don't know everything. History is always written by the conquerors."

"Who taught you all that?"

"My father did."

"Your father sounds so wise." As they continued to walk around, her eyes rested upon a mosaic. "What's that?" she asked, looking excited.

"It is a mosaic," replied Costa. "This church was full of them at one time. This one was uncovered after Santa Sophia was converted to a museum."

She looked surprised. "What happened to the rest of them?"

Costa wondered how he could explain all that without offending her Islamic sensibilities. As a rule, the Turkish educational system never revealed that the mosaics had been defaced on purpose.

"It is not that important. In its glory days, this church probably looked like an art gallery."

"You are avoiding my question, Costa."

"Well, Islam does not permit any images to be displayed within a mosque."

She was quick. "Now I know why my mom calls the mosques artless places of worship."

"You mean you did not know about that?"

"Costa, I go to the mosque because my father insists. It pains me to think about the loss of these mosaics."

"It pains me, too, Süheylā, but there is nothing we can do. Religion does funny things, but time marches on and things change."

"I love it here," exclaimed Süheylā. "Are all the other churches covered with mosaics like these?"

Costa smiled. "These mosaics are priceless and timeless, Süheylā. They were prohibitively expensive to produce, even then. Modern-day churches are adorned with icons that look like this one," said Costa, pointing at a large mosaic depicting Jesus Christ.

"Süheylā looked up, stunned. "Who is that, Costa? It is incredible."

"That is Jesus Christ. It is called the 'Deesis.'"

"What does it mean?"

"It means, 'Prayer' or 'Supplication.'"

"When can we go see a church, Costa? My curiosity is killing me!"

It was one thing to be visiting an ex-church converted to a museum, but quite another to visit an active church with a Muslim girl. Süheylā, however, was beyond the boundaries of Islam or any other religion. She did not have a preconceived idea; her interest was purely artistic. "I will take you to a church, Süheylā, at the next opportunity," replied Costa, hoping to slow down her galloping curiosity.

During all this time, the two sisters were enthralled listening to the many tour groups that spoke so many different languages. There were very few Turks in the museum—mostly security guards and tour guides who unfortunately had minimal knowledge of the Greco-Byzantine culture, a fact that infuriated the Westerners. While they were walking around the museum, they came upon a group led by a cleric explaining the religious and historical significance of Santa Sophia, in a language other than Turkish. Süheylā's seemingly infinite curiosity led her to ask Costa what language it was.

"Greek," replied Costa.

By coincidence, a museum guard, hearing Costa's answer, walked over to the cleric, frowning. "Mr. Priest, you are not supposed to lecture here."

"Why not?" asked the cleric politely in broken Turkish.

"Because this is no longer a giaour's church; it is a Turkish museum. We have guides who can explain things to your group."

The cleric ignored the rudeness. "Do you have any guides who speak Greek?"

"We don't study the giaour's language," responded the guard tersely.

"What do you expect my group to do then?"

"I don't give a damn what they do," snapped the guard. "If you don't like it, you can leave."

Süheylā, who was following the exchange, had heard enough. She stepped in front of the guard, scowling. "Aren't you ashamed of yourself? Why are you calling these people 'giaours?' " She was practically spewing flames.

"Who are you?" he barked.

"I am Süheylā Gülpinar," she said crossly. "My father is a judge. I am going to report you to the Ministry of Justice."

Costa was surprised. Up to this point she wore her Madonna-like persona, but now she looked like a raging

61

tigress. At five foot ten, she towered over the diminutive guard.

"You are giving Turkey a bad name," she fumed. She grabbed her sister by the hand and motioned to Costa that it was time to leave. They left immediately—the shocked guard looked like a wet cat.

"I am sorry, Costa. I was not going to let that idiot get away with it. Sultan Ahmet's Mosque can wait for another day."

They drove to Bosporus with Süheylā still smoldering. "I am proud of you, Süheylā," complimented Costa, impressed with her tenacity. "No one, especially a woman, would dare talk to a guard like that."

"Thank you, Costa. I am surprised I did that."

"You did it for me. This sort of thing could put you in trouble."

"I felt embarrassed. Why some people conduct themselves like that is beyond me."

"Just do me a favor; never come to my defense."

"I was defending common decency, Costa; I was defending Turkey."

Gülēngül kept quiet up to this point. "Süheylā, can you turn on the radio please? You and Costa are boring me!"

Strangely, the radio was playing "I want to Hold Your Hand" by The Beatles. Costa reached out and took Süheylā's hand. They were already very close to the Bebek region, one of the best spots of the straits. They parked and got out for a walk.

Bosporus had an alluring effect on Costa like no other place. His favorite pastime was watching the maritime traffic move up and down the narrow passage. He always fantasized about Jason and the Argonauts, who sailed the straits into the Black Sea. There was no place like Bosporus anywhere in the world.

Süheylā, too, found the sight magnificent, skipping for joy across the boardwalk like a child. When she saw several girls wearing the traditional Islamic 'chador,' she winced. Leaning into Costa's ear she whispered, "I feel sorry for those girls. This outfit is a testament to ignorance; it has nothing to do with Islam. Religion resides behind the temple, in the heart, and not behind a cape. These fundamentalists want to force us back into the caves."

For the third time today, Costa was impressed. He began to realize how rapidly Süheylā was revealing her persona. "Why don't we drop this conversation?" he suggested. "We came here for fresh air."

She extended her hand. Gülēngül ran to his other side. "I love the Bosporus straits. Now I see what you mean, Costa—it is incredible."

The giant oil tankers, the freighters, the cruise boats and the small sea crafts were rushing up and down Bosporus like a colony of ants. Süheylā was in a happy mood, and she was not about to let go of Costa. He suggested dinner before heading back. He knew of a reasonable restaurant near the center of the Bebek, renowned for its fresh seafood. Among several dishes, such as sautéed eggplant, arugula salad, roasted beans with tomatoes and herbs, and broiled octopus, Costa ordered a sautéed Kalkan (Turbot), a native species of these waters. Brushed with fresh herbs, virgin olive oil and lemon juice, it was incredible. The two sisters went wild with the food.

"We never had a dinner like this," Süheylā exclaimed. "We thank you very much, Costa."

"We will be back, I am sure."

On the way to the car, Süheylā stopped. "Costa, I have something to tell you."

"What is it?"

"I told my mom."

"You told her what?"

"I told her I have been seeing you."

Costa felt his throat dry up. "I thought we had agreed to keep it secret."

"I could not hide it anymore. She would not let me go out until I told her who I was seeing."

"What if she tells your father?"

"She will not."

Costa swallowed hard. *She might be of Austrian decent, but she is a Muslim convert.* "We are treading on taboo ground, Süheylā, and we both know it."

"You are right, Costa. I thought about it a great deal. But . . ."

"What?"

She started to say something but stopped. She asked her sister to wait in the car.

"Don't leave your answer in the middle," Costa pleaded.

She looked into his eyes as if she wanted to reach down into his soul. "Seeing you may be taboo, but not to me. So what if your parents are Christian and mine are Muslims? What difference does it make?"

"It makes a big difference."

"It does not matter to me at all, Costa. You have opened my mind to another world. I think about you every day."

Before he had a chance to say something, she hurried away. He caught up with her and clasped her hand. "I liked what you told me. Did you mean it?"

She nodded. Costa looked around and not seeing anybody, grabbed her chin and kissed her. Just as she began to wrap her arms around him, they heard Gülēngül calling.

"Costa, can you help me turn on the music?" she begged, sticking her head out the window. "There are too many buttons on this radio," she protested.

"Count on my sister every time," smiled Süheylā, looking around and quickly giving Costa a hot kiss.

He led her by the hand, opened the car door for her, and then buckled her into her seat. He walked around and slipped behind the wheel, still feeling her lips on his.

"I liked it when you strapped me in, Costa," she teased giggling. "It makes feel secure."

He did not know what to say and started the engine. This girl was a dynamo. He turned on the radio. "What kind of music, Gülēngül?"

"You know what I like!"

He dialed a station with popular European and American tunes. Gülēngül knew most of them—songs like "Portrait of My Love" by Steve Lawrence, "Volare" by Dean Martin, and "Love Me Tender" by Elvis Presley.

" 'The portrait of my love'; what does it mean, Costa?"

" 'The image of my loving heart,' Gülēngül; It is an American song."

"I know it is an American song, Costa."

"Do you know how to dance then, Gülēngül?" Costa inquired jokingly.

"Don't be so shocked," chimed in Süheylā. "Although my mother has converted to Islam, she didn't lose her Euro-culture. She taught us how to waltz. She and my father waltz in our living room all the time."

"What kind of waltz?"

She raised her eyebrows. "Is there more than one?"

"Yes, there is," replied Costa. "There is the Viennese Waltz and the American Waltz. I assume you have learned the Viennese Waltz."

"How do you know all that, Costa?"

"My English teacher owns a dance studio here in Istanbul. In exchange for my part-time services, she has been teaching me some ballroom dancing."

"I can't believe it; a dance studio here in Istanbul?"

"Believe it!"

"Maybe some day we can dance the waltz, Costa!"

"That would be great," he stammered, feeling completely amazed.

"What about music, Costa; what music do you like?"

"My favorite music is opera, although I still like Greek and Turkish music; not necessarily in that order."

"You like Turkish music?"

"It is one of my favorites."

"Are you joking?"

"No. My favorite artists are Zeki Mûren, Emel Sayin and Behiye Aksoy.[31]" It was Süheylā's turn to be surprised.

"Can you turn on some Turkish music, then? I cannot tolerate Western music for too long. It lacks soul."

Gülēngül made a few sounds of protest as Costa switched to a Turkish station. "Gülēngül," Costa advised, "try to enjoy this music. It soothes the soul."

"Maybe we can switch back later," she grumbled. "I don't need my soul soothed."

They were close to their apartment. "I will be gone next week," Costa said.

"Where are you going?"

"I am driving an American couple to Ephesus. I will be back next Friday."

Süheylā looked dejected. "I was counting on seeing you Wednesday. Now I have to wait for a week?"

Costa was surprised and pleased. They were outside their apartment. She moved closer and gave him a long kiss. "I will miss you, Costa. Call me when you get back," she winked and got out of the car.

Costa hugged the steering wheel and closed his eyes, still feeling her arms around him. *Was she real or was she a temporary breeze in the middle of a desert?*

---

31. One of the best vocal artists of the Sixties, Seventies and Eighties.

Chapter 10: The Vixen

Driving the Andersons around the Aegean coastline was an amazing experience. The route was more than three-hundred miles. Troy, the city of Izmir, and the beach towns of Çesme, Alacati, Ilica, Urla, Şerefhisar, along with Ephesus and Kuşadasi—all were incredible. The harbor of Bodrum[32] was the highlight of their trip.

Mrs. Anderson—Erika—was an energy-driven woman, commanding Mr. Anderson's constant attention. The car's divider curtain remained closed most of the journey. She exhausted her husband to happy oblivion, pulling him to every ruin and stopping at every beach. Mr. Anderson was all too happy to indulge her every wish—nothing but the best for his goddess.

From the first night, the Andersons had insisted that Costa stay in the same hotel with them, picking up his expenses. As the trip wore on, Erika's flirtation toward Costa grew from pretend innocence to outward boldness. At first Costa was defensive and even reserved, but when he noticed Mr. Anderson's tacit approval, he relaxed. By the time they got to Bodrum, Erika was openly salivating at Costa.

"You look well and fit, Costa. You are an attractive young man," complimented Erika when she saw him in his swimming trunks. "You look like Apollo."

Costa blushed. Warily he looked at Mr. Anderson.

"Coming from Erika, that is a real compliment, Costa. That means she likes you!"

"Thank you, Mrs. Anderson," replied Costa nervously.

"Erika, please call me Erika, Costa. I insist."

"Thank you, Erika; you are very kind."

---

32. Known in the ancient world as the harbor of Alikarnassos.

"And call me James," added Mr. Anderson. "Erika and I would like to know you better."

"I am honored to be at your service," replied Costa, catching their enigmatic smiles.

"Do you lift weights, Costa?" inquired Erika, looking at him seductively behind her enormous sunglasses.

"Whenever I can; now that I have a job, I will be pressed to keep up."

"Don't give it up, Costa. It becomes you."

"Thank you, Erika."

"Tonight we are having dinner at our suite, Costa, and we would like you to join us," said Mr. Anderson, looking slyly at Erika.

Costa's mind went numb and before he could say anything, Erika placed her palm on his chest.

"Dinner will be at eight-thirty, Costa, in our suite. We really want you to join us; we insist."

This was an invitation he did not expect. Erika's touch reminded him of the last time she'd slid her palm across his thigh at the restaurant. Should he decline? It would probably be unwise to do so.

"How can I refuse? You have been a pleasure to be around," he replied, still not knowing what he was agreeing to.

"Great," said James Anderson. "Erika and I are going to do some shopping. You can lounge around the pool if you like. We will take a taxi. We will see you back at our suite at eight-thirty."

Erika gave Costa a tussle on his hair and winked. She took her husband by the hand and sauntered into the hotel's lobby, swaying her hips like the Aphrodite of Paphos.[33]

Costa lay back in his chair, feeling his heart pounding. He did not know whether he was scared or excited.

---

33. A seaside location in the Southwestern Cyprus, considered the mythical birthplace of Aphrodite, the goddess of beauty and love.

Having dinner with Erika Schmidt and James Anderson in their suite? Did he have a choice? What should he do?

At eight-thirty he knocked on their door.

James Anderson opened it. "Come in, Costa," he greeted cheerfully. "Erika is on the veranda; follow me."

He followed Mr. Anderson through the spacious suite. Erika was standing by the railing sipping champagne. One look at her outfit and his eyes popped. She was hardly dressed. Visible under her diaphanous night coat was the sexiest underwear Costa had ever seen.

"Glad to see you," greeted Erika cheerfully. She pointed to a chair and sat beside him. Mr. Anderson poured a glass of champagne and handed it to Costa.

"To our friend, Costa; thank you for deciding to spend the night with us."

The night? Costa managed a smile. *You must mean the evening,* he thought. He got a little nervous, stood up and went to the railing to look over the harbor of Bodrum. Sparkling under the setting sun, the luxurious yachts looked like floating pearls. The numerous fishing boats and sightseeing boats were maneuvering in and out of the harbor like musical notes on water. He stared out into the open sea, inhaling the fresh breeze of the Aegean—but Erika, with her tantalizing perfume, was playing havoc with his loins. The three of them made small talk while hanging over the rail admiring the view. After Costa's second glass of champagne, Erika squeezed closer and placed her arm across his shoulders. Warily, he looked at Mr. Anderson for any sign of disapproval, but he seemed unconcerned. When Erika began to slide her hand up and down his chest, Costa again searched Mr. Anderson's face, but he only winked at Costa as if to confirm his approval. Erika by now had abandoned her glass and had wrapped her arms around Costa, rubbing her body against him seductively. Room service rang the doorbell and Mr. Anderson excused himself. Erika grabbed Costa by the neck and gave him a long kiss, rolling her tongue in and out of his mouth. He tried to keep his senses under control, but it was impossible.

"James and I like you, Costa; we like you very much. Are you a virgin?"

"Costa became red in the face.

"So much the better, Costa; I am really excited," she said and again slipped her tongue into his mouth.

His bulge was shooting up. Erika rubbed her pelvis against it and peered into Costa's face. "Have you ever heard of *ménage a trois*?"

Costa's French was limited but he understood immediately. "No, Erika," he replied hastily, feeling intimidated while dying with anticipation.

"Don't worry, Costa. You will have fun with James and me. Now let's go have dinner." She pulled Costa by the hand and guided him to the dinner table.

"Here he is, James; he is ours for the night."

Excited and out of his mind, Costa cracked a smile and took a chair. Erika was so distracting he had hardly noticed Mr. Anderson's attire. This man knew how to dress; his white slacks, silk shirt and navy blue jacket were an antithesis to Erika, who was wearing next to nothing. Her breasts were so distracting, Costa could not even hold his fork straight. At the end of the dinner, they moved to the couch and Mr. Anderson opened more champagne.

By this time, Costa was halfway drunk and blind with lust; Erika had shed her nightgown and was all over him. To his amazement, Mr. Anderson—camera in hand—was content to watch his wife undress and fondle Costa, while he snapped away. Costa by now did not care. The fact that he was about to make love—for the first time in his life—to a woman like that, made him giddy with desire.

He woke up the next morning with Erika sleeping between him and Mr. Anderson, both stark naked and looking beautiful. If there was such a thing as a 'sexy couple,' it was Erika Schmidt and James Anderson. Costa was just their temporary toy, a prop. He knew they'd used him, but this was an unimaginable experience.

The night with Erika and James was beyond fantasy. In the bottomless sea of lust, he had lost his inhibitions and his mind. Could he have said no? He had no idea. He had visited the land of the Lotus, tasted the fruit, and was sleeping between two virgin hunters.

He glanced at the two blonde gods, rubbing his eyes. One of his biggest surprises from the night before was that both of them were completely shaven. He had never expected that. Erika's glistening body by his side looked inviting and luscious. He thought of waking her up and making love to her one more time, but the thought of seeing James Anderson in the mix again stopped him. When he saw the curtains flutter, he sensed Süheyla's face peering behind and recoiled in horror and guilt. His mother had warned him that he should never consider premarital sex. "It is immoral," she had said. There was a red-light area in Istanbul, but he'd never dared visit, for his mother warned him about that, too. "If you ever visit that area, you are going to get a disease and your thing is going to fall off." He never thought he would cross the line in this fashion. No matter what, he was never going to do this again—with the Andersons or anybody else, no matter what they offered. He slithered his way across the bed, dressed quickly and ran to his bedroom. He lay there for a while, questioning his sanity. His phone rang and he picked it up. It was Erika.

"Good morning, Costa; we missed you this morning."

"I apologize," he said in haste. I did not want to disturb you."

"Disturb? No, James and I had fun last night."

He felt the flash of red in his face and guilt creeping all over him, but he kept his cool. "Yes, it was fun," he replied demurely, not wishing to send the wrong signal.

"Well, good," cheered Erika. "We will have to do it again. By the way, James and I decided to leave this afternoon. My friend Monique is flying in from France in a couple of days."

"Okay, Mrs. Anderson, I will get the car ready."

"After last night, why are you still calling me Mrs. Anderson? Erika, please."

"My apologies, Erika; what time do we leave?"

"Be ready about twelve."

Driving back was easier. Costa's familiarity with the Andersons made the return more pleasant. They took the same route, with an overnight stop in Çanakkale. The following morning they boarded the ferryboat across the straits and drove through Thrace, keeping the coastline of Marmara on their right. The closer they got to the city of Istanbul the more excited Erika seemed to get. From all looks and sounds, Monique, a model from Paris, was more than a friend. When they stopped at the city of Tekirdağ for a quick lunch, Erika wanted to use the phone right away. She came back to the table beaming from ear to ear.

"James darling, Monique is already at the bungalow waiting. You are going to love our *ménage a trois*." She looked at Costa smiling. "Costa you are invited, too; what do you say?"

Cost swallowed hard and smiled. "Can I think about this, Erika? I am still reeling from last night's experience. I am a small town lad."

"What is there to be concerned about, Costa?" chimed in Mr. Anderson. "Life is too short; live it in full."

"Okay, Mr. Anderson. I will try."

About fifteen miles outside Istanbul, the Andersons instructed Costa to drive them to their beach resort. This one in particular was reserved for wealthy foreigners, sun worshippers and topless bathers. It was off limits to all natives. This complex was one of Mr. Sariyer's real estate developments. They stopped at the gate, where Erika introduced Costa to the resort manager, who at her request issued him a season's pass.

"I want you to become familiar with this area," she instructed. "We will be entertaining our friends here. It is well maintained and very clean. The best part is its privacy and its luxurious bungalows. James and I are going to relax with Monique at our bungalow this afternoon. If you want anything by the cabana, just sign our name."

He drove them in front of their bungalow and parked. Erika seemed so excited she flew out of the car. To her delight, Monique was at the door waiting. The two models were in each other's arms hugging and kissing madly—on the lips—while James Anderson smiled and waited patiently. Costa had never seen women kiss one another on the lips before, and with so much passion. *This must be a new European trend,* he thought, although the picture was beginning to register.

Finally, the two models let go of each other and Erika turned around to introduce James Anderson to Monique, who grabbed him by the nape and gave him a kiss on the lips, too.

Costa took their suitcases out of the trunk and carried them inside. He asked them if they needed anything else.

"Be back at our bungalow about seven-thirty tonight, Costa. We are going to take Monique to the Hilton with us," Erika smiled while holding hands with Monique.

"Okay, Erika."

Costa found a spot closer to the cabana and parked. He took his swim shorts out of the trunk of the car, went into the cabana's bathroom, and changed. He swam and lounged around all afternoon, soaking up the sun. By seven-thirty he was at their door.

Please come in, Costa." Erika pointed at the bags in the middle of the salon. "Just these three; we will be right out."

Within minutes, Mr. Anderson came holding Monique by the hand while Erika followed behind. Costa opened the door for Monique, but she stepped aside, inviting Mr.

Anderson to go in first, and then sat beside him. Costa saw Erika walk to the other side and Costa rushed to close her door. These two gorgeous women had Mr. Anderson pinned in the middle like a sandwich. Costa sat behind the wheel and started the engine.

"To the Hilton, Mr. Anderson?"

"Just drive us around Bosporus a little, Costa. I will let you know when it is time to turn around."

Costa drove out into the traffic, mindful to be careful. The minute he was out in the road the threesome began to chat and giggle uncontrollably. Both models had their arms around Mr. Anderson, kissing him. From time to time, they would leave his lips and kiss each other. When Costa saw them sticking their tongues into each other's mouths, his mind went numb. He did not know what to think. When he stopped at a red light, he turned around and asked Mr. Anderson if he wanted him to draw the curtain.

"No, Costa," instructed Erika. "We want Monique to enjoy the view."

What view? They had no time to do anything else other than ravage one another and play in Mr. Anderson's pants.

Trying to keep his eyes on the road, Costa pursed his lips. Although Erika had placed her huge pocketbook between the two front seats, most of the rear was still visible. When he saw them working their hands up and down on Mr. Anderson's middle, he did his best to look straight ahead. He heard Mr. Anderson's moan and the two models clapping. Not even a monk could keep calm, and Costa was not a monk. He drove for a while longer. Finally, when he looked at the rear view mirror, Mr. Anderson seemed to be sleeping while the two models were now really at each other with passion. They seemed to be feeling each other's breasts and working their hands under their miniskirts, too. They finally quieted down and Erika asked Costa to drive them back to the Hilton.

"Do you have a girlfriend, Costa?" asked Erika unexpectedly.

"Yes, Erika, I do," replied Costa trying to suppress his discomfort. The fact that he was unfaithful to Süheylā bothered him greatly.

"Does she like the beach?"

"She comes from Muslim family. Muslims do not go to the beach."

"Why?"

"Nudity is considered immodest."

"What is her name?"

"Süheylā."

"Does she speak any English?"

"She speaks some French and some German; her mother is Austrian."

"Fascinating; why don't you ask her to come along next time?"

"I will try, but as I said, Muslims girls do not go to the beach."

"But you said her mother is Austrian."

"She is a Muslim convert. She cannot go against the wishes of her husband. The laws of Islam call for total submission."

"What does the beach have to do with submission?"

"Muslim women must submit to their husband's commands and be modest at all times; nudity of any sort is frowned upon."

"Going to the beach is immodest? The world of Islam sounds very strange to me."

"Well, it might be, but Turkey is a Muslim country. My girlfriend's mom is finding the Muslim world difficult, and she is trying to find help."

"What kind of help?"

"She wants to reconnect with her Austrian culture."

"Why don't you give me her phone number? I will call her."

"That would be very nice. Thank you, Erika."

Chapter 10: The Vixen

They were almost to the front entrance when Mr. Anderson woke up. Erika gave him a kiss. "We had a nice ride, James. Wasn't that great, Monique?"

"Oui, mon petite."

Costa opened the car doors and let them out. Mr. Anderson pulled two fifty-dollar bills out of his wallet and handed them to Costa."

"You have been a most wonderful companion; thank you."

The two vixens slipped under Mr. Anderson's arms and sauntered with him into the lobby. Costa took out the luggage and handed them to the bellhop. "Take them to the presidential suite," he instructed.

He drove back to Park Hotel, parked the car and took a cab to his apartment. He felt the two fifty-dollar bills in his pocket and smiled. What a fortune! Before heading up the steps, he checked his mailbox. Just as he had hoped, there was a letter from Süheylā.

Hello Costa:

I hope you are home by now. As you know, my father came to spend time with us. He and my mother argued a lot. We all had a miserable time. My mother is determined to trace her relatives in Austria, but my father will not allow her to travel. He left this morning. Call me when you get back.

Regards.

Süheylā.

He picked up the phone and dialed. It was Gülēngül on the line.

"Hello, Gülēngül, this is Costa."

"Süheylā, it is for you."

"Welcome back, Costa. It is good to hear your voice."

"It's good to hear your voice, too," replied Costa, closing his eyes to inhale her lilting sound.

"How was your trip?"

"Costa chuckled. " I will tell you some day when I am brave enough."

"That interesting, huh? Well, you must tell me when you see me."

"I will try."

"Did you get my letter?"

"I just read it. How is your mom?"

"Right now she is painting. It relieves her frustration. She misses her relatives, her childhood friends and her culture."

"I understand. I know somebody that might be able to help."

"Really! Who is that?"

"It is this lady I met. She is from Germany. She promised to call your mom."

"Oh, Costa, that is really nice. My mom will be very pleased."

"Let's wait and see what happens. Would you like to meet this Friday?"

"That will be perfect."

"How about the Garden of Taksim?"

"That is great. I missed you," she said quickly and hung up the phone.

Costa lay on the couch and took a deep breath. It felt nice to know that Süheylā missed him. The escapade with Erika and James Anderson was bothering him to no end. How could he do this to Süheylā? He was not even sure he could face her tomorrow.

Chapter 11: Gezi Park

To Costa's surprise, Süheylā was standing in front of the tea garden, all alone. "Where is your sister?" he asked as they hugged.

"At home," she replied, as if it were nothing.

"How did your mother allow that?"

"Erika Anderson visited us in our apartment. Not only did she and mom become instant friends, she also convinced her that I could go out on my own. "

"I am glad to hear that," Costa commented cautiously.

"Erika is a fascinating woman," said Süheylā. "I have never met anyone like her."

Oh, no, Costa wanted to say, but he bit his tongue, trying to shake off his discomfort about his recent dalliance with Erika and her husband. Costa still felt troubled, but he thre was no going back. "Would you like to go for a walk in Pera[34]?" he followed, still trying to shake off that memory with Erika and James Anderson.

"No, let's have something to eat here. We can stroll around the park later."

They ordered tea and sandwiches. When they finished, they walked around Gezi Park, and when Süheylā spotted a bench shielded by shrubbery, she invited Costa to sit.

"I want to be alone with you, Costa. I have a surprise."

Costa looked at her with curiosity.

"My sister and I can go to the beach with the Andersons," smiled Süheylā, looking pleased.

"Your mother will let you go to the beach?"

"Aren't you happy?"

"Of course I am, but if she knew that I would be coming along, she would block you."

---

34. The old Greek name for Beyoglu; the European section of Istanbul.

"I am not going to tell her."

Costa struggled with this thought for a while, but he let it go—for now. "Do you know how to swim?" He knew that as a rule most Muslim girls never take to the water.

"You know I can't swim. I am counting on you to teach me."

"You cannot be wearing any clothes other than a bathing suit." Costa joked, inviting an elbow to the ribs.

"I am still having a hard time convincing myself to wear one, Costa."

"But why?"

"I don't want you to see me!" she said, raising her eyebrows playfully.

"Don't worry, I won't look."

Süheylā let out a giggle. "Promise?"

"Süheylā, on my island everybody wears bathing suits; some even swim naked."

"Do you?"

Costa blushed, "no, never."

She rolled her eyes. "Oh come off it, Costa. My mother draws naked people all the time. She even drew my father, but since he has become a devout Muslim, those paintings disappeared."

This new revelation got Costa over his embarrassment. Finally, he did what he had wanted to do for some time. He reached over and started to untie her head cover.

"What are you doing?"

"I want to play with your hair. Can I do that?"

"Sure, let me do it." She loosened the double knot and pulled off her head cover. She shook her head sideways several times, and her golden hair flew about her shoulders like strands of gold.

He had seen her hair exposed only once before, because as a rule Süheylā never took her head cover off. He ran his fingers through her soft locks and she closed her eyes. He continued to play with her hair, caressing her head, running his palm over her cheeks. When he buried his nose in her hair, Süheylā smiled.

"Süheylā, I love your hair with its smell of basil, mint and Ottoman roses."

"You mean Turkish roses?"

"No, I mean Ottoman roses."

"I don't know how to handle that; you are making me blush."

"Don't. Your hair conjures images of the Golden Fleece."

"What is that?"

"It is from a mythological story about Jason and the Argonauts, who sailed the Bosporus straits up into the Black Sea, looking for it."

"Did they find it?"

"I think so, but I have found mine."

She raised her eyebrows and smiled. "I wonder who that might be," she exhaled.

Costa winked and met her lips. "It is this girl I met in Troy."

She cozied closer. "Your knowledge about things leaves me feeling inadequate, Costa. How am I going to catch up to you?"

"You have no worries in that department, Süheylā. You are the brightest girl I have ever met."

"You've met others?"

"I attended a co-educational elementary and middle high. None of the girls had your smarts or your looks."

She looked at him with her enormous eyes, cupped his face and kissed him hard, practically gluing her lips to his mouth. "You are unique, Costa. I am so happy I met you," she added between several kisses. She pulled back and stared into his eyes with a sly smile.

"I too wanted to sink my fingers into that thick black hair of yours since the day I met you." Without waiting for his reply, she combed her fingers through his hair. "Your hair feels so strong."

She drilled her eyes into his face for a few seconds and smiled. "You have the greatest dimples I have ever seen; I love your face, Costa."

Nobody had told him anything about his dimples before, or his face. "I will look in the mirror next time I am home," he smiled, putting his arm around her.

She gazed back at him. "You look so tanned, Costa. Did you lie on the beach a lot when you were with the Andersons?"

"I did. As I said, it was an experience."

"What happened?

"It is a bit risqué."

"That good, huh?"

"It was something I never imagined."

"Something about Erika?"

"Yes, and her friend Monique," said Costa, trying to forget his own adventure with James and Erika Anderson. He could not even look Süheylā in the face.

"What about them?"

"I saw them kissing and ravaging one another," said Costa, feeling somewhat embarrassed.

She giggled. "That is really 'sexý', Costa!"

She pronounced it the Turkish way, by accenting the last syllable, and Costa cracked a smile.

"Why are you smiling?"

"The way you pronounced the word 'sexy' as 'sexý.' "

"What is wrong with my pronunciation?"

"I love the way you say it, Süheylā. It sounds a lot sexier!"

"Okay, if you say so. So, what about Erika and Monique?"

"What I told you was only a fraction."

"I am dying to know the rest!"

"I am not bold enough to tell you."

"Costa, believe me, I can handle it."

"Okay, but not today."

"What did they do again?" she asked, probingly.

Costa lowered his head. *I am not going to tell you what they did and I will never tell you what I did.* "I told you, Süheylā; they ravaged one another, by kissing and groping."

"Groping their what?"

"Their breasts."

"That is unbelievable. Is there more?"

"I am not going to tell you anything else."

She looked dejected. "I promised to go to the beach with you; you have to tell me!"

When Costa told her about the sexual activity of the two models in the back seat, Süheylā was astounded. "That Erika must really be something. I am looking forward to meeting her come Sunday."

Costa was afraid that once he told her a few things about Erika, she would change her mind about the beach, but instead she did the opposite. She had the capacity to absorb the unusual and the unexpected as if she had experienced them herself. He wanted to hold this girl in his arms forever and never let go.

Chapter 12: A Bathing Suit for a Muslim Girl

Today was Sunday, a beach day with Süheylā and Gülēngül. Although the Andersons had agreed to serve as chaperones, Costa was still unconvinced that the girls would actually come. He pulled up to the Hilton's entrance to pick up the Andersons.

"I have talked to Mrs. Gülpinar," said Erika cheerfully. "She agreed to let her girls go to the beach with us. Costa, please drive us to their apartment."

Costa drove in front of Süheylā's apartment, pulled up to the curb and let Erika out. Within fifteen minutes or so, Erika walked out of the apartment followed by Süheylā and Gülēngül. Costa opened the rear door and let the two sisters and Erika in. Mr. Anderson took the passenger's seat.

"Mrs. Gülpinar entrusted me with her daughters. Is that all right with you, gentlemen?"

"Of course darling," replied James Anderson cheerfully. "I hope it is okay with you, Costa," he winked.

Costa, who was watching the two sisters in the rearview mirror, smiled. "Yes sir, it is fine with me!" Costa felt his heart racing. He had never been to the beach with a girl before, but this was going to be with a Muslim girl, not any girl.

When they arrived at the bungalow complex, the beach was teeming with sunbathers. Mr. Anderson headed straight to the tennis courts; he had a tennis lesson. When Süheylā saw that most females wore bikinis, her jaw dropped. This was not what she expected. She heard Erika inviting her and Gülēngül to their bungalow to change into bathing suits, and she froze. Gülēngül volunteered immediately, but Süheylā was on the verge of panic.

"Can I wait, Mrs. Anderson?" she begged.

"You are not going to be wearing a bikini, Süheylā. I have a full bathing suit for you."

"Not now, please," pleaded Süheylā, looking to Costa for help.

Costa understood immediately. It takes a lot of courage for a Muslim girl, even for Süheylā, to get into a bathing suit. Even though her mother was an artist and an Austrian, the influence of Islamic culture weighed heavy on her. He took Süheylā by the hand and walked her through the sunbathers toward the water's edge. She was the only one on the beach wearing pants, jacket and a head cover.

"These people are all Europeans, Süheylā. They do not really care what you wear. You can stay dressed all day long if you like," Costa said, trying to calm her down. When they reached the edge of the water, she stopped cold. A group of females was tossing a beach ball; they were all topless. She pulled Costa to a secluded spot and sat looking out into the void of the open sea.

Costa was sympathetic. He did not want to push this Muslim girl into anything she did not want to do. "Süheylā, why don't you stay here?" he suggested. "I will get us something to drink."

"No," she begged, "don't leave me alone."

"I will only be a minute."

Without giving her a chance to reply, he headed straight to the concession stand. By the time he got back, Süheylā was gone. He scanned the beach and, to his surprise, he spotted her far off, running in and out of the lapping waves. She had taken off her shoes and her socks. She'd even rolled up her pants to her knees. He called her name. She turned around and waved.

"Süheylā, I brought you a cola."

"Thank you, Costa. This is fun," she giggled and kicked into an onrushing wave.

"You are the only girl at the beach with a head cover. Take it off; nobody will notice!"

She sipped on her cola, looked at him mischievously, flung off her head cover, threw it on the ground and took off like a gazelle.

Surprised at her speed, he picked up her scarf and ran after her.

"Let's go find chairs," Costa suggested to Süheylā after he'd caught up with her.

"Let's walk around a little first," she replied as she took Costa's hand. "I like the feeling of the sand under my feet."

Her blonde hair now exposed to the sea breeze flew about her face and shoulders in all directions. She began to feel hot; she shed her jacket and handed it to Costa.

"Please, Costa, you carry it. I am hot."

They walked along the beach for a while, found a group of chairs and sat. They spotted Erika scanning the beach for them and waved. She was holding Gülēngül by the hand; both were wearing bikinis.

"I thought you were not going to wear a thing like that," protested Süheylā, pointing her finger at her sister; the prospect of having to wear anything like that horrified her.

"You don't have to wear a bikini, big sister," snapped Gülēngül. "Mrs. Anderson has a regular bathing suit for you. I am going into the water and I want Costa to teach me to swim," she declared, but Costa wanted to change into his swimming trunks, too. He left the two sisters with Erika and ran to the cabana.

When he got back, both sisters were knee-deep in water, jumping up and down into the breaking waves. Costa saw Süheylā edge a little deeper and braced himself. The wave broke, soaking her from top to bottom. She jumped up immediately, looking distraught. Seeing her wet shirt clinging to her chest, with her pronounced breasts, she stooped forward like a hunchback.

"Süheylā, why don't you come with me?" beckoned Erika. "Your clothes are all wet; you need a bathing suit."

Reluctantly, Süheylā followed. Gülēngül on the other hand took to the water easily. Seeing her sister walk away, she grabbed Costa by the hand, imploring him to teach her swimming. Costa tried; she would need time. He was relieved to see Erika and Süheylā return.

"Here she is, Costa. Thank goodness, she understands some German."

Dressed in tennis shorts and a tee shirt, the full bathing suit was clearly visible below. Even more bizarre, Erika had collected Süheylā's hair into a ponytail. Before Süheylā had time to think, Costa pulled her by the hand toward the water's edge. She resisted at first, but his hand was firm. Subtly, he guided her deeper when a large wave hit them. Terrified, Süheylā jumped into his outstretched arms as Costa lifted her up and held her against his chest. She did not know how to respond. After a few seconds, she wrapped her arms around Costa, as Costa repeatedly dipped her into the onrushing waves.

Erika Anderson was watching Süheylā's reaction in total amusement. "Now you must take off your tennis shorts and your shirt, too, Süheylā," she advised.

For a Muslim girl, taking off her clothes in front of so many eyes was another ordeal, but she had no choice. Slowly, she pulled off her wet shorts, casting worried looks around her as if people were really watching. She started to pull off her shirt and looked for Erika's approval. The shirt was her last vestige of security, but with Erika's encouragement, she relented. Costa had to turn his face away to keep from laughing. Erika patted her on the back.

"You will get used to it, Süheylā; you will love the beach. I'm going to join my husband now, but we want the three of you to join us for dinner this evening."

"Thank you, Erika," replied Costa. "That is very kind of you."

Gülēngül tried to get Costa back into the water, but he did not want to leave Süheylā alone. With the bathing suit on, she was cutting a fascinating figure.

"Gülēngül, why don't you stay near the edge of the water?" instructed Costa. "I will be watching you; don't go above your waist."

He sat next to Süheylā for a while without saying anything. Although uncertain at first, gradually she lay back on her chair and began to soak up the sun.

"Süheylā, you must not stay in the sun for more than forty-five minutes," Costa advised.

"But why? This is the first time I have ever been in the sun; I like it."

"Overexposure will give you sunburn."

"Will it hurt?"

"Yes it will. It will make your skin peel off and give you blisters. If you want to avoid that, you must rub suntan lotion on your body."

"Did you bring any?"

"No, but I'll go get you some."

He returned within a few minutes with the suntan oil." He handed the bottle to her, not daring to rub the oil on her. To a Muslim girl that would have been offensive.

She lifted up on her chair and began massaging the suntan oil into her skin. "If my father ever saw me in this bathing suit, he would kill me."

"If I had a camera, I would take your picture and send it to him."

"You wouldn't dare."

"You are the prettiest girl at the beach."

"Thank you, Costa. You look great, too. I never thought you would be so muscular."

"I spend a little time lifting weights at the Beyoglu Health Club."

"Are there any clubs like that for women?"

"I don't think so."

"That is just too bad."

"You really want to lift weights?"

"I want to do something for my physical wellbeing. I am not going to be like all those other girls—staying home and having babies."

Costa could hardly disguise his surprise. He wanted to help, but he had no idea how. "We can explore such a possibility, Süheylā. Why don't you let me look around?"

"That will be great, Costa. Until then, the least I can do is go jogging with you."

There she goes again . . . from one thing to another.

"You would be the only female runner in Turkey!" hastened Costa, terrified at the thought. A girl running through the city of Istanbul would elicit catcalls, disapproval and even physical attacks.

"Costa, I don't really care if I were the only female; I am not just anybody. I am me."

"The only females I know of who ran were the ancient Spartan women; they were equal to men in speed and athleticism."

"Then I want to be one of them! Where can I read about such women?"

"I don't really know, Süheylā." He was perplexed to no end. This Muslim girl was pushing the norms, and he had no idea how to handle her. Hoping to shake her off, he said, "maybe we can find a secluded spot, a far-off beach."

"Which beach would that be?"

Think quickly, Costa. "Maybe the beach of Kilyos," he blurted out, just to say something.

"Where is that?"

"It is at the farthest spot of Bosporus by the Black Sea."

"When can we go there?"

"Soon," he replied, hoping that she would change her mind eventually.

'Okay, I am looking forward to that."

Costa, who was keeping his eyes on Gülēngül, called her to come out of the water.

"I like the water, Costa; why do I have to come out?"

"Because, you will get sunburn; take this towel, dry up and rub some of this lotion on you. You'll thank me for it later."

Costa left Süheylā and her sister sunning on their chairs and went for a swim. On his way back, he spotted Süheylā standing by the water's edge, scanning for him. With so many swimmers around, she had difficulty spotting him. When she saw him wave, she jumped up and down and called his name.

She waded into the water knee deep and extended her hand. "I want you to teach me swimming, Costa."

"That may take a while. You will have to overcome your phobia of the water first. Unfortunately, in a couple of months or so the season will be over."

"In that case, I want to start now."

"Okay." Costa gave her a quick demonstration. Holding her by the hands, he instructed her to kick her legs like a frog.

The more she splashed the more she relaxed. She now wanted Costa to guide her into deeper water. The first wave was so big it knocked them both down. Süheylā disappeared into the wave and when she surfaced, she was panting with fright. She saw Costa extend his arms and she jumped into them, holding on to him for dear life. When she realized the water was not that deep, she started to laugh hysterically, beating on Costa with her palms. Costa squeezed her a bit more and she rewarded him with a quick kiss.

"The beach is great, Costa; I love it."

Neither Gülēngül nor Süheylā were going away from the water that day. Between swimming instruction and trips to the cabana for snack and colas, they kept Costa busy the entire afternoon.

Costa looked at his watch. It was time to join the Andersons. The two sisters went straight to the Andersons' bungalow, while Costa took a shower by the cabana and changed. He always carried extra clothes in the car's trunk. When he got to the pavilion, he noticed almost everyone was wearing special outfits. He asked one of the attendants what was going on.

"It is international beach wear night," the attendant replied. "Mrs. Anderson is the hostess this evening."

Suddenly Costa was concerned. The two sisters were not going to be very comfortable in this environment. Not only did they not have any appropriate clothing, he was also worried that an evening like this might be too much for the Muslim girls. He was probably better off taking them home and returning for the Andersons later. He sat at the table pondering what he should do when he saw Erika walking across the dance floor followed by the two sisters. All three were dressed in harem outfits: golden silk pantaloons wound tightly around their ankles, high heels, an Eastern style vest, exposed navel along with a long, diaphanous silk shirt tucked under their pantaloons with a Gobarah[35] belt. Trying to get over his surprise, Costa blinked. It seemed as though every eye of the pavilion were on Erika and these two sisters.

"I convinced them to wear these outfits I bought for the States. Luckily, Süheylā and I are the same size. The other one was for my husband's teenage daughter, who is Gülēngül's age. Don't they look beautiful, Costa?"

"Yes, Erika, they do," he mumbled in haste, peering through Süheylā's diaphanous veil. He saw her glinting eyes and sensed her ambivalence about this whole thing.

Gülēngül sat immediately while Süheylā glanced around her with concern, but only for a moment. The stares of several German bucks eyeing her made her

---

35. A wide silk belt adorned with fake gold coins.

blush. She sat by Costa and immediately slipped under his arm. This was a typical reaction for a Muslim girl. *I am spoken for and off-limits; go away.*

Trying to ease her apprehension, he patted her on the back.

The band started to play a tango and Mr. Anderson took his wife onto the dance floor. Erika, in the sexy harem's outfit and her overflowing bosom, was a moving seduction. James Anderson, tall and handsome, was an excellent dancer; the two of them were an impressive couple, commanding the envy of many.

The tango ended, and the Andersons returned to the table. Costa wanted to ask Erika about Monique, but changed his mind; it would have been inappropriate. Just at that time, Erika looked at him, smiling.

"Costa, before I forget, you will need to pick up Monique from the airport tomorrow. She had to go back to France for a show. I will give you her arrival details later."

"Of course, Erika; anything else?"

She put her hand on her chin and smiled enigmatically. "James and I like you and Süheylā a lot. We would like you to join us for dinner at our bungalow some time."

Costa did not know what to say. He wondered if Erika had an ulterior motive.

"What are you two talking about?" chimed in James Anderson.

"Nothing, darling," said Erika, planting a kiss on her husband. "I was just asking Costa if he and Süheylā would like to join us for dinner at our bungalow some time."

"Of course," replied James Anderson, looking enthused. Almost immediately, he called the server over.

When Süheylā saw the waiter pour champagne into her glass, she looked uncertain. "Mr. Anderson," she managed mildly, "my father never allows us to drink alcohol."

"Why not?" inquired Erika looking surprised.

"Because it is against the rules of Islam," explained Costa, wishing to rescue Süheylā.

"Just take a taste, Süheylā," encouraged James Anderson; it is not going to kill you."

She looked at Costa for his approval. "Go ahead, Süheylā. Nobody is going to tell your father," he teased, winking his eye.

"Okay." She lifted her glass and took a sip.

"I like it," she said, puckering her lips.

The waiter poured cherry juice for Gülēngül, who was not paying any attention anyway; she was fascinated watching all the dancers. The band started a new song, and Mr. Anderson invited Gülēngül to the dance floor. She jumped up immediately as if she had done it countless times before.

"Go on, Gülēngül," cheered Süheylā, looking relieved that it was not her.

Gülēngül smiled and took Mr. Anderson's hand. Rudimentary Tango was one of the dances their mother taught them. She knew the basic steps.

Süheylā could not get over her sister's nerve. She took a couple more sips of her champagne, looked at Costa, and cracked a smile. When Erika suggested that Süheylā and Costa dance, Süheylā lost her smile.

"I have never danced in public before, Mrs. Anderson!"

"Süheylā, call me Erika, please."

To her relief, dinner was in service and the band took a break. By mid-dinner, Süheylā drank at least half of her champagne. She now was grinning at Costa constantly, dipping her long eyelashes to show her contentment. The band started to play again—this time a Viennese Waltz.

Costa extended his hand and led her to the dance floor. With great effort, she followed, keeping her head down, sensing the many eyes on her. She looked stunning. Behind that diaphanous veil lurked a Eurasian face, a mysterious beauty. With some effort, she rested her arm on Costa's shoulder, looking ready to faint.

"Don't worry, Süheylā," smiled Costa. "Your mother taught you the basic steps for waltz. Just do as I do."

He took a few steps, and she tried to follow. After all, she had never been in a place like this before, but even more so in the arms of a man.

"This is a simple dance, Süheylā: One, two, three— one, two, three. Right left right, left right left. That is all there is to it."

"I know, but I am nervous. My parents waltz all the time."

"You are doing just great." By the middle of the song, she was catching on. As Costa whirled her around, she began to relax and let the music take her along. The song ended and as they walked back to their table, Erika stood up and clapped."

"Süheylā, you have great potential. You and Costa will need to come to our bungalow for lessons. I will teach you."

"Can you really teach me how to dance, Erika?"

"Of course I can. I am a professional ballroom dancer."

Süheylā was delighted, but Costa not as much. He was worried about Erika's motives.

"Where did you learn to dance like that, Costa?" Erika interrupted his thoughts.

"My English teacher owns a dance studio here in Istanbul. I took private lessons."

"I had no idea that there is a ballroom studio in Istanbul!"

"We are not that backward, Erika."

"Kemal Atatürk, the founder of The Republic of Turkey, was an avid waltz dancer," Süheylā chimed in.

Süheylā's reply threw Erika completely off stride. "That is amazing."

The band started to play a familiar tune. "I love this song," whispered Süheylā. Can we dance to it, Costa?"

Costa jumped up and led her onto the dance floor. "This is Rumba, Süheylā. Do you know it?"

"Who cares?" The champagne is making me light-headed already."

"Süheylā, you are the prettiest girl I've ever met."

She blushed and clasped Costa's hand a little tighter. "Costa, you make me feel so free. I want to be with you every day."

"I feel the same way, Süheylā."

They could have danced forever, but it was time to go. Costa dropped off Süheylā and Gülēngül at their apartment and the Andersons at the Hilton. He parked the car and walked home. It was a great day, a perfect Süheylā day. In her harem's outfit, she could have been the Sultan's favorite, and yet, she was his girlfriend. *How lucky could he get!*

Chapter 13: At the University of Istanbul

It was a perfect time of basil, mint and Ottoman roses. Costa and Süheylā fell madly in love. In spite of their different cultures, religion and ethnicity—he a Greek-Christian and she, an exotic beauty of Turko-Austrian lineage—the two lovers defied all the odds. The beach of Kilyos and the Anderson's bungalow became their places of escape. These were the only areas where the two lovers could go jogging and kiss—unencumbered from the strange looks of the city's dual[36] personality.

The Andersons had fallen in love with Süheylā from the first day they'd met her. If Erika was looking for a project to alleviate her boredom, she found one; it was Süheylā. With her large wardrobe, she kept up a constant flow of clothing, taking pride in Süheylā's looks; she even taught her how to use makeup. Under Erika's coaching, Süheylā discovered shampoo, hair dryers, perfume, miniskirts and intimate apparel. Movies, rock and roll, and the beach were pushing Süheylā to the edge of cultural rebellion. Maybe because of the influence of her Austrian mother or because of Costa or Erika, her proclivity to adapt and experiment was bottomless.

The University of Istanbul was a classic Turkish institution that provided gender and race equality, managing to stay away from all the anti-minority hysteria. In this university, Armenians, Greeks and Jews found acceptance and graduated alongside one another. It was located at the old city, in Beyazit Square, originally built by the Emperor Constantine the Great as the Forum Tauri and later enlarged by Theodosius the Great as the Forum of Theodosius. Sultan Mehmet, the Conqueror,

---

36. Partly Islamic and partly westernized.

reestablished the University in 1453. It was equivalent to Roman universities consisting of the schools of medicine, law, philosophy and the letters. Venerated as the prime educational institution of Turkey, it had a student population of over seventy thousand. When Atatürk came into power, he reorganized the learning institution more along secular lines. He also made university education free to all those who passed an aptitude test. Some of the notable alumni were Yitzhak Ben-Zvi, president of Israel; David Ben-Gurion, prime minister of Israel; several Turkish prime ministers, such as Yildirim Akbulut and Nihat Erim.

Like thousands of other students, Costa and Süheylā took the university entrance exam. Today was the official posting of the results. They were hoping to see their names on the list.

"Are you ready for this, Süheylā?" Costa asked. Süheylā placed her palm over her heart while they waited behind a long line of other hopefuls.

There it was! Süheylā Gülpinar: number eleven. *Major: Law. Minor: Ethnology.* Süheylā jumped up and down and clapped her hands joyfully. Others in the line clapped at her spontaneous reaction.

"All right, Costa," said Süheylā, "let's go to your bulletin board and find out how you did."

"Not yet," said Costa as he scanned the list. He pointed to his name down near the bottom. *Costa Rigas; Minor: Ethnology.* "I did this for you," Costa smiled. "I decided to take ethnology as a minor so that we can attend at least one class together.

"For me?" she smiled, giving Costa a hug. She looked overjoyed.

"Yes, just for you. Now let's go to the business section and see how I did."

They hurried to the other side of the building, where the line in front of the bulletin board was even longer.

There it was, Costa Rigas, number 23—*Business Major*.

And they shared a class: Ethnology 1, which met every Friday. Their first week at the University of Istanbul went like a blur. The two lovers could hardly wait for their first class together. They arrived in the lecture hall ahead of time just to make sure they found space next to each other. The professor asked the students to introduce themselves.

After Costa's turn, dead silence. The students had noticed his Christian name on the bulletin board before, but that was okay. What was vexing was that this giaour, was the companion of this beautiful Turkish girl. For most Turks, this was an effrontery.

Costa felt the stairs directed toward him, but he did not care. Purposely, he leaned closer to Süheylā just to antagonize them.

Eat your heart out, fellows; she is mine.

He saw Süheylā scribble something on a piece of paper, fold it and push it to his side with a big smile. He opened it on the sly.

"You are the handsomest guy around. I wish I could kiss you right now."

He sent her a quick smile and put the note in his pocket. When the class was over, Costa and Süheylā walked down the stairway on their way to the bus stop. Two students rushed from the opposite direction and blocked their way.

"Excuse us," said Costa, feeling uneasy. "Can we get by?"

"No, you can't."

"Why not?" shot back Süheylā visibly annoyed.

"Don't you know that socializing with a giaour is immoral?"

"You dare to lecture me?" she shot back angrily. "Get out of our way."

"You are a prostitute. You should be ashamed of yourself, sister."

Süheylā slapped him so hard he staggered. Immediately, Costa stepped between Süheylā and her victim.

"How dare you insult my friend?!" he shouted, feeling angry. He was not about to waver.

"What are you going to do about it?" jeered the other as he took an aggressive step forward.

"Nothing," replied Costa, pretending to cower.

Emboldened by Costa's passive stance, he swung to his face, but Costa had been in these scrapes before. He deflected the blow and hit the student square in the jaw. The student dropped immediately. The other one pounced on Costa from behind and wrestled him to the ground. Quick as a cat, Costa grabbed his foot and put it into a lock. A police officer patrolling nearby heard the fracas and blew his whistle.

"What is going on here?" he questioned, looking at the yelping student. "Who hurt you?"

"This giaour," he pointed.

"Did you hit him?" asked the officer.

"Yes sir; this jerk and his friend over there wanted to beat me up."

"Why?"

Costa shrugged his shoulders. "I have no idea."

"I know," shot Süheylā furiously. "These two men have been harassing me since my first day at school with catcalls. They were jealous because I was walking with my friend."

"You are wrong, sister. I wanted to inform you that you have no business socializing with giaours."

The commotion in the meantime attracted several bystanders. One of them, hearing the derisive comments, scolded the jerk aloud. "Aren't you ashamed of yourself? This is the University of Istanbul, not Dolapdere[37]."

Costa recognized Ozan immediately; he was a classmate in *Applied Economics.* Taking a giaour's side was unexpected for a Turk. The police officer looked at Costa and scratched his head.

"Why don't you leave right now? Do not let me catch you fighting around here again. Next time, I am going to take you in."

The two lovers headed for Beyoglu, where they'd had their first date. It was where they felt most comfortable. It was also the location of the movie theaters, the cafés, all the fast-food restaurants and the American library. They found a corner and sat without saying much. The fight left both of them feeling perplexed.

Finally, Süheylā nudged Costa in the arm and looked at him in admiration. "Costa, where did you learn to fight like that?"

"From my father, Phillip," Costa replied with bravado. "He is an expert on the ancient Olympic sport Pankrateon."

"What is that?"

"It is a combination sport of boxing, kicking and wrestling."

"Can you teach me Pankrateon?"

Costa was at a loss. "First, you started jogging with me at the beach. Then you have started taking dance lessons from Erika and now you want to learn fighting? Is there anything a girl like you won't do?"

"I am not just any girl, Costa. I want to be independent and strong," she shot back.

"Slow down, Süheylā. As you saw, any Turkish girl who socializes with a giaour like me can get in trouble."

---

37. A notable slum of Istanbul.

"Aren't you getting carried away?" She glanced around and seeing no one, gave him a quick kiss. "I will try, but as you said, I am a Turkish girl. We Turks have very little control of our emotions."

"You don't have a monopoly on this one. Greeks are no different!"

"What about the Kurds?"

"What about them?"

"Do they have the same temperament?"

Her question left Costa scratching his head. *What was that all about?*

He remembered the note she had handed him in class, about wanting to kiss him, took it out of his pocket and waved it in her face. "You could not kiss me in the lecture hall, and that kiss you just gave me was not much. What are you going to do about it?"

She glanced at him seductively. "Okay, let's go."

"Go where?"

"To your apartment!"

"Are you serious?"

"You have a kiss to collect. Besides, I want you to teach me fighting." She stood up and started to walk away.

Her offer was so unexpected, Costa felt glued to his chair.

When she glanced back and saw him still sitting with his mouth open, she winked. "Are you coming, *Monsieur* Rigas?"

Chapter 14: A Special Assignment

It was a banner year for the travel business. Hermes Travel kept Costa busy and the Gregorys very happy. School, part-time work and time with Süheylā were working to perfection. Costa had just returned from a ticket delivery when Mrs. Gregory asked him to go into the hotel's coffee shop to meet with Mr. Gregory. He found him in the company of a very serious-looking man.

"Good evening, Mr. Gregory."

"Costa, this is Mr. Orhan Akduman; he needs your help."

Mr. Akduman shook Costa's hand and invited him to sit.

Wondering what this was all about, Costa took his seat with trepidation. He avoided looking the man in the eyes; he looked important … even scary.

"Mr. Akduman requires your interpreter skills," Mr. Gregory continued.

Costa looked toward Mr. Akduman, wondering.

"Costa, do you know who I am?"

Costa swallowed, trying to think. "I am sorry, sir; my apologies."

"I am the chief of the secret police of Istanbul."

Costa's antennae went up. *Was he in trouble?* Mr. Akduman spoke before he even had a chance to think.

"I need your services this weekend, Costa. Friends of my younger brother, who is studying at M.I.T, USA, are visiting Turkey as my guests, and I am trying to entertain them. Unfortunately, I hardly speak any English and nobody else in my circle does, either. We will also need the Mercedes. I have already spoken to Mr. Sariyer; he is okay with that."

"Yes, Mr. Akduman, at your service."

"It is settled then. Here is my address. Be at my home Saturday by six-thirty p.m."

Before Costa could say anything, Mr. Akduman got up from his chair and shook his hand.

"Thank you, young man; I shall be grateful."

Costa looked at Mr. Gregory, who smiled and gave Costa the sign to go.

Costa walked through the lobby and out into the courtyard, wondering. He had never met such a high functionary in the Turkish government before. Was it good luck or should he be scared? Thankfully, it was Friday, a night out at the movies with Süheylā.

Chapter 15: A Mystical Connection

The Seven Hills Café and the American Library were their favorite places to socialize. Here, Costa began tutoring Süheylā in English. Within the short time of their courtship, under Costa's influence she began to read Greek and Roman classics, voraciously; and her sketching abilities were amazing. Every time they met, she would hand Costa the sketch of some Greek or Roman statue. She drew them just as they looked; pronounced muscles, genitals and all.

In the span of several months, they saw *The Marriage of Figaro* and *The Barber of Seville.* When they saw the movie *Topkapi*, Süheylā fell in love with Melina Merkouri[38], the star of the film. She was so taken with the actress, not only did she start to dress like her, she also copied her accent to perfection; their similarity of voice was uncanny.

The Ottoman music masters—Emel Sayin, Behiye Aksoy, Zeki Müren and several others—were their favorites. When it came to movies, they loved early American and Turkish films. Although most Turkish films were in black and white, their melancholic cultural depth gave them a sense of country, a sense of belonging. Even more so, the Turkish actors were more compatible with their eastern temperaments. Invariably, most Turkish films featured the music genre of Tùrkùs[39], which always tugged at their heartstrings.

Due to a late airport run, Costa asked Süheylā if she could meet him in front of the movie theater—Emek[40].

---

38. The famous Greek movie actress, who played the role of Ilya in "Never on Sunday" filmed and produced by Jules Dasin.

39. The folk songs of Anatolia.

40. A classical theater considered a cultural treasure of Turkey.

This was a sold-out event starring the grand dame of the Turkish Cinema, Fatma Girik. Costa bought the tickets a few days earlier.

When Costa arrived, he spotted Süheylā amidst a group of girls talking excitedly. He knew immediately; Süheylā was wearing one of her mother's designer Islamic head covers. They all wanted to know where she got it, how they could make one, so on and so forth. As an artist and an aficionado of fashion, Süheylā's mom foresaw the need for Islamic clothing, and her daughter Süheylā was the perfect candidate to model her Islamic wares.

At the beginning, Süheylā was very happy to sport this fancy Islamic head cover, not necessarily out of religious sentiments but for the sheer joy of wearing something different and original. As the time marched on, the head cover became Süheylā's mystical connection to culture, and country; it became a metaphorical bond to her platonic relationship with the Divine. Costa had seen Süheylā in fancy head covers before, but this one was a cut above all the others. Wrapped across her forehead was a Ninja-like black bandana, topped with a multicolored silk head cover. Not only did it contour around her face and cover her ears, it also wrapped below her chin, wound around her neck and ruffled under her rose-colored, fitted V-neck jacket, accentuating her oval face into a portrait of classical beauty. With contoured eyelashes, red lipstick and light makeup, she was a statement of Islamic sophistication, a worthy Delacroix, the sexiest Turkish girl in Istanbul.

When Süheylā spotted Costa, her spontaneous smile sent his heart racing

"Excuse me, girls," she apologized tactfully. "my fiancé has just arrived." She walked briskly and gave him a kiss. The maidens now trained their eyes on Costa. One in particular nudged him on the elbow.

"Excuse me, sir; you are very lucky. Your fiancé is a beautiful Muslim girl."

"Thank you," said Costa graciously, wrapping his arm around Süheylā's waist. The girls swooned with excitement.

"We will see you inside the theater, girls," added Süheylā as she slipped under Costa's arm, leaving them gasping.

They presented their tickets and walked into the theater. The usher took them to their seats.

"Your fiancé? When did we get engaged?" inquired Costa half-seriously.

She gave him her trademark, that giant smirk of hers. "It sounded rather nice, don't you think? Besides, a male in the company of a Muslim girl has to be either her husband or her fiancé. Singles dating is a 'no-no' in our country," she said, winking her eye.

"Clever girl, you think so quick on your feet."

"I learned from you."

"No, you did not. You either have it or you don't."

"Have what?"

"It."

"You know, Costa. I never thought I would ever meet anyone like you."

"You say that because you have not met any others—yet."

She elbowed him in the ribs. "I don't want to meet any others; you are *It*."

"You really are something, Süheylā. This yashmak[41] unlike all the others is breathtaking."

"Thank you, Costa; I wanted to surprise you."

"Not only did you surprise me, you invited head-turning."

---

41. Turkish head cover for girls.

"Oh stop it. I just wore it for effect. My mother has been experimenting with this design for a while. She is already beginning to sell them to fashion stores."

"I think your mother is on to something. If I were a girl, Muslim or Christian, I would buy one, too," Costa joked.

"Thank you, Costa. This theater is too hot. Please help me take my jacket off."

Süheylā was wearing a sexy, sleeveless tightly fitting pullover. Her healthy chest popped up in front of his eyes, startling him sensually. He also caught a whiff of a tantalizing smell, which seemed to be coming from her underarms. When she placed her arm across his backrest, he was astounded. Her underarms looked completely shaved. She caught him looking and giggled.

"Are you surprised?"

"Yes, I am. When did you start this?"

"About two weeks ago." She moved closer. "Take a good look; no underarm hair."

"I see; you have the sexiest underarms I have ever seen."

"Don't get too excited. I have more surprises for you."

"What is that aroma?"

"Erika calls it "underarm deodorant." It is meant to mask the smell of perspiration."

"That deodorant is great, but I don't think anything can replace your natural scent, Süheylā."

"Ooh! I love that," she exclaimed and nudged herself closer.

The room was now dark. Costa grabbed her face and gave her a hot kiss. Instantly her eyes glistened, ready to swallow him. "After the movie, can we go kiss, Costa?"

"I thought you'd never ask. I am dying to explore what is under that head cover of yours!" he teased.

"Let's go now!" she whispered.

Chapter 15: A Mystical Connection

They left the movie theater in a hurry. His apartment was ten minutes away. He was anxious to peel off that head cover, and hopefully even more!

Chapter 16: You Are Nothing But a Slave

The good thing about Istanbul was that one could ride public transportation almost everywhere. To get to the university from the European section required a combination of a trolley or tram, bus and a short metro ride called "The Tunnell," or just a single bus, depending on where you lived. Costa and Süheylā were riding home. Close to the Golden Horn, two porters boarded the bus. After a day of carrying heavy loads on their backs, as all porters do in Turkey, they looked filthy, unkempt, and reeked. They walked down the aisle eyeing every female lecherously, found seats, and immediately began directing catcalls at the female passengers. At the next stop, a young woman assisting an older man boarded the bus, who unwittingly took seats in front of the porters. The old man seemed hard of hearing so the woman had to speak to him a tad louder. Costa recognized the spoken Greek.

When the porters heard the sound of the foreign language, they began cursing. One of them stood up and yelled at them to shut up.

The woman spoke to the porter and in perfrect Turkish: "Excuse us, Mister; my uncle is visiting from another country and does not speak any Turkish."

"We don't care," yelled the porter. "You are giaours. When in Turkey you speak Turkish."

"Greek is the only language he understands," pleaded the woman.

Before she could finish, the porter slapped her. "Giaour prostitute; we are the masters of this land, and you are nothing but a slave. Shut your mouth or I will take you down and fuck you hard."

The bus driver, who saw the commotion in his rear-view mirror, stopped the bus and opened the doors with the intention to throw the porters out, but before he could get out of his seat, the porters grabbed the old man and the young woman and shoved them out of the bus like trash.

"Get lost, giaour dogs," one of them cursed at the old man as he and his companion tumbled to the pavement.

Süheylā and Costa, who were sitting a couple of rows behind, jumped from their seats to the aid of old man and his companion, but the porters blocked their way and glared at them.

Süheylā, who was in front of Costa, pretended to turn around, but suddenly she kneed the porter in front of her in the groin. The blow has so hard the porter collapsed to his knees, screaming like a soprano. Looking surprised, the other porter attempted to jump over his writhing buddy, but before he could so, Costa stepped in front of Süheylā, grabbed the porter by the hair and slammed his head into the steel railing. Dazed from the blow, the porter attempted to swing, but Costa warded ohh his blow, grabbed his arm and twisted it into a lock behind his back, incapacitating him. When the porter began cursing, Costa slammed the porter's head against the open window frame. The porter collapsed on the seat, bleeding from his head.

The two lovers hurried out of the bus and knelt by the side of the old man who was lying on the ground. He had a bleeding nose and a couple of gashes on his forehead. His lady-companion was hysterical. Costa looked at Süheylā with concern.

"This man is really hurt, Süheylā; call a cab. He needs to go to the hospital."

Süheylā hailed a passing cab and she and Costa assisted the old man into the cab. The hospital was only five minutes away."

Thankfully the hospital staff attended to the old man immediately. In the meantime, the old man's companion—apparently, she was his niece—could not thank them enough. Costa and Süheylā waited until the doctors stitched up the old man; he looked well enough to walk. By the time Costa and Süheylā made it back to Costa's apartment, it was dark. They sat on his couch saying nothing, but Süheylā seemed very animated.

"Now you see why I wanted to learn Pankrateon, Costa. That knee trick you taught me really worked." She was beaming from ear to ear.

"You are probably the first woman in Istanbul to have done this," Costa said seriously. "I never thought I would see a thing like that."

She gave him a kiss. "Besides meeting you, it was the most exciting thing I ever did in my life, Costa. I am proud of myself."

"You should be, Süheylā, but what are you going to do when those porters spot you alone some day? They will be looking for both of us."

"We might have to change our bus route."

"There is no other route."

"What should we do then?"

Süheylā remained silent for a few seconds. "I got it," she murmured. "I will speak to my Kurdish friends."

Costa was alarmed. He knew of Süheylā's sympathies toward the Kurds, but he'd never given it much thought, even when she had joined their social group. It was just a passing fancy, or so he had thought. "Oh no," he protested. "We don't want any more trouble."

"Who spoke of trouble? My Kurdish friends might know a way."

Costa attempted to say something, but Süheylā cut him off with a kiss.

"Go get us something to eat and we will talk about that later," she winked. "After dinner I want my Pankrateon lesson," she winked.

"Such an offer I cannot refuse," replied Costa pensively, his mind already troubled with the Kurds. They were a troublesome lot. He left Süheylā in his apartment making tea and went to pick up dinner. On his way back, he opened his mailbox, and when he saw his mother's letter, he sat on the steps to read it.

Dear Costa:

I hope you are in good health.

We have bad news. The Turkish government forbade the teaching of Greek at our schools and your brother needs private tutoring. We decided to send him to Greece. There is no safety here.

We are scared to death. The military, purposely, allows the hard criminals to roam the island freely so that they can terrorize us. They found the grocer's body in a well; he had been missing the past three months. Apparently, they robbed him and then killed him with a steel rod right through his heart. Our island now is teeming with belligerent Turkish neo-immigrants from the mainland.

A mass exodus of the Greek natives is inevitable. We are also concerned about you. You must consider leaving.

Do not do anything foolish. If you are still seeing that Turkish girl, stop. You are playing with fire.

Love, Mom

Costa read the letter, put it in his pocket and walked up the steps. The news was unsettling. He regretted his present predicament, but leaving Turkey was out of the question; he was in love. No Süheylā, no nothing.

Chapter 17: Muslims and Christians Never Intermarry

After the incident with the porters, Costa and Süheylā made sure to ride the later bus, to avoid running into them again. They were having tea at the café Diyarbakir when a bus driver walked in and nonchalantly looked around. When his eyes rested on their faces, he grinned and walked toward their table.

"I want to shake your hands; you really gave it to those porters!" smiled the driver approvingly at Costa and Süheylā.

Costa looked at the driver with concern. When he and Süheylā fought with the porters, he was hopeful that nobody would remember their faces. "It was self-defense, we had no choice," Costa replied apologetically.

"You are a crafty young man," said the driver. "But you lady, are a brave girl. I never thought I would see a thing like that. Who taught you to fight like that?"

Without any hesitation, Süheylā pointed at Costa. "My friend," she said proudly.

The bus driver gulped for air and looked at Costa. "Are you a boxer?"

"Nothing of that sort; my father taught me Pankrateon."

"I have never heard of it. What is it?"

"It is a combination sport; it involves boxing, kicking and wrestling all at once."

"You are an impressive pair," said the driver smiling. "You are safe from those brutes."

"How can you be so sure?" inquired Süheylā.

"Didn't you read the papers this morning, Miss? Those porters got into a fight last night at some meyhane in Dolapdere. They are dead."

Costa choked on his tea. He looked at Süheylā with consternation. *Did her Kurdish friends have anything to do with it?* "I really don't know how I feel about this," replied Costa, feeling a knot in his stomach.

"They got what they deserved; Allah Ekber," smiled the driver and patted Costa on the back.

"You don't mean that, do you?" replied Costa, still in disbelief.

"Maybe they deserved punishment, but not death," added Süheylā.

"I mean every word I say, Miss. You were the only ones who went to the aid of that old man. The other passengers ran like chickens." He shook their hands again and sat down at a nearby table.

Costa and Süheylā left the coffee shop immediately. The minute they were out in the street, Costa was ready.

"Did you speak to your Kurdish friends about those porters?"

"I told Dersim," she smiled coyly.

"Who is Dersim?"

"He is a member of my Kurdish Club."

"Is it possible that your Kurdish friends had anything to do with this?"

"That is impossible, Costa. They did not even know them. How can that be?"

"I am getting a bad feeling about this. I need to get going. I have to pick up Mr. Sariyer from the airport. I am not sure when I will be back; I will call you tomorrow." They took the next bus and Costa escorted Süheylā to her apartment.

His main concern was Süheylā now, who in spite of his admonition had joined that Kurdish Club. "It was a pure social one," she maintained, but Costa knew better. These semi-secret Kurdish social clubs around campus were springing up everywhere lately, and their main purpose was to agitate for Kurdish independence.

Mr. Sariyer's flight from Geneva was late. When he finally returned to his apartment, Costa was surprised to see light through his window. As a rule, he never left the lights on. He walked up the steps and put his ear to the keyhole. Inside his apartment were his parents, talking. He opened the door with trepidation. His mother was standing in the middle of the small living room.

"Do you always come home this late?" she frowned. His father on the other hand was sitting on the couch looking pensive.

"Hello, Dad. Are you all right?"

"I am fine, son. My apologies for the surprise visit; I could not shake your mother off."

Costa looked at his mom. "What is going on?"

"Have you lost your mind?"

"About what, Mom?"

"That Turkish girl, Costa."

"What about her?"

"I want you to stop seeing her immediately."

"You came all the way here to tell me that?"

"If you don't stop, you will have to leave Turkey."

"Aren't you going a little too fast?"

"You are embarrassing the family."

Costa got angry. "What does this have to do with our family?"

"We are Christians, and don't you forget it."

"So?"

"Christians and Muslims don't intermarry."

"Who spoke of marriage, Mom? She is my best friend."

"I don't give a damn about that. What are you going to do about this friend?"

"Nothing," replied Costa with annoyance.

"You are liable to get us all in trouble."

"I appreciate your advice, Mom, but it won't happen."

His mother continued as if she had not heard his reply. "Sooner or later this relationship will ruin your life."

"Mom, stop."

"Turks will always be Turks. We can never trust them."

"There are good Turks and bad ones, Mom. Good Greeks and bad Greeks."

"Islam and Christianity don't mix."

"I have read the Koran, Mom. Frankly, I do not see much difference in the two religions."

"Reading the Koran is blasphemy. You can be excommunicated from the church."

"What do I care about the darn church? Organized religion is tyranny."

"I am frightened for you, son."

"Don't worry, Mom. I am not going to do anything to disgrace our family."

"That girl will be the end of you, Costa. You must leave Turkey as soon as possible."

"I am not going anywhere; I love Istanbul, I have a job, and I drive a Mercedes for a powerful man."

"I don't care if he is the Sultan of Turkey."

Costa looked at his father for support, but his father simply shrugged. "You are on your own, Costa. A little encouragement from a vixen and you are off to the races."

"Dad, don't be like Mom."

His mom cut in. "Stop with all that nonsense, Costa. Your father and I came here to order you to stop seeing that Turkish girl. It looks like we are not making any progress."

"Mom, I told you. I am not going to do that."

"Listen to your mother," advised his father. "When her father finds out about your relationship with his daughter, he is liable to go to extremes. You will have no place to hide."

"Your father told you right," added his mom. "But it looks like we are going to leave empty-handed."

Costa had never seen his mother like this before. When she placed her hands on her hips, he prepared for more.

"Where did you get that dresser?"

"It is not mine. It belongs to a friend."

"I bet I know who that friend is."

"Okay, Mom, you know that, too. So what is wrong with that? Her father is very strict, so she keeps her stuff in that dresser."

"Why is it locked?"

"Because it is hers; I don't really care what she keeps in there."

"Is she an anarchist? Stuff like that will land you in jail."

"Aren't you carrying this thing a bit too far, Mom?"

"I am not getting through, am I? Your father and I will be in the city for a couple of days. I hate sleeping in that room with that dresser, but I guess we have no choice. We will continue this conversation tomorrow. Good night."

The next two days were hell on Costa. He was never so glad to see his parents leave; their backward attitude was suffocating.

Chapter 18: Volcanic Passion

Süheylā had a dance lesson that evening, but Erika had called it off. Costa thought about a movie, but Süheylā had other ideas.

"Let's spend the evening at your apartment, Costa," she suggested, smirking.

They took the trolley. Süheylā hurriedly pushed through the door. "Your apartment is cold," she observed as she sashayed into the spare bedroom.

Costa lit the fireplace and sat on the couch. *Why was she taking so long?*

"Are you ready?" she yelled from behind the door.

"Ready for what?"

He heard the turning of the door handle and turned to look. In pranced this creature in high-heels, silk stockings and a pitch-black miniskirt. All he could see were two gorgeous legs up to her mid-thigh. Finally, when he managed to inch his eyes higher, the tight pink blouse, ruby-red lips and the long eyelashes astounded him.

"What do you think?" she teased as she paraded in front of him, swaying her hips like Erika Anderson.

Costa was agape. "You look fantastic, Süheylā. What in the world have you done?"

"Do you like it?"

"Like it? I am having a heart attack!"

"Slow down, *Monsieur*," she challenged with her Merkouri imitation.

"Did you keep this outfit in that dresser all this time?"

"I did. Erika told me to wear it when the time was right."

"Did Erika teach you to walk like that, too?"

"Yes."

"I noticed the change in your walking style the past few weeks—now I know."

"I wanted to surprise you."

"This is beyond surprise."

"I am so glad you like the new me!" she winked. She blew him a kiss and walked to the kitchenette. "I'll make us some tea."

"I like the new you and the old you," he complimented. "I love them both. You would look good in a burlap bag." With his heart racing, he put a few more logs in the fireplace and picked up a magazine from the coffee table, pretending to read, but his eyes were on Süheylā's back.

"Costa, stop staring at my legs," she admonished him without turning around. "Will you put on some music?"

He dialed Radio Istanbul. It was Emel Sayin, their favorite artist.

"Perfect timing," she said as she placed the teapot on the coffee table.

When she sat on the couch and crossed her legs, Costa thought he was going to pass out. Her miniskirt was generating more heat than a hot day at the beach. They gazed at one another amorously; their faces were aflame, and their warmth was creeping into their loins.

It had been almost seven months since they'd met. Spending time together in his apartment had been a gradual journey of discovery, but tonight it was electric. When Costa ran his hands behind her back, she writhed and wiggled with excitement. He unbuttoned her blouse and slid it off her shoulders, exposing her bra. He trailed his hand over her breasts, feeling her firm nipples beneath her bra. She gave him a seductive smile, lay on the couch and pulled him on top of her. Chest against breasts, their lips met. Ravaging each other, they were inhaling one another's breath like fumes of nectar.

"I am hot," she whispered.

This is it, thought Costa. *This cannot be happening.*

They lay side by side, exploring their bodies, getting bolder by the minute. When he slipped his finger under her bra to play with her erect nipples, she gave him a hot kiss and started to unbutton his shirt. He in turn reached behind her back and unclasped her bra.

In front of his eyes popped two of the most magnificent things he had ever seen. She pulled him onto her tightly as if to shield her breasts from his vision. They stayed embraced for a while, feeling their desire accelerating.

They knew where they were going and it was deliriously frightening. This was going too fast with dangerous consequences, but Süheylā surprised him by acting as if she had done this hundreds of times before.

Feeling the insides of her thighs, he pulled off her miniskirt. Her stockings, her high heels and her panties were the only things left. His eyes were ready to pop out of their sockets.

"Come on," she challenged, "don't be so helpless. You have seen me before!"

"But never like this!"

She made a dismissive notion. "Are you going to take off your pants or do I have to?" Without waiting for his reply, she unbuckled his belt.

Intimidated by her boldness, he removed them himself.

"That is better," she smiled, nuzzling into his chest while he ran his hands around her beautifully curved bottom.

The first time he'd seen her, he'd dreamed of intimacy, but he was convinced it was pie in the sky; and now she was naked in front of him. Slowly he inched his hand up to her mid-thigh; she moaned with excitement.

His blood was tumbling in his loins like a raging river while his brain was racing in reverse; he was in panic. There was no premarital sex, in a Muslim country like Turkey; even more so, this was a Muslim girl, and he was a Christian.

"Let's go to your bed, Costa," she suggested, startling him. Before he could react, she got up off the couch and walked to his bedroom.

Mesmerized, he followed. He watched her pull the coverlet off the bed, spread herself on the white sheets, and beckon him to lay by her side. It was as if Eve had just invited Adam to her bed, and she was not wearing a fig leaf.

To go with an angelic face, Süheyla had a fantastic body. He lay beside her marveling at her unashamed composure.

"You are my dream girl, Süheylā. The first time I saw you, my heart stopped. You looked like a rose on fire. It never crossed my mind that we would lie naked together."

"Here is your chance, Costa. Now you have to make love to me," she challenged.

He took a couple of gulps of air. "I have to master my courage about that," he apologized humbly.

"You are a coward," she shot back tempestuously.

"Why are you calling me that?"

"I just told you; you don't want to make love to me."

"It is because I love you too much."

"Why is it that I feel I can do anything with you, Costa?"

"I don't know, Süheylā; frankly, you are taking me beyond my limits."

"Don't be so modest, Costa. Our friends Firyāl and Ali make love every day."

Costa was not amused, but Süheylā was irresistible.

He was at his wits end when Süheylā shocked him further. She ran into the living room and came back holding her pocket book. She sat beside him, opened it and took out something wrapped in plastic. "Here, put it on, quick. I cannot wait."

"Costa had never seen one before, but he knew immediately. "What is it?" he asked somewhat shocked.

"It is called a prophylactic."

"Where in the world did you get it?"

"Erika gave it to me."

"What about the Turkish law of virginity?" he managed, feeling his loins quivering in temptation. His mother had admonished him long ago 'no sex before marriage.' He broke the rule with Erika and he was not about to break it with Süheylā. It would be a dishonor.

"I really don't care," she replied and nuzzling closer.

The consequences of making love, especially for Süheylā, would be severe. If her father found out, he could put her through a virginity test. A broken hymen would place her future in jeopardy. As the male perpetrator, Costa would probably be in even worse shape. Balancing himself between depths of fright and heights of desire was pure torture. Costa struggled with that thought, and yet he could not think at all. After some gigantic effort, he looked deeply into her eyes. "Süheylā, please dress."

"What?"

"Please dress," he begged, feeling sorry the minute he said it. *What if she changed her mind?*

She got furious. "Are you scared?"

"No. It is because I care for your honor."

"Are you insane? We got up to this point and now you are cowering?" she challenged, feeling spurned. "I want the real thing, Costa."

"I am afraid of the consequences."

"Nothing is going to happen to me, I assure you."

"May I remind you that this is Turkey, not Europe?"

"I told you, I don't care. I want you now, Costa."

Holding the prophylactic in his hand, he was trembling with excitement.

Süheylā grabbed it from his hand. "I will show you how to put it on.

The feel of the prophylactic assuaged his fears immediately; He could no longer wait.

"Go slow," she murmured and lay down.

He searched for her opening. With his first thrust, she let out a shriek of delight and clasped her arms around him tightly. "Oh, Costa, Costa," she whispered. As his thrusts grew stronger, she dug her fingernails into his flesh like claws. With his loins on fire, he sealed her mouth with a long kiss while her vagina began to suffocate him. When his thrusts grew more frenetic, she began to scream—"oh Costa, I am in heaven—dear God I am in Heaven." Sensing his explosion, she bit him on the lips, mumbling his name.

"That was how I fantasized about us making love, Costa. I feel great all over and I love you deeply."

"And I love you too, Süheylā; you shall be mine always and forever."

Their torment was now sheer ecstasy. Glued to one another, they lay on his bed, exhaling with delight.

Finally, Costa caught his breath. Süheyla, who taught you all this?" he asked, still trying to recover from her boldness.

"Erika," she said coyly.

"Even how to shave?"

"Yes."

"What about the prophylactic?"

"She taught me how to put it on a banana. It is the only way not to get pregnant."

Costa was aghast. "How much time do you spend with Erika?"

"Enough! Next time I see you, I want you shaved," she teased.

Costa pretended surprise. "What else?"

"The time I spend with Erika opened my eyes in areas I never knew existed."

"I'd like to lock you up in my room and never let you out of my sight. Erika is corrupting you," he teased, half seriously.

"Costa, since I have met you, I have lost all my inhibitions. The idea of making love to you was following me since the day we met; you are my Apollo."

Apollo? Wasn't that what Erika had called him a few months ago? "That is the greatest compliment I ever heard, Süheylā. I started to get delirious about you since I saw you in that bathing suit with your skin of milk and your great body; I dreamed about you every night."

"Funny you should say that; every time I think of you, I get excited," teased Süheylā.

Costa absorbed her words as if they were manna from heaven. He never thought a young girl like her could be so open and so bold. She was mature beyond her age.

Finally, Costa got up.

"Where are you going?"

"I'll go get us a towel, Süheylā."

"Not yet; here is another prophylactic; one more time."

Costa took the loaded prophylactic off, and slipped the other one on quickly.

This girl was beyond fantasy. He never wanted her to leave his bed. This time their lovemaking was even hotter and steamier; it was heaven. Süheylā was a cauldron of passion. Finally, he managed to go to the bathroom, flush the prophylactics down the toilet and return with a towel. He nudged her off a little to the side and handed her the towel. Just at that time, he spotted the bloodstains on the white bed sheet.

Süheylā understood immediately. "Don't worry, Costa. That is natural. It is the rupture of my hymen. It means that you took my flower away. Now, you either have to marry me, or I will kill you."

Her serious tone was menacing.

Costa swallowed. "Any time you say so, Süheylā. I could never love anyone but you."

"Me too, Costa, "now let's clean these blood stains."

"No," protested Costa. "I have a better idea. "I will be right back." He went to the kitchenette and returned holding a pair of scissors. "I will cut out the bed sheet stains and keep it as a memento."

Süheylā looked at him as if he were a lunatic. "What kind of crazy custom is that?"

"It is practiced by the people of Mani, Greece," Costa replied seriously.

"Do you want to tell me about it?"

"According to this tradition, during the first night of the newlyweds, the mother of the groom keeps guard outside their bedroom. At some point after the couple makes love, the bride opens the door and invites the mother in-law into the bedroom to show off the bloodied bed sheet, as a testament to her purity. The mother-in-law replaces the bloodstained bed sheet with a fresh one, and leaves them alone for the night. The following day, she gives a breakfast in honor of her daughter-in-law to all the friends and family. At some point, she proudly displays the bloodstained sheet on a clothes line, where the party participants—male and female—shoot out the blood stains off the bed sheet to smithereens. This ritual is followed by wine offering, other spirits and libations in honor of the bride's virginity and good fortune."

Süheylā was following Costa with such stupefied attention he had to nudge her back to reality.

"Costa, that is a scary custom. Woe to me if I am not a virgin the day of my wedding!"

"You don't have to worry about that. I will vouch for your purity," Costa teased.

"That is not funny. Is the reason you want to have the bloodied sheet because you want to show it to your mother?"

"No," Costa protested. I want it to remind me of the greatest day of my life!"

"Ooh, I like that. How do you know about this custom?"

"My grandfather Alexander told me. He is from Mani."

"Where is that?'

Costa had to think for a minute. "It is in Southern Greece; about fifteen-hundred kilometers from here, I think."

"How did your grandfather ever end up in Imvros?"

"He and his crew were shipwrecked on the island. When they came ashore, they found a young maiden tending a flock of sheep. That was my grandmother. They got married within six months and my grandfather settled on the island permanently."

"So, did your grandfather keep the stained bed sheet?"

"He did. It hangs in their bedroom behind glass; they are still in love."

Süheylā shook her head. "In that case, I want half of that bloodstained sheet too—as a memento."

"What?"

"It is my virginity on that sheet. You don't have a monopoly."

Costa cut through the blood stains and folded the two halves."

"Thank you, Costa," said Süheylā giving him a peck on his cheek. She gathered the two sheet halves, went into the kitchenette, and wrapped each one neatly in paper. "Now we are even; half a bed sheet for you and half for me."

Costa was at a loss for words. She placed her packet by the nightstand, opened her pocket book, took out another prophylactic and handed it to Costa. "Make love to me one more time before I go home."

It was an exhaustive delirium. Finally, Süheylā collected the rest of her clothing. "I am going to change," she smiled. "That miniskirt outfit was only for you. If I walked home with that, my mother would kill me."

He escorted her to the taxi stand. Just before she got in the cab, she pressed her bed sheet packet into his chest.

Chapter 18: Volcanic Passion

"Costa, if you ever make love to another girl, I will kill you with my bare hands," she threatened, pointing at his face.

Chapter 19: The Kurds

"Don't show up at the party, tonight, giaour. You and that Kurdish bitch are going to get it."

Costa put the phone down. *Did he care whether she called herself Turkish or Kurdish? She was all a man could ever want!* Her sympathetic stance for Kurdish autonomy did not make her Kurdish. Lately, however, he'd begun to wonder whether Süheylā had any racial affinity with the Kurdish race, since many other Turks, out of fear of political retribution, chose to keep their identity secret. More alarming was the semi-secret social group of Kurdish students who drew Süheylā to their cause. Although he warned her against it, Süheylā ignored his advice even when he told her that the Turkish Secret Police did not view organizations like that kindly. When Süheylā tried to enlist his sympathies for Kurdish independence, Costa refused. He got further upset when she began to study the Kurdish language in secret; this was beyond bizarre. Worse, she began to keep banned Kurdish literature in his apartment, something that could land them both in jail.

The phone call was enough to keep him in his apartment, but now he was worried about Süheylā. He tried calling her, but she had already left her apartment. Out of concern for Süheylā's safety, he decided to go to the party.

To mark the end of the semester, the chair of Ethnology, Professor McLaughlin, invited his class to his house for a party. Each student had the option to dress according to his cultural affinity. "If you are students of Ethnology, dress accordingly and demonstrate you have grasped the ethnological composition of our globe," he challenged.

Dressing as a Greco-Roman soldier crossed his mind, but he thought it would look foolish. Wearing a tunic would not go well with the conservative Islamic Turks, so he dressed in blue jeans and a flannel shirt. He was not about to invite any attention.

When he arrived, the place was already packed. To his disappointment, most of the students were dressed in various outfits dating from the Ottoman Empire. As usual, the male students outnumbered the females. This was because some of the Turkish women lately have been under the influence of Islamic fundamentalists and refused to come to the party at all. To them, a social gathering of this sort was a degenerate Western custom. To flaunt their religious purity, these females began sporting their Islamic outfits of black headscarves and long, shapeless, black capes around the university. Earlier, they voiced their opposition openly in the classroom, accusing the professor of corrupting their culture and tampering with the moral fiber of Islam. To their chagrin, Professor McLaughlin, a Scotsman, stood his ground and dismissed their behavior as an immature paroxysm. This was his apartment, and attendance was not mandatory.

In spite of their protest, several radicals were there, probably to take notes. Their publications were eager to print any trash that would discredit the West. Except for Ozan, his classmates ignored Costa completely. A giaour like him had no business in Turkey. Luckily, there were a couple of Armenian students with whom to kill time. Noting that Süheylā had not yet arrived, he began to get concerned; and then four beautifully dressed young women walked in.

A hush fell over the room, and every eye turned and looked. Dressed in the traditional Kurdish colors of red, white and green, these maidens commanded the attention of all. Sheer fabric gowns over fluffy pantaloons, Gobarah belts, red sandals and multicolor black velveteen turbans adorned with amber and turquoise beads. They looked like the Nymphs of Persia. Süheylā, the tallest of the four, looked stunning. Her golden hair flowing beneath her turban over her shoulders gave her the look of Roxellana[42]. She was breathtakingly gorgeous; the males eyed her with lust and the females with envy.

In the eyes of these Turks, this group was treasonous. The Kurdish colors in particular were symbols of insurrection.

The four girls moved about the crowd saying hello and exchanging pleasantries until they made their way to Costa. Like all the others, Costa complimented Süheylā on her outfit; she smiled while making a slight curtsy. She then introduced her friends.

"Bināz, Eminē and Firyāl," said Süheylā, making sure to pronounce their names distinctly to accentuate their Kurdish ethnicity.

While they were talking, several men were casting menacing looks toward their group and making disapproving gestures. It got worse when Süheylā and her friends moved to converse with a group of Kurdish students. Even though the Kurds were Muslims, as a matter of national policy Turkey did not recognize the Kurds as an ethnic group, but instead considered them a bunch of wild mountain Turks. Turkey had even outlawed the Kurdish language.

As the party was winding down, Professor McLaughlin thanked everybody for coming. He proceeded to take pictures with Süheylā and her friends, and many others too. Costa and the two Armenians decided to leave together after they escorted Süheylā and her friends to a taxi. To save money they decided to take

---

42. A legendary beauty and the wife of Suleiman the Magnificent and the mother of Mihrimah Sultan, Sultan Selim 11 and Shehzade Beyazit. She was of Ukrainian descent born as *Anastasia Lisowska:* 1506 to 1558.

the bus; the bus stop was some distance away. Hoping
that the phone call was just a hoax, Costa was glad to be
leaving with a group.

As soon as they passed through a side street, several
figures pounced on them out of nowhere. "Get ready to
die, giaours," they shouted.

Before Costa and the Armenians could react, the
assailants were punching and kicking them. One of them
swung a board, hitting Costa above the kidneys. Costa fell
to the ground, writhing in pain. One of the Armenians
managed to run away, but the other was not so lucky.

As if out of nowhere, another group of men rushed to
their aid. Swinging wooden poles, they put their assailants
to flight. They helped Costa and the Armenian to their
feet and walked them to a nearby taxi. Costa could barely
walk. His eyes were almost swollen shut. Blood was
oozing from his head, and the blow to his kidneys was
excruciating.

"We're taking you to the hospital," said one of the
good Samaritans when he got behind the wheel. Costa
recognized his voice. He was a Kurdish student he had
met a couple of times with Süheylā.

"No," pleaded Costa, "just take me to my apartment,
please."

"You are in no condition to look after yourself. We
will take you to our apartment. One of our friends is a
medical student."

Before Costa could utter another protest, he heard the
Armenian.

"Yes, take us to your place. That would be much
better."

When they got into the apartment, the Kurdish students
assisted Costa and the Armenian up a stairway. They put
Costa on a bed and in a few minutes, the student doctor
arrived. His friends called him Barzani. Costa told him
about the blow to the kidneys and the excruciating pain.

Barzani asked him to urinate in a bottle. The presence of blood was alarming.

"I'll take it to the lab in the morning," Barzani said. "You might have a dislodged kidney stone. Your friend is not hurt that bad."

Barzani left for the nearest drug store. He returned with supplies and gave Costa a strong sedative, which put him to sleep almost immediately.

When Costa awoke in the morning, he could barely lift his eyelids. The pain in his lower abdomen had increased. He heard conversation coming from the next room and tried to call, but his voice failed him. He got up slowly, wobbled, and collapsed on the wooden floor with a thud. The noise alerted the people in the next room and two young men rushed in.

"You are not supposed to move," Barzani, scolded. He helped him to the bathroom. Costa had difficulty standing. When he tried to urinate, he felt his interior being scraped as though with coarse sandpaper. He was scared. He asked for a glass of water. He tried a spoonful of yogurt, but he could hardly swallow. Barzani gave Costa another sedative.

He must have fallen asleep. The voice in the hallway was familiar and so was the language. By the time he opened his eyes, in walked Süheylā. She rushed to his bed and took his hand.

"Hello, Costa. How are you?"

"How did you know I was here?"

"My friends called me last night."

"All these people are your friends?"

"They are members of my club."

"What club is that?"

"The Devils of the Sun!"

"Who are they?"

"It's a Kurdish organization, dedicated to an independent Kurdistan."

"But I thought your Kurdish club was purely social."

"Yes and no."

"Did I hear you speak Kurdish?"

"Yes."

"How did you learn Kurdish so quickly?"

"I did not."

"How then?"

"It is my grandmother's language."

"You grandmother is Kurdish?"

"Yes she is."

"And just because of that you call yourself Kurdish?"

"I identify with the plight of the Kurds."

Costa was lost.

Did he care whether she called herself Turkish or Kurdish? She was all a man could ever want! When her fingers began to massage his neck, he forgot about his pain.

"My father is one of those Kurds who does not like to admit his ethnic identity."

"Now wait a minute. You father's dad was a Turk who married a Kurdish girl. That does not make him a Kurd— or you."

She frowned. "I love my grandmother. I want to help her people."

Are you a romantic vagabond or are you out of your mind? he wanted to ask her, but he could not. "Did you learn Kurdish from your grandmother?"

"Yes. She lived with us when we were in southeast Turkey—Kurdistan between us two."

She got up, closed the door, and sat beside him.

"I need you back healthy Costa, so that I can look at your pretty face." Here is an incentive for you." She unbuttoned her shirt, exposed her bra and pushed her chest into his swollen face. "You see what you are missing?" she challenged.

Suddenly, Costa's pain went away. He wrapped his arms around her and closed his eyes. If there was any medicine for his pain, she was it. The knock at the door startled him. Süheylā on the other hand, said "just a minute," and calmly collected herself. "Come in," she said after she had buttoned up her shirt.

It was Barzani, who came to inform him that the lab test showed blood and urine crystals.

"It's most likely a kidney stone. Do not worry. You will pass it within a few days."

"Is that why my kidneys are killing me?"

"Yes, I brought you a couple of painkillers."

"I don't know how to thank you."

"You are among friends," Barzani smiled, winking at Süheylā.

"When can I go to my apartment?"

"Not for a few days," said Barzani. "Süheylā will bring you what you need," he added, and left the room.

"I can take care of myself," Costa protested, trying to reclaim his physical dignity.

"You can't take care of yourself," scolded Süheylā, giving Costa a kiss on his swollen lips. "You are staying right here. I will be back tomorrow and bring you clothes."

She placed her palm on his cheek, "Costa, never reveal to anyone that you know these people, please."

"I understand."

"Remember that I am a Turkish girl."

"I'll just remember your name. Is that okay?"

She gave him another kiss. "Don't worry, Costa. Everything will be fine."

"My physical state is only temporary, Süheylā. My concern is about you and that social club of yours."

"Costa, stop; get well and we'll talk," she said, straightening his bed covers before leaving the room.

Süheylā's revelation made his head spin; but more so, he now wanted to get well as soon as possible. In spite of the hospitality he was receiving, it felt like Hell. His hotel was Süheylā's bosom.

Maybe they could run away before things got any worse, but he had only known her for a few months. He was prepared to leave Turkey and take her along, but he had no money, no profession and hardly any clue about life. Where could they go? No matter what, his parents would demand her conversion to Christianity. Costa would never go for that. She was what she was, a Turkish girl, a Kurdish girl, a Muslim girl . . . it did not matter.

He moved his face slowly on the bed dent she left, and his nose caught her exquisite scent. Afraid to let go, he held his breath, closed his eyes and pictured her. That determined chin, the round nostrils, the puffy lips, her silky blonde hair and her distinctive smell invaded his senses like a narcotic. She could be an angel carrying him on a flying carpet above the Zagros Mountains[43]. The thought of having her in his arms by the lush shores of the Tigris River tantalized his senses and quickened his pulse. Sensing the cascading river caressing their naked feet, he wiggled his toes. Slowly, that pleasant sensation, accelerated by the sedative, sent him into a deep sleep.

---

43. A large mountain range between Iran and Kurdistan.

Chapter 20: Zelal Hanum

"Marry a Turkish girl and have my curse." His mother's words still echoed in his ears. If Süheylā was ambivalent about her ethnicity, so was he. He was confused about her and about himself, too; was he a Turk, a Turko-Greek or just a Greek?

"Muslims and Christians don't mix," his mother had warned. The fog was swirling in his brain when he awoke.

He'd lied to Süheylā the night before when he'd told her he was feeling better. His urinary tract was still killing him. He had a fever, and his throat was dry. In spite of all his pain, he felt hungry. He had not eaten solid food for two days. To his relief, someone walked through the door with a food tray.

"Hello. I am Dersim. I brought you something to eat."

Dersim? Costa's antennae went up. *That was the man Süheylā had told him about. Was he capable of murder?*

"Thank you, Dersim. Can you help me to the bathroom? I have to go." Holding on to Dersim, he wobbled slowly. Just walking made him dizzy.

Afterwards, Dersim helped him back into his bed, propped him against the headboard, and placed the food tray of yogurt, chicken soup, and tea on his legs. Swallowing was still difficult, and he ate slowly. The chicken soup and the tea made him feel warmer.

"You cannot have any solid foods for a couple more days," advised Dersim. "You got hit everywhere; face, throat, abdomen and kidneys."

"I feel it everywhere."

"They were out to kill you."

"Do you know who they were?"

"We are not sure. We suspect they are a paramilitary group of Turkish radicals."

"Why did they pick me?"

"Like all giaours, you are expendable. Their tools are fear, intimidation, abductions, torture, and even killing. They want all non-Muslims to leave Turkey; and, they do not like Christians socializing with Turkish women. They would like to keep us Kurds suppressed forever, but we are too many.

"I don't think that would be possible."

"You never know. We just have to keep on fighting for a better life."

"Who would argue against that?"

"Maybe you can help us."

"Help you?"

"Why not?"

"All of us Greeks have a hard time surviving in Turkey as it is. The Turkish military has militarized my island, and she is going to hell. I appreciate your taking me into your confidence, but you cannot include me in your group."

"It is too late," said Dersim seriously.

Costa felt a lump in his throat. It sounded like the end of the world.

"Remember the Turk who harassed Süheylā at the university?"

Costa held his breath. He wanted to plug his ears.

"He is not going to bother you anymore," continued Dersim as if it were nothing.

Costa understood what he meant, and to his surprise, he did not feel a touch of sorrow, If anything, he wanted to beat that that basrtard himself. "Why are you telling me all this anyway?" Dersim he asked, sensing that there was something behind this story.

"Because, as I said, you can help us."

Exasperated, Costa lay back on the bed, trying to think. *Kurds and Greeks? Strange bedfellows,* he mused. Tha last thi ng he wanted to do is get into a revolutionary group like that.

The phone rang. Dersim went into the hallway to pick it up. He came back with the phone cord trailing behind him.

"It's Süheylā." He handed Costa the phone and left the room.

"Hello, Süheylā. What a pleasant surprise."

"How are you?"

"I am getting better, although my kidneys are still killing me. I do not know how to thank your friends." He took a deep breath and swallowed. "How am I going to get out of this?"

"So, Dersim had a talk with you?"

"Yes."

"You are safe where you are. Once you get well, we'll chat."

"I think I should go home."

"You are in no condition to go anywhere. See you Wednesday."

If Süheylā's voice was a tonic, it did not last long. The terror weighing on his mind was too much. Where was he anyway? He slowly rose from his bed. For the first time he parted the window drapes to look out. Peering through the dirty panes he observed a back alley; it looked like a typical slum. Rows of three- and four-story buildings nestled together like sardines—good for nesting pigeons, rodents . . . and Kurds. Covered with clothes and ugly underwear, the railings of the small balconies looked like rat nests. Every apartment with a radio had it on full blast. The haunting Turkish melodies blending with the arias of the mating felines all around betrayed a dysfunctional beehive. Snaking for several blocks, the alley looked like a tunnel of Hell, a perfect prop for *Dante's Inferno.*

It must be Dolapdere, he thought, one of the worst slums of the city, populated by drug dealers, addicts, robbers, Communists, racists, pimps and prostitutes. This was a hornet's nest for unruly Kurds and revolutionaries. Maybe he was better off in an asylum. This was Istanbul, the heart of Turkey—his homeland. His fellow Turko-Greeks spoke glowingly of Greece as if she were the Promised Land, but Costa was conflicted. He had no idea where his loyalties lay. No matter how bad, he loved Turkey with all his heart. He had heard of other great cities, but for Costa there was no city like Istanbul.

The student doctor must have been right—in all probability, a kidney stone was making its way down his urinary channels. The pain was killing him, and more sedatives would be a real blessing. *Where was that Barzani,* he wondered? Barzani had the same last name as the fiercest Kurdish guerrilla fighter in all of Turkey. *Are they related? Should he ask him?* Such a question might be inappropriate; the Kurds do not play around. With Allah and Islam as their allies, they were famous for vendettas, honor killings, drug running, contraband, and many other clandestine activities. If cornered, they fought back to the death.

Slowly he headed to the bathroom. The kitchen was crowded; his fellow students were having breakfast. When Barzani saw him stumbling through, he jumped up to help him.

"You must call one of us when you want to go," he admonished. With his help, Costa went to the toilet, and when he returned, Dersim already had hot tea ready for him.

"I'll give you a sedative shot," said Barzani.

"I don't know how to thank all of you."

"No need for that," responded Barzani. "Some day you can do the same."

"I wouldn't bet on it," Costa joked politely.

"You and Agop will be alone today," said Barzani. "Besides classes, our group share-owns a couple of taxicabs, which we drive for a living. Zelal Hanum will take care of you."

"Who is Zelal Hanum[44]?"

"She is the owner of the meyhane[45] across the street."

"Is that where the loud music is coming from?"

"Yes. She will bring you lunch."

Costa ate a little breakfast of goat cheese, soft bread, black olives, and drank tea. Barzani helped him back to his bed. "I am touched by your hospitality, Doctor Barzani."

"You are the first one to call me Doctor. I have a way to go, my friend."

"Dr. Barzani, you must be very careful. You are playing with fire."

"We must have an independent Kurdistan. Our homeland has been ours for millennia, way before the Turks came from Central Asia."

"I know, Dr. Barzani, but insurrection is not a good option. There has to be a better way."

"Turkey denies our ethnic existence. They call us "Mountain Turks." They even forbid us from speaking our language."

"Can I ask you a question?"

"Anything."

"Are you a Peshmerga[46]?"

Barzani's face remained expressionless for a few seconds. "What do you think?"

"I think you are a patriot."

"We all are, my friend. What are you?"

"I thought I was a Turko-Greek. I sang the Turkish National Anthem in school twice a week. I have known no other country. Now, I am not sure what I am."

---

44. The honorable term for "Mrs."

45. Turkish typical café of various standards and degrees, some of ill repute.

46. A Kurdish guerilla—it means "not afraid to die."

"I share your dilemma. Now let me give you this injection. It will put you to sleep until noon. By then, Zelal Hanum will be here."

The pain fled immediately but when he woke up, his bladder was again on fire. Collecting himself as best he could, he wobbled into the kitchen. Agop was sitting across from a very large woman who immediately rushed to his side. Her cat-like agility surprised him.

"You must be Zelal Hanum," greeted Costa, extending his hand.

"Yes, and you are that handsome Greek my boys have been telling me about."

"You mean all these students are your boys?" Costa joked.

"All Kurds in this neighborhood are my boys," she said seriously. "I have brought you lunch."

"Thank you, Zelal Hanum."

"Now sit and eat, my boy," she commanded in a motherly tone.

The woman, dressed in the traditional Islamic black abaya[47] all the way down to the floor, cut a foreboding figure. A shapeless halter hung about her shoulders with a pair of large straps tightly wound around her mid-section, looked like a makeshift bra—probably to prevent her huge breasts from sagging any lower. Her torso was massive blubber on top of which rested a fat chin. Knife cuts on the face attested to a few scrapes in her life. A huge nose wedged between her black eyes gave her the appearance not-to-be-taken lightly. If it were not for a dozen or so golden arm bracelets wrapped around her wrists, she could be mistaken for a monster. Costa speculated her age to be about her mid-forties, maybe even younger.

---

47. An Islamic-style black gown; it covers the entire body from the neck to the toes.

She watched them eat in total silence, keeping a matriarchal composure about her. The rice pilaf with pine nuts and poached chicken was delicious, just as that great ekmek kadayif[48]. Agop excused himself to go back to his bed; Costa chose to stay.

"Thank you, Zelal Hanum; may God give you health and freedom."

"May Allah be praised, but for some reason, he has been denying our freedom for centuries." She cleared her throat and spat on the dirty floor, pulled her skirt slightly and rubbed her cutout slipper over it. Her bare feet looked like an elephant.

"Who knows, Madam Zelal; all things change in time."

"Maybe they will, but tell me; are you really in love with that skinny one?"

The question caught him off guard. He thought of giving her an evasive answer, but he changed his mind. *Tell the truth and earn her respect. A dishonest answer was certain to earn her scorn.*

"Yes, I am."

"Barzani told me I'd like you. You are straightforward and honest."

"Thank you."

"Do you plan to marry her?"

Costa knew this was coming. "Some day!"

"Why don't you marry her now?"

"Because I don't know if she wants to marry me."

"Why not?"

"Because I am a Greek and Süheylā is Turkish and Muslim. How will that work?"

She shook her head. "Don't be foolish."

Costa swallowed. "Maybe, but I have not asked her yet."

---

48. Turkish-style bread pudding.

"You don't ask, you tell her."

"Marriage right now would be foolish. It will slow down our education."

"Women need no education. They get too smart and tell their husbands what to do."

"Zelal Hanum, with all due respect, times are changing."

"They are changing, all right. Parents are losing control. I arrange the marriages of my children. They marry whom I choose."

She fumbled below her halter into her huge chest, found a knitted wool-wallet and took out several pictures. "These are my girls. This one is Aisha; she is fourteen. This one is Esmeray; she is seventeen. I would be glad to give you one of them; both if you like," she added, laughing.

In one picture, the two girls were standing in front of a fierce-looking Kurd with a black patch over his left eye. He was dressed like a Pesh-Merga (Kurdish guerrilla). A Kalashnikov rifle slung on his shoulder spoke plenty about this man.

"Nice girls!" commented Costa politely looking at the pictures. "Who is that impressive man?"

"He is my husband. I am his first wife, his favorite."

Costa hesitated, but he asked anyway. "How many wives does he have?"

"Counting me, three."

"Where are the other two?"

"Back with him, good-for-nothing bitches. They only take bed space. Tell me if you want to marry any of my daughters," she said jokingly.

"Please, Zelal Hanum, marriage for me right now is out. As I told you, I am not a Muslim."

"We can convert you in a minute."

Costa let out a laugh with Zelal Hanum giggling along.

"Muslim or Christian, there is no difference," she thundered. "Both believe in Allah. These Turks believe in

146

nothing. Some day we are going to have our own country. You will see."

Zelal's zeal for drama matched her fanaticism. God pity anybody who crossed her; she would probably wring his neck. *I must stay on her good side, at least until I can get out of here.* He got up and walked to the stove to get more tea. The rumble of engines on the street below drew him to the window; he lost his color. In front of Zelal Hanum's tavern, two police officers were dismounting from their motorcycles. Zelal Hanum understood his concern immediately.

"Sit, my boy. I will be right back."

Dragging her slippers on the kitchen floor, she lumbered away. The wooden steps creaking under her heavy weight sounded like piano chords out of tune. He watched her through the window as she headed straight to the police officers. After they chatted for a few minutes, the police officers followed her back up to the apartment.

Costa was horrified. *They will probably take me to the jail of no return.* Running crossed his mind, but he was in no condition. Besides, there was no other escape except down the same steps. He felt he was going to lose control of his bladder. With hands shaking, he took a couple of sips of tea. Within moments, Zelal Hanum was in the kitchen with the two police officers.

"I brought you company," said Zelal Hanum cheerfully.

"How nice, Zelal Hanum," said Costa, wondering what was next.

One of the police officers extended his hand. "Glad to have you in the neighborhood. Are you feeling better?"

Costa did not know what to say. "Yes, I am fine, officer. Thank you." The other cop did the same thing, except that he called him by name.

"Costa, you are the first Christian ever to step into this area. We are glad you are in good hands."

Costa's heart skipped. *Was he dreaming or were they toying with him?* Meanwhile Zelal Hanum invited the cops to sit for tea.

"These cops are my friends," she said, slapping them on their backs. "They are good Turks," she sniggered.

Costa was flabbergasted. "I am so glad to hear it," he said politely, still not believing what was going on.

"Zelal Hanum is the mother of us all," said the cops. "We want to make sure that all people around here are safe."

Safe from whom?

They drank some more tea and, to Costa's relief, they signaled it was time for them to go.

"We are traffic cops," they apologized. "We have to be at our posts before the streets begin to jam."

They shook hands and left the room with Zelal Hanum trailing. Costa was glad to see them ride away. He was sitting at the table feeling relieved when Agop walked in.

"I heard the whole thing, Costa. I thought we were going to be rounded up."

"Me too, Agop."

"I know why we are not, Costa. These cops are Kurds, not Turks. I heard them talking in Kurdish with Zelal Hanum when you were in the bathroom."

"How in the world did they ever get to be police officers?"

"There are many Kurds in the Turkish government ranks," said Agop. "Some are pro-Kurdish sympathizer; others, such as these cops, play a double role."

"They look like regular cops to me."

"Cops like them can be very dangerous. They will sell anybody down the river; they are probably collecting information."

"You mean about us?"

"We are small kabobs, my friend. It is the Kurdish revolutionaries they are after."

"How can you be so sure?"

"Don't be naive. You think the Turkish police are stupid?"

Soon after, Costa felt he could urinate, but something was blocking the flow. The pain was intense, he called for Agop, who ran over and steadied him over the urinal. After some agonizing moments, something shot out of his penis like a missile. Luckily, the urinal screen stopped it from falling into the sewer. Costa reached down and picked it up. It looked like a large olive pit with rough edges all around. He washed it and put it into a cup for Barzani. Agop helped him back to his bed.

Barzani came late. "So you passed the stone. It is the largest I have ever seen."

"You are going to be a great doctor," Costa complimented.

"I hope so; my people need me."

"Do you intend to go back home and practice medicine?"

"Yes, I do."

Barzani gave Costa another shot. "This will be your last one. Your urinary tract will heal in a few days, and you should no longer have any pain."

Costa fell asleep right away. He dreamed of Zelal Hanum, murderous Turks and Kurdish radicals, but mostly he dreamed of Süheylā.

Chapter 21: No Charge For a Virgin

The next day, Agop, the Armenian, felt better and left for his apartment. Although still weak, Costa was happy the pain was less. He felt well enough to make breakfast on his own. The fresh clothes Süheylā brought him from his apartment gave him euphoric confidence. Although his face was still swollen, he did not look that scary anymore. Better yet, Süheylā had promised to come by in the evening.

In the meantime, Zelal Hanum invited him to her tavern for the afternoon. This was a dive—dark, smelly, smoky, mysterious, and dangerous. Gambling, dealing in hashish, pimps peddling their prostitutes and a host of other activities were the norm of a place like this. Costa had read about such places in the newspapers. Murders and other violent crimes were common. Rough citizens of all kinds were always ready to knife each other for the price of nothing.

When Costa stepped into the tavern, his nose caught an overpowering smell of a peculiar smoke. *It must be hashish,* he thought, for he had never experienced such a smell before. He looked around trying to familiarize himself with the place. Zelal was busy behind the counter with some dubious-looking characters. If they were conducting any fishy business, this seemed the right place for it. This was definitely a drug house, maybe something even worse. A friendly old man noticed Costa standing around and invited him to a game of backgammon.

By the end of the game, a couple of prostitutes, accompanied by their pimps, walked in and started to bargain with a group of fierce-looking Kurds. One in particular was very argumentative about her rates of comfort. She and her pimp were ready to come to blows with a couple of rough-looking characters. One of them—

a typical dayi[49]—was fumbling through his pockets, perhaps for a knife or even a gun. Costa was relieved when Zelal charged into the middle of the group like a bear.

"You bastards," she hollered, shaking her fist at the face of a tall mustachioed scallywag. "You don't argue around here for anything."

She next turned to the vocal prostitute. "Mehtab, if you want to lift your legs around here, leave, or I will throw you out. This gentleman is our guest, and you are giving him a bad impression."

Mehtab, who now took note of Costa, was quick with an apology. "Oh, I am sorry Zelal. I did not notice the fellow," she smirked as she sashayed toward him. "What is your name, pretty boy?"

Before he could open his mouth, Zelal Hanum shouted. "His name is Costa; keep away from him!"

"Oh my," lilted Mehtab, "such a gorgeous Christian." Nudging herself closer, she placed her hands on his shoulders, massaging them. Abruptly, she lifted her miniskirt, placed it over Costa's head and pushed her pelvis into his face, gyrating playfully.

Everybody let out a big laugh, including Zelal. Mehtab gyrated for a few more seconds and stepped away. "Did you see anything, pretty boy?"

Everybody roared. Costa had to laugh, too. The joke was on him.

In the meantime, Mehtab leaned over to Costa. "No charge for you," she winked. "You can make love to me any time, for free!"

Costa attempted to get up from his chair, but Mehtab pushed him down and bestrode herself across his legs. Rubbing the insides of his thighs, she slithered her hands

---

49. A typical ruffian: drooping jacket, exposed chest, big mustache and wild eyes.

closer to his box. She peered into his eyes seductively and raised her skirt to show him her see-through panties.

"I always wanted to make love to a young man like you," she smiled lecherously. "Would you like to spend the night with me? What do you say?" Her black eyes sparkled as she ran her tongue over her lips seductively. She was an attractive woman.

Costa, not wishing to cower, "I am sure you are joking."

"I am serious."

Suddenly, her pimp stepped in. "Mehtab, you don't have time for freebies," he scolded, and tried to pull her away.

Mehtab got angry. "Aziz, you cannot tell me who I can spend my free time with." Furiously, she opened for her purse, took out a bundle of cash and flung it in his face. "Here is your percentage from last night. Take it and fuck off!"

Zelal caught Mehtab's fury. She stepped between Mehtab and the pimp and spoke to her in Kurdish. Costa had no idea what she said. He noticed the rest of the Kurds nodding while Mehtab appeared to be apologizing. She walked back to Costa and gave him a protracted kiss.

"Just playing with you, young man; I meant no disrespect. Anyone in love with a Kurdish sister deserves my friendship. Count on me as a friend." She took a polite bow and went back to bargain her market prices.

Costa left the café and climbed the steps to the apartment in anticipation of Süheylā's arrival. He wanted to put some order in that awful-looking room. It was the worst place he had ever slept. Thankfully, he felt well enough to leave. He'd started to gather his belongings when Barzani walked in.

"Dr. Barzani. I am feeling better. When Süheylā gets in, I would like to go to my apartment."

"While you were at the tavern, Süheylā called; she will not be coming by. Dersim will drive you home."

Costa felt dejected, although he was relieved. He did not want to see Süheylā around here anymore. He wanted to say goodbye to the students, but they were all missing. He went back to the tavern and thanked Zelal Hanum for her care. Drug dealer or not, she was a nice woman, perhaps a noble one.

By the time they got to his apartment, it was dark. Before Costa could get the key out of his pocket, somebody opened the door, startling him. Standing in the middle if the living room was Süheylā flanked by her friends, the Kurds.

"Welcome home, Costa," they shouted.

They all took turns giving him the traditional Kurdish welcome, a kiss on both cheeks. They sat him down on the couch. Süheylā brought him a glass of cherry juice. Another girl walked from behind the kitchenette and sat across from Costa.

Costa looked around and blinked his eyes. Süheylā and her friend were dressed in the same Kurdish outfits they wore at the Professor McLaughlin's party. Even more, the men were also dressed in the traditional Kurdish outfits, with the large pantaloons, wide cummerbunds and head turbans.

Before he could ask a question, the girl that sat across from him "I am Esmeray, Dersim's sister. My brother asked for my help tonight," she added, pointing toward the kitchen. In that traditional costume not only did she look mysterious, she was beautiful and vivacious.

Costa started to wonder whether he had seen her before, but with all the aromas of the various dishes coming out of the kitchen, he lost his train of thought. He'd not had a decent meal for a few days. Are you responsible for all that?' he asked Esmeray, pointing toward the kitchenette.

"I had a lot of help from Süheylā," she winked, jumping from the couch and clapping her hands.

As if on cue, a couple of Kurds moved the coffee table away and set a low, round table about one foot tall in its place. This was a sofra, requiring everyone to sit on the floor on pillows. They covered the table with a tablecloth, a striking piece of handiwork with all the Kurdish colors. Esmeray and Süheylā were setting all the spicy food down, assisted by the males, who were dutifully following their orders. Esmeray in particular was zipping around with great fanfare, swaying her hips to the Halay tunes[50] playing on a tape deck.

Finally, the table was set. The door opened and in walked Barzani holding two bottles of raki[51], an indispensable party libation to any Kurdo-Turkish festivity. He poured a glass for everyone and then lifted his own glass.

"To health and friendship, to our friend, Costa Rigas. May our friendship last forever!"

Costa, in whose honor this dinner was prepared, was touched. "I welcome all of you. I deeply value your friendship. I thank you."

They all sat down on cushions and crossed their legs. Dersim, a devout Muslim, offered a short prayer. "May Allah be praised and let the eating begin."

It was the first Kurdish dinner Costa had ever had. Lamb casserole with couscous, long-grain rice pilaf with pine nuts, raw lamb meatballs spiced with hot paprika and wrapped in lettuce, dolmas[52], eggplant salad, and much more. Süheylā sat next to Costa. She took only a sip of the raki and so did Esmeray.

Some of the men began to get a little tipsy, but Dersim seemed downright euphoric. Dr. Barzani asked him if he could sing a song.

---

50. A Kurdish folk dance.

51. The national spirit of Turkey.

52. Stuffed grape leaves with rice, meat and herbs.

"Dersim, your father is a Dengbej[53]. I am sure you know a tune or two."

Dersim closed his eyes and took a couple of deep breaths:

A Kurdish girl fell in love with a handsome prince on a summer's day.

On a dark night still, he came by and took her home for life to stay.

Her dad got mad to get revenge, to find the prince and kill that hare.

Her mom she begged him not to dare, because he now was their daughter's fair.

But he galloped forth, found that prince, and laid him bare to bone and hair.

He broke his daughter's heart apart, who wailed and plunged into the Tigris's path.

A Kurdish girl fell in love with a handsome prince on a summer's day.

On a dark night still, he came by and took her home for life to stay.

His voice was heavenly and even more so the moment was of another world. Although Costa could not understand a word, he could not hold back his tears and neither could anybody else.

"This is against the law," muttered Dersim. "Turkey can lock me up in jail if anybody heard this song beyond these walls."

"It is against the law to be a Kurd in this country," Dr. Barzani commented sarcastically. He looked at Costa,

---

53. A Kurdish storyteller singing *a capella* a traditional song of life, love and homeland.

who was still in some pain. "It is time to go and leave our friend alone."

The Kurds cleaned up the table, put the apartment in order, said goodbye, and carried their belongings downstairs, leaving Süheylā and Esmeray alone with Costa.

"Ladies, I am in your debt. How are you getting home?"

"I am taking a taxi," said Esmeray. "Süheylā is staying to look after you," she winked. She kissed Süheylā and Costa goodbye, put on her long Islamic coat over her Kurdish outfit and left the apartment.

"Finally," exhaled Süheylā. "I have you all to myself. "You need a shower; you will also need my help to wash yourself," she winked.

Suddenly his pain went away. He started to walk toward his bedroom.

"Don't run, Süheylā challenged. "Let me help take off these dirty clothes; but before I do, I'd like to take a couple of pictures of you. With that black eye you look beautiful." She snapped away a couple of flashes and then put her camera on the coffee table. First she took off his shirt, then his pants, and finally his shorts. She stepped back and looked at him.

"Ooh, Costa, the shower will help those black and blue spots, I am sure."

Slowly, she peeled off her Kurdish outfit down to her panties, took him by the hand and led him into the shower. "I am obeying Dr. Barzani's orders," she whispered, kissing him along the way.

Chapter 22: Christmas With a Muslim Girl

It was the holiday season and like all Orthodox Greeks of Istanbul, the Karas family had a Christmas gathering. Costa knew the Karases through his employers, the Gregorys. Weeks ago, Mrs. Karas had invited Costa and Süheylā to their party. In spite of his injuries, Costa felt well enough to go. The Karas were the owners of the biggest automotive import business in all of Turkey. Several years ago, Mr. Karas had received the government's citation as the biggest taxpayer in all of Turkey. Just as all the guests settled down to dinner, the doorbell rang with a simultaneous loud door knock. Mrs. Penelope Karas rushed to open the door. She hurried back to the table looking ashen.

"There are two police officers at the door," panted Mrs. Karas at her husband Themis. "They demand to see you right now."

The table of about a dozen people or so went silent. One of the Karas' sons jumped up and turned down the stereo.

"Did you say police officers, Penelope?"

"They demand to see you right now, Themis," she repeated, barely audible.

Themis Karas tried to appear calm, but his face registered impending doom. He walked to the entrance with Penelope trailing behind. Süheylā squeezed Costa's arm.

"Good evening, officers," greeted Themis Karas. "Please come in."

Ignoring his greeting, the officers shoved him aside and stomped through the living room as if it were their personal turf. They leered at the guests contemptuously and glowered at Themis Karas.

"Is this the house of Karas?"

"Yes it is."

"Are you Themis Karas, the automotive importer?"

"I am," replied Mr. Karas respectfully. "What can I do for you?"

"You will see in a minute," shot back the fat one. He cleared his throat and began to read.

To: Themis Karas

By order of the General Security Department of the Fourth Police precinct of Sirkeci, Istanbul, Themis Karas is ordered to appear at the station tomorrow at 9:00 a.m. to answer charges of tax evasion, fraud, and for harboring anti-Turkish sentiments.

Signed:

Nihat Karamanoglu, Security Director

Sending another scornful leer toward the guests, he put the document in front of Themis' face demanded his signature. Mr. Karas attempted to protest, but the police officer stopped him cold.

"Don't try any tricks," he warned. "You are liable to go to the station right now."

"For the love of God," begged Mrs. Karas. "This is Christmas Eve, our holiest day."

"We don't give a damn. This is a working day for all Turks, and you giaours are celebrating."

He turned to Themis Karas. "And don't be late," he threatened, pointing his finger. High stepping like Yenitsars[54] on the march, the policemen walked out and slammed the door shut behind them.

---

54. The elite troops and personal guards of the Sultans of the Ottoman Empire. They were taken away from Christian families as children and raised to be solders for life under a system of collection called "Devşirme," instituted by Sultan Murat.

Mr. Karas slumped on his seat. His house had turned into a morgue. Christmas Eve celebrations and holiday dinners in Istanbul for Turko-Greek Christians was a tradition for centuries. However, like all Greek families of this city lately, the Karas family had lived their daily lives in impending doom. They knew their turn would come. Turkey's plan to force the Turko-Greeks to abandon their businesses, property and their homes was unwavering. Themis Karas collected himself as best he could.

"Come on, friends," he beckoned "Let's have a drink and eat this food. This is what we get for having the misfortune to live in the land of our ancestors."

Mrs. Karas, still in shock, attempted to say something, but Themis put his arm around her shoulders. "You and I have been through a lot, dear. Do not worry. We will weather this as well."

His comforting words had the opposite effect. Mrs. Karas started to sob. Themis Karas, trying to find a way to rally everyone, grabbed a bottle of raki and went around the table filling their glasses. "Come on, brethren," he implored. Let us drink to the Holy Night. Let us have a Christmas cheer. God will look after us."

Themis' cheers were of no use; the evening was ruined. In all probability, they too were next in line for the Fourth, the most dreaded police station in all of Turkey. They also knew that all Greeks in Turkey were in the same predicament. Mrs. Karas begged everyone to eat, apologizing as if it were her fault. "I am sorry, I am sorry," she kept mumbling incoherently.

Most guests hardly ate anything. Several of them, too upset, began to leave, and so did Costa and Süheylā.

Thanking the Karas family for their hospitality was awkward, even uncomfortable. Mrs. Karas, still in shock, reached out and gave Costa and Süheylā a hug; she also had a Christmas gift for everyone. Costa and Süheylā accepted theirs graciously. They wished the Karases

Merry Christmas; it was not. Deep in thought, they found themselves in the city's main artery.

"I am sorry, Süheylā, I am upset. Those policemen are worse than Nazis."

"I have finally seen the light, Costa. The Kurdish people must have their own homeland."

Costa was startled. The Kurdish social club was influencing Süheylā more radically than ever. She had no idea what she was getting into.

"I am getting concerned with your radical attitude, Süheylā. You are playing with fire."

"If it weren't for you, Costa, I would have done something by now."

"I don't want to hear that ever again," scolded Costa loudly. "Think of your family. Once you get involved in anything like that, you will cause them great hardship."

"And what should I do?"

"Why don't you wait? Time changes many things. I ask you to sever all contacts with any radicals. Do it now before it is too late!"

"They would feel betrayed."

"There are many ways to fight for freedom. Violence is not one of them. Acting like a radical is foolish. Once the Turkish police pull you in, it will be the end of you. Don't you know that they monitor all radical activity?"

"How do you know that?"

"I have reliable information."

"You are scaring me."

Costa abruptly shook Süheylā from her shoulders. "Am I getting through?'

"If not now, when?" she snapped.

"Never," Costa replied, surprised at her militancy. "Not now and not ever. If Turkey wants to grant autonomy to the Kurdish people, she will do it in her own time. You and your Kurdish friends are acting silly."

Süheylā looked at Costa seriously. "What can I do, then?'

"Get your law degree and work within the system. Have you ever heard of Gandhi?"

"I have."

"So you know that he led India to its independence through nonviolence."

"Okay, I get that, but tell me; what is going to happen to Mr. Karas?"

"At the very worst, he will come home mentally broken."

"What do you mean?"

"He will be interrogated severely until he confesses to all fabrications against him and signs his property away. He will be lucky to leave the country with his underwear."

"Can't you do anything about it?"

"Me?"

"I was thinking about Mr. Sariyer."

"I don't know about Mr. Sariyer. Even all decent Turks would not dare raise their voice."

"What about Mr. Akduman?"

Costa bit his tongue. Mr. Karaduman was the chief of the secret police of Istanbul, who had engaged Costa's interpretive services on several occasions. Mistakenly Costa had told Süheylā about him."

"All I do is translation work between him and his American guests; frankly, I don't really know him."

"But you said that he was the chief of the secret police of Istanbul."

"So? I am telling you, Süheylā, you have got to give up those Kurdish independence ideas of yours."

"How can we be so helpless?" she protested angrily.

"There are things we cannot change. Let's go get something to eat."

"I don't feel like eating. Can we go to your apartment?"

"Okay," replied Costa. Süheylā's offer was like an anesthetic, making him forget—at least temporarily—

what had just transpired. Holding Süheylā by the hand, he hailed the next cab. Things would be better in his apartment.

Chapter 23: Icons for Süheyla

Once again, anti-Greek hysteria has gripped the Queen City. Mob violence can erupt at any moment, ready to loot and burn like a fire-spewing dragon. The justification this time is the Turkish Minority of Cyprus egging their brethren Turks to mayhem, just because the Greek Cypriot Majority is looking to confederate with Greece. The Turko-Greek minority of Istanbul is their convenient scapegoat. The rampaging mob has them marked in their homes, in their businesses and in their social clubs, but their favorite targets are the Greek Orthodox churches. Numbering about a hundred or so, these churches have been under siege by the city mobs off and on during the past thirty years. With the constant outflow of the city's Greek population, most of these churches were bereft of any parishioners, managing to hang on behind locked doors. The Greek Orthodox priests were scared to venture out anywhere, even to buy groceries. From a cosmopolitan metropolis, Istanbul was gradually descending into a cultural desert. Instead of racing forward, Turkey was going in reverse. Such was the myopic post-Kemalist policy: monolingual, monoracial and monoreligious.

In spite of all the turmoil, Costa and Süheylā's relationship continued to grow. Her curiosity to visit a Greek church was unrelenting. Her fascination with the art of iconography was a rare interest including most Christians, but for Süheylā, it was purely artistic. For such a visit, Costa chose the church of the Holy Trinity, by Taksim Square, instead of St. George, the church of the Orthodox Patriarchate. Although this church would have been his preference, he wanted to avoid having to explain to her the Gate of the Hook[55], a very sad chapter in the world of Orthodoxy under the Ottoman Empire.

He heard the knock and opened the door. In walked a tall silhouette led by two sparkling eyes, the rest of her face hidden behind a silk scarf, while her entire body was covered under a long Islamic style grey coat all the way down to her shoes. With black gloves and a large black pocketbook hanging from her shoulder, she looked like the ambassadrix of Saudi Arabia.

Before Costa had time to recover from his surprise, Süheylā said, "Costa, I am really excited today. I am looking forward to seeing that church," and she gave him a long hug.

"Shall I make us some tea," he offered, hoping she would take her coat off. He was curious to see what she wore under it.

"No, Costa. We don't have time, let's go."

"Okay, Süheylā, I am ready."

"Before we go, is my outfit okay?"

He wanted to tell her that she did not have to dress that conservative, for the dress code in a Greek church was not that strict, but he changed his mind. "It looks perfect," he replied

"Really?"

"My mother wears something similar to yours, and so does the Madonna."

"Is there an icon of her at the church?"

"There is."

"Does the Madonna wear a head cover like mine, too?"

---

55. The hanging of Patriarch Parthenius by Sultan Mehmet the 1V, under false accusations of treason that he conspired with Russia, against the Ottoman Empire. Given a choice to convert to Islam, the patriarch chose death. In 1757, Parthenius walked from his prison to the "Parmak Kapi," where he was hanged. He stayed on the gallows for three days, after which he was thrown into the sea.

"Almost!"

She hesitated. "You are not joking, are you?"

"No, I am not."

They took a taxi. The church was two blocks from Taksim Square. When they arrived, Costa put some coins on the tray and lit a candle.

"What is that for?" asked Süheylā.

"In remembrance of my relatives who have departed; it's customary."

"Should I light one, too?"

"If you wish."

She deposited a coin in the tray and lit a candle. She looked up and was instantly transfixed. "Is that the Madonna?" she asked in a hushed voice, tugging at Costa's arm.

"That is she."

Süheylā was concerned that someone might hear. "Costa, can a mortal really be the mother of God?"

"I wish I could explain all that; I don't understand it either."

"Why do you believe it then?"

"I was raised with the belief that the Virgin Mary was the mother of God."

Sensing Costa's quandary, she dropped the matter. "I like her," she said looking at the icon once again. "Now I see what you mean. She looks beautiful."

"If it weren't for that halo, she would look just like you."

She gave him a smirk. "That icon is a beautiful piece of artwork, Costa. I am impressed. Who draws these things?"

"They are called iconographers."

"Are there any in Istanbul?"

"None in Turkey; they are mostly in Russia, Greece and other Christian countries."

"I get it; I am sorry."

"Why should you be sorry about that?"

"I really don't know, but I am." She looked up around the church marveling at the many icons. "Costa, I read that the ancient Greeks believed in many gods. The books you lent me depict them as great statues. Are all these icons gods too?"

"No, they are saints."

"Why did that old lady cross herself in front of all those saints then?"

He wanted to change the subject, but Süheylā continued.

"My father tells me that Mohammed was a prophet, not a god."

"That is a far better claim."

"Well then, you cannot call yourself a Christian, can you?"

Costa started to look for an out. Süheylā was giving him fits. He felt relieved to see Father Issidore walking toward them.

"Hello, Father Issidore," greeted Costa. They embraced and kissed each other on both cheeks.

"Nice to see you, Costa; who is the young lady?"

"This is Miss Gülpinar, a fellow student."

"Good to meet you, Miss Gülpinar. Are you an Antiochan Christian?"

Noticing Süheylā's helpless expression, Costa interjected politely. "Father, she is a Muslim girl; we met in Troy."

"Everybody is welcome in the house of God," said Father Issidore, shaking Süheylā's hand warmly. I hope you like our church, Miss Gulpinar."

It is beautiful, Father Issidore. Thank you."

"Father Issidore," is it okay if I show my Muslim friend around the church?"

"Of course it is; please walk around."

"Costa, do you call the priests 'Father'?" inquired Süheylā politely.

"Yes, it is a form of reverence."

"We call the imams "Hodja[56]"; of course you know that. They dress in robes, too."

"So what is wrong with that?"

"I am always leery of men who claim that they speak the word of God."

Costa shook his head and led her into the interior of the church. It was an impressive building. The divider wall between the Solea and the altar was at least twenty-four feet tall, all hand-carved wood inlaid with gold. Precious icons of various sizes were everywhere.

"It is beautiful," commented Süheyla. "Why the steel bars across the windows?"

"For security reasons."

"If this is a place of worship, why does it need security?"

"Lately, the churches have been under increased vandalism."

"I am beginning to see; those newspaper articles incite them, don't they?"

They went outside for a while, to rest. They found a bench under a tree and sat. Finally, Süheyla lowered her scarf below her chin.

"Is this better, Costa? Finally, I can breathe easier," she exhaled, moving her eyelashes rapidly.

"What made you think you needed to cover your face?" asked Costa with curiosity.

"I assumed that is how the Madonna dressed," replied Süheyla innocently.

You are the Madonna, he wanted to tell her, but he smiled instead.

"Now that I have seen the icons with exposed faces, I feel better, though I still like the looks of the nude statues," Süheyla continued, training her eyes on his face as if to imprint her soul. She scanned around and not

---

56. Teacher, swami, master.

seeing a soul, she unbuttoned her gray coat and parted it slightly for Costa to take a look. The short silver-sequin skirt just above her bare knees made Costa dizzy. Quickly he put his arm behind her waistline and sealed her mouth with a kiss.

"Maybe that is how the Virgin Mary seduced Joseph," he commented feeling the exquisite taste of her lips.

"We are past that stage, Costa," she scoffed. "You are the guilty party on this one!"

Just as that moment, they saw a familiar figure crossing the courtyard and Sūheylā buttoned her coat quickly. It was Mrs. Karas. Forced out by the Turkish government, the Karas family was leaving the country for good. Under the threat of imprisonment, Themis Karas had confessed to all the trumped-up charges and signed away his property to the Turkish state. They kicked him out of the country months ago, but allowed Mrs. Karas an additional thirty days. Costa knew all about the injustice done this family, something very similar to most other Greek families of Istanbul.

"Hello, Mrs. Karas," waved Costa.

Mrs. Karas, who was keeping her head down, looked up.

"Costa, nice to see you,' she said looking at Sūheylā inquisitively. It was obvious she did not expect to see a Muslim girl anywhere near church grounds.

"Hello, Sūheylā," she greeted. "What are you doing here?"

"Hello, Mrs. Karas,' replied Sūheylā, kissing her on the cheeks. "I am visiting this church with Costa. I am interested in iconography."

Mrs. Karas looked pleasantly surprised. "So you like icons, Sūheylā?"

"I love the art form, Mrs. Karas," replied Sūheylā politely. "I really don't know much about them, but Costa is my guide," she said smiling.

"Guide Mrs. Karas I am not," protested Costa politely, looking at Süheylā. "I really do not know much about the artwork either. I am doing the best I can to keep an artist's mind like Süheylā's occupied."

Mrs. Karas seemed to be tearing up and Costa and Süheylā held their breath.

"Are you all right, Mrs. Karas," inquired Süheylā.

"As well I can be. I have thirty days to leave the country. My husband left already. I stayed behind to dispose of all our personal belongings."

"Is there anything we can do?" inquired Süheylā sympathetically.

Suddenly, Mrs. Karas' face lit up. "Yes, there is Süheylā. Can you and Costa come to my apartment this afternoon? I have something to entrust you with."

"Of course," replied Süheylā without any hesitation. "What time?"

"Any time after two; now, if you excuse me, I am sort of in a hurry."

"See you later, Mrs. Karas," Costa said and got under Süheylā's arm.

"I am now depressed, Süheylā. Can we continue another time?"

"Okay, Costa, if you promise to bring me here another day. I love this church. It is fantastic!"

"I promise. Let's go get lunch and then visit Mrs. Karas."

They took a light lunch and strolled around Gezi Park, their favorite garden. Mrs. Karas' apartment was ten minutes away.

"The Turkish police gave me very little time to prepare for my departure," cried Mrs. Karas, after a short greeting. "Imagine that; being thrown out of your country," she lamented. "I have something for you, Süheylā. I would like to entrust you with our family icons." She pointed to a neatly wrapped box on the floor. "These icons have been in our family for generations.

171

Turkish Customs will not allow us to take them out of the country."

"But why?" asked Süheylā looking disturbed.

"Because they are considered state property; I trust that you will keep them safe, or donate them some day to a worthy cause. Please do not sell them."

Süheylā did not have any comforting words, and neither did Costa; both were hesitant.

"Please accept my request, Miss Süheylā, I beg of you," pleaded Mrs. Karas with tears running down her face. "You are the only one I can entrust with my icons."

"Maybe my friends can help, but I cannot guarantee their safety, Mrs. Karas," replied Süheylā."

Costa had nothing to say. It was Süheylā's decision. His preference was to burn them. That was what the Turkish mobs were doing—until they realized that they were worth a lot of money. The art dealers of Europe paid dearly for icons like these.

They kissed Mrs. Karas goodbye and took the box of icons back to Costa's apartment.

Costa was excited to peel the scarf off her face, and Süheylā was eager to show him her sequin skirt. The minute they entered his apartment, Süheylā was in a hurry to take off her coat, but Costa stopped her.

"Before you take your clothes off," he joked, "I want to snap a few pictures of you in that outfit."

"You mean you like it that much?"

"You are the most mysterious thing I have ever seen, Süheylā. I have never seen an Arabian princess in person, but except for your cerulean eyes, you are it."

"You are already making me hot Costa; will you hurry up?"

"Okay, okay. Please put your scarf on just as you had it before—that is right, just above your nose—and stand over there by the chair."

He unbuttoned the lower part of her coat up to her knees and guided her to place her right leg on the chair.

Her sequin silver skirt shot right up to her mid-thigh, exposing her gorgeous legs.

"Are you a photographer, Costa?" Süheylā teased, slinging her pocketbook over her shoulder.

"I can be anything you want me to be," Costa replied, looking at her with fascination. "This is a sexy pose, Süheylā. You look incredible," he continued to mumble as he snapped away.

He paused and looked at her for a few moments. "Now take of that long coat. I want to snap a few more pictures in your sequin dress."

She frowned. "You are taking too long, Costa." She took off her coat and threw it in his face." She strapped her pocketbook back on her shoulders and assumed the pose one more time, looking like an angry tigress.

After a few more shots, Costa put the camera down. He led her into the bedroom, laid her on his bed and pushed her sequin skirt up her mid-belly, beholding her tigress eyes.

Chapter 24: The Garbo Club

They were the 'Garbo Club' of Istanbul, the fanatic fans of Greta Garbo, Marlene Dietrich, Lauren Bacall and Melina Merkouri. These were the sons and daughters of Turkish aristocrats of western education, led by Ozan and Gönül—brother and sister—the children of the foreign films' distributor in Turkey. Sharing the same major, Ozan and Costa became great friends the minute Ozan discovered that Costa was fluent in English and had an encyclopedic knowledge of foreign films. Even more so, Gönül and Süheylā—having the sultry looks and husky voices of Melina Merkouri—were natural soul sisters.

The Seven Hills Café was a popular spot for the group, who, in spite of Turkey's anti-minority hysteria, intermixed and socialized with Greeks, Armenians, Kurds and other ethnicities. This café was one of the few places where Costa and Süheylā could socialize without any concerns. No more than two dozen or so, these friends converged around the café sharing experiences, art, music, movies and fun.

The fourth Friday of every month was 'Garbo Night.' The café was the jump-off point for a late lunch, cards, backgammon, and an evening at Ozan and Gönül's family villa to watch a movie, preferably one with Marlene Dietrich, Lauren Bacall or Greta Garbo. Without exception, every female of the group dressed in the style of the Forties and Fifties. They were the most colorful group of Istanbul.

Before heading to class, Costa decided to stop by the Seven Hills Café. To his delight, Ozan and Ali were playing backgammon. When the two friends saw him, they immediately stopped playing.

"Why are you out on the streets today, Costa?" asked Ozan with concern, waving the morning's newspaper at his face.

"What do you mean?" Costa laughed. "I have a class today, and tonight is 'Garbo Night!' "

"Look, my friend," said Ozan, unfolding the newspaper and pointing to the main headline.

"What does it say, Ozan?"

Ozan bit his lip. "Bad news, my friend," he said seriously and handed him the newspaper.

Costa took a seat and after reading the first few paragraphs, put the paper down. It was another invective against the peoples of Greek descent. Articles like this were published routinely by the leading newspapers of Istanbul, but this one was pure bile.

He remembered the massive pogrom of 1955 against the Greek community of Istanbul, and he cringed. Turkey's design for the eradication of all Greeks was not going to waiver. His ears were ringing so hard he could not even hear his friends' apologies.

"You are not taking that class today, are you, Costa?" pleaded Ozan.

"What would you advise?"

"Come stay with our family."

"Thank you, Ozan. If anybody wants to harm me, they know where I live; I cannot hide in your house forever."

"Ali and I will ride the bus with you; we insist."

Even had he known about the article before, it would not have mattered to Costa. In a country like Turkey, Greeks, Armenians and Jews learned to live with danger all their lives long; verbal abuse, physical attack, even death, were normal. He left his friends by the students' forum and, clutching the newspaper under his arm, walked into the lecture hall. He saw Arda, a familiar classmate, and set next to him.

Professor Kismet called the class to order. Today she had scheduled a lecture by a renowned economist, but he was late. On a whim, she invited the students to bring up any topic they wanted for discussion.

"Professor Kismet," shouted Arda, grabbing the newspaper from Costa. "I would like to discuss the irresponsibility of our press today," he said waving it at the professor.

Complete silence; there was not a peep from anyone.

Finally, Professor Kismet spoke. "I don't think it is an appropriate subject for this class."

"Professor, I disagree."

"You are out of place, Mr. Arda!" shouted the professor.

"I think our country is out of place. The purpose of this article is to inflame the masses again; it is irresponsible and criminal." Arda turned to his classmates. "You know about this article, yet all of you are cowards; you ought to be ashamed of yourselves." Not getting a response, Arda mumbled a couple of expletives and sat down, staring at his classmates scornfully.

A few students glared at Arda, but most of them put their heads down or stared into the void. Just at that moment, the guest lecturer arrived—perfect timing for Professor Kismet to avoid any further discussion.

When the class was over, to Costa's surprise several of his fellow students surrounded him to offer their apologies.

"Can I escort you home?" offered Arda with much concern.

"Thank you, Arda, but my friends Ozan and Ali are waiting by the forum. Why don't you come and meet them?"

Costa introduced Arda to Ozan and Ali, who immediately invited him to join their Garbo Group for the evening, although Costa was no longer in the mood for any entertainment. The only thing that was going to take his mind off was Süheylā.

When they arrived at the café, Süheylā immediately rushed to him. "Did you see the article, Costa?"

"Yes I did," he replied stoically, "but with Turkish friends like these, I have nothing to worry about," he smiled, trying to make her feel at ease.

They all sat around for tea and a late lunch, before leaving for Ozan's villa to watch 'Key Largo' with Lauren Bacall and Humphrey Bogart.

Finally, they were on their way. The variegated colors of the women's outfits made the Garbo Club members stand out like roses in the middle of the Sahara, as if Hollywood were transported to the heart of Turkey. On their way to the bus stop, the group had to walk by a side street leading to a mosque, which had just let out worshippers from Friday afternoon prayers.

As the Garbo Club stepped onto the sidewalk, it came face to face with a group of men and women holding placards with inscriptions like, 'Bati Bok[57] and 'Giaourlar Vazgeçĩn[58]', slogans that conveyed the worst xenophobia of Turkey and Islam. Egged on by today's article, these fundamentalists were heading to the square to demonstrate against the few remaining Greeks and all things western; and right in front of them was the enemy—the Garbo Club, the scourge of Islam, the height of Western decadence and immorality.

As if on cue, they positioned themselves in front of the Garbo Club to block their progress. One female in particular, dressed in a chador[59], moved closer to Gönül and started to shout. "Infidel prostitute, infidel prostitute."

Incensed, Gönül punched her in the face. That was when things turned ugly. The two groups were at each other shoving, punching, kicking and swearing. It did not

---

57. Western shit.

58. "Infidels, leave."

59. A black cape—down to the ankles—worn by most females of Islam. See the glossary section for further details.

take but a minute for a group of police officers to rush in, blow their whistles and put a stop to all the commotion. Soon they lined everybody up against the wall, threatening to lock them up. Costa was in the middle of the line, with Süheylā hanging from his arm.

"Your identification," demanded the police officer, without even bothering to look at Costa's face.

Costa gave it to him. The police officer looked at the identity card and lifted his head.

"Aren't you Mr. Akduman's English interpreter?"

Costa swallowed. "Yes, sir, I am."

The officer turned to his fellow officers. "Give them back their identity cards; I know these people." He then turned his attention to the group holding the placards with derision. "You are all under arrest for disturbing the peace."

Costa was elated. Although this police officer knew him, he could not place his face. Maybe he was one of Mr. Akduman's lieutenants. This was the first time that a Turk had come to his rescue. He said "thank you" to the kind police officer, who motioned the Garbo Group to go.

The minute they found themselves at the bus stand, his friends surrounded Costa. Ozan was ecstatic. "Thank you, Costa, for saving us from all this trouble. How do you know the policeman?"

"I don't really know him, but I know his boss—I think," he replied nonchalantly.

"Süheylā gave Costa a hug and so did the rest of the girls. Gönül especially gave him a kiss with much gratitude. "You are not alone, Costa," she said. "Some of us Turks are just as scared. These fanatics want to send our country back to the Dark Ages."

In spite of Gönül's effort to cheer him up, Costa did not feel like celebrating. He wanted to spend his time with Süheylā. The fact that he was leaving for a week to visit his parents weighed heavily on him. She must have read his mind.

"Let's go to your apartment, Costa, and snuggle," whispered Süheylā into his ear. I want to forget about today. You are leaving me alone for a week," she protested.

"I am sorry, but I have to."

"That is why I want you to kiss me all over this evening! I will miss you too much. Let's take a taxi."

Costa and Süheylā apologized to their friends and hailed the next cab. They were in his apartment in a few minutes. As usual, they rushed up the steps as if their world was in a hurry. Süheylā wanted to go into the bedroom immediately, but Costa slowed her down.

"Let me look at you, Süheylā," he pleaded. "That maybe-nautical dress of yours is so sexy. Where did you get it?'

She winked. "Erika, who else?'"

"Would you like to dance, Süheylā? That dress of yours is all music to me!"

"Of course I would; I can always melt in your arms!"

He dialed radio Istanbul and to his delight, the program was the swing music of the Forties. He turned around and invited Süheylā to dance. She gave him a smile, took off her jacket and walked into his arms. Her contoured navy dress above her ankles with a large side pocket gave her the look of a fashion model in the middle of Hollywood. He looked at her in admiration.

"Do you want to see what's below? she winked.

Costa blinked his eyes. "Yes," he replied. "Don't rush, I love seeing you in that dress." They danced to the sounds of swing for a while, while Costa struggled to hold his composure. Süheylā was like a rose on fire, emitting her gentle aroma and stoking his loins. When she took off her dress, exposing her glamour-waist-cincher, he could not hold it any more. He lifted her into his arms and carried her to his bedroom.

They seldom smoked, but it had become a ritual at the end of each lovemaking session. Süheylā took a deep drag and looked at Costa.

"Costa, will you do something for me?"

"Anything."

"Can you write me at least one letter?"

"What if your father gets hold of it?"

"Send it here, to your apartment. I have the keys."

"In that case, I will write you every day."

"Thank you." She reached for her purse and pulled out a white silk handkerchief. "This is for you," she winked and handed it him. "It will keep you company."

Costa took it and brought it to his nose. When he began to trawl the handkerchief between her legs, she wiggled with excitement.

"I like the feel of it, Costa. It is sexy. Why are you doing that?'

Because I want to imprint your scent," he said. "I will carry it in my pocket to keep me calm."

Chapter 25: That Turkish Bitch

The six-hour bus travel from Istanbul to Çanakkale and a ferryboat ride to the island of Imvros took more than twenty hours. His parents were waiting at the harbor. Although he was glad to be home, he was already missing Süheylā. The first thing he did was to go to his room and write her a letter.

Dear Süheylā:

I just made it home. I already miss you terribly.

Things look different. The entire island has an eerie feeling.

I will keep your handkerchief under my pillow every night. Your scent is all over it. In your absence, it will do.

I love you.

Costa

He sealed the letter and called his brother Alkis. "Little brother, will you mail this for me?"

"Is it for that girl?"

"Yes."

"Are you in love, Costa?"

"How do you know?"

"Mom and Dad say so."

"There is nothing I can do. Why don't you and I spend time in our cabin tomorrow?"

"That will be great." Alkis took the letter and left the room.

Costa went to bed immediately. It had been a long day.

His grandfather's booming voice woke him up. He brushed his teeth and walked down into the kitchen. The fireplace was roaring, and the table was set. Breakfast time was always fun around the house of Rigas—freshly baked bread, cured black olives, rose-petal marmalade, goat cheese, cured pork, smoked island sausage, and island tea.

He took a seat by his mother.

"So, what happened, Costa?" inquired his grandfather, Alexander.

"What happened what, Granddad?"

"Don't be evasive. Friends told us about the fight."

"It was not that serious."

"Is that why you did not come home for Christmas?" cut in his mother, Electra.

Costa hesitated. He did not want to tell her that the real reason was that staying away from Süheylā for a two-week holiday would have been too long. "It was nothing to worry about, Mom."

"Don't lie, Costa," snapped Phillip, his father.

"I was beaten by several students, Dad. They pounced on me unexpectedly."

"My God," recoiled his mom, looking horrified. "How did you get out of it?"

"Some Kurdish students saved me from great harm."

"Kurds; what are you doing with them?"

"They are just friends, Mom."

"Since when did you start calling the Kurds friends?"

"Keep away from those Kurds!" thundered his grandfather. "They are worse than the Turks."

"That is all we need," added his father. "First we have the Turks and now the Kurds."

"Are you still seeing that Turkish girl?" inquired his mom; she wanted to get to her main concern as soon as possible.

"Yes, Mom."

"Aren't there any Christian girls around?"

"No, Mom."

"Our village is abuzz with your relationship with that girl. We are embarrassed."

"There is nothing to be embarrassed about, Mom."

"Muslim girls do not belong in our circle," she said, looking angry. "Worse, she is Turkish."

"Don't generalize, Mom. Some of my best friends are Turks."

"Let me get straight to the point. Stop the relationship immediately or we will cut off your allowance." She was fuming.

Costa stood his ground. "She is the only one I want, Mom. If you cut me off, I will never set foot on this island again." He regretted his words the minute he'd spoken them. He saw his mother contract in pain, and he apologized immediately. Thankfully, his father came to his rescue.

"Electra, don't say things you don't mean. Costa can do what he wants. I wish he did not date anyone." He looked straight at Costa. "Do you love her, son?"

Costa thought of saying no to please his mom, but he could not. "I love her very much, Dad."

"You fell in love with a goddamn Muslim?" screamed his mother in disgust. "You are going to ruin our family name!"

"Our family name has nothing to do with her," replied Costa defiantly. He was getting angry. Süheylā was beyond any girl he'd ever met, Christian or Turk. "There is no one like her, Mom."

"Do you plan to become a Muslim then?"

"That is silly, Mom. She does not subscribe to any religion and neither do I, but if she asked me I would consider it."

He saw his mom turn ashen. "I bet you have not been to church since you met that girl!"

"That is correct. I am giving up Christianity for good!"

"Mary and Jesus, you have become a nonbeliever just because you met a Turkish girl?"

"She is not any girl, Mom; I cannot breathe without her."

"What is her name?"

185

"Her name is Süheylā."

"This Süheylā has corrupted you, Costa. You are going to rot in Hell."

She was a stubborn woman. Costa was venturing into unfamiliar territory, and she was frightened.

"We are sending your brother to a boarding school in Greece. We will be in Istanbul in a couple of months to see him off. God help me, I will find that Turkish bitch and chase her all the way to central Asia."

Costa winced. "Don't call her that name, Mom. I really take offense to that. Once you meet her, you will change your mind."

"I don't ever want to meet her, mark my words!" screamed his mother as she strode defiantly out of the kitchen.

Costa looked at his father expecting a nod of sympathy, but he remained impassive. His grandfather and his brother acted the same way. He understood their predicament. Five-hundred years of Turkish oppression was a heavy deposit upon the soul of every Greek. Costa was not immune to that either, but Süheylā was pushing him into a different world. Her raw innocence was defusing all lines of hatred. He hated to leave the table, but he had no other option. Writing Süheylā another letter might just calm his nerves.

Dear Süheylā:

Things are not going very well with my family. They are furious at me for being in love with you.

Federal criminals on the loose are roaming the countryside, frightening the natives to death. They beat people up and chase them from their farms and fields. The looting of the chapels around the island is an everyday occurrence. The worst thing about these criminals is that they have prevented the harvesting of the olive crop this fall, depriving the island of most of its income. Nothing is sacred, and no one is safe.

The government by decree has shut down all the Greek schools. My family has decided to send my brother to a boarding school in Greece.

Because of all this, the natives are leaving the island in droves. The youth are leaving faster than most everybody. Sadly, the elderly are the ones left behind.

Thank goodness, I have my brother Alkis and Grandfather Alexander to keep my sanity.

I refused to go to the church anymore. My parents are convinced I have converted to Islam.

Remember my advice: Cut off your activity with our friends.

I miss you a lot. I will be there soon.

I love you forever.

Costa.

He'd come to spend a week on the island, and this was his fourth day. But its tragic condition and the family discord were too much. "I am going to leave tomorrow," Costa announced.

His parents did not say a word. His mother looked very angry and his younger brother sad. Grandfather Alexander did his best to keep up a happy face.

"I am writing to your aunt in New York," said his mom. "I will ask her to sponsor you for the United States as soon as possible."

"I don't want to go to the United States, Mom. I want to join my cousin in his bakery business in Congo. No matter what I do, I need a sailing permit from the military."

"Maybe we can bribe someone. There are many who will sell their mother for money. What about that Turkish girl?" pressed his mom; "will you continue seeing her?"

"If I have to leave the country, I will have to take her with me. I am not going anywhere without her." He saw his mother seething. Costa had no appetite for this sort of conversation all over again. He excused himself to go up to his room.

His brother followed behind. "I picked up the mail today. I kept it away from Mom's prying eyes."

"Thank you."

"I am really worried about you, Costa."

"I can take care of myself. Now let me read it."

Dear Costa:

Today, I have received your first letter ever. I will keep it forever.

I am sorry to hear about all the troubles of the island. I also have some disturbing news. The police picked up Dersim and locked him up. He has been accused of clandestine activities. He is liable to go to prison for a long time.

I am frightened for the rest of our Kurdish friends, and of course for me too. I can now see your concern. Thank goodness, I did not venture into anything radical. Still one never knows what might happen.

I have been visiting your apartment every day, reading and spending time with myself. It is my best therapy next to having you close. I strip down, put one of your shirts and lay in your bed thinking about you. Your scent is so arousing!

Please get here soon! I love you.

Süheylā,

"Did you have sex with her, brother?"

Her letter was the sweetest thing he ever read. His brother's question snapped Costa from his daydreaming. He got angry. "It is none of your business."

"Just be careful, Costa. Turks can kill you."

"You, too? Thank you for your concern, Alkis. I have advice for you: Stop your hatred. I know the Turks have inflicted many calamities on us Greeks, but we cannot change history nor continue along the same path. It leads to nowhere."

"It seems to me that this Turkish siren has messed up your mind, big brother."

"If you ever meet her, you will think differently, Alkis. I will see you tomorrow at breakfast."

Costa was glad he was leaving tomorrow. In comparison to Istanbul, his village was dull and boring. There was nothing to do except play cards at the coffee shops, and inhale thick, second-hand smoke. Even worse, the haranguing he was receiving from his parents about his relationship with Süheylā was getting on his nerves.

Chapter 26: Tonight You're All Mine

Costa had returned to Istanbul earlier because he missed Süheylā. He was disappointed to find her note in his mailbox. Unexpectedly, her father had come to town, and she would not be available tomorrow, their standard night out.

With nothing to do, Costa decided to hang around the office. With the travel season a couple of months away, things were slow, so he moped around, feeling depressed. The phone rang, and he picked it up. "Hermes Travel, can I help you?"

"Can you use some company?" It was that husky voice at the other end.

"Not really, I have a better offer," he mumbled, trying to hide his excitement.

"Don't play games with me, Costa; pick me up at about six-thirty?"

"What happened with your father, Süheylā?"

"I will explain later; *a bientôt Cher Monsieur.*"

She hung up before he had time to reply. Her voice inflection along with her French was always a dead give-away; she was up to something. He rushed home, took a shower, and drove to pick her up.

Süheylā was standing by the curb wearing very conservative clothes: black head scarf that covered most of her face, a drab jacket down to her knees, an olive-green maxiskirt and flat black shoes. She looked like a black phantom, except for those eyes, which sparkled of mischief. Even more bizarre, she was holding a large duffle bag as if she were on her way to Haj[60].

---

60. The religious pilgrimage to Mecca.

Costa got out of the car and opened the door. She handed him the bag to put in the back seat. He pulled the seat belt, looped it carefully around her, mindful not to brush against her chest; her alternating looks of piety and tempestuosness were a clear warning to stay away from that area! He closed her door, walked around the car and got behind the steering wheel. "Where to?" he asked, wondering. *Will it be Mecca or the red light district!*

"How about Emiryan[61] for tea?" she asked mischievously.

Her question vis-à-vis her conservative outfit had him wondering. He had never before seen her in such drab clothes. *Did she turn into a Muslim nun?* His mind rested on the duffle bag. *Why a duffle bag?* His curiosity was killing him. "What is in the bag?" he asked.

"It is a surprise," she smiled enigmatically.

"I like surprises, Süheylā. I was expecting you to be with your parents tonight. Where are they?"

"They went to Yalova. I told them I had a big test Monday."

"And Gülēngül?"

"They took her along."

"How was the mosque service today?" Costa teased, knowing she had stopped going to the mosque some time ago.

She glared at him., "Drive, Costa. You are in for some rough time!"

Rough time? Lucky me!

He took the coastline road. The shoreline of Bosporus is one of the most picturesque drives of the world: monuments, magnificent villas, greenery, trees and flowers are in every turn. To his delight, Süheylā took off her head cover, cracked open the car window and let her

---

61. A notable area of Bosporus, known for its restaurants, tea gardens and lively street life.

blonde hair fly about as if she had not a care in the world. They were in Emiryan in forty-five minutes.

"Here we are, Süheylā, that famous teahouse."

It was the Emiryan Palace, one of the great spots of Istanbul. Like most places of Bosporus, it was across from the road that ran along the shoreline. It served the best tea fare in all of Istanbul. Costa pulled in front of the entrance and let her out.

"Costa, please give me that duffle bag. I want to go to the bathroom first."

He handed it to her, wondering what kind of surprise she had. He found a spot, parked the car and walked up the steps. The tea palace was on the second floor. The *maître d'* recognized him immediately.

"Good evening, Mr. Rigas, how many tonight?"

"Just two, Mr. Bülent; I prefer a table at the back."

"I am sorry, Mr. Rigas. There is a private party there this evening. We have a table by the band."

He gave Mr. Bülent a large tip and asked him to hold the table. A couple of weeks ago, he chaperoned a group of American bankers for an entire weekend for a fee of one-hundred dollars. He went back to the lobby to wait for Süheylā. Her conservative outfit among this modern crowd was making him a bit nervous. Looking out the window, he kept himself occupied with the marine traffic of Bosporus. He felt a tap upon his shoulder and turned around.

"Did you get a table, *Monsieur*," whirled Süheylā. She had stuck one of her legs out and was twirling her purse like a dame of the night looking for customers. This gorgeous thing was dressed in pink—tailored jacket, tight skirt barely above the knees and high heels. Her lips were pink as well, and so was her purse. He tried to say something, but she put her finger on his lips.

"Allons-y Monsieur."

His male ego shot several degrees above normal. When the *maître d'* saw Süheylā hanging on Costa's arm, his eyes flickered wildly. "Follow me, Mademoiselle, Mr. Rigas."

The place was already crowded. Costa felt the many eyes looking at Süheylā and smiled. Mr. Bülent led them to their table, pulled the chair out for Süheylā, and invited her to sit. Costa sat across, rested his hands on the table and gawked at her; she could have been the Ethereal Nymph. Sending him a foxy smile, she opened her purse, took out two cigarettes, and placed them between her lips.

Costa fumbled through his pockets for the lighter, but she was quicker.

"I am going to light your fire tonight, *Monsieur*," she teased.

He watched her light up, take one of the cigarettes out of her lips and put it between his. Taking a long drag, she tilted her head back and sent a puff of smoke into his face, letting her husky giggle cascade all over him.

He blinked his eyes, wishing he could inhale all of her.

Looking at him seductively, she rested her back on her chair, crossed her legs, took another drag and puffed him a smoke-kiss.

It was *déjà vu. Was it Greta Garbo or Melina Merkouri?* He could not remember which one. Tonight, her tempestuosity was beyond fantasy. Her body language conveyed the stance of a tigress on the prowl, and her prey was Costa.

Grrrrrrrr!—how lucky can I get? Costa grinned.

"Tonight you are all mine," she hissed between her teeth, furrowing her eyebrows, ready to pounce.

He wanted to rip her outfit off her body right then, but all he could do was shake his head. "You amaze me, Süheylā. I never know what you'll do next."

"You, mon Cher," she said pointing her finger, "when I get you back into that car, I am going to punish you."

She dragged her words slowly and deliberately as if she were determined to set the waters of Bosporus on fire.

Before Costa could think of something clever to say, the captain approached their table.

"Good evening, Mademoiselle, Mr. Rigas. What will it be tonight?"

Costa knew the routine. "Two glasses of champagne, tea for two, a tray of sandwiches and sweets, please."

"Thank you, Mr. Rigas." The captain bowed politely just as the band started to play.

Süheylā stared at Costa. "How do you know all these people?"

"I have been here several times before."

She collected her face into a frown. "Entertaining other ladies?"

"Absolutely not," protested Costa defensively. "I have been here with the Sariyers. I also brought several groups of American VIPs through Hermes Travel."

"I am glad to hear that; I was ready to scratch your eyes out!" she threatened, forming her hand into a cat's paw.

The champagne came. "To you, Süheylā," said Costa, "with all my heart."

"No, *Monsieur*, to you; the night is yours," she lilted. Sending bolts of lightning toward him, she drank at least half of the champagne from her glass.

"Easy, you will get drunk."

"I am not driving, you are."

"Why do you want to punish me?"

Holding her cigarette between her fingers, she drew a smoke ring and leaned forward; "for corrupting an innocent Muslim girl like me."

He attempted to protest, but she shushed him. "Don't worry. I will go easy on you; I promise."

The anticipation was killing him. Thankfully, the glorious Turkish tea arrived in a sparkling double silver samovar set—brewed tea on top, hot water on the bottom, sugar cubes in a silver ramekin, and tea glasses encased in silver meshing. The tray of Turkish delights was outstanding—mini baklavas, künefe[62], hanim göbeĝi[63], acibadem kurabiyeleri[64], revani[65], ameretti, dilber dudaĝlari[66] and various finger-size sandwiches. Halfway through the evening, Süheylā began to get tipsy.

"*Monsieur!* Aren't you going to ask me to dance?"

Costa was so busy gaping at her, he forgot about the band. He jumped up from his chair and pulled her onto the crowded dance floor.

"What is this rhythm, *Monsieur?*"

"Rumba."

"I know this one. Erika taught me."

"You are spending too much time with that vixen. Is there anything you are not telling me?"

She pursed her lips into a seductive frown. "You won't believe, *Monsieur!*"

"I believe anything about that lady," Costa replied. He'd learned a few things about Erika several months ago.

"She was Germany's playmate of the year."

"What is that?" Costa asked, pretending ignorance.

"It is a magazine for men called Playboy."

"I never heard of it."

"She showed me the magazine, *Monsieur.*"

"Really?"

"*Oui, Monsieur;* I had to cover my eyes. Right in the middle of the centerfold was Erika, completely naked."

"No joke?"

"No, *Monsieur.* This magazine features naked young women in all sorts of provocative poses. It is devoted to articles of intimacy and related sexual subjects."

---

62. Shredded wheat pastry with melted cheese on top.

63. Woman's navel.

64. Bitter almond biscuits.

65. Semolina cake with almond syrup.

66. Woman's lips.

Costa's mouth was getting wider. "What else?"

"I'll tell you another time."

"My curiosity is killing me."

"In time, *Monsieur*. Right now, I want to dance forever," she lilted, holding him tighter.

"Don't you have to be home before curfew?"

"No, *Monsieur*; my parents will be back tomorrow. We have all night!"

Now Costa was *really* getting excited. "Do you have anything in mind?"

"Yes. I want more champagne. Your surprise is coming . . . later," she smirked, puckering her lips.

She was breathing fire. Between more champagne, the sandwiches and the sweets, they danced several sets. Süheylā had the waiting-staff making somersaults.

Finally, it was time to go. Costa called the captain and paid the bill. The *maître d'*, Mr. Bülent, came by to say good night.

"Excuse me, *Mademoiselle*; have I seen you on the screen before?"

She gave him a condescending glance. "Not on your life, *Monsieur*. I only act for this one," she grinned, batting her eyelashes at Costa amorously.

The *maître d'* winked at Costa. "I beg your pardon, *Mademoiselle*. You are the most gorgeous lady we have seen around here in a long time; it has been our pleasure."

"Thank you, *Monsieur*," she said, offering her hand like a grand dame, which the *maître d'* kissed enthusiastically.

She turned to Costa and winked. *You see? I can put anybody in my pocketbook!*

Süheylā left to go to the bathroom while Costa brought the car around to the front entrance. She sashayed out the door in her high heels, smiling slyly. Behind her walked the captain holding her duffle bag. Costa held the car door open while the captain placed the duffle bag on the back seat. When he pulled the seat belt to loop it around her, she stopped him.

"I know you enjoy strapping me in, *Monsieur*, but not tonight."

"But . . . it is company policy," smiled Costa, feeling deprived of the opportunity to brush against her chest.

"Pease indulge me, *Monsieur*, for a while."

"Okay," exhaled Costa, mindful of the treacherous shore of Bosporus. He walked around and slipped in behind the wheel.

"Before you drive, *Monsieur*, I have some conditions."

"What conditions, *Mademoiselle*?"

She gave him that rapid-eyelash-move of hers: I-am-so-hot-Monsieur-I-am-going-to-blow-your-mind.

"We are going to play a game. First, you must drive very carefully. Second, you must keep calm. Third, at no time will you attempt to look at my face."

"I can promise you all that except the last one."

"The last one is very important. The minute you look me in the face, the game will be over, *Monsieur*."

Costa was getting too excited about this game. "Okay, okay."

"Excellent, *Monsieur*. This escapade will require at least an hour."

"*D' accord*[67]," replied Costa, writhing with anticipation.

The shores of Bosporus are very misty this time of the year. One can hardly see clearly ten meters ahead. *Costa, drive carefully and avoid all distractions,* he mumbled to himself. The minute they were on the road, he saw her push a tape into the player, "Misty Night." It was one of their favorite songs.

The music and the pink oasis by his side were giving him goose bumps. He had no idea what the temptress was

---

67. "Agreed."

up to. Although he was careful not to peek, his side vision was on total alert; she was opening her purse. The sound of spray wafted to his nose immediately. It was one of those perfumes Erika Anderson wore to drive her husband nuts. He coughed to get her attention. "Can I ask at least some questions?" He was careful not to look her way.

"You may by tapping your hand on the dashboard twice. If I choose to reply, okay. If I tap three times, the answer is no. Is that understood, *Monsieur*?"

"*Oui, Mademoiselle.*"

"Tap, tap; what kind of perfume is that?"

"*Chanel Nombre Cinq*[68], *Monsieur.*"

"It is driving me out of my mind."

"No comments until the game is over. Understood?"

"*Oui, Mademoiselle.*"

The mist was getting thicker. Many have died on this shore during times like these, and he had to be careful; thankfully, his side vision served him well. She was pulling her jacket off. *She must be getting hot.* When she took off her blouse, his loins went into convulsions. But when she leaned forward and unclasped her bra, he lost his concentration, veered off course and made a sudden correction with the wheel.

"Easy, *Monsieur*," she scolded. "I want to sleep in your bed tonight, not with the fishes."

The thought that she was completely naked above her waist drove him nuts. *What if a passing car saw her?* He exhaled with relief when she put her jacket back on, but it was only temporary. Her firm breasts, partially protruding through that leather jacket, accelerated his pulse. When she blew her minty breath on his face, he was overwhelmed with lust. He grasped the steering wheel and trained his eyes on the road, quaking with anticipation. Her hand was now searching for his shirt

---

68. "Chanel Number Five."

buttons. She unbuttoned a couple of them and ran her hand up and down his chest, pulling at his hair playfully.

He could not hold his tongue. "What are you doing?"

"Tap, tap, tap."

He shut his mouth. *Was it Heaven in Hell or the other way around?* He did not care. When her hand meandered about his knee, his spine quivered. With his heart racing, he managed to stay in control until he felt her hand slip between his legs. His breathing now became erratic.

"You are a merciless sadist," he wanted to thank her.

It was sheer torture. Feeling her tight lips clamp around his sex, he started to blink; he had the feeling of being sucked into the surrounding fog. His convulsive explosion echoed through the shores of Bosporus in ecstatic euphoria. He did not even know he was driving. After a few minutes or so, he spotted a deserted parking space. "*Mon Chèrie*, can I pull in here for a few minutes?"

"*Oui, Monsieur*, drive close to that trash bin."

He stopped the car, lay back in his seat and covered his eyes with his hands.

"Can I look now?"

"Tap, tap, tap." She was putting on her bra. Her blouse was next, and then the jacket; the lipstick was last.

"You may look at me now," she said, sealing his mouth with her pink lips.

He opened his arms and engulfed her with all his might. "You are the sweetest angel I have ever met!"

She sent him a scolding glance, reached for her seat belt and strapped herself in, letting her skirt inch higher. "Drive *Monsieur*," she murmured.

How? Her gorgeous thighs were like a magnet. He did not want to drive into the sea.

She caught him looking and giggled. "Keep your eyes on the road, Costa. More punishment is coming your way . . . later."

She was taunting him by showing off her thighs, and he was not about to lose this game. "I know what you are up to, *Mademoiselle* Gülpinar, but I am not going to fall for that."

"Bravo, Mr. Rigas, bravo." She leaned over, gave him a kiss, and pulled her skirt down to her mid-thighs.

"No more distractions for you," she admonished, "until I get you into your bed."

Costa grabbed the steering wheel with determination. How did they ever get to this point? He, a Greek-Christian from the island of Imvros, and she, a Turko-Muslim, the exotic daughter of an Austrian mother and Turkish judge, were the most unlikely candidates to fall in love; they were a paradox. In a country of fifty-million Turks, how could he be so lucky? She was everything a man could ever dream of and more. He was convinced that his only reason for coming into this life was to be part of her world; he loved her before he even met her. There could not be anyone like her. He never wanted a single moment to end, and yet he could not wait to experience her next act.

Every day with Süheylā was a new adventure. To go along with her flirtatious personality, her passion was unlike any other. She transported him beyond race, beyond religion and beyond any flag. Süheylā was his earthly connection and his Heaven too—the nuttiest, the sexiest, and the most sensual Muslim girl in the world. If she asked him to convert to Islam, he would do it in a minute. It was either Süheylā or eternal Hell.

Chapter 27: Tea and Marmalade

Costa was playing backgammon with his friend Ozan at the Seven Hills Café. He was surprised to see Süheylā walk in. She greeted them cheerfully and then pulled Costa aside.

"I tried to call you, Costa. My parents are going to France with Gülēngül."

"Without you?"

"My father did not ask me."

"Why Gülēngül?"

"She wants to study voice; they found the perfect academy."

"Would you like to go to Kilyos then?"

"I prefer we stay in the city. I want you to come to our apartment."

"Wouldn't that get you in trouble?"

"No, it would not. The doorkeeper will let you in."

"What am I going to say?"

"Nothing. Just show up at the door."

"Okay, but I am still worried about you."

"Don't. I will see you tomorrow at about six-thirty." She gave him a quick kiss and ran down the steps.

Süheylā's coming to his apartment was one thing, but visiting her in her family's flat did not seem right. He shaved all over, took a shower and dressed. He stuffed his pajamas along with his toothbrush and the Delacroix's art books into his duffle bag, stopping by the florist on his way. The taxi ride was too short. He rang the bell of the apartment complex with apprehension.

"Just a minute, I will be right there."

The voice sounded familiar. The door opened. In front of him was Firyāl, Süheylā's friend, and her boyfriend—members of the 'Garbo Club.'

"Come in, Costa, we are expecting you."

"Thank you, Firyāl; I did not know you lived here."

"Just for the last two months; we live and work here. The Gülpinars are on the fifth floor, apartment D."

He entered the elevator and pushed number five. Apartment D was at the end of the hallway. Before he even had time to press the bell, Süheylā opened the door.

"Ooh, Costa," she lilted, looking animated and puckered her lips.

They kissed quickly. "Excuse me Süheylā; I still can't believe I am in your apartment."

"You are in for a rough time," she winked. "Are those flowers for me?"

"Who else?"

"Thank you."

He followed her into the living room. It was just as he imagined it. Dozens of pieces of art hanging on the walls gave the room the look of an art gallery; paintings of all kinds—landscapes, sketches of animals, whitewashed houses by the shore, etc. A few of them were in chiaroscuro[69] but most in color. One large piece, a tall granite mountain awash in silver-grey, eclipsed all others in size and style. The large living room was furnished very tastefully—matching fixtures and furnishings and a huge oriental rug covered most of the wooden floor.

Süheylā nudged his arm. "Come sit, Costa," she said, pointing to the couch. "You will have plenty of time to admire my mom's artwork."

"This salon is an art gallery. Your mom is an exquisite artist, Süheylā. I am impressed."

"Thank you. I wish I had her talent."

---

69. The art of the use of strong contrasts between light and dark, affecting the whole composition. Chiaroscuro is also a technical term used by artists and art historians for using contrasts of light to achieve a sense of volume in modeling three-dimensional objects such as the human body.

She excused herself to arrange the flowers. She came back and put the vase on the coffee table. "What have you got in that duffle bag?" she asked and sat by his side.

"Some personal belongings."

"Should I put it in my bedroom?"

"Not yet." He reached into the duffle bag and pulled out Delacroix's art books. "These are for you. They are from my cousin Demos."

When she saw Delacroix's '*La Liberté*[70] *Guidant le Peuple*', she appeared mesmerized; her eyes rested on the cover for a long time.

"Do you like it, Süheylā?"

She woke up from her daydream. "This is incredible, Costa. I never expected to see anything like this. Do you know anything about it?"

"According to my cousin Demos, it symbolizes liberty of the people, liberty of humanity, liberty of women, liberty from tyranny and liberty from chauvinistic oppression."

"If I were looking for a symbol to identify with, this is it; I love it. Thank you for bringing these books to me." She nuzzled closer. "Welcome to our apartment, Costa, I am really excited!"

"Süheylā, what if your parents find out?"

"They are in France, and like all good Muslim girls, I am at home with you!"

"What about your neighbors?"

"They are all foreign diplomats; all of them are away for the weekend."

She was wearing jeans, a shirt and a tasteful vest, no head cover, and bare feet. She had collected her hair into a bun. Costa reached out and touched it. "I always like this look," he complimented. "It makes you look sophisticated."

---

70. Liberty leading the people, one of Eugene Delacroix's masterpieces, housed in the Louvre.

"Thank you, sir; now put on some music while I make us some tea." She gave him a quick kiss and disappeared into the kitchen.

It was a Grundig radio console encased in a wooden cabinet, equipped with a tape deck and a record player. He dialed Radio Istanbul, always the perfect radio station for Ottoman music. He sat back on the couch still trying to get used to the idea that he was in Süheylā's apartment. He heard her calling him.

"Costa, will you put these sandwiches on the coffee table, please?"

He followed her into the living room with the tray of sandwiches while she placed the teakettle on the table.

"While we are waiting for the tea to steep, let me show you around." She extended her hand. "As you noticed, our kitchen is small but very functional. My mom wanted more space for the living room. This room over here is my parent's, and the one next is Gülēngül's—mine is off to the far right." She gave him a wink.

They walked to the end of the hallway. Süheylā opened the door and let him pass. She then crossed the room and pulled the heavy drapes to expose a huge bay window. Suddenly, the filtering sunlight through the silk sheers danced about the room as if it were Monet's garden. This was not a bedroom, it was a studio. Several pieces of artwork—some finished—were arranged randomly around the perimeter of the studio on tripods; easels, paintbrushes, various paints and pencils and crayons were everywhere. A bed in the far corner with posts was covered with a beautiful bedspread.

"This is it, Costa. This is where I watch my mom paint; I love it."

Costa took a deep breath. He now understood the passion of an artist. Regina Gülpinar and his cousin Demos were of another world, one that amateurs like Costa could not fathom. When he got over the spectacle, he noticed Süheylā's desk by the other corner and walked over to look. Right in the middle of it was one of the art books he had lent her; the page of Kouros was open.

"I don't leave these books around here like that, Costa. I keep them locked in my personal closet over there. Do you want to see it?"

"If you want to show it to me!"

She took out a key from her desk drawer, walked to the closet door and opened it. "Don't be shy," she said and flipped the switch. She stayed behind to let him pass. The closet was huge. In the middle of it was a large easel, on top of which was a human-size sketch of Kouros, genitals and all.

"I have been working on this in my spare time. I wanted to surprise you. As I told you, I can sketch all right, but I cannot paint that well. I have a way to go. Probably, I will never get to my mom's level."

"Does your mom know about this Kouros?"

"She does."

"How about your father?"

"I have the only key," she winked.

"I am impressed with your talent, Süheylā. Words fail to describe my amazement."

"Thank you, Costa, I was hoping you would. Now let's get to our tea." She locked the closet, put the key in her pocket and led him into the living room. She filled their glasses.

Costa took his glass. "To you, Süheylā; you are an amazing girl."

She gave him a quick smirk. "We are going to have a great time, Costa, you and me this weekend."

The sandwiches were great—grilled sardines on fresh bread, goat cheese on toast, shrimp and muscle canapés, and mini sweets of all sorts. The tea was exceptional.

"This is a feast, Süheylā; thank you. Did you work all day for this?"

"My mom prepared it all; she was worried I would starve."

"I love these biscuits."

"They taste even better with that rose-petal marmalade."

"Good suggestion."

Rose-petal marmalade was his favorite preserve, but this one was extraordinary. He took another spoonful. Before he'd even had time to chew, Süheylā sealed his mouth with a protracted kiss, causing the marmalade to meander between their lips. On a whim, Costa pushed some of that marmalade into her mouth. She made an "oh" sound and swirled the marmalade about their mutual cavity with gusto. Between more spoons of marmalade, they gnawed at each other's faces beyond suffocation. Süheylā finally pulled back.

"Slow down, Costa; let's finish this food first. You will need all your strength for later," she challenged.

He gazed at her angelic face, convinced that behind her facade was a lurking tigress.

Staring at him mischievously, she pulled out a pillow and stretched out on the couch. "Massage my feet, Costa," she pleaded. "I have been sketching all day."

"Just your feet; can I go any higher?"

She giggled. "You can only go up to my knees."

"Okay." She had gorgeous feet, and great calves, too. He pushed her jeans halfway up her legs and massaged her feet for a few minutes.

"Oh, that feels good, Costa; you have great hands."

He inched higher. She looked as if she were going to scold him, but instead she gave him her devilish side-glance.

"You are doing great; keep it up!"

"Are you sure you want me to?"

She lifted her foot and tamped it down on his thighs teasingly.

He massaged her knees for a while and moved up to her thighs one inch at a time. He saw her close her eyes, and stretch herself on the couch like a kitten. He continued to inch higher up to her flat belly. Her vest had no buttons, but her shirt was tucked under her jeans. He undid the top button and slowly pulled her shirt out. This was a silk shirt, very expensive. *Another gift from that devil Erika, he thought. He wondered how he could ever thank her.* He ran his hands up and down her chest, feeling her breasts and nipples pushing under her bra searching for air, and buried his face in her cleavage.

"Costa, will you excuse me; there is too much light around here."

She went about the living room, pulled all the drapes, lowered the radio volume, and switched on a single night lamp at the far end. She sat back by his side and straddled her legs across his thighs. This was one of her most endearing traits—never sitting close to him without touching some part of his body.

When Costa slithered his hands on her chest, she grinned. "You have the fingers of an artist, Costa!"

"Maybe, but I don't have that kind of talent."

"You have the talent to drive me crazy." She threw her arms around him, locked her lips on his, and slipped her tongue into his mouth. Her distinctive aroma of basil, mint and Ottoman roses was driving him over the cliff.

"Costa, will you excuse me again?" She rose from the couch and sauntered off into the hallway, giving him a wink before she disappeared around the corner.

Costa poured himself more tea and rested on the enormous couch. *What was she doing now?* He heard hard steps on the wood floor and turned to look. Standing in high heels and hiding behind a black leather eye mask was a blonde angel, dressed in a diaphanous camisole and lace panties. Her flickering eyes behind the mask honed into his face like a lasers; she had the look of a menacing tigress.

"Well, *Monsieur*," she challenged. "What do you think?"

He was dazed. He took her in his arms. "Who are you?" he asked.

"I am the black fury, *Monsieur*. Touch me and be consumed in fire!"

He lifted her in his arms and placed her gently on the couch. Slowly he undid her bra. His mind raced to the marmalade. A spoonful at a time, he laced the marmalade around her nipples. To the touch of the cold spoon, she let out an "Arrggh—arrggh!"

"Do you want me to stop?"

She stared at him behind that black mask, ready to claw him.

Gently, he began to suck on her nipples, rolling his tongue around them. She was now gyrating. She tugged at his belt. He took off his pants and his shorts.

"Ooh Costa, I love your looks," she complimented. She spread herself on the couch like a Mona Lisa, and beckoned him in her arms smiling mischievously. When he burrowed his face between her legs, she wrapped her thighs around him and climaxed, calling his name.

Slowly she calmed down. "You take me to another world, Costa; every time. You are my dream man come true."

They continued this love game nonstop, declaring their love forever. Finally, after several combustions, Süheylā calmed slowed down . . . sort of.

"We will take a shower in a while, Costa," she whispered and wrapped him in her arms tightly again, squeezing him as if he were her lifeline.

The radio was still playing in the background. "This is Radio Istanbul; time is twenty-two thirty."

"We were at this since seven-thirty?"

"Maybe," she said. "Erika and James Anderson sometimes play all night."

"She told you that?"

"No, she showed me."

"She showed what?"

"A movie; they made a movie of themselves while making love."

"Keep away from that vixen, Süheylā; she is corrupting you." Her close relationship with the Andersons was making him uncomfortable, even jealous.

"Erika is a free woman," continued Süheylā, ignoring his discomfort. "Between you and the Andersons, I have freed myself from all cultural taboos. Delacroix's '*La Liberté*,' it is me, Costa, it is me!"

He loved her liberated mind, but maybe not too much. He wondered whether he was strong enough to handle a girl like her. He never imagined that such a relationship was even possible. "There is no one like you, Süheylā; no one! I mean it."

She glued her lips and pushed her tongue into his mouth. "Let's take a shower, Costa. We have to wash off all this marmalade," she teased trawling her palm across her chest.

"Keep doing that and I will not sleep tonight."

"Yes you will. You will sleep in my arms," she lilted, caressing him with her eyes. She jumped from the couch, pulled him up and took his arm. "It is time to play, Costa," she purred and pulled him into the shower.

Spending time in Süheylā's apartment was one thing, but sleeping in her bed? He would follow her to the ends of the earth; his mind was making somersaults.

Chapter 28: A Cross for a Muslim

It was Byzantium first, Costantinopolis later, and now Istanbul; this was the city where east met west, disparate cultures competed, and religions clashed. This was the place where Islam, riding on the shoulders of the Ottoman Turks, defeated Christianity and displaced it forever. The original natives of the city were in their last gasp. After twenty-five-hundred years, modern Turkey was determined to wipe out the remaining Greeks. Not even the conquerors of the Americas succeeded so well.

The smaller pockets of ethnicities—Armenians, Jews, Italians, Bulgarians, French—had left long ago. From a multi-lingual city, Turkish was the only language spoken. Ethnophobia[71] was the norm. This was the new Istanbul.

By the second year Costa and Süheylā were beyond lovers; they could not breathe without one another. Their volcanic passion had incapacitated them to assess the consequences; their relationship was sacrilegious to their respective cultures.

Tonight Costa and Süheylā were dinner guests at the Gregorys. With no special occasion to think of, the two lovers wondered what was in the offing. Usually, the Gregorys called a dinner event to either celebrate an occasion or just for the fun of it. However, the Gregorys had been acting very reserved lately and Costa was beginning to get concerned. He knew that the Turkish Tax Service recently audited Mr. Gregory's businesses, and if it were not for his connections, they would have already thrown him out of the country. Auditing any Greek business was Turkey's standard practice, an underhanded

---

71. The hate of all ethnicities other than your own.

way to fabricate tax evasion and confiscate their businesses and properties.

Costa and Süheylā arrived at the Gregorys much earlier than everyone else. Mrs. Gregory, already several months pregnant, could use their assistance.

"We are so thankful to you for coming early to help us," said Mr. Gregory. "We appreciate it very much."

"Don't even mention it, Mrs. Gregory; why don't you let us do the rest?" replied Süheylā in her usual cheerful manner.

Within an hour, the guests arrived. After some social time, they sat down to dinner. From the looks of things, the Gregorys did not seem cheerful. Usually cordial and funny, Thomas Gregory said very little. It was dessert time before he rose to offer a toast.

"Dear friends, you're probably wondering why Martha and I have invited you in our home tonight. I am sorry to inform you that Martha and I are leaving the country."

This was unexpected. Everybody was in shock.

"We are leaving, my friends," stated Thomas Gregory. "We are no longer welcome in our homeland. As you know, Martha is expecting, and we wish to raise our child in safety. Turkey will no longer do."

"But where will you go, Mr. Gregory?" asked Costa.

"Our first stop will be Greece, and after that, who knows?"

"What about your businesses, Mr. Gregory?" asked somebody dejectedly.

"With Hermes Travel, we were lucky. Our partner, Mr. Sedat Sariyer, paid us at full market value; the rest of our businesses, including our apartment, we were forced to sell them for very little." He looked at his wife, who stood up.

With dark hair and black, penetrating eyes, she was a tall and impressive woman. Dressed impeccably, she carried herself like a princess, a testament to her long, aristocratic lineage dating back to the old Greek families of Istanbul.

"Look, friends," she said with her arresting gaze. "Every year some of you leave, and our group is getting smaller. Our community can no longer survive this land. The Ottoman Empire had a touch of humanity, but modern Turkey is from another mold. I would like to ask a favor of you. Before you leave our house tonight, we want you to take whatever you like. Take it even if you don't need it."

A chorus of protest arose from the table. They were proud people. Besides, their departure was imminent, too.

"You all know that we can take none of these things with us," Martha continued. "And frankly, Thomas and I do not wish to sell them; we would rather smash them or burn them. A few more Turkish liras are not going to make much difference."

Costa gathered his wits. "Mrs. Gregory, Süheylā and I would gladly take something that we can save and pass back to you at some future time. If it weren't for you, I personally would have been out on the street."

"In that case, Costa," said Martha, "if you don't mind, I would like to give you and Süheylā a special present."

Her words were weighty, sad and enigmatic. Everybody looked up, wondering.

Martha walked to her icon stand and genuflected reverently. She reached up and took down a wooden cross, inlaid with gold and precious stones, and held it up for everyone's view.

"This cross is very old and probably valuable. It has been in our family for generations. My prayers to this cross helped me conceive after the doctors in Switzerland declared me sterile. We would like to take it with us, but Turkish Customs will confiscate it. Costa and Süheylā, we want you to have it."

Costa gulped for air, and Süheylā squeezed his arm. "But Mrs. Gregory," protested Süheylā, looking at the cross, "how can we accept such a gift?"

"There is a reliable Antiochan dealer at the bazaar," Martha continued. "Gregory and I have already spoken to him. You can sell it if you wish; I am sure you and Costa can use the money."

With great veneration, Martha placed the cross in Süheylā's hands.

This was *déjà vu*; they had just gone through the same thing with Mrs. Kara's icons a couple of months ago. Costa looked at Mr. Gregory for some answer, but he only nodded with kindness.

"We will gladly accept it, Mrs. Gregory," Costa relented, "but we will not sell it. On the other hand, we cannot vouch for its safety."

"As long as you are safe, it will be safe," added Mrs. Gregory assuredly.

"Here are the legal documents," said Mr. Gregory, taking an envelope from a drawer. "It is a notarized bill of sale. If you decide to sell it, all you have to do is sign one of your names. If you do not, please keep it safe. Who knows, it may be useful someday."

Martha Gregory in the meantime came back from the kitchen with a wooden box. She lifted the cross from Süheylā's hands, wrapped it in a velvet cloth and carefully placed it inside.

Costa and Süheylā did not know what to say. The last thing they needed was to worry about a relic like this.

"We will try to keep it safe," assured Costa. "I am sure Süheylā feels the same way. If we ever sell it—and only under extreme need—we will sell it back into the realm of Orthodoxy. It would be a dishonor if it ended up in the hands of strangers. We promise you it shall never reach the hands of art dealers."

"It is all yours," said Mrs. Gregory, putting her arms around Süheylā. She looked over her guests kindly. "The rest of you, walk around the house and pick up whatever you like. We are moving into a hotel in a few days, and we no longer have a need for any of these possessions."

"What about the icons?" someone asked.

"We are going to burn them in our fireplace tonight," said Mr. Gregory, looking sad. "You are welcome to take them, but unfortunately, you will never get them through Customs; they will be confiscated."

"That would be horrible, Thomas," commented one of the guests.

"Such is life, my friends. The people that desecrated our churches have just realized that they can sell these icons in Europe for big money. Vandalism has been replaced by greed and profiteering."

Looking very sad, the guests began to leave. Costa and Süheylā decided to do the same. Mr. Gregory escorted the group down the stairway. The door attendant jumped out of his post, pulled Mr. Gregory aside and started to talk to him rapidly. The guests saw Mr. Gregory get animated and stopped; he seemed upset.

"You are nothing but a heartless pig. You have been employed by my family for over fifty years, and you are now behaving like a vulture."

"Mr. Gregory, I have bought your building from the government," shot the door attendant back.

"How could you afford to buy my building? The government took it from me by fabricating tax evasion so that they could give it to you? Once more, you cannot have it a single hour before its agreed time. I have the statement from the Department of Interior. Your takeover date is January one."

"But Mr. Gregory," screamed the door attendant. "I have renters whom I promised your apartment by December."

"I don't give a damn about that. Get the hell out of my face."

It looked as if Mr. Gregory were going to punch the door attendant. Costa and a couple of others stepped between the two and pulled Mr. Gregory away.

"Let it go, Thomas," said one of his friends. "It is not worth it. That is all you can expect from this country we once called home."

It took Mr. Gregory a few tense moments to calm down. Finally, he composed himself, hugged all his friends and bade them goodbye.

Costa escorted Süheylā to the taxi stand and handed her the box.

"Take the cross with you, Süheylā."

"What am I going to do with it?" she protested.

"Put it in a safe place. You never know where it might end up with me."

"You are scaring me."

"Just do as I ask, please."

"Al right, Costa; I love you." She gave him a kiss and got into the cab.

Costa and Süheylā had no idea whether the cross was valuable. The Gregorys' imminent departure had shaken them to the core.

Chapter 29: The Sketch

Süheylā's father, Judge Mehmet Gülpinar, had an arthritic problem and loved the thermal springs of Yalova. With her parents gone over the weekend, this was another opportunity for Süheylā to invite Costa to spend the night with her at her family's apartment. He woke up with Süheylā wrapped around him like an octopus. She was sleeping so blissfully, he did not dare move. Inhaling her gentle breath, he could have gazed at her angelic face all day long, but she opened her eyes.

"How long have you been awake?"

"For a while."

"And you were watching me sleep?"

"Yes."

"You are a hopeless romantic."

"Romantic yes, hopeless no!"

"When did we go to bed last night?"

"I think it was after two-o'clock."

"You wore me out."

"No, you wore me out. What are we doing today, anyway?"

"Um, let me see." She gave him that devilish look of hers. "Today I am going to sketch you," she winked, tracing her finger around his chest.

"You want me to pose for you?"

"Yes, but let's get some breakfast first."

"Here is your nightwear, Süheylā; I found it under my pillow."

"I don't need them—come closer." She brushed her breasts against his chest. "You see; I am hot."

"Don't start any games, Süheylā. I want to go brush my teeth."

"Okay, me too."

"You don't need to. Your breath is fresh as the valley of roses."

"Liar." She gave him a wink, flung off the sheets, and sauntered into her bathroom completely naked.

He shook his head. He would be content to lie on this bed all day long as long as she was by his side. He found his sleepwear and went to use the other bathroom. He was in the kitchen brewing tea when she wandered in barefoot, wearing only a see-through silk robe all the way down to her ankles.

"Good morning, Costa; kiss me."

"I will . . . if you promise to behave."

"I promise. First, we will make breakfast. We have eggs, cheese, biscuits and fruit; anything else?"

"That is plenty. I will fry the eggs; I am an expert with eggs."

"Okay, I will do the rest. Do you want any marmalade?"

Costa cracked up. "If it is rose petal!"

By the time they finished breakfast, it was noon.

Süheylā looked at Costa. "Are you ready?"

"Ready for what?"

"Your sketch."

"We have all day."

"No, we don't. I can sketch only in full daylight."

"How long will it take?"

"It depends on how you behave."

Something in her voice told him that this was going to be another adventure. "Okay, Süheylā, I am game."

"Come with me, *Monsieur*," she commanded, assuming Melina's voice again.

He followed her into her bedroom. She parted the drapery to let in the sunlight. He assisted her in setting up a very large easel off to the side of the room, on which she placed a huge sheet, holding it in place with pushpins. She gathered up a few pencils and crayons, put them in a box, and placed it by the easel.

"*Monsieur*, will you bring me that bar stool from the kitchen?"

"*Oui, Mademoiselle, a votres service!*"

"Put it over there, at forty-five degrees from the window, *Monsieur*."

"Okay, what now?"

"Go brush your hair and sit on the stool; I am ready."

When she saw him wander back into the studio, she lifted her eyebrows. "Not that way, *Monsieur*; take off your pajamas."

"Are you serious?"

"Of course I am. I want you to look like that Kouros."

Costa took off his pajamas and sat on the stool, feeling funny. This was a new experience. He was going to live under her microscope all day. When she slanted the easel off to the side, he was disappointed. The angle would make it impossible to see anything from where he was sitting. She stuck a pencil between her teeth, picked up a long ruler, and divided the canvas paper in half; she then drew several more parallel lines. Costa was familiar with this technique. He had seen his cousin do it whenever he drew large landscapes and other larger pieces.

Finally, she was ready.

"You must stand erect at all times and look directly at me. Turn your body to the right slightly and lower your right leg and put it on the floor. Lift your other leg and rest it on the cross bar of the bar stool. I also want your genitals in full view. When I tell you to flex a particular muscle, especially your pectorals, please do. She gave him a hot kiss, rolling her tongue in his mouth.

"This is the last thing you are going to get from me, *Monsieur*, until I am finished. Remember: you are my first live model." She slipped out of her robe, winked at Costa, and stuck another pencil behind her ear. "While I am sketching you, I want you to direct all your energy at me," she admonished him seriously.

Costa tried to adjust himself on his stool.

"She looked at him approvingly. Now that is more like it. I want you excited and agitated; stay that way. She sharpened her pencil and slowly began to draw his outline. Looking back at him for a second or two, she would draw a line or erase it and start all over again. He was surprised with her speed and confidence. It was obvious she had her mother's skills, and she was all business. Occasionally she would ask him to shift his body slightly, but other than that, she did not say anything else; she was all business. He took a bathroom break, but that was all. She must have been at it for two hours when she finally dropped her pencils, looked at him and smiled. "Do you want to take a look?"

Happy to leave the wooden stool, he walked around the easel. He had never seen a sketch like this. Mostly in black and a hue of blue, it was so proportional and so real. He could not get over the look of his genitals. He stared at Süheylā with admiration.

"This looks fantastic. I am speechless."

"You like it?"

"I love it. I am so glad you drew an abstract face."

"Not intentionally. I did it because I do not have that kind of confidence. In due time, your face will be real, when I mature a little. For now, I am pleased."

"You cannot leave that thing around here, Süheylā."

"I am going to roll it up and ship it to my grandmother in Diyarbakir. The climate there is very dry. If I packed it right, nothing is going to happen to it. Now, *Monsieur*, it is your turn."

"My turn for what?"

She threw her arms around his shoulders, glued her hot naked body to him, brushing her pelvis against his. "You will have to make real love to me. I need my reward, Costa."

"What do you mean by real love? We have been doing that for the last year!"

"I mean real love, Costa . . . no prophylactic!"

"Are you insane?"

"No, I am not."

He ignored her reply, searched for his pants and found one.

She looked at it with disdain, grabbed it from his hand and flung it on the floor. "I mean the real thing, Costa. I want to feel you inside me."

"What if you get pregnant?" he replied, feeling terrified.

She winked her eye and gave him a passionate kiss. "I am on a special birth control medicine," she replied.

"What kind of crazy medicine is that?" he asked, although he'd read about this birth control pill some time ago.

"Erika gave it to me; I have been taking it for the last two weeks."

"I am not sure I want to take that chance, Süheylā." Although he was delirious with passion, he was not going to give in to her demand—at least not yet.

"Why do you think Erika does not get pregnant?"

"I don't care about Erika," Costa replied, looking determined. Making love to Süheylā without any protection would be suicide.

"Have it your way," she exhaled and led him to her bed.

Chapter 30: An Unexpected Visitor

The hard knock startled him. Who could it be so early in the morning? He opened the door of his apartment halfway. Even though he had not met her before, he knew immediately who it was. He fumbled for something to say.

"I am Mrs. Perihan Gülpinar. May I come in?"

"Yes, of course," Costa stammered.

She walked in and stood in the middle of the small living room. Tall and slim like her daughter, she was impeccably dressed. Nothing in her attire attested to her Islamic conversion. "I think you know why I am here," she said, glaring at him.

Costa gulped for air. "I think I know, Mrs. Gülpinar. Please sit down."

"I am not here for a social visit," she replied tersely, placing her hands on her hips.

"I know why you are here, Mrs. Gülpinar."

"In that case, let me be quick; you have to stop seeing my daughter Süheylā," she stated, fuming.

Costa raised his eyebrows. "Mrs. Gülpinar, with all due respect, I cannot do that."

"Why not?"

"Because I love your daughter."

"Love, what do you know about love? You and my daughter are crazy."

"I beg your pardon?"

"Look, young man, this is Turkey; it is a Muslim country."

"Mrs. Gülpinar, I was born here."

"Then you should be aware that Islam does not allow for inter-religious friendship or love."

"Pardon me, Mrs. Gülpinar, but as I understand it, you are Austrian. Why are you lecturing me on inter-religious practices?"

She leaned closer into his face. "I converted to Islam before I married my husband."

"Yes I know; your daughter told me."

"Did she also tell you that my conversion resulted in my excommunication from my family?" She looked rather sad; "can I sit down?"

"Yes, please Mrs. Gülpinar. Can I get you some tea?"

"That won't be necessary. As I was saying, you and my daughter are treading on taboo ground. Both of you are lucky that my husband does not know a thing—yet. When he finds out, you and my daughter will be in big trouble."

"Mrs. Gülpinar, I cannot worry about me. I am worried about Süheylā."

"So you are aware of the consequences?"

"Yes I am, but I cannot change a thing."

"Yes you can; stop seeing my daughter. I am warning you, my husband will have you punished."

"If that is a threat, you have made your point, Mrs. Gülpinar. As you know, I am of Greek lineage; I don't even call myself a Christian."

"That is what my daughter told me; she is no longer a Muslim."

"Mrs. Gülpinar, Muslim or not does not matter to me."

"It matters to my family. My daughter was born Muslim, and she is going to stay that way."

"That would be her choice, Mrs. Gülpinar. She is the brightest girl I've ever met."

"I am not getting through to you, am I? Even if you converted to Islam, my husband would never tolerate your relationship with my daughter. For your information, my husband received a promotion within the Ministry of Interior. Are you aware that people like you are expendable?"

226

Costa this time got angry. "You really don't mean that, Mrs. Gülpinar."

"It does not matter. What I am telling you is reality."

"You are not telling me anything I don't know, Mrs. Gülpinar. All people of Greek descent are being chased out of their homeland by post-Kemalist Turkey; you should know better."

"Don't lecture me, young man. I know all about that; there is nothing I can do."

"So, close your eyes and let us perish?"

"I told you, there is nothing I can do. You and that Erika Anderson have corrupted my daughter."

"Nobody can corrupt Süheylā. She has a mind of her own."

"I know she does. I have a sneaky suspicion that while we were in France, Süheylā invited you to our apartment. Tell me it is not true."

Costa raised his brow. *Hold on to this one, Costa; otherwise, you are toast.* "I know where your apartment is, Mrs. Gülpinar, but I have never seen the inside of it."

She frowned. "Heed my warning, young man, or bad things will happen to you." She jumped up from the couch and stormed out of the apartment.

Costa closed the door behind her and sat on the couch shaking; was it anger or fear? Maybe both; his mind was racing. Deep in his heart he knew that his relationship with Süheylā would come to one thing: acceptance. Mrs. Gülpinar's warning was not a veiled threat. Even if he graduated from the university, remaining in Turkey would not guarantee a future with Süheylā. Her parents would never accept him; nor would his parents accept her. The phone rang and he jumped.

"This is Costa Rigas. Who is calling?"

"Costa, this is Mr. Akduman. Can you meet me at the Park Hotel in an hour?"

Costa swallowed. "Yes, sir," Costa replied mechanically.

This was weird. He had spoken with Mr. Akduman just yesterday; guiding his American friends about the city was not until next week. As if Mrs. Gülpinar were not enough of a worry, it was now the chief of the secret police of Istanbul. He took a quick shower and before boarding the trolley, he stopped by the newsstand to buy a 'Hürriyet[72], the largest newspaper of Istanbul and the leading mouthpiece of Turkish propaganda. He found a seat on the trolley and unfolded the paper. When he saw the article, "The *Hate*[73]," he froze.

The poem had an additional eighteen verses, all pure venom. By the time Costa finished reading the article, he could not breathe. He could not understand the depths of such human depravity. Thankfully, he had a circle of Turkish friends who in spite of all the state propaganda were ready to protect him at any cost, but these friends were the few, the exception. Finally, it dawned on him that he must leave Turkey. Any country would be better; Turkey was no place to live.

His nerves were on edge. He arrived at the café holding the newspaper in his hand and took a seat. Within a few minutes, he saw Mr. Akduman walking toward him and stood up.

"Good morning, Costa. Did you order breakfast yet?"

"No sir."

---

72. Freedom.

73. The poem, called 'Hate, was published by Istanbul's leading newspaper, "Hürriyet", on July 18, 1974, 48 hours before Turkey's invasion of Cyprus:

As long as in this world exists the Greek prostitute
I swear to Allah, I will never forget my hatred
As long as there is a Greek dog standing across from me
May the mighty Allah help me perpetuate my hatred
Not even the heads of a thousand of these infidels
Will they help me cleanse my hatred.
My only purpose in life is revenge . . . etc.

Mr. Akduman called the waiter over. "Bring us some breakfast rolls, hard-boiled eggs, olives, cheese and tea, please." He looked at Costa and cracked a faint smile. "I see that you read the article, Costa. How do you feel about that?"

"It is scary, sir."

Don't worry. I have instructed my unit to keep you safe." Do you have any idea why I called you?"

Costa looked bewildered. "No, Mr. Akduman, I have no idea."

"You must leave Turkey as soon as possible. Do you understand?"

Costa felt his heart skip. "What did I do, Mr. Akduman?"

"You have broken the moral code."

Costa was beginning to see. "Why is it that falling in love with a Turkish girl is against the rules, Mr. Akduman?"

"It is an unwritten law, and you know it. Your girlfriend's father will not stand for a relationship like that—ever."

"Is it because I come from a Christian family and of Greek decent?"

"Yes and yes. The reason I am here is that I like you. You know who I am. I can have you locked up, or worse."

"So what am I supposed to do, Mr. Akduman?"

"Leave the country as soon as you can. There is no future here for you."

"I appreciate your advice, Mr. Akduman, but leaving Turkey without Süheylā is unthinkable; I could not live without her."

"Don't you think I know that?"

"So you know everything?"

He raised his eyebrows. "I advise you to leave this country and succeed elsewhere. Maybe then you can send for Süheylā."

"Mr. Akduman, I am humbled by your advice, but the idea of giving up Süheylā is worse than death."

"I am sure of that, but her father will never accept you. He will not let her out of his clutches."

"How can he do that?"

"He can place travel restrictions. She could be denied a passport and not be able to travel out of the country at any time."

"And leaving the country is my only option?"

"What other choice do you have? You do not have the financial means to stay in the university. Even if you graduate, you will never be able to go near his daughter. Sooner or later you will have to leave."

Costa lowered his head. Breakfast arrived, but he did not look at it. He watched Mr. Akduman eat while he sat in silence. "Mr. Akduman, you are a powerful man. Can't you help me?"

"What am I doing right now? Do you think that a man in my position would be wasting his time? I am doing it because I owe you a favor."

Costa raised his head, wondering.

"The reason I am leaving you alone, Costa, is because you have spared us an embarrassment. You managed to prevail upon your girlfriend and some of her Kurdish nuts to stop their radical activities."

Costa managed a faint smile. "Mr. Akduman, if I did such a thing, I have no idea."

"You are too modest, young man."

"So what are my best options, Mr. Akduman?"

"You have only one: leave Turkey and hope for the best. By then, who knows? Judge Gülpinar might have a change of heart."

Costa did not remember saying goodbye or thank you to Mr. Akduman. The realization that he must leave Turkey was slowly sinking in. He and Süheylā had already discussed such an eventuality several times before, but he could not fathom life without her

When he arrived at the travel agency, Süheyla was at the door. Costa had no idea what to say; the feeling of powerlessness was overwhelming. He saw Mr. Gregory in the middle of the reception area and showed him the article.

"I know, Costa. I have been thinking of closing the office. I have sent all the employees home. You and Süheyla take the day off, too; you never know."

At that moment, a rock crashed through the main window. They ducked, but it was too late. A shard flew into Mr. Gregory's face, opening a gash above his forehead. Costa saw a group of rowdies outside the office shouting obscenities and pointing toward the travel agency. By luck, a police cruiser on patrol drove by and the rowdies took off running. Süheylā bandaged Mr. Gregory's bleeding forehead. It did not seem that serious. Fortunately Mrs. Gregory was not in the office that day. The incident was unnerving enough to scare a pregnant person into a miscarriage.

They locked the office and drove Mr. Gregory to his apartment. The radio was reporting that Turkish military forces were massing in the south, poised to invade Cyprus. Suddenly, Costa's future with Süheylā in Turkey looked very bleak indeed. He had to find a way out—and a way to take her with him.

Chapter 31: Kilyos

Kilyos by the Black Sea was their favorite beach. Because it was an hour's drive from the city, there was hardly anybody around, especially in late summer. The two lovers drove there with one thing in mind and one thing only.

It was a crisp, late summer evening, close to twilight. Costa and Süheylā walked down the beach until the small harbor was almost out of sight. They found a perfect spot behind a sand dune hidden by tall reeds. Süheylā spread a blanket, and Costa gathered driftwood and lit a fire. They lay on the blanket holding hands, kissed and gazed into each other's eyes with much love. The sound of lapping waves punctuated by the sparks of the burning driftwood urged their passion even more.

Süheylā loosened her hair clasp, letting her golden hair flow freely. Looking at Costa amorously, she unbuttoned her blouse and unfastened her bra. His hands found her nipples while Süheylā ripped off his shirt. Just like every time, their surging desire had morphed into a pendulum of ecstasy and mind-numbing sensuality. They were aflame. They had done this many a times before, but tonight was going to be different.

"You promised to make love to me without a prophylactic on the beach," she challenged. "This is your chance."

He took a few breaths.

According to Turkish law, the male is the absolute power and authority over the woman. It is the law throughout the land that all women must be virgins at the time of marriage. The state has the power to order a virginity test at any time, without any recourse from the female concerned.

His mother had admonished him long ago: *'no sex before marriage,'* and he'd already passed that point.

"What if you get pregnant?" he asked, feeling scared. "If that happens, it will mean the end of both of us."

"I am on birth control, Costa. Besides, I love you beyond death."

In the waning twilight, the rays from the fire were dancing over Süheylā's breasts like the rippling waters of the Black Sea. Costa unbuttoned her jeans, pulled them off and yanked her panties away.

"Go slow," she murmured. "This is the real thing," as she wrapped him in her arms.

In their delirium, they lost themselves in time. In the chasms of Heaven, they felt the earth move and their loins explode. The elation was indescribable. The circling seagulls above were their only witnesses.

"I love you so much, Costa," Süheylā kept repeating, with her long legs wrapped around his body like a vice.

"I loved you the first time I saw you, Süheylā. My heart leaped and I nearly fainted!"

"Oh, Costa, you have a way with words. Let's go into the water."

Costa stood and pulled Süheylā up. Clasping her hand, he led her into the surf. Her breasts bobbed above the rolling waves like two giant sapphires. Holding and touching with passion, they let their hands roam free over each other's bodies. Süheylā now pulled him to the edge of the water, asking for more.

Once more, their lovemaking was relentless as the lapping waves caressed their feet into a happy exhaustion. They stood by the fire, gazing into each other's eyes, feeling completely in love.

By the time they dressed, they had chased away the twilight and invited the myriad stars above to supplant the flickering embers. Holding hands, they walked to the Tayfun[74] tavern, their favorite spot in all of Bosporus. A

---

74. The Tempest restaurant.

Turko-Christian Greek and a Turko-Muslim girl had crossed all the taboos of the land, convinced that nothing could ever separate them.

As they were about to go up the steps to the tavern, Costa spotted a car pulling out of the parking lot. He had a funny feeling.

"What is it?" asked Süheylā.

"Nothing," he shrugged, pretending indifference.

Süheylā gave him a nudge. "Did you see a ghost?"

"Just a car," he said and guided her up the steps.

The restaurant was an open-air place with a thatched roof. Built on piers, it had the beach to the left and the entrance to Bosporus straits to its right. This spot was the place for seafood and the magnificent view of the Black Sea. With crisp, white linen and turquoise napkins, it was a romantic spot unlike any other. Hassan, *'the maître d'*, took them to their usual table by the water.

"Will it be grilled mackerel and arugula salad?" Hassan asked.

"You have such a memory, Hassan," complimented Süheylā. "What shall we have, Costa?"

"We would like grilled swordfish tonight."

"But, Costa; isn't it expensive?"

He leaned over and whispered into her ear. "Today is our special day."

"Grilled swordfish then, Hassan," Süheylā smiled.

"And bring us two beers, please," Costa added.

"But Costa, I haven't had beer before."

"Why don't you try it? I think you'll like it."

The beer came, and Süheylā took a sip. She did not realize that the foam left a slight mustache on her upper lip. Costa reached over, wiped it off with his finger, and brought it to his lips.

"I like it," she winked.

As they were waiting for their dinner, Süheylā took a small package from her purse. "This is for you."

With much anticipation, Costa removed the wrapping and opened the small box. Inside was a golden pendant with a chain. Etched on its face was the church of Santa Sophia, surrounded by its four minarets. On the backside was the inscription in Greek, *"To Costa with all my love, Süheylā."*

He was in tears.

She reached out and stroked his face. "I love you, Costa. I've waited for the right moment to give it to you."

"It will be my most prized possession, Süheylā. You are a most unusual girl."

"And you are a beautiful man, Costa."

"I want to build us a castle in the middle of the Black Sea and stand by your pillow every night so that I can inhale your every breath. All I want is you; you are my Roxellana," said Costa, running his palm up her cheek.

She planted her eyes on his face for several seconds. "Does this mean you want to marry me?" she asked.

He took her hand. "You beat me to it, Süheylā. I want to live in your arms forever!"

"Let's set a date right now," she suggested, as this was a natural thing to do.

When, how and with what? Costa was astounded. "I suggest the year we graduate from the university," he replied excitedly.

"It might take longer than that," she mused. "We will need to convince our parents."

"Oh, them! And if we don't?"

She shrugged. "With or without them; they cannot stop us."

"That might be true, but you know we cannot live in Turkey."

"Maybe things will change by then; we can always go live in Vienna."

"Why Vienna?"

"I am a dreamer. I want us to get married on New Year's Eve, and then spend New Year's Day waltzing in the halls of Vienna. Maybe we can sneak in the Schönbrunn."

"Pardon my ignorance; what is that?"

"It is a magnificent palace, in the Rococo style."

"How do you know that?"

"You forget. My mom is from Austria. She told me all about its magnificent palaces, its waltz culture with Strauss and its music with Mozart."

"That is a most romantic idea, Süheylā. I can hardly wait."

At the end of their dinner, Süheylā asked Costa to get his guitar and serenade her with a song or two, something he had done before. Costa soon had the attention of all the diners. A group of Turks from the nearby tables joined in.

In a moment of pause, Süheylā leaned into Costa's ear. "Can we leave now? Let's go back to your apartment and make more love."

Amidst a chorus of protest, Costa and Süheylā rose from the table, hating to leave these fun-loving people. They all shook hands with Costa and kissed Süheylā on both cheeks. These were the real Turks Costa knew: loving, generous, gay and friendly. Costa called Hassan to pay the bill, but he refused payment.

"It's on the house," he said kindly.

Hassan escorted them to the parking lot. Costa let Süheylā in the car, and as he walked around, Hassan pulled him aside.

"You have been coming here for the past two years. Please tell your girlfriend not to call you by your true name in close earshot. You know how some of us Turks can be. Keep safe and come here as often as you like. May Allah be with you." He turned and hurried back to the restaurant before Costa had a chance to say a word.

"What was that all about?" asked Süheylā.

"He wanted to tell us how much he appreciated our patronage."

"That was nice of him. Now can you hurry up? This time I will make love to you, and I will be in control," she said and burst into her husky laughter.

Costa swallowed hard. He did not know how to take this one.

She saw his expression. "Relax, Costa. Erika does it to her husband all the time."

Finally, he recovered from this new titillation. "You mean you saw that, too?"

"Yes, I saw them making love."

"Where?"

"In their bedroom."

"Are you joking?"

"No. I was resting in the next room when I heard all that sexual activity next door; they had left the door open . . . purposely, I think."

"And you crept in?"

"I stood by the door."

"Did they not see you?"

"They did. They did not care."

Costa did not know whether Süheylā was attending a sexual academy or there was something else beyond that. "I am curious, Süheylā. Is there something you are not telling me?"

She looked at him mischievously. "They invited me to join them," she said. "I ran out of there as fast as I could. You are my only man."

Costa shook his head and exhaled. "You are a tantalizing temptation!"

"I am glad you think so. Can you hurry up, please?"

"Süheylā, I will not drive like a maniac."

"Now don't get uptight, but I am really angry," she smirked.

"Angry for what?"

"For taking my virginity away!"

"After all this time? I thought you gave it to me willingly a long time ago."

238

"Did I now? You seduced me, Costa. You are guilty of deflowering an innocent Muslim girl," she chuckled.

Her distinctive smell of basil, mint and Ottoman roses stoked his imagination and set his senses on fire. He was going to drive carefully . . . but fast.

Chapter 32: Roxellana

They raced each other up the steps to his apartment. Costa tried to pull off her jeans, but she stopped him.

"I don't want you doing anything tonight," she warned.

"Okay, I am all yours," he challenged, mesmerized by her tigress-like attitude.

"Good man," she complimented; "now come with me."

She led him into his bedroom, pulled off the bed cover and patted the sheets, beckoning him to sit. Next, she turned on the night lamp and drew the window drape.

"What do I have to do?' he asked, feeling paralyzed with excitement.

"Very little," she smirked as she loosened his shirt. When he attempted to embrace her, she stopped him.

"I was yours on the beach. Now it is my turn to get even."

"So you hold grudges?"

"Yes, I do," she giggled and unbuttoned his shirt. "Your ordeal is just beginning," she teased as she kicked off her sneakers and pulled down her stockings. When he tried to do the same, he caught her scolding, stern look.

"I told you not to do anything, but you have a thick skull. I am going to double your punishment."

She pushed him on his back, took off her jeans and pulled the belt out. "Give me your wrist," she commanded.

She strapped the belt around his wrist and secured it to the bedpost. She did the same thing for his other hand by pulling off his own belt." She stepped back and sniggered. "Now I have you under my control. Your ordeal is just beginning!"

He never felt so aroused. He tried to move his arms, but there was no wiggle room; it was deliriously frightening. When she ran her fingers over his sex, he bit his lip.

"Raise your hips," she commanded and pulled off his pants as if they were paper.

He tried to roll off to his side, but she pushed him back, surprising him with her strength.

"I told you not to move," she hissed. "Your ordeal is going to get worse."

She got up and walked to the end of the bed. Beholding him languidly, she took off her jacket and her shirt and threw them on the floor. She then began to trail her palms over her bra, pretending to hyperventilate; he wondered whether he was hallucinating. When he saw her pick up her nylon stockings, he knew.

"I thought you weren't going to tie up my feet!" he protested.

"I lied," she smirked, wrapping his ankles with her stockings one at a time and securing them to the lower bedposts.

He was now defenseless and in hedonistic panic. "You are a sadist," he protested, grinning. "If I were free, I would take you down right now."

"You are in no position to make any threats, *Monsieur*! I am in control." She gyrated her hips like a belly dancer, unclasped her bra and threw it in his face. Her breasts danced in the dimly lit room like two diamonds; she sat by his side and jutted them into his face.

"You like?" she teased, pushing her nipples about his lips. "I am going to take you to the white clouds, *Monsieur*, until you beg me to stop."

Costa wanted to scream. She was the sexiest thing in the universe.

"Excuse me a minute, *mon Cher*."

She rushed into the living room and returned with her pocketbook. Out of it she pulled a small bottle, opened it and poured some of the fluid onto her hand. Rubbing her palms together, she jumped on the bed, straddled him and lubricated his sex. He was moaning in ecstasy.

She stopped and turned around. "Did I not tell you not to make a peep?" she admonished.

"No, you did not!"

"I have a remedy for that," she smiled lustfully. She took off her panties and tugged at his chin. "Open up," she ordered and stuffed them into his mouth. "This will keep you quiet, until I am through with you."

When he tried to mumble, she shook her finger. "Don't move," she warned and continued to tease him mercilessly.

You are a merciless angel, he wanted to tell her, relishing this game even more.

"You had it coming," she admonished. "I was an innocent Muslim virgin; now look what you have done to me!"

When he felt her inserting him into herself, he was in delirium. Her rhythmical gyration was unlike anything he'd ever felt . . . or fantasized. He could not hold it any longer.

Their harmonious explosion was indescribable. She collapsed on top of him, breathing hard.

"I am still mad at you," she teased.

"Why?"

"I told you; you took my virginity away," she protested and bit him on the lip.

"Ouch!" He was bleeding.

She trawled her finger on his bleeding lip. Before he even had time to say anything, she brought it to her mouth and licked his blood.

Are you a wild beast? he wanted to ask her, but he held back.

She glued her lower lip between his teeth. "Bite me now," she demanded.

"Are you insane?"

"Bite me, Costa. Do it!"

He hesitated. "Cut my lip, Costa, draw my blood."

He bit her hard, but all she did was giggle.

When he saw the blood trickling down her lip, he turned ashen. *I must have lost my mind.* "I am really sorry, Süheylā," he apologized.

"You obeyed my wish," she teased, as she swirled her lips around his mouth. Lip to lip, mouth to mouth, they tasted each other's blood as if it were nectar.

Finally, she pulled back and looked at him. "You know, Costa, we are not just lovers anymore. Do you know what we are?"

He looked at her in amazement. "I have no idea, Süheylā."

"We are blood brother and sister. Our lives together are sealed."

"Is this some kind of Ottoman ritual?"

"Yes, it is."

"You know what you are, Süheylā?"

"What am I?"

"I told you; you are my Roxellana."

"Oh, I love that, Costa. I wish I had met that fascinating woman," exhaled Süheylā nostalgically.

"I met her," replied Costa, looking at her playfully.

She raised her eyebrows, "Costa, I don't know what to make of you. Any time I think I am ahead, you throw something unexpected; I am really flattered."

"Well, in that case are you still mad at me for taking away your virginity?"

"Never assume that," she with a fiery look in her eyes. "As a Muslim girl, always; for now, I got even," she smiled and wrapped her legs around him tightly.

Once again, the sensation was beyond the stratosphere. Feeling spent and exhausted, they rested on their sides kissing with all the love they could master.

"I never thought it would be like this, Süheylā; it is unreal."

"We make love better than the Andersons."

"Them again! Did Erika show you all these tricks?"

"She showed me everything."

Costa was not amused; "like what?"

"They have a library of sex films; I have seen some of them."

Costa was flabbergasted. "You are joking, right?"

"I am not; do you want to see them?"

He coughed. "I don't believe you."

"Well, believe it. Tomorrow we are going to their villa."

"But the Andersons are in the United States."

"I have the keys. Erika gave them to me. We can use their villa any time we want."

Costa by now was getting alarmed. Something was going on between Erika and Süheylā. "You and Erika are a pair of mischief," he said, trying to keep his jealousy under control.

"I am glad you feel that way; tomorrow then?"

"Go to their villa and watch the love-making movies of the Andersons?"

"Yes, that . . . we can make love in their huge bed; we can also practice our waltz."

"Right now I am worn out. Can we take a shower?"

"Sure, Costa, you can wash my hair. I love your fingers around me," she teased pointing between her legs. "We can have so much fun in the shower!"

Chapter 33: Back in Five Days

Costa's younger brother Alkis left Turkey for the boarding school in Greece. The family took it hard, but rejoiced that at least one of their sons would be safe. His parents, like all Imvrians, were getting poorer by the day, and young people like Costa were leaving. If it were not for Hermes Travel and the Sariyers, Costa would have had to leave the country, too. The alternative was induction into the Turkish military, a waste of time; whether he completed his military duties or not, Turkey did not have any use for giaours. The few remaining Greeks were on a constant lookout. The See of Orthodoxy, the Patriarchate, hemmed in by the worst slum of the city, feared for its very existence. Bomb threats were a frequent occurrence. A tossed Molotov cocktail now and then over its walls was a reminder that their time was up. If there was a bright spot in Costa's life, it was Süheylā, and to his delight and because of his pressure, her pro-Kurdish fervor had begun to evaporate.

The friendly warning about 'leave Turkey' Costa had received from Mr. Akduman, the chief of the secret police of Istanbul, was eating at him daily. October 29 was Turkish Independence Day; he had not been home for several months. He took advantage of the holiday to visit his parents and discuss with them such an eventuality; the Belgian Congo was his best option.

Süheylā escorted Costa to the bus station. She glued herself to his side, looking distraught. Although she was aware of her mother's threatening visit to Costa and Mr. Akduman's warning, her concern was her father, now a high functionary in the Ministry of Interior, who had begun to exert great pressure to terminate her relationship with Costa—or else. Süheylā took her father's threats seriously, and Costa's safety became her main concern.

Her father was determined to pry her away from Costa by any means. She did not want to tell him, afraid he might do something irrational. Her best option was to wait until Costa found a way out of Turkey and sent for her.

"Please, Süheylā, this is not a goodbye."

She buried her face in his chest. "Don't do anything foolish," she admonished him.

"I am only going to Imvros, Süheylā; I will be back Friday. That is only five days from now." Congo is at least three months away."

"That is not soon enough. I will be waiting for you in your apartment Costa, with dinner and me ready," she smiled halfway.

"Just you Süheylā; forget the dinner," Costa said and put her in his arms.

"I am petrified, Costa; I am afraid of losing each other."

"Who said a thing like that?"

"Turkey. We need to run away to another country; right now, Costa!"

Her unsettling tone caught him off guard; she was expecting an answer. He tried to collect his thoughts. Running away in Turkey with a girl after a love affair was pretty much a custom. It was a standard practice between Turks but never between Greek men and Turkish girls. This was taboo.

"Where could we go, Süheylā?"

"As far away from Turkey as we can."

"Süheylā, we had this conversation before. We have no money and we don't know anything about this world."

Her eyes were searching his soul. She began to cry.

"Please, Süheylā, do not cry. Things will turn out okay; I assure you."

"I am afraid of losing you, Costa; if that ever happens, I will kill myself."

"Don't say a thing like that, please."

"Can't we go to the United States?"

"I told you, no matter where we go, we still need money and visas, especially for the United States. Besides, your father will not allow you to travel anywhere."

"I am going to try to get a passport. I should have done that before."

"That is good, Süheylā. I still need a sailing permit from the Turkish military. They will not allow me to leave Turkey before I complete my military duties. To get that sailing permit, I have to bribe a Turkish general. That will cost a fortune."

"Since Turkey does not want you, why will they care?"

"According to Turkish law, military service is a must for all males over eighteen."

"In that case why don't we escape from Imvros? The island of Samothrace, Greece is only an hour's ride by boat, isn't it?"

"What if we get caught by the Turkish Coast Guard? You know what happens to a Christian like me for kidnapping a Turkish girl?"

"Yes I do."

"I am not worried about me, Süheylā, I am worried about you. If we are caught, it will be scandalous and your father will force you to marry someone you do not even know. Would you like to be in misery for the rest of your life?"

"But what else can we do?"

"The best thing is for me to leave and send for you as soon as I settle down somewhere; right now, Congo is my best option."

"That is way too far off, Costa, and iffy at best. I still think our only salvation is to leave Turkey together and by any means before something really bad happens."

"Is there something you are not telling me?"

"No, no," she assured him in haste, looking distressed. "Costa, no matter what happens, you and I will be together and forever."

"Süheylā, my first priority will be to send for you the minute I settle down."

They hugged, but she would not let go. She cried so much that Costa grew alarmed. He tried soothing her, but she only held onto him tighter. The bus was ready to pull out of its slot, and Costa pried her away gently. He saw her running along the bus for a while, trying to keep up, and waved.

Chapter 34: Like a Vanishing Thief

The minute he stepped onto the harbor, gloom and doom gripped his heart. To intimidate the islanders, the Turkish military brought tanks and artillery, as if some enemy from outer space were going to invade. It was an effective strategy. Frightened to death, the Greek natives were leaving Imvros as fast as they could.

The depopulation of the island was a catastrophe. The value of the land went down to zero. To resettle Turks and Kurds from the interiors of Anatolia, the Turkish State confiscated most of the valuable properties. Like the other remaining natives, Costa's family became poor—strangers in their own home. Even though his parents were still young, it was impossible for them to leave, for now. His maternal grandmother was blind and needed care, and to a lesser degree, Grandfather Alexander; the family Rigas was trapped.

As if this were not enough of a worry, his fear of losing Süheylā had turned into sheer dread. Her parents would never accept him, and Turkey did not have a place for him. His only salvation was to leave as soon as possible. He had no idea where.

His preference was the Belgian Congo. His cousin Steelian had established himself in the bakery business. He was anxious to get there, work, and send for Süheylā; that was priority number one. Just in case anything happened, they would be in touch through Zelal Hanum, their friend and confidante.

After much agony, the family had decided that Costa should be prepared to leave. It was a misty morning. A heavy fog had blanketed the village. As if tolling all happy times away, the church bell sounded like a dirge.

Grandfather Alexander and his parents had gathered around the kitchen for breakfast, but nobody was eating.

Chapter 34: Like a Vanishing Thief

His mother looked sad, and Costa did not dare lock eyes with her. Unlike most of the women of the village, she always wore bright colors, but not this time. She was dressed in black and had covered her head with a black scarf. Her face wore the tragic mourning of the Virgin Mary. Costa caught a tear in his mother's eye and lowered his head.

Phillip, his father, was sipping tea as if it were poison. He was watching his family disintegrate, and he had no power to stop it.

"Well, Costa. Life will never be the same. I have confidence in you, son. You will make an honorable citizen wherever you go!"

Costa cracked a faint smile. His father, the philosopher, always knew what to say. He ate breakfast slowly, wishing to prolong his stay, but it was time to go.

His father hugged him long and hard.

It was his grandfather's turn. He was sobbing. "I will miss you, Costa," he mumbled. "May all the fish die of loneliness! I am not going fishing until you return. Do you hear me?"

Costa nodded. "I am determined to come back, Grandfather; you can bet on that."

They hugged. The waiting taxi blew its horn. It sounded like the end of the world. It was time to say goodbye to his mother. It was difficult for Costa, but unbearable for her.

"Keep safe," she admonished. "Remember my advice: never dishonor the family name."

"Yes, Mom" he whispered, wiping her tears away with his fingers. He ran out of the house like a fleeing rabbit.

The taxi took off in the thick fog like a vanishing thief. As it descended the mountain slopes, his beloved village faded away like a ghost. One more look and he choked. Life would never be the same. He slumped into the cab seat and hid his face in his palms, crying.

Süheylā never left his mind. He saw her darting blue eyes and felt the puff of her breath through his nostrils. Her scent permeated the interior of the cab like a perfume. Inhaling that becalming effect, he lay back. Right now, she was his only tonic.

Chapter 35: Roses for Sūheylā

The ferryboat could not carry him fast enough and the bus from Çanakkale to Istanbul was too slow. The minute he stepped off the bus, he hailed the next cab for Kapali Çarşi[75]. The diamond ring for which Costa had been saving over the past year was ready. He stopped by the Çiçek Palas[76] and bought a dozen of roses. By the time he got outside his apartment, he was a complete wreck. With his heart pounding, he began to climb the steps; his anticipation of what awaited him behind the door, was giving him goose bumps. Would she be dressed in one of his shirts and her bikini panties, her lace underwear, his jacket or one of his ties or nothing at all? He knocked at the door...nothing. He knocked again...not a sound. This was strange.

He put his suitcase down, found the key in his pocket and opened the door, expecting the tigress to pounce. Maybe she was asleep. He ran into his bedroom. She wasn't there either. He scanned the apartment around for a note or maybe a sign. He put the roses on the coffee table and dialed her number... no answer. He waited a few minutes and tried again... nothing. Maybe they were out for the day. He would wait till later. By seven, he tried again. This time there was not even a ring tone. By now, he was in panic. Something horrible was going on. He picked up the phone and dialed Firyāl.

"Firyāl, this is Costa. Do you know where Sūheylā is?" he asked, trying to mask his quivering voice.

"You'd better get over here, Costa."

"Okay, but do you know where Sūheylā is?"

---

75. The famous covered market of Istanbul.

76. The flower market of the European section of Istanbul.

"They left three days ago."

"Left for where?"

"For Ankara, I think. I have a letter for you from Süheylā."

He ran down the steps and took a taxi. Firyāl was at the door waiting for him, holding the letter; she handed it to Costa. With trembling hands, he opened it.

Dear Costa:

It is over between the two of us. My family and I are moving to Ankara.

My father finally convinced me that there is no way that a relationship between a Christian and a Muslim will ever work.

Turkey is not a desirable place for you. Leave the country and find your future elsewhere.

Goodbye.

Süheylā.

He felt the air rush out of his lungs and sank to his knees. He read the letter once more. This could not be true. Maybe somebody else wrote it, but it was her writing and signature. With tears rolling down his eyes, he looked up at Firyāl.

"How can this be?"

"I don't know, Costa. They left so abruptly, nobody had any inkling."

"But I thought Süheylā would stay in Istanbul to finish her semester!"

"Süheylā did not say a word to me."

"How did you get this letter?"

"Her little sister brought it to me."

"You mean you could not even talk to her?"

"No, I couldn't. They would not let anyone near her."

"Who were they?"

"The police."

Chapter 35: Roses for Süheylā

"Can I look in her apartment?"

"Yes; you can see with your own eyes."

They took the elevator, and Firyāl opened the door. No furniture, nothing. Costa sat in the middle of the living room and cradled his head in his hands. Firyāl shook him by the shoulders.

"Didn't you know they were leaving?"

"Yes, I knew but not so unexpectedly. Did they leave an address?"

"Sorry, Costa, they didn't."

Costa wobbled out of the building. Maybe Zelal Hanum knew something, for he and Süheylā had agreed to use Zelal Hanum as a forwarding address, just in case. He took a cab to the café. He found Zelal sitting by the kitchen. Panting and sweating, he explained what happened and asked her whether Süheylā had left a forwarding address.

"She didn't," lamented Zelal, looking upset. "How could she do a thing like that?"

"I wish I knew, I wish I knew," he cried in agony.

Zelal tried to console him, but Costa shook his head and ran out into the street. The shock was unbearable.

He found himself on his couch. He had no idea how he got there. The only person that meant to him more than life had bid him 'farewell.' He'd never before felt pain like this. He needed time to sort things out, and yet he could not think at all.

Chapter 36: Throw a Stone Behind

His first inclination was to track down Süheylā, but even if he found her, she probably would be in her father's clutches; in all probability, he had her under house arrest. The best option was to leave Turkey and send for her as soon as possible. Things could not have been any worse. His passport was not worth a damn unless he got his sailing permit from the military. He thought of Zelal Hanum again and took a cab to her tavern.

"Hello, my boy. Did you find her?"

Costa was in tears. "I wish I had. I need your help, Madam Zelal."

"Anything."

"I need a sailing permit out of the country. Can you get me in contact with a Turkish general?"

"I don't know anybody in the military; maybe I can ask our cop friends. Come by tomorrow."

The phone rang. Zelal talked for a few minutes and hung up; she seemed very upset. "Bad news, my boy: The Turkish military went through our village yesterday and took my husband and several other men to prison."

"I am sorry to hear that, Zelal."

"Those were our cop friends. The Turkish Secret Police are going after everyone who harbors pro-Kurdish sentiments. I must be careful."

Costa came to Zelal for help. Instead, he found himself in the middle of another crisis. He started to leave, but Zelal pressed him down.

"My cop friends should be able to find somebody. Some of these generals never turn down a bribe. Do you have any money for this?"

"I have three-thousand Turkish liras, but I need two-thousand of that to purchase two-hundred dollars in foreign exchange, to leave the country; it is required by law."

"That leaves you with one-thousand liras; that might not be enough."

Zelal Hanum called the next morning. She told him the cops had made a connection, and that he should be at her café by noon. When he arrived, Zelal was sitting on a chair looking troubled.

Costa looked at her with concern. "What is the problem, Zelal?"

"Three-thousand liras; the general won't take any less."

Costa immediately thought of Mr. Sariyer, but unfortunately he was in Switzerland seeking a cure for his cancer.

"How am I going to get that much, Madam Zelal? I need the rest to get out of the country."

Zelal lifted her cape and took out an envelope with a pile of cash. She counted out two-thousand Turkish liras and handed them to Costa. She called for Mehtab, who was meandering about the café looking for customers.

"Oh my!' she exclaimed; "what brings you here?"

Zelal cut her off and spoke to her in Kurdish. Mehtab opened her purse, counted out a thousand liras, and handed them to Costa.

"Take it. I am doing well. My pimp has gone to Diyarbakir to visit his family."

"Thank you, Mehtab. I will be forever grateful."

"You can still thank me by spending the night with me," she winked. "If you are ever successful, just remember Mehtab, the prostitute who cares." She gave him a kiss and sauntered into the back of the café.

"I wish you were not leaving, Costa" said Zelal. "Take care of yourself and maybe I will see you again."

Zelal Hanum was the noblest woman Costa had ever met. As for Mehtab, as far as he was concerned she was a saint. He hung around waiting for the cops. After an hour or so, they walked in and headed straight to Costa.

"Do you have the money, young man?"

Costa took out the envelope with the three-thousand liras and handed it over.

"We can't guarantee anything. It may take a week. The general will be in the city in a few days." He had no choice; it was going to take time.

Zelal called before the week was out. His sailing permit was ready, but there was more. The Ministry of Interior must stamp his passport. To save time, he took a taxi. The place was packed. Most were Turkish workers heading to Germany. Others were giaours like him: Greeks, Jews, Armenians, Italians and Kurds. After standing in line for hours, it was his turn.

The clerk behind the service counter lifted his hand without looking. "Your passport."

Costa handed it to him along with the sailing permit.

"What is this?" asked the clerk rudely.

"It's a sailing permit from the military."

"Why?"

"I want to visit my sick brother in Greece."

"I didn't ask you about that. Why do you need a sailing permit?"

"It is a requirement by the military."

"Do you know why it is a requirement?"

"No, sir, I have no idea."

"To make sure that giaours like you do not skip out on their military duty."

"Why do you say that?"

"Because all giaours take advantage of Turkey."

"Look, sir, I brought you my passport and my sailing permit from the military. All I am asking you is to process it."

"Wait over there."

The clerk took the passport, went to another counter and began thumbing through a large file. He came back looking mad. "I'm going to keep your passport. You can come back tomorrow."

"What is the problem?"

"I said tomorrow; now fuck off."

Costa went back the next day. Thankfully, the line this time was shorter. He saw the same rude clerk behind the counter and cringed. "Good morning, sir, I am here for my passport."

"What's your name?"

"Costa Rigas."

The clerk fumbled around his disorganized desk, found the passport and handed it over. Costa flipped through the pages looking for the official sailing stamp. "But, sir, my passport has not been stamped for sailing."

"So you noticed," said the clerk sarcastically. "You have no permission to leave the country."

"But I brought you an authorization from the military."

"You did what?"

"I brought you a written authorization from the military."

"You brought no such thing. You're a liar."

Costa wanted to jump behind the counter and beat the clerk, but he restrained himself. "Listen, sir, I brought you that document yesterday. You told me to come back today; you are the one who is lying."

A police officer on duty overheard the argument and moved close to Costa. "What are you yelling about?"

Costa attempted to say something, but the clerk cut him off.

"This giaour claims that he brought in a sailing permit from the military, and that I have lost it. He is calling me a liar."

"Follow me to the station. I'm going to teach you a lesson," barked the police officer. He grabbed Costa by the arm and started to pull him through the hallway. Costa had to think fast.

"Listen, sir, you are messing with the wrong man. Once Mr. Orhan Akduman learns what happened to me, you will be knee-deep in . . ."

As soon as he mentioned Mr. Akduman's name, the police officer stopped.

"Do you know Mr. Akduman?"

"Of course I do. You and that clerk will hear from him, I guarantee it." Costa had no idea what he was saying. His bluff might put him in deeper trouble, but it was worth the gamble.

"Give me your passport," said the police officer "and wait here."

Within five minutes, Costa saw the police officer hurrying back. "Here is your stamped passport, Mr. Rigas. You have two weeks' permission. Have a nice trip."

Costa looked at the passport and saw the official stamp. He did not know whether he should be happy or sad. Maybe he was free at last! On his way back to his apartment, he stopped by the post office to drop off a letter to his parents, along with a packet of his cherished mementos with Süheylā.

Dear Mom and Dad:

I have managed to work things out. I am leaving for Greece tomorrow. I do not know what is in store for me. I am going to stop and see Alkis at his school in Thessalonica for a few days.

I am not sure where I want to emigrate; my preference is Congo.

Süheylā has disappeared without a trace. My life without her will be meaningless. Please forward any letters you receive from Süheylā, I beg you.

Mom, please keep my mementos in a safe place. You can mail them to me when I have finally settled somewhere.

Love, Costa.

The hardest thing was looking at the wilting roses, as if his life was going the same direction. His plan to propose to Süheylā ended badly, and now that she was gone, all he could to do was hug the bouquet. He took a rose out of the bunch, peeled off its petals carefully and placed them between the pages of his high-school yearbook. This along with the ring and all their other mementos he put into a small wooden box, which he was going to mail to his mother on his way to the bus station. Suddenly he thought of Gezi Park, where he and Süheylā spent many a romantic evening. Holding the bouquet in his hand, he hailed a cab. The minute he found himself in the middle of the park, he began to disperse the rose petals all around the area one by one, trying to keep his heart and tears under control.

He sorted out his meager belongings and packed his suitcase with some clothes, a pair of shoes and a few travel items. For good measure he strapped some rope around the old suitcase to prevent the contents from spilling out. His passport, high-school diploma, along with the six-hundred German marks he stuffed into his shirt's pockets. He locked the apartment and took the keys to the real estate company, leaving instructions to hand the dresser over to Süheylā Gülpinar if she came by. He stopped by the post office and mailed the box of mementos to his mother and the letter to the Sariyers, thanking them for all they had done and wishing Mr. Sariyer well. He was going to be in touch with them when he made it to the Congo. The cheapest transportation out of the country was by bus across Thrace. He was leaving Turkey one way.

Chapter 37: Twenty Years Later

It was late spring 1994, and although Turkey was under the civilian leadership of its first female prime minister, Tansu Çiler, the island of Imvros, now renamed Gökçeada, Costa's homeland, was still under the grip of the Turkish military. With much anxiety, Costa boarded the ferryboat from Çanakkale, excited to be visiting his birthplace. Way out there, bathed in the hazy blue sky was his home. As the ferryboat neared the pier, Costa got behind the wheel of his rental car eager with anticipation. He was surprised to see the checkpoint. Two police officers were checking everybody's identity. Finally, it was Costa's turn.

"Your papers," asked the police officer. When Costa handed him his American passport the police officer looked it over intently.

"We have to keep it with us," he said. "You will get it back when you leave."

Costa's blood rushed to his head. This was a stark reminder of his last experience at the Turkish border when he'd left the country two decades earlier. The police officer was doing his job; in all probability, he had noticed that Costa was born in Imvros, clearly stated on his passport. Expatriates like Costa were considered dangerous giaours and Turkey was on the lookout, just in case one of them decided to lead an armed insurrection. Three-hundred Greek elderly men with sticks and stones against ten thousand transplanted Turks and a garrison of soldiers, tanks and machine guns were a formidable adversary! It was obvious that the Turkish paranoid attitude against its minorities had not changed at all. This small incident alone was a reconfirmation of Turkey as one of the leading countries of human rights abuses. The deprivation of his passport made him feel naked and even nameless. He'd come back to his homeland prepared to forgive and let live, but this incident jolted him back to reality. He had buried the bitter memories of this land long ago and now that he was back, Turkey reminded him of what he did not miss. Maybe this was just a stupid bureaucratic glitch. He did not have the stomach to protest against this indignity. He drove out into the open road mindful of the safety of his child, riding in the back seat with her Turkish governess, Kadife. His five-year-old daughter, Nilüfer, was infinitely more important than the entire lot of Turkey.

Immediately the aroma of pine and sage rushed through the car window, soothing his anger and heightening his sense of nostalgia. Awash in silver gray, the granite mountain towered above the village like a shepherd looking after his flock. His heart started to pound; anxiously he searched for his first glimpse of the village. Suddenly, the not-so-whitewashed houses came into view. The steep, winding road was rushing by like a film-noir, frame by frame. Every bend reminded him of a time past. Some twenty years ago when he'd left Turkey, he promised himself that the minute he stepped over the border, he would throw a stone behind him, but he'd forgotten; and now that he was back to visit his parents' graves and reconnect with his youth, his feelings about his homeland were like a rollercoaster.

After ten minutes of climbing the mountain slopes, he arrived on the plateau and parked by his old elementary school. Nilüfer was still sleeping on Kadife's lap, so he motioned her to stay in the car.

The minute he stepped on the ground, all the memories of his boyhood began to swirl around in his head. Gone were the almond trees, the mulberry trees, the fig trees, the pear trees and the small gardens and mini-vineyards. The only life visible was the chirping sparrows, darting sheep and wild bushes. There was no laughter of a single child, as if the gods had cursed the village barren. Those who remained, most of them elderly, were clustered around the village square; but first, he would visit his parents' graves at the cemetery.

Why in the world did my parents choose to give birth to me in a godforsaken corner of the world like this? Couldn't they have found another place? The thought was unsettling. He felt guilty for even thinking it. Amidst piles of conflicting sentiments, he took the side road, traipsing through the piles of rubble of the crumbling houses. He kept his head down, mindful not to stare into the eyes of lurking ghosts.

The rusty gate barely hung from its hinges, but the cemetery looked clean. In the stillness of the twilight, he walked slowly, afraid to disturb all those who slept in this sacred ground.

There they were—the graves of Electra and Phillip Rigas, his parents. His mother had died very young from esophageal cancer, and his father had been lost at sea. He took a deep breath and traced his fingers over the chiseled lettering. The weathered tombstones reminded him that time had no sympathy for anything or anyone, but rolled on unconcerned, trampling everything in its path.

He knelt between their graves, keeping silent for a few moments. Electra and Phillip had wanted what was best for him; it was not what he wanted. Their pure hatred of Süheylā was a lingering pain, even after twenty years. "May you rest in peace," he whispered, and stood up. He would revisit tomorrow.

Slowly he traced his steps back toward the gate, but the small chapel drew him in. The mournful souls of the ossuary were begging for his companionship. Afraid to gaze into their hollow eyes, he lit a candle and said a silent prayer in their memory. This was where his ancestors rested while their seeds had sprung elsewhere. Nilüfer's sweet face, popped into his mind and he smiled. She was the green grass, the new life, the hope for a better tomorrow. Slowly he walked back to the car and drove up to the village square.

Chapter 38: A Home Welcome

The first to arrive was his grandfather, Alexander. The café, the only public space of the village, was his main hangout. In a way, it was his second home. He took a chair, lit a cigarette and puffed away.

Auntie Sappho—everybody called her Sappho—was the operator of the café and the gatekeeper of the square. Potluck supper was the best part of the lives of these elderly. Their children had left them long ago for foreign lands. With no grandchildren to care for, socializing at Sappho's was the only break in their tedium.

One by one, women in black and old men in scruffy beards—some with canes—placed their dishes on the table and sat, mindful of Alexander. His habit of sneaking food was never welcome; the women especially watched him like hawks. "You lecher, keep your dirty hands away from that food," they admonished, shaking their fingers. With pretentious indifference, Alexander curled his handlebars and grinned.

The age of eighty-seven meant nothing to him. His silver hair—not one missing—protruding below his leather cap gave him the look of an eccentric. Black garb, Cretan style, was his trademark, along with a leather vest over a pirate's shirt, a wide cummerbund wound tightly around his puffy pantaloons. The knee-high spit-polished boots were his exclamation mark. He was an old seafarer, a captain of a cargo ship. Everybody called him 'Captain.' Tapping his foot impatiently, he spotted a car making its way up to the square and raised his eyebrows; he had never seen this vehicle before.

The car stopped in front of the café and out stepped a tall stranger, who bent down and kissed the ground. Meanwhile, a young lady in her twenties opened the car's rear door for a little girl, about four or five, in pigtails.

"Oh my God, it is Costa," screeched Auntie Rose, scrambling to hug him. The other elderly surged after Costa to mob him with sobs and happy tears. The village of Agridia[77] was claiming back a native son they had not seen for a very long time.

Alexander, paralyzed from joy, was unable to move. He sat on his chair to await his turn and watched all the commotion in silence. Costa spotted him and rushed forward.

"I am here, Grandpa Alexander!" shouted Costa, opening his arms. As Alexander tried to hug him, he lost his balance, but Costa steadied him on his feet. He led him back to his chair, stroking his wet cheeks as if he were a lost child. The old man sobbed softly, letting his emotions run unchecked.

"I never thought I would see you again, my dear Costa," he mustered. "This is the happiest day of my life." Stroking Costa's hair, he looked at him lovingly while tears streamed down his face.

Costa pulled out his handkerchief, but Alexander grasped his hand. "Let the devil take me now, Costa. I am not afraid of him!"

"You are not going anywhere," assured Costa, but Alexander clung to him and would not let go.

"I owe you my life, Costa," he continued, resting his hand on Costa's shoulder. "Listen," he shouted. "This is the man who supported me in my old age. He is the noblest grandson I know."

The young woman accompanying Costa could not understand a word of Greek, but she could not hold back her tears; the emotion was overwhelming.

Costa lifted his daughter in his arms. The crowd held their breath. "This is my daughter, Nilüfer," he said smiling.

---

77. "Little fields."

Nilüfer gazed at the crowd with some ambivalence, then broke into a broad smile and waved.

"And this young lady over here," added Costa, "is Kadife, Nilüfer's governess. She is helping me ease my daughter into my life. Let us sit down. There will be plenty of time to get reacquainted."

Grudgingly they sat down, especially the women. They wanted a piece of the little girl. Kadife took Nilüfer from Costa's arms and sat her on her lap. She had the sense that Nilüfer was already the star of the village.

Another car stopped in the middle of the square. To Costa's delight it was Father Nestor. How could he forget that face? Father Nestor spotted him immediately.

"By the love of the Virgin, is that you, Costa?" Father Nestor exclaimed with open arms as the two men embraced.

"It is me, all right, Father Nestor. You have not aged a bit."

Father Nestor stepped back to look Costa over; he shook his head. "You are taller than I expected. It is a pleasure to see you again." Feeling just as emotional as Alexander, the tears streaked down his face, "You were the best altar boy I ever had," he jabbed, "and a great voice in the choir. I am so happy you have found your daughter," continued Father Nestor, reaching out to touch Nilüfer's hand. "What is your name, little one?" he asked in Greek.

Nilüfer scrunched her face. "She understands only Kurdish and Turkish," explained Costa. This got everybody's attention.

"I am Apo," croaked Alexander to Nilüfer, pointing at himself. The little girl cracked a smile and snuggled up to Costa. It was the first word of Kurdish she had heard in this village so far. Everybody looked at Alexander, trying to understand what he said.

"It means '*uncle – in Kurdish,*'" explained Costa.

271

"I know a lot of Kurdish," boasted Alexander. "I learned it from Ekrem, the Kurd."

Costa laughed. "So you have been learning Kurdish?"

"Just a few words, Costa; I was hoping to see this great-grandchild some day. What do you expect when a little girl gets lost in Kurdistan?" commented Alexander, looking pained. "She can only speak the language of her people," he continued. "Thank goodness she is alive. Come on, Nilüfer," he said in Turkish. "I am your great-grandfather. I will teach you anything you need to know."

"Listen, everybody," interrupted Sappho. "Let us eat. Alexander, there is plenty of time to get acquainted with this cutie," she admonished, giving Nilüfer a squeeze on the cheek. "Father Nestor, grace, please."

Island tea, rice pilaf with fresh herbs, dandelion salad, spanakopita[78], fresh-baked bread, virgin olive oil, feta cheese, black olives and fried sardines; even wild asparagus was part of the fare.

"The octopus stew is still in the oven," said Sappho. "It will go well with the raki Alexander brought earlier."

Alexander read Sappho's lips. He gave his curled mustache a couple of twists, slurped hard on his tea and rolled his enormous eyes upwards. There had not been such happy laughter in this village for years.

"Attention, everybody," begged Father Nestor. "Sappho tells me that the Captain brought raki. We ought to drink to our returning son, Costa. Sappho, where is the blessed thing?"

"It is chilling," she blurted and skipped into the kitchen to get it.

Father Nestor rose to offer a toast. "Dear God, we thank you for sending us our beloved son, Costa, and little Nilüfer. Please accept our prayers and grant us peace."

---

78. Spinach and cheese baked in filo sheets.

It was Costa's turn. "To all the good things granted to us here on Earth: the friendship, our families, our departed parents and all our loved ones, to the dispersed Imvrians all over the world, and to you, the remaining heroes of this village, I pledge my undying love."

It was the best welcome Costa could have imagined. As the conversation flowed, so did the glasses of raki. Costa hated to leave their company, but Nilüfer looked tired. He excused himself to take Nilüfer to bed.

His family home was across from the café. After twenty years, he crossed the threshold and once again stood in the middle of the entry hall, feeling dejected; his parents were not there to welcome their first grandchild. Holding his daughter by the hand, he climbed the steps to the second floor one by one. Aunt Rose had already prepared their rooms—one for Kadife and Nilüfer and another for Costa. He watched Kadife prepare Nilüfer for the night, gave his little girl a hug and a kiss, and walked into his room.

Chapter 39: Letters From the Past

He lay on his bed and shut his eyes. This was the same room he'd been born in and nearly died before he had the chance to look at the world. In her haste, the midwife had cut his umbilical cord short, and he almost bled to death. He was barely three when his mother gave birth to his younger brother Alkis. Her labor screams still echoed off the walls as if it had happened yesterday.

Heartbroken and hoping for a better life, some twenty years ago he'd left parents, home, country, and the love of his life. Now that he was back in his homeland, his feelings were all over the place. The loss of Süheylā, the death of his parents, his marriage to Lale and her tragic death, the Gulf War, the abduction of his daughter—all these thoughts and more were swirling in his head.

He'd married in his late thirties, and when he did, he thought he had found the perfect girl. Alas, Lale had died tragically in the helicopter crash. Miraculously, his daughter survived but was lost for three years. A nomad-child among a million Kurdish refugees, she became homeless and nameless. Finally, she was in his care. He would never again let her out of his sight.

The knock on the door stirred him from his thoughts. It was Aunt Rose holding a box.

"This is for you, Costa. I am not sure if this is the right time, but I don't know when that might be."

"Do you know what it is?"

She looked at him with sad eyes. "In her dying days, your mother instructed me to hand this to you personally when I saw you." She deposited the box on his bed and quietly left the room.

Costa sat up in his bed and looked at the box, trying to guess its contents. Just before he left Turkey, he had shipped this box to his mother, with instructions to send it to him when he settled down somewhere; she never did. With great reservation, he opened it. A stack of letters bundled together in a red ribbon stared at him as if they were ready to talk. Feeling his breath quicken, he pulled off the ribbon and lifted the first letter; it was from his mother Electra.

Dear Costa:

If you ever open this box, please forgive me. I tried to do what was best for you. My love and ambition for your success made me hide these letters. I have kept this secret for so long because I did not dare to tell you. As I am dying, I cannot take this burden to my grave.

In fact, Sūheylā never stopped loving you. I was going to mail these letters to you, but just before I could do so, I found out that she got married. I did not have the courage to tell you; I knew how much you loved her.

Go on with your life and be happy, and do not think about me when I am gone. It is my dying wish that you find love.

Forever.

Your Mom, Electra

Costa put the letter down. He felt angry, even claustrophobic; his stomach was churning. He ran to the bathroom and vomited. His ghost in the mirror stared back at him. He was not prepared for something like this. He dragged himself back into his room, feeling trapped. When he looked into the box and saw the name of the sender, he froze.

Sūheylā Gülpinar
11 Sokak # 24
Bahçeeviler,
Çankaya, Ankara
Turkey

With trembling hands, he opened the letter.

Dear Costa:

After seven years of searching for you, I have given up. I know you are either in Congo or in the States, but I cannot find you. I graduated Law School a year ago, and I am working as a lawyer in Ankara. For cosmetic purposes, I decided to get married. My wedding is next weekend.

Farewell, Costa.

I will love you forever.

Süheylā.

He felt his hands shake uncontrollably; his head was exploding. The four walls were closing all around him while his tears were flooding his face like a river. In the stillness of pain, he was in shock. He had experienced unimaginable trials before, but this one was the worst. Although he was sitting, he felt a disconnection from his feet. Levitating between depths of despair and chasms of acrimony, he was scared to open Süheylā's many other letters. The large envelope, containing all the photographs, was the living calendar of a time lost. There was a particular picture dearest to him, which he and Süheylā had taken at a photo studio. They looked so young, so untested and yet so full of optimism. Nothing ever scared them, or so they thought.

The tiny red box pierced him through the heart. It contained the diamond ring with which he planned to propose to Süheylā. After so many years, he thought he had buried that past, but suddenly, it roared back like a cyclone. He started to pound on the matress with his fist. Kadife, who slept in the next room, rushed in.

"Colonel, is everything okay?"

"No, Kadife, it isn't."

"Is there anything I can get you?"

"Is there any medicine for heartache in Turkey?"

277

"I did not know you have a heart problem," said Kadife, looking concerned.

"I've had it for a long time. I thought it left me, but now it is back."

"Isn't there any medicine for it in America?"

Costa smiled bitterly. "No, there isn't, Kadife. I am sorry to alarm you, but there is nothing physically wrong with me. These letters have transported me back in time and made me ache what I missed; I wish I could turn back the clock."

"Now I understand, Colonel. I will get you some water."

"I know I said we'd be spending a month here, but I have changed my mind. We will be going back to Istanbul. As soon as I can process your papers, we will be leaving for USA. There is nothing for me to do here anymore."

"I am sorry, Colonel. Good night."

Finally Costa found the courage to read the rest of Süheylā's letters—many times over—until fatigue finally took him and he drifted off to sleep.

A tingling sensation in his nostrils woke him up. It was the unmistakable aroma of his favorite herb. Twitching with delight, he opened his eyes. Standing by his bedside was his little girl, Nilüfer, brushing his face with a sprig of fresh basil. He inhaled the scent nostalgically, but almost immediately it pierced through his chest as if it were a double-edged knife. Basil was Süheylā's distinctive smell. His eyes welled up with tears. He pulled his daughter into his arms and squeezed her tenderly, as if she were Süheylā. All his feelings of yesterday now took a second seat behind Süheylā's memory. That sprig of basil blew apart the gates of Hell. He saw Aunt Rose looking at him anxiously and managed a smile.

"I am all right, Auntie Rose. I could use some tea."

"Just tea? It is time for breakfast, Costa," she smiled, begging Nilüfer from his arms.

He meandered into the bathroom, brushed his teeth, combed his hair and walked down the familiar steps, holding onto the old bannister, still coarse from the claws of Odysseus, the family's tomcat.

He scanned the kitchen and the adjacent family room. The ghosts of his parents seemed to be walking around as if they'd never left. The presence of the rose petal marmalade on the table was another shock. The memory of that night in Süheylā's apartment came roaring back as if it were yesterday. Reluctantly he spread some on his toast and offered it to Nilüfer; he did not want any of it. The fresh-brewed island tea, cured black olives, goat cheese, the fresh fruit and native bread were plenty.

Aunt Rose sat silently across from him, content to watch the three of them eat. Costa's eyes continued to roam until they fell upon his mother's portrait. With much sadness he remembered her parting words at Boston's Logan Airport so many years ago.

"Some day when you get back to Imvros, please remember that I loved you; I am sorry."

He had wanted to ask her what she meant, but her esophageal cancer had left her bereft of voice; she could barely whisper. She was so frail that Costa had to carry her onto the plane, hoping that she could make it home alive. Her cancer was beyond cure, and she did not want to die in a foreign land. He hugged his mother farewell and sent her back to Imvros, knowing that she was already dead. He wished he could have gone with her, but his reservations about his safety in Turkey held him back. His absence from his mother's funeral gnawed in the abyss of his guilt. Electra was a noble mother. She wanted what was best for him.

Guilt can creep in when it is least expected. His quest for opportunity and his blind ambition had pushed him to leave behind parents and loved ones—all for the sake self-preservation. Although his peers had done the same, he should have stayed in Turkey to face the consequences; his arrest warrant was bogus. Being absent from home when his father was lost was another stab to the chest. Phillip the philosopher, the heathen, the fanatic sailor, had drowned at sea during a tempest—he was probably happy to be resting in its bosom.

Where was Süheylā now? How many children did she have? Where did she live? The urge to see her once more overwhelmed him. He would fall to his knees, kiss her feet and beg forgiveness. Even more so, he would give anything if he could hold her in his arms again. Finding her might be his only redemption. Aunt Rose must have sensed his turmoil.

"You did the right thing, Costa. Your parents thought the world of you."

"You are kind, Auntie Rose."

"Is there anything special you would like?"

"Can you bake a su-börek[79]? I have not had one since I left Imvros."

"Gladly; anything else?"

"We are going to leave in a few days. I need to get back to Istanbul."

"Is it because of those letters, Costa?" she asked, looking unsettled.

"Yes, Aunt Rose, it is."

"My sister warned me about this. I am sorry. I hope the best for you."

"Thank you."

"Will you be coming back next year?"

Costa shrugged his shoulders.

Aunt Rose started to cry. "The village was looking forward to your company, Costa. We were so happy to get to know your daughter and spoil her."

---

79. A baked Turkish dish made of poached sheets of egg dough and layered with native cheeses and herbs.

"I promise you, Auntie Rose, I will be back sooner than you think. It will depend on what happens in Istanbul.

Alexander was not very happy about Costa's abrupt departure either. He calmed down when Costa assured him that he would be back soon. The ferryboat was not leaving until mid-week. Costa spent the next three days supervising some minor house repairs. It was a spacious home, constructed of granite stone and at least three-hundred years old. Spending time with Nilüfer in his home village of Agridia was going to rekindle his boyhood years and reconnect with his past. Süheylā's letters changed everything—he had to find her.

Chapter 40: The Queen City

The slithering about his feet brought a smile to his face. It was Nilüfer, trying to crawl under his bed covers; he pulled her into his arms.

"Do you want breakfast?" he asked her in Sorani[80]. She nodded; he picked up the phone and dialed room service.

"Nilüfer, where are you, where are you?" It was Kadife. She barged into his room looking distraught. Seeing Nilüfer in her father's bed, she placed her palm on her heart.

"Excuse me, Colonel," she said looking tousled. When I woke up and did not see Nilüfer in her bed, I panicked."

"Breakfast will be delivered in a few minutes Kadife," said Costa, squeezing his daughter, who opened her arms and gave him a big hug. Tears of love ran down his cheeks. Kadife, who never missed anything, excused herself and went back to her room to get ready.

Unlike her mother's light complexion, Nilüfer had Costa's olive skin. Although skinny, she was very strong. Her deep green eyes reminded Costa of her mother's homeland, the rolling hills of Kurdistan. The pitch-black hair was from his family's side. In the absence of Lale, his departed wife, Costa now had to be both parents, a challenge for which he was unprepared.

Long ago, Costa left Turkey laden with pain and hating it. After all, it was the Turkish military that turned his home island into a base, frightening away his fellow Greeks to the four corners of the world. Ironically, the same military rescued his abducted daughter. Without their assistance she likely would have been lost forever.

---

80. The dialect of the majority of the Kurdish people.

After missing for three years, Nilüfer was located in a Kurdish refugee camp. Just before Costa could claim her, terrorists abducted her for ransom, *"Three million dollars for Nilüfer's freedom, along with the release of 12 prisoners from the Turkish jails. The money is to be deposited in a secret Swiss bank account. Once our terms are met, information about her whereabouts would follow."*

The sticking point was the release of prisoners. General Ersoy, the commanding general of the SE Turkish Military Forces—Costa's childhood friend—promised to help, but he had no authority to negotiate any terms like that. It was up to the Turkish government, and her policy was 'never to negotiate with terrorists.'

Nilufer's kidnapping became a news sensation in Turkey. As a Turkish ex-patriate, Costa's face, was all over the place. It did not matter whether Costa was an American citizen and a Colonel of the American Army. As far as the news were concerned, Costa was one of their own and Turkey had to deliver his abducted daughter safely and expeditiously.

Hoping for a good outcome, Costa continued to negotiate with Nilüfer's abductors. Just as the negotiations hit an impasse, the kidnappers sent word they were setting Nilüfer free. A Turkish commando unit braved a helicopter flight over the Iranian border and retrieved Nilüfer from a dark cave. Even more bizarre, an anonymous stranger or strangers had paid the ransom and facilitated her release. Costa was overjoyed and very grateful to that benefactor, whoever it was. If General Ersoy knew anything about this, he was very evasive. It was obvious he was holding back information, and Costa chose not to press the matter.

During all this turmoil and in spite of all the recent positives, Costa's bad memories about his ex-homeland were in constant conflict. Generations of debasement were not that easy to swallow. The dust of five-hundred years of enslavement and humiliation was not going to blow away any time soon. The annals of history had been stamped for eternity on the bones of every dead and living Greek. Süheylā, Ozan, Emine, General Ersoy and the Sariyers were the exceptional Turks, the mini oasis in the middle of a heartless Sahara. He'd gone to Diyarbakir searching for Nilüfer and could not have been any more pleased with the courtesy he'd received. All his bad memories about Turkey were now comingling with happy times, bad times and nostalgia. In a way, he was happy to be back, although his feelings about Turkey were in constant flux.

The doorbell rang; it was Hayri, the security guard provided by General Ersoy as a precaution against a copycat abduction of Nilüfer. The general wanted to make sure that Nilüfer was safe until Costa took her out of Turkey. Hayri wanted permission for the server to wheel the cart into the suite.

Kadife had already changed Nilüfer from her pajamas into a bright skirt and pulled a chair out for her to sit down, but Nilüfer refused. She walked around the table and nuzzled closer to Costa, who lifted her onto his lap.

They had no schedule today other than an appointment at the American Consulate. Although Costa had been in Southern Turkey several times before as a military officer, he never stepped away from the American base. He had no desire to see any of Turkey and that included Istanbul. With bad memories and a lost love, he had no appetite for the city; but with his daughter Nilüfer at his side, suddenly the city came alive.

He took Nilüfer by the hand and walked out to the small balcony. Independence Avenu was clogged with traffic. His heart raced at the familiar sounds of the city. Istanbul had a population of three million when he left, now she had more than twelve. The air was much heavier, but still it had the wonderful odor of the city he loved. Trying to rekindle his sense of smell, he breathed in the air, practically swallowing it. The excitement of being back in the queen city was wreaking havoc on his nerves, but Süheylā's memory was stabbing at his heart with every beat.

He walked back into his suite. The phone book on the coffee table was staring at him; there were several Gülpinars, but none with the name 'Süheylā.' He knew she was married, but he did not know her maiden name. *I must find a way.* The city of Ankara was her last residence. He dialed the operator. Yes, there was a 'Süheylā Gülpinar,' but the number was unlisted. He thought of catching a plane for Ankara but restrained himself; knocking at some door without any information would be inappropriate. He flipped through the phone book pages for a detective agency and jotted down several numbers. He could also call Errol Sariyer, Sedat Sariyer's son. Kadife interrupted his thoughts.

"The hotel operator wants to talk to you, Colonel."

"Good morning, Colonel Rigas. You have a message from Mr. Errol Sariyer. He would like to know when he can call you."

Speak of the devil! "Did he leave a number, operator?"

Her pure Istanbul accent was music to his ears; the Turkish language sounded more refined now and more pleasing.

"Yes, Colonel Rigas, may I dial it for you?"

Errol's secretary put him through immediately. "Hello, Costa, welcome to Istanbul! How are you?"

"Errol! How did you know I was at this hotel?"

"General Ersoy. Isn't he a friend of yours?"

"How do you know the general?"

"It is a circuitous story; I will tell you some day."

"You must; I am intrigued already."

"I promise. Anyway, would you care to join me Friday night? There is special evening with two great artists, whom I know you will like; one of them is Emel Sayin."

Emel Sayin was the artist he and Süheylā went to see only weeks before that fateful separation over two decades ago. Costa was well familiar with this famous artist. In fact, he loved traditional Turkish music more than any other. After he left, he had refrained from listening to it because it brought back so many painful memories. Nevertheless, he was now in Turkey, his ex-homeland, and all these familiar sounds were tugging at his soul; going to hear Emel Sayin meant a telepathic touch with Süheylā. He thought of asking Errol about her immediately, but it would have been tactless. "Errol, how can I refuse?"

"I'll send my driver over. Shall we say seven-thirty?"

By coincidence Costa had Friday evening free. The hotel manager's daughters, both Nilüfer's age, had invited her to spend the night. Although Costa was uncomfortable with the idea, he felt it was important that Nilüfer transition into a normal life as soon as possible.

He hung up the phone and went to the bathroom to shower. His appointment at the American Consulate was not until eleven. Kadife was going to take Nilüfer to the playground for the morning under the watchful eyes of Hayri. He let Nilüfer and Kadife out the door; Hayri, who stood watch outside the suite, saluted. Suddenly Costa remembered something; he scribbled all he knew and gave it to him.

"In your spare time, Hayri, can you track down this individual? I have only a first name, the approximate age and the neighborhood."

What kind of time frame am I looking at, Colonel Rigas?"

"About twenty years."

"That might be difficult, Colonel. I wasn't even a policeman then."

"Just give it a try, Hayri."

"Give me a couple of days, Colonel."

"I would appreciate it if you did not divulge my name."

"Absolutely, Colonel."

"Thank you, Hayri."

He rode the elevator down with Kadife and Nilüfer and watched his daughter skip across the hotel's lobby holding Kadife by the hand, while Hayri trailed discreetly behind.

The minute he stepped onto the avenue, the sea of humanity rolled over him. Peddling their imitation Rolex watches for twenty dollars, Bill Blass shirts and Chanel Number Five perfume for ten dollars, the street hawks immediately pounced on him; his perfect Turkish stopped them.

Indulging in his favorite Turkish snacks along the way, he made his way to the American Consulate and took possession of Nilüfer's passport. Kadife's papers were still in process. He also executed a power of attorney for his brother in Greece. He appointed Alkis Nilüfer's legal guardian, just in case anything happened to him.

Chapter 41: The Big Surprise

Costa was back at the hotel in time for lunch. The minute Nilüfer saw him she ran into his arms. Her reserved personality was disappearing fast. They ate at the coffee shop while Kadife struggled to teach Nilüfer how to use a fork. Using her hands to eat was normal; her nomadic ways were not going to go away that soon. They spent the afternoon walking around Gezi Park[81] and the playground. It was May in Istanbul and the park was in full bloom. The familiar paths of his youth were still there and the trees were magnificent as ever. Roses were everywhere and every one of them reminded him of Süheylā. When he saw the same bench where he and Süheylā used to sit and kiss, he invited his daughter to sit next to him, holding onto her for dear life. The park was a perfect, romantic spot for young lovers like Costa and Süheylā at night and a great place for young families during the day. There were many playmates Nilüfer's age, helping her along in overcoming her shyness. Her favorite thing was the swings, which kept Costa and Kadife busy all afternoon. Gezi Park had awakened so many memories, and if it were not for Nilüfer and Kadife, Costa would have broken down and cried.

For the evening, Hayri drove them around the city. The site of Hagia Sophia brought Costa to tears. He visualized Emperor Justinian and Empress Theodora driven into the church in their golden carriage with a chorus of a thousand chanting monks. There was Sultan Mehmet the Conqueror, riding on his horse to pray in the same church. They ended up on Bosporus, another memory lane.

---

81. Known as the garden of Taksim, the largest green space in the European section of Istanbul.

Chapter 41: The Big Surprise

Dinner at the Çinaralti restaurant in the heart of Ortaköy brought back his college years. He had difficulty managing the floodgates of his past. USA was his country now, but his reconnection with Turkey was wrecking him emotionally. By the time they returned to the hotel, it was time to put Nilüfer to bed. He walked into his room, his mind swirling about Süheylā. Every place, every sound, was a reminder of her.

The knock on the door woke him up; he had overslept. When he saw his daughter running toward him, he jumped from his bed and took her in his arms. She was all his; nobody would ever take her away.

"I took the liberty of ordering your breakfast, Colonel."

"Thank you, Kadife." He wanted to use the bathroom and freshen up; his entire day would be Nilüfer again. What more could he ask?

When the evening came, he walked Nilüfer to the hotel manager's suite. She was going to spend the night with his girls. He dressed up for the evening and took the elevator down to the lobby; Errol's driver was waiting. He drove him to Errol's club, a fifteen-minute ride. The *maître d'* escorted Costa to his table, where Errol was sitting in the company of two women.

"I am so glad to see you, Costa!" exclaimed Errol. "Of course you know my mom, and our governess, Mademoiselle Neriman."

"Mrs. Sariyer, you look marvelous. After so many years, I am so happy to see you again."

Mrs. Sariyer rose from her chair and gave him a protracted hug, while Costa kissed her in reverence. She was older now, yet she looked remarkable. Coming from the lineage of the Sultans, she was a bona fide aristocrat.

"I am happy to see you, too, Colonel Rigas. How many years has it been?"

"About twenty, Mrs. Sariyer," Costa smiled, looking at Mademoiselle Neriman.

"Such a long time!" lamented Mrs. Sariyer.

"I am sorry to hear of Mr. Sariyer's passing away."

"Thank you, Costa. His pancreatic cancer was incurable. I don't think you could have saved him," she added, "like you saved me!"

Suddenly that memory flushed into Costa's mind. Some twenty-one years ago, he had performed CPR on Mrs. Sariyer, who was having a heart attack. It was sheer luck that his cousin Tina, who was a nurse in USA, had visited Costa's village and taught him the procedure. "I wish I could, Mrs. Sariyer, Costa lamented. Mr. Sariyer was a noble man. Again, I am sorry for your loss."

"Thank you, Costa. I will always be grateful. I'd better sit down. Neriman is waiting."

"How are you, Costa," exclaimed Mademoiselle Neriman, hugging him madly.

"I am delighted to see you, Madam Merriman. Why in the world hasn't some dashing Turk swept you off your feet by now?"

"Besides Errol and you, nobody could compare in looks!" she joked.

"Thank you, Mademoiselle Neriman. You are kind." He pulled out her chair; "please."

"Thank you, Costa. As you know, I never married, and of course, no children. Errol is my adopted son. Had you stayed in Turkey, I would have adopted you, too," she cried. "Besides Errol, you were the best son I could ever have."

"My mom passed away years ago, Mademoiselle Neriman; you can adopt me any time," smiled Costa, and assisted her to sit.

A warm-up band was playing traditional Turkish music, songs Costa loved passionately. Along with all the bad memories about Turkey, Costa had buried this mystical music genre long ago, and he just realized what he missed. The Turkish melodies were stirring his senses in quick reverse—he had the feeling he'd never left.

"One more guest is joining us tonight," said Errol, interrupting Costa's nostalgic indulgence. "You will meet her later. Now let's have a toast."

Errol lifted his glass. "A toast to our old friend, Colonel Rigas, and his daughter Nilüfer."

Costa was touched. "Never in my wildest imaginings did I think that I would I be visiting my ex-homeland under these circumstances. I am forever grateful to your family, Errol. Thank you."

"Costa, I am the one who is grateful to you for having saved my mom from her heart attack."

"It was just pure luck, Errol," replied Costa humbly. "What about the entertainment tonight, Errol? Costa followed politely.

"Oh, you will love it, Costa!" Errol replied with assurance.

The show started with a couple of warm-up artists, and then Emel Sayin, the ambassadrix of Ottoman music, made her entrance. After two encores, the crowd stood and clapped for more. Finally, the announcer quieted the crowd.

"We have a surprise guest this evening. We are going to be entertained by the new sensation of Ottoman music. Ladies and gentlemen, I give you 'Gülēngül!' "

Costa's heart skipped. *Could she be Süheylā's sister, Gülēngül? No, it could not be,* he thought. There were many others with the same name. When he left Turkey, Gülēngül was no more than fourteen. Suddenly, a beautiful blonde-haired creature walked onto the stage in a black Costaine gown. She walked so similarly to Süheylā that his heart leaped in his chest. She took the microphone and begged the crowd to quiet down.

"Ladies and gentlemen, before I start, I have an announcement to make. I want to tell you something." For a few seconds, she allowed her words to sink in for effect. The crowed shifted in their chairs. "I am in love with traditional Turkish music," said Gülēngül, punching her last words hard; the kanun[82] eased into her song.

Misty night, the rain is cold, with empty arms, an aching heart

Looking for you, maybe a dance, hoping to catch your kissing glance

Too many cafés, I am already drunk, tired of searching, my knees have sunk.

My breath is short, I dare not walk, I am killing time, but never hope.

Misty night, the air has gone, in silent space, I float alone

I hear my breath, in deepest song, I drooped so low, to bare and bone.

With soul so thirsty and arms weary, I row and row a night so dreary

I long to touch your loving face, hoping to melt in your embrace.

By the middle of the song, Costa's eyes were tearing up. It was his and Süheylā's all-time favorite song; it awakened his most powerful emotions. He thought it was Süheylā on the stage—a song they sang together so long ago.

Gülēngül finished the song, and the crowd went wild. Costa was angry with himself for allowing his emotions to deprive him of such wonderful Turkish music. Gülēngül sang two more songs, and the crowd would not let her go.

"Ladies and gentlemen, I appreciate your love. I will do one more. With your permission, I would like to dedicate this song to my husband," she said pointing to Errol, who stood up and blew her a kiss. She blew him a kiss in return and launched into her final song. Finally, she stepped off the stage gracefully to the fading sounds

---

82. A hammer dulcimer struck with steel fingers.

of the kanun. She was more than a special guest. Costa was dying to know.

"Hello, my love," she said, kissing Errol. She gave Mrs. Sariyer a hug, calling her "Mom," and kissed Mademoiselle Neriman. Costa stood up; Errol introduced him.

"I am pleased to meet you, Miss Gülēngül," said Costa, shaking her hand. He looked toward Errol. "I heard you got married but never did I imagine to a gorgeous creature like Gülēngül," complimented Costa, trying to guess who she really was.

"Thank you, Colonel Rigas; welcome to Turkey!" smiled Gülēngül.

Costa pulled out her chair. When she sat and crossed her legs; Costa's heart jumped; she was all Süheylā.

The servers poured more champagne and the group settled down for conversation. As Costa looked at Gülēngül, he could hardly contain his excitement. The more she spoke, the more he was convinced she was Süheylā's younger sister. Impressed with Costa's Turkish, her next comment was inevitable.

"Colonel Rigas, your Turkish sounds so perfect for an American."

"I am an expatriate."

"Errol told me. I am also familiar with your daughter's abduction. I am so happy you found her."

"I am, too," chimed in Mrs. Sariyer.

"What are your plans after all you went through?" asked Gülēngül, looking at Costa seriously.

"My priority is to ease Nilüfer into my life; everything else is secondary."

"Since you are an expatriate, are you planning to stay in Turkey long?"

"As soon as I have her nanny's traveling documents, I plan to leave for USA. Nilüfer needs a permanent home and schooling. I have already visited my parent's graves in Imvros[83]. I plan to be back next year, although I find Turkey very exciting; I have lots of memories here."

"All good, I hope!"

"Most of them; some not so good."

"I am sorry to hear that."

Costa was dying to ask the burning question—*aren't you Süheylā's sister?*—but he was determined to wait for the right opening.

"Memories, we all have them, Colonel. Some are more intense than others, but sooner, or later we must confront them," commented Gülēngül with a touch of an enigmatic composure.

"I have a specific memory I would like to come to grips with, but I don't dare," Costa blurted out.

Before Gülēngül could ask a follow-up question, Errol, her husband, invited her to dance. This left Costa alone with Mrs. Sariyer and Mademoiselle Neriman. Politely, Costa invited Mrs. Sariyer onto the dance floor. They danced without saying a word for a while. It was at the tail end of the song when Mrs. Sariyer stopped.

"Costa, have you figured out who my daughter-in-law is?"

Fumbling for an answer, he led Mrs. Sariyer to their table and pulled out her chair. As her intense eyes were still searching his face, Gülēngül rescued him.

"Don't sit down, Colonel; may I have this dance?"

"Such an offer I cannot refuse." With a racing heart, he excused himself and followed Gülēngül onto the dance floor.

"With all your memories about Turkey, is there anything that sticks out?" asked Gülēngül the minute she settled into his arms.

Costa was cornered. "I am looking for a lost love. I am determined to find her."

---

83. Renamed Gökçeada today.

Gülēngül stopped dancing. "Why don't we take a seat by the patio, Colonel?"

He followed her mechanically. They took a table way off to a corner. Gülēngül leaned forward. "I am sure you know by now who I am, don't you Colonel Rigas?"

"Yes I know, but tell me anyway."

"I am Sūheylā's younger sister."

It was as if Sūheylā had just jumped out from the closet of history. Sensing her inquisitive eyes on him, he tried to collect his thoughts.

"A long time ago I met the love of my life. In my darkest hour, I thought she left me out in the cold, until recently. So much has happened. I have never been able to make any sense of all this."

"I feel your pain, Colonel Rigas," she replied, pausing for a moment. "Do you want to know what happened to her?"

"Of course I do. I wanted to believe that somehow she was okay, even if she had stopped loving me."

"I am very touched, Colonel," said Gülēngül. "Would you like to see her?"

Costa felt dizzy. "When?" he blurted out, afraid that what he had just asked might come true.

"Any time you are ready, Colonel."

Costa leaned back in his chair and closed his eyes. He did not expect this turn of events. Gülēngül, sensing his turmoil, reached across the table and touched his hand.

"You do not need to decide that right now, Colonnel."

"Thank you. I need time to decompress from this shock."

"I will call you tomorrow some time after ten o'clock. Now let's go back to the table before Errol starts to get suspicious about us," she joked.

Trying to keep a brave face, he followed her and took his seat. He had a keen sense that the entire table knew his predicament. They all pretended complete indifference.

After half an hour of additional social time, Costa felt it was time to go.

"I need to get to my daughter, Nilüfer," he apologized to the group. "Errol, your driver does not need to drive me, I will take a taxi." They all kissed goodbye, but Mrs. Sariyer insisted on another big hug.

"I am proud of you, Costa. In spite of all the odds, you have succeeded brilliantly. I love you as my son."

Costa could not utter the right response. Another Turk was making his past melt away. Back at the hotel, Costa was surprised to see the police guard sitting outside his suite.

"What is going on, Hayri?" he asked with a lump in his throat.

"Not to worry, Colonel," replied Hayri standing in attention. "Nilüfer did not want to spend the night away from you."

"Nothing serious, I hope?"

"Everything is fine, Colonel."

"Thank you, Hayri. Costa opened the door, and when he saw Kadife watching TV on the couch, he relaxed.

"I am sorry, Colonel Rigas,' Kadife apologized. " Nilüfer did not want to stay away. She wanted to sleep in your bed." She walked to his bedroom and cracked the door open. There was Nilüfer, in the middle of his bed, sleeping.

Costa was elated. He thanked Kadife and told her to go to sleep. It was already past midnight. Nudging his daughter to the side, he lay down, feeling emotionally spent. Unexpectedly, Süheylā had roared back into his life and he did not know if he could sleep. Although he'd had enough to drink, he dialed room service. A double gin and tonic would be good.

Things happened so unexpectedly. Errol had set the whole thing up. His emotional condition was like a churning sea. A few days ago, he planned to leave Turkey without going through the pain to learn anything about

Süheylā, but after he'd read her letters, he was determined to see her—at least just one more time. After so many years of longing, he now felt uneasy, insecure and ambivalent. Was he afraid to face her? What had happened to the young woman with whom he had fallen so madly in love? The question kept popping into his mind. If he saw her, what was *he* going to say? What was *she* going to say?

Chapter 42: Gülēngül

The sounds of a child's laughter woke him up. He opened his bedroom door and walked into the small salon of the suite. Nilüfer was sitting on Kadife's lap having breakfast. She jumped from her chair and ran into his arms.

"She came to my bedroom complaining you were still sleeping, Colonel. She wanted to wake you up, but I stopped her; you needed your rest."

"You are so kind, Kadife. I must say, last night finding her in my bed was a pleasant surprise."

"The müdür[84] and his wife invited her again. Their kids had a nice time playing with Nilüfer."

"I will make sure to thank them," replied Costa. "Now if you excuse me, I would like to get ready. Can you order breakfast for me?"

"Will it be the same, Colonel?"

"What else?" Costa laughed. "This is Turkey, my homeland!"

When the hotel's staff found out that Costa was an expatriate, they were eager to accommodate him. By the time he had dressed, his breakfast was ready. He ate with Nilüfer on his lap. The phone rang and Kadife picked it up.

"It is for you, Colonel."

He knew who was at the other end. "Hello," he whispered.

"Good morning, Colonel Rigas, this is Gülēngül."

"I knew it would be you. How are you today, Gülēngül?'

"I am fine, but how are you, Colonel?"

---

84. The hotel's general manager.

"You really don't want to know," he answered politely.

"Why don't we meet at the hotel's coffee shop in about an hour?"

"That is a good idea; thank you."

Gülēngül hung up the phone with a "see you then" in perfect English.

Costa looked at his watch; he had an hour to kill.

"Kadife, take Nilüfer to Gezi Park for a while. Be back about noon."

"Okay, Colonel."

Nilüfer, hearing the word 'park,' was eager to go. "Kadife, please remember to take the policeman along."

"Yes, of course. Hayri will not let us venture out without him anyway."

His nerves were on edge, so he went out for a brisk walk. He returned on time and took a seat in one of the corners of the coffee shop to wait. When he saw people looking at the entry and gesturing with excitement, he knew immediately. It was Gülēngül, the famous singer. He stood up and pulled out her chair.

"Good morning, Colonel Rigas. The host told me where to find you."

"Call me Costa, please."

Dressed in a pair of white slacks and a light sweater over a silk shirt, she was beaming with charm.

"You have so many admirers," complimented Costa, trying to keep his heartbeat in check.

"You are so kind, Costa. Thank you."

"I was going to ask you last night, Colonel Rigas; how is your daughter, Nilüfer?"

Costa smiled. "She is doing fine, thank you; she at the park with her governess."

"I am so glad she is back with you safe and sound, Colonel. I can not even imagine the nightmare you went through."

"Thank you Gülēngül. I must confess that I had chills up and down my spine last night. You sang my favorite song. I am not ashamed to tell you, I could not hold back my tears."

"I sang it for you. I knew it was an all-time favorite of yours and Süheylā's."

Costa brought his palm to his heart. Süheylā was already reaching down inside him, freeing his memories like a tumbling waterfall. The mere mention of her name conjured much emotion. Skillfully he sidetracked Gülēngül.

"How did you get to become such a great artist?"

"After my prep school academy, I went to the University of Sorbonne for further voice studies. At first I dabbled in Turko-Western pop and became successful. However, the last five years I found a home in the traditional Turkish music."

Costa collected himself as best he could. "May I ask how Süheylā is doing?'

"She is doing great; she manages her own law firm."

He dreaded the next question. "Is she still married?" he asked, not knowing what to expect.

"How did you know she was married?"

"From General Ersoy when we met at the US Army Staff and Command College, in Fort Leavenworth, Kansas, several years ago."

"She is a widow. Her husband passed away a few years ago from wound complications."

"What wounds?"

"Wounds he sustained on the Iraqi border."

"I am sorry to hear that. What was her husband doing there?"

"He was a military doctor. He and his unit went to retrieve wounded soldiers. Unfortunately, they ran into a minefield."

Costa became pensive for a while. "Do they have any children?"

"No children."

"Where does she live?"

"She lives mostly in Ankara, although she keeps an apartment here in Istanbul."

"Last night you transported me back in time. You reminded me so much of your sister."

Gülēngül leaned over the table and placed her palm over Costa's cheek. "Süheylā would love to hear that."

He fell silent. He wanted to ask a few more questions, but he stopped. Seeing Süheylā was the only way. "When can I see her?" he asked resolutely.

Gülēngül smiled. "Any time, Costa; name the place."

"A place of her choosing; it has to be in private."

"Yes, of course."

"I can reserve a conference room at the Hilton. Will that work?"

"Funny," said Gülēngül. "I am performing at the Hilton this weekend for a convention. Errol and I have already reserved the presidential suite. We have also invited my sister to spend time with us. Why don't you meet her there?"

This is it. There is no escape. "Thank you, Gülēngül. I will be forever grateful. "

They said goodbye and parted company. With much apprehension, Costa took the elevator up to his suite. After twenty years, he was going to see his lost love. He'd been in some harrowing scrapes in the Iraq War, but meeting Süheylā after twenty years was going his biggest challemge.

With her limitless energy, Nilüfer was getting bolder by the day. Her acquired English of "I love you, Daddy" lifted his heart every time. About a week ago, he was convinced that Nilüfer and the U.S. Army would be his only interests, but with Süheylā now on the horizon, he had no idea how it would end.

Gezi Park became Nilüfer's favorite playground. For some reason, she loved this park as much as Costa and Süheylā had so long ago. With so many kids around, the swings, the teeter-totter and the sandbox were active conduits for making friends. Her unusual accent was a dead give-away. Her playmates, noting her father was always nearby, would ask him where she was from. He would wave his hands with a smile. The last thing he wanted to say was that she was an American who did not speak a word of English.

His anticipation of meeting Süheylā was driving him insane; and that was tomorrow. To calm his nerves, he decided to visit his boyhood friend, Bishop Nicolas, at the See of Orthodoxy, the Patriarchate of Istanbul. He took his daughter along and gave Kadife the afternoon off. Nicolas was delighted to see him.

"I must say you look so distinguished in your robes and that big cassock, Nicolas."

"And you Costa look young and fit. How is it going with this little one?"

"As well as I can expect. We both need time."

"We have a kid's playroom. Would you like to take her there?"

Their conversation was in Greek; Nilüfer looked lost. "Would you like to play with other kids?" Costa asked his daughter in Turkish.

"Evet Baba[85]," she nodded excitedly, but Costa was still hesitant to leave her alone.

"Don't worry, Costa," reassured the bishop. "We have security around the clock; nobody gets through."

Although he had heard these words before, Costa relaxed. They left Nilüfer with the other kids and went back to the bishop's offices.

"Tell me, Costa," asked Nicolas. "What are your plans?"

"Nilüfer; everything else is secondary."

"Why Nilüfer? Isn't that a Turkish name?"

"Should it matter whether it is Turkish or Greek?"

"No, but you might consider baptizing her here before you leave for the States."

"Thank you for the offer, Nicolas. I am sure you know that I no longer subscribe to any religious rituals. My wife and I chose that name because we liked it."

"You have always been a rebel, Costa; straight and unambiguous," gibed Nicolas.

"Nilüfer can choose any religion she wants when she grows up, Nicolas."

"Excuse my impertinence, Costa. I was trying to be of service."

"You are kind."

"Are you hungry? We can have lunch brought here."

"That would be nice, Nicolas, but what about Nilüfer?"

"They feed all the kids. I assure you she is having a great time."

The attendant deacon brought sandwiches, coffee and fruit. They ate while making small talk. The topic came around to precious icons and other religious relics that were being spirited to the antique markets around the world for great prices."

---

85. "Yes, Daddy."

"We are making some progress, Costa, although the political climate is still rocky. Turkey has a hard time letting go of its past, but we are optimistic."

"I know," said Costa sympathetically. "What is the size of the Greek community in Istanbul now?"

"About three thousand; mind you, in the year 1918, there were two-hundred-forty thousand of us."

"Such a calamity; Turkey will live to regret it."

"Turkey is for the Turks only, Costa. They have literally chased away every minority—Greeks, Jews, Bulgarians, Italians and French. On the other hand, they expect the rest of the world to accept them within their ranks, falsely pretending that they have aggrieved no one."

"Let's not give up hope, Nicolas."

"You must know something that I don't."

"Just think for a minute, Nicolas. What if Turkey were to declare an annual pan-Islamic-Christian conference in Istanbul and designate Santa Sophia as the common place of worship?"

"Wow, Costa; you just blew my mind!"

"Can you imagine the millions of faithful—Muslims and Christians—that would flock to this annual occasion? It might rival 'Haj!' The possibilities of reconciliation between the two great religions would be tremendous. This action alone would catapult Turkey's prestige throughout the world by a hundredfold!

"And one more thing, Nicolas; Turkey should reinstall the huge golden cross on top of the dome of Santa Sophia!"

Bishop Nicolas looked breathless. "Costa, do you have any more crazy ideas like that?"

"I do, but in comparison, they are minor."

"You have my undivided attention, Costa!"

"Well, two more things Turkey can do.

"A: Move the Patriarchate to the Church of Santa Irene or some other Byzantine structure and grant it semi-autonomy.

"B: Restore all the rights of Tenedians and Imvrians and provide compensation."

Bishop Nicolas rang for his attendant. "Deacon, brandy, please; we need a couple of brandies fast." He gaped at Costa as if he were some alien. "You are either nuts or you are ahead of everybody; I cannot decide which. Turkey is not that farsighted."

"I disagree, Nicolas; all that is required is leadership; maybe another Atatürk."

"Is he visible through the telescope?" he scoffed.

"Not at the moment, Nicolas, but everything is possible. There are some bright Turks around."

"Get real, Costa. Right now, our biggest struggle is trying to hang on for dear life."

"What about the Museum of Byzantium."

"It is a start. Turkey realized that it is in her interest to preserve her Christian heritage. So far, she has a hard time granting us the permit, but we are hopeful. The present regime wants to go slow, but they also promised to fund the museum—in secret of course. "

"I assume you are accumulating a collection, Nicolas."

"Yes, we are, and we are running out of space."

"I read you are the curator."

"By default, I am afraid."

"Who knows? Some day it may rival the Vatican Museum."

"Nice try, Costa," Bishop Nicolas chuckled laconically.

"I think the museum is a great idea. What else is going on?"

"Can you keep a secret?"

Costa looked at the bishop with curiosity. "A secret kept is a secret not told, Nicolas."

"You are right, but I will tell you anyway." Bishop Nicolas cleared his throat. "I have in my possession a most precious relic that predates the fall of Constantinopolis[86]."

"You have an item more than six-hundred years old?"

"Yes. I had it appraised by two experts I flew in from Florence, Italy."

Costa's curiosity was piqued. "What is it?"

The Bishop blinked his eyes. "It is a gilded, wooden cross adorned with stones—about 20 centimeters long. " Do you want to see it? It is still in my vault."

"Yes, I do; I am curious!"

The bishop got up from his chair. "Follow me," he motioned, opened a side door and led Costa into a smaller interior room. He flipped a light switch and pointed at a vault. He dialed the lock's combination and signaled Costa for help.

The two men pulled on the heavy door slowly. Nicolas walked into the vault and removed a wooden box from the shelf. Carefully he carried it out and placed it on a small table, opened it, and invited Costa to look.

The gilded cross looked familiar. Costa knew instantly "What a relic," he exhaled in admiration. What is it appraised at?"

"The consensus is more than ten million dollars, maybe more."

Costa whistled. "How did you come by this?"

"It is an extraordinary story," stated Nicolas seriously and placed the cross back into the vault. "You are one of the few laymen to see it. It will be housed in the museum when it opens—some day!"

"I am honored."

The two men closed the heavy steel door and the bishop scrambled the combination. They went back into

---

86. Istanbul today.

the office. Nicolas sat behind his desk beaming from ear to ear.

"You still did not tell me how you came by this relic, Nicolas."

"I get too excited whenever I set my eyes on this piece." He cleared his throat and took another sip of his brandy.

"Several weeks ago I was working in my office late when my phone rang. My attendant told me that a woman wanted to talk to me; she would not give her name. It was strange, especially for a woman calling me late at night. 'Bishop Nicolas,' I said, 'who is calling?'

" 'This is an anonymous call,' said a distinguished, husky voice on the other end. 'I have something to show you. It might be very valuable to your museum.'

" 'And how would I know it is valuable? I get a lot of calls like that.'

" 'I know it is, especially to the Orthodox Church,' replied the woman without any hesitation. She had no phoniness in her flexion. I deduced she was a woman of means, and very educated. She spoke perfect Turkish."

Costa leaned forward. This was getting very interesting. The bishop continued as if he were in a trance.

" 'Okay, Madam,' I said, 'when can I see it?'

" 'It will have to be tonight. I have no time to waste.'

" 'Okay Madam, tonight then.'

" 'I will be there in an hour. Please instruct security to let me in.'

" 'Our security will not let anybody in, unless you tell me your name and what you look like.'

" 'I cannot tell you my name. I am five nine and will be wearing a veil. Is that enough?'

" 'I need to think about this,' I said, stalling. 'Can you give me a minute?' "

"Well Nicolas, then what?"

"What I was about to do was foolish. Letting anybody into the complex without any identification was against security rules, but my curiosity got the better of me. It was the best decision I ever made."

"Go on," urged Costa impatiently. He was dying to know what happened next.

"My deacon ushered this lady into my office. She walked in with her face covered by a veil and took a seat without even asking. Her stately gate exuded a pronounced self-assurance. She reached into an enormous pocketbook and took out a box, placed it across her knees, opened it and invited me to look. My eyes have never popped before. They are still popped."

Costa was at his wits' end. He could hardly contain himself, "Then?"

The bishop buzzed his attendant. "A couple of more brandies, Deacon." He lay back in his chair and exhaled in triumph. "This is where it gets interesting, Costa. I asked the woman what was the asking price. Can you guess?"

"I have no idea."

" 'Three million dollars; not a dollar less.'

" 'How would I know it is worth that much?' I replied, trying to think. As you know, Costa, I have studied religious antiques at the University of Sorbonne for two semesters. I knew this was no ordinary item.

" 'You don't,' she said, 'and neither do I. My guess is it is worth more than ten million.'

" 'How do I know this item is not stolen?'

" 'I have a notarized bill of sale. I will transfer it to your museum if you decide to buy it.'

" 'Can I see the Bill of Sale?'

"She reached into her pocketbook and pulled out an envelope. 'This is a copy. I have blurred out the names. I will transfer you the original once you decide to buy it.'

" 'I cannot promise you anything, Madam. You will need to leave it with me so that I can have it appraised.'

"She rose from her chair and handed me the box.

" 'Bishop, you have a week.'

"I was impressed with her poise. She was not a woman to be trifled with. 'How can I trust you?' I asked, stalling for more information.

" 'You don't, and neither do I trust you, Bishop. For security reasons, I have photographed all pertinent documentation, which I am keeping in my bank vault. I have also taped our conversation.'

"She reached under her lapel and pulled out a mini microphone. The wire leading in the inside pocket of her jacket was now visible. She took out a mini tape recorder and showed it to me.

" 'It has recorded everything we discussed,' she said. 'Do you want to hear it?'

"I smiled. 'That will not be necessary, Madam.' As I said, this woman was really something.

"She reached inside her pocket again and handed me a note with a Swiss bank name and an account number. 'If you decide to buy it, you must deposit the money in this account.'

" 'How can I get in touch with you, Madam?' "

" 'You can't; I will be in touch with you. Remember, seven days, Bishop.'

"My attendant walked her to a waiting car. The driver behind the wheel was also wearing a veil. He surmised she was another lady."

Costa was so engrossed he had lost track of time. "I need to check on Nilüfer, Nicolas. Can we continue later?"

"Yes, of course."

Bishop Nicolas led Costa into the playroom. There she was in the middle of several kids, jumping and laughing. Nilüfer spotted him and waved.

"Let's go back to your office, Nicolas."

They walked back to the Bishop's quarters and partook of some more brandy.

"This story is intriguing," said Costa, his curiosity at its zenith. "How does it end?"

"If you can call it that. Within two days, I flew in two experts from Florence, Italy to examine the item. Their findings were as I told you.

"We did not have three million, but I found them. I took a leap of faith and deposited the money in that Swiss account."

"Excuse me, Nicolas; three million is a lot of money. Can your treasury handle an amount like that?"

"You know it cannot. Let's say it came from a secret source, which I cannot divulge."

"I don't need to know that; please, continue."

"Seven days exactly after my first meeting, I was sitting in my office, anxiously waiting for her call. It was getting close to midnight when my attendant knocked on the door." 'It is that veiled lady at the gate again. She says you are expecting her.'

" 'Show her in without any delay, please.'

"She wore the same veil, but a different business suit with a skirt barely above her knees. I must say I had never seen prettier legs in my life—may God forgive me. She sat in the same chair and opened her pocketbook."

" 'Thank you for depositing the money,' she said, dispensing with any nonsense talk. 'Before I hand you the Bill of Sale, here is an affidavit for you to sign. The sale will be invalid if the buyer divulges the sale particulars; I reserve the right to reclaim the relic and return the money.'

"This lady had me cornered; I had no choice.

" 'Thank you,' she said, pocketing the affidavit. 'Here is the Bill of Sale. It is signed and notarized; it is perfectly legal.'

" 'How did you know I would buy this relic?' I asked with curiosity.

" 'I didn't; not until I saw the expression on your face when you looked at the cross.'

" 'You are too clever for me, Madam. This relic might be worth more, but I am not a merchant. I am at the service of the church.'

" 'I know it is worth more, but it is in the right place.' She reached into her jacket and clicked off her tape recorder. 'I am sure you were aware I was recording you?'

" 'Yes, I knew. That is why I had stated that the value of this relic was infinitely more valuable.'

" 'It is money well spent, Bishop.'

" 'What is the money for? I know it is not for you.'

" 'How can you know that?' She looked surprised.

" 'If it were for personal gain, you would have asked for more,' I replied, feeling I had measured up to her in some way.

" 'You are right Bishop; it is not for me. As a matter of fact, before I was in this predicament, I was going to donate it to the Orthodox Church.'

"I did a double-take. This woman was a noble one. I had to ask a follow-up question.

" 'Are you a Christian, Madam?'

" 'Just a Turkish citizen, Bishop,' she giggled. We shook hands. Just before she exited my door, she turned around.

" 'Some day I might be able to return that money, Bishop,' she added, and left my office.

"I stood in the middle of my office completely taken aback. I wanted to run after the lady and hug her, but by the time I made it into the courtyard, she and her companion had disappeared into the night."

This was a most unexpected twist. After some additional chitchat with Bishop Nicolas, Costa collected Nilüfer and left the compound; his head was getting cloudier by the day.

Chapter 44: An Old Friend

Holding Nilüfer by the hand, Costa took the elevator up to his suite. Hayri, the security guard, saluted and handed him an envelope.

"We have found the individual you are looking for, Colonel. Here is the information."

Costa was impressed, "How did you manage it so fast, Hayri?"

"I consulted my friends at the secret police. I told them it was for a worthy cause."

"Thank you, Hayri."

"My pleasure, Colonel."

Costa opened the door. Kadife was sitting on the couch. "Good evening, Kadife. Please look after Nilüfer; I will be back in an hour."

He took a cab to the address Hayri had given him. The driver drove straight to Dolapdere, an area very familiar to Costa, and stopped in front of a drab café. Costa asked the driver to wait, and walked in.

It was a decrepit place—dark, smelly, pungent, full of smoke. Draped over their chairs were several men, obviously stoned from hashish. A frumpy little woman spoke to Costa from behind the counter.

"I am looking for Madam Mehtab."

"Is she in trouble?"

"No. I am just a friend of hers from way back. I would like to say hello."

"How far back?"

"About twenty years ago."

She scratched her head. "Where have you been all this time?"

"I live in America."

"You speak perfect Turkish for an American."

"It is a long story; I was born in Turkey."

"Surprises never end. Have I seen your face before?"

Costa ignored her question. "Can we sit down?"

Mehtab stepped out and led him to a table. "Can I get you some tea, Mister? I am Mehtab."

"No, thank you, Mehtab," said Costa and pulled out her chair.

She smiled, "nobody pulls out a chair for a used-up bitch like me!"

"My name is Costa. Do you remember me?"

"After thousands of tricks, I don't remember anybody."

"I was not a customer. You remember Zelal Hanum and a student doctor Barzani, don't you?"

Mehtab tensed. "I remember them all right, but what do they have to do with you?" she replied tersely, examining Costa's face with more suspicion.

"Relax. I am the Christian you wanted to make love to."

Mehtab's face lit up. She jumped up from her chair to hug Costa madly. "You are Zelal Hanum's friend," she sobbed. "Now I remember you. You came to Zelal's café to play backgammon."

"I am glad you remember."

She looked into Costa's face again. "Now wait a minute. You are that American colonel. It was your daughter those bastards had abducted, wasn't it?"

"How do you know, Mehtab?"

"Who doesn't?" She seemed breathlessly animated. "From Turkey into the American military? she comented. "What kind of crazy country is that?"

"More that you can imagine, Madam Mehtab."

"You were handsome then; you look like a movie star now!"

"Thank you, Mehtab. You are kind."

"As you can see, I lost all my beauty; I am worn out." She started to cry. "What is your name again?"

"Costa."

314

"Sorry, Costa; people like you never set foot in my place, except that lady who walked in here some time ago. She too mentioned the names of Barzani and Zelal Hanum. Do you know her?"

Costa's antennae went up. Before he could think of something, Mehtab continued as if she were relishing her conversation.

"The lady was dressed in a dark suit and wore a veil. She handed me some money and asked me if I remembered Zelal Hanum and some her Kurdish friends. I told her that Zelal was dead, but I had no idea where her Kurdish friends were; some of them had become guerillas, who besides killing Turkish soldiers, they kidnapped people for ransom."

"Yes, I know. Were you able to help the lady?"

"My husband did, for money of course. That s.o.b. never misses an opportunity. He is my ex-pimp, a master of extortion."

"What happened then?"

"Well, the lady said, 'I will pay you five hundred dollars for information.'

"My husband said, 'make it a thousand,'.

" 'Here is a thousand,' said the woman; and sure enough, she just counted out the cash. Then she said, 'If your information is correct, I will mail you another thousand.'

"This was a lot of money. More than we earned for the entire year. I let my husband take it, although I still feel that we might have betrayed someone—I hope not. My husband gave her all the information he knew about the Barzanis—they are his cousins. About three weeks ago, we got a registered letter with a thousand-dollar check without a name."

Costa had the entire picture. After his conversation with Bishop Nicolas and now Mehtab, he knew exactly who this woman was. "Do you have any children, Mehtab?"

"My profession left me sterile," she moaned. "I have no children and no money. Look at this place; it is a pig sty."

Costa was beginning to feel bad; he had to end this soon. "I am here to pay you my debt, Mehtab."

"What debt?"

"You gave me a thousand liras to help me get out of the country."

"You are joking, right."

"Do you remember Zelal Hanum asking you for a thousand liras for someone who needed help? It was me." Costa took out an envelope from his pocket and handed it to Mehtab.

Mehtab held it in her hand and screwed up her face as if this were some kind of prank. Seeing Costa smiling, she tore the envelope open. When she saw the pile of cash, she nearly lost her mind, and started to sob. A frail-looking man staggered out of the kitchen, wondering about Mehtab's crying. Mehtab looked at Costa one more time and attempted to kiss his hands, but Costa stopped her. He patted her on the shoulders and assisted her back onto her chair.

"Do you want to know what really happened to Zelal?" she sobbed.

"I know all about Zelal Hanum, Mehtab; I am sorry."

"This goddamn country," she groaned. "I am not afraid of these Turks any more, but as you can see they are not afraid of me either," she sniggered, looking at herself contemptuously.

"A debt must be paid, Mehtab. I am sorry for the late payment."

"I never loaned money to anyone. If I gave you any money, it was out of the goodness of my heart. So don't tell me it was a loan." She stood up and clung on Costa's neck like a child.

"Mehtab, I will always be your friend," consoled Costa, and sat her back on her seat again.

She noticed the cook standing behind her. "This is my husband, the pimp," she croaked derisively. "He is good-for-nothing; I was drunk when I married him."

"Aziz, meet my American friend. You probably do not remember him. You were too stoned with hashish to notice anybody."

Aziz extended his hand weakly, offering a faint "welcome."

"That hashish ruined his mind, Costa," lamented Mehtab. "He no longer smokes it because he is dying from lung cancer. There is no time left for him."

Costa took out his business card. "Call me when you need something."

Before Mehtab had any chance to say anything, Costa walked out briskly and into the waiting cab. He saw Mehtab in the rear-view mirror waving frantically.

He smiled that in some way he was able to help. Surprisingly, Mehtab has added more mystery to his suspense. The thought of meeting Süheylā tomorrow constricted his chest. He tried to visualize her. Would it be the Muslim Madonna or the Ottoman Lava? He could never tell them apart.

Chapter 45: Hold Me and Do Not Move

Pacing back and forth in the Hilton's presidential suite was not doing anything for his nerves. Although the view of Bosporus was breathtaking, it did not help much. His mind meandered about the Black Sea. The beach of Kilyos was out there, the place where he and Süheylā trampled their cultural taboos and made love. Her arrival was getting perilously close. The jingling of the door lock exploded like a canon. He turned around. In the middle of the salon walked in Süheylā. Their eyes met.

For a few moments, they stared at one another. It felt like an eternity. Then they were in each other's arms, holding tightly, longingly. Her chest was pressing against his, heaving. Stroking her hair, he was caressing her cheeks and drinking her tears. Holding each other tight, they sat down on the couch, staring at one another in disbelief. It had been twenty years.

"I have finally found you, Süheylā," he managed in a whisper.

She wrapped her arms around him. "Hold me, Costa; hold me and do not move. It is such bliss to see you again! Kiss me as you did long ago. I want to taste you and listen to your heartbeat."

Her breath was as fresh as he remembered it. They kissed lovingly and passionately.

"Rip off my clothes, Costa," she murmured.

He guided her into the bedroom, shedding her clothes along the way. He could not wait either.

Their love was furious and wild.

Finally, when their fury subsided, she stood up. "What do you think; do I still look good?"

"You have the athletic look of those ancient Spartan women, Süheylā. You are a wonder."

"Ooh, that is flattering."

"Your face is radiant, just as I remembered it. Even more, you still look skinny, and so young."

"Thank you. You look handsome as ever."

"Keep talking," he teased. "I've always loved your husky voice, especially when you called over the phone pretending to be Melina Merkouri."

"I could do her voice, but never could match her accent."

"What else," she continued, thrusting her chest while she posed like a ballerina.

"You look so fantastic. Teenage girls would kill for your figure."

"Don't get carried away!"

"How do you do it?"

"There is a gym in my apartment complex. I use it all the time."

"That explains it, but not all. One of your best assets was your breasts. They were the firmest I ever touched."

"Now wait a minute; you touched other breasts before mine?"

"I did not mean that. It was just a figure of speech."

"In that case, I forgive you," she smirked as she lay back down.

"You look so complete, Süheylā. You are a gorgeous woman. I should be so lucky to avoid the jealousy of Apollo!"

"You were always a charmer. You have occupied my heart ever since I first saw you. I loved you then. I loved you to death, Costa, in spite of your complete silence."

Costa abruptly sat on the bed and clasped his head in his palms, feeling distraught. The time lost, the heartache, the years of pain. He turned toward Süheylā, looking pale, and contemptuous of himself. "I know now why you chose to leave me, Süheylā."

Süheylā, who up to that moment was stroking his shoulder, stopped. She did not know what to say. "When did you find out?"

"A few days ago."

"After twenty years? I don't understand."

Costa put his head down. "I found all your letters in a box in Imvros. My mother never forwarded them to me."

She looked crushed. "Not even one?"

"That is correct."

Süheylā was beside herself. She looked distraught; she was ready to scream.

"My mother was no worse than your father, Süheylā. They both wanted the best for us," mumbled Costa, trying to comfort her, but she looked as though she had been kicked in the gut.

"For the love of God, Costa, you did not get even one?" she repeated, as if she did not hear him at all.

Costa lost his voice. He had no answer.

"I sent them to the only address I knew, Costa; I thought your mother loved you."

A dagger in his chest would have been less painful. His admiration for his mother took one more down turn.

Süheylā, who was trying to recover from her shock, ran into the bathroom and brought a couple of robes. "Let's sit for a while, Costa," she beckoned.

They sat on the sofa staring into the void.

"This is a difficult thing to comprehend, Costa. It is beyond tragedy; it is criminal."

"We have been murdered by our parents many times over."

"I could not have said it any better." She remained pensive for a while, trying to make sense of all this. "The tragedy is that we cannot turn back the clock, Costa, can we?" she whispered, looking painfully nostalgic.

"I wish we could,' Costa lamented out loud, still feeling lost; he tried to pull her close, but she stopped him.

"I have waited over twenty years to hear your explanation, Costa," she wailed in anguish. "I cannot wait a minute longer."

"I am not sure I know where to start."

"Start from anywhere. I don't care." She got up and walked to the mini bar, "what do you like to drink, Costa?"

"Gin and tonic," he whispered, feeling the weight of her gaze. "I think I need the tonic more than I need the gin."

"Tonic, with some gin then."

"What about you, Süheylā?"

"The same!"

"You have been corrupted by the Western ways," he joked.

She smiled bitterly. "I am no more Westerner than you are. No matter what, remember that you are still a Turk." She placed the drinks on the coffee table and sat, looking at him with her enormous eyes.

Costa took a sip from his drink, trying to compose himself.

"When I got your farewell letter, Süheylā, my world crumbled. I rushed to your apartment like a lunatic. I did not care whether your parents were there or not. I begged Firyāl to let me in and see with my own eyes."

"That is when it hit me. I understood right then that you meant every word you wrote. It was the most shocking thing I ever read. I left my soul in your living room and dragged myself into my apartment, feeling angry and even bitter; I felt betrayed."

He paused for a few seconds and took a sip from his drink. Süheylā was listening with stupefied sadness.

"From then on it was an uphill battle all the way to the Greek border. Your face followed me everywhere; I could not concentrate about anything. As you know, about a month earlier, I received my draft notice from the military. My induction into the army was within six months. I could have deferred it by staying in the university, but remaining a Turkish citizen no longer mattered. You had gone, and left me dry. I had no incentive to remain in this godforsaken land. The trial I went through crossing the border was unimaginable. When I read the article of Zelal's death, my world crumbled further. I had no way of ever getting in touch with you. The thought that I would never see you again gnawed at me for twenty years. I stood on that bridge, that neutral ground between Turkey and Greece, and cursed in all directions. I had no country, no money and I was facing an uncertain future, but I was not scared; anything would have been better than Turkey."

By the time, Costa finished telling Süheylā of his border-crossing experience, she had lost her anger. The more he spoke the more teary-eyed she became.

"I am numb," she whispered, and started to cry. "I have no words to comprehend all that." She rested her head on his shoulder; "this was sheer terror, Costa."

"After I was done with cursing, I walked across the border into the Greek Customs house. 'I am a refugee from the island of Imvros, Turkey,' I stammered.

"They were expecting me. That little old woman with that icon had informed them of my detention. Hoping that I would make it across the border, she left me fifty dollars along with her address and phone number. They gave me a grilled-cheese sandwich and a glass of orange juice. I thanked the guards and boarded the next bus."

"You are killing me, Costa. I know how you felt," muttered Süheylā, hugging him tighter.

"I was poor in Turkey, but in Greece I felt rich, even if the border guards had robbed me of my six-hundred Deutch marks. I could speak any language I wanted, and nobody called me a giaour. My suitcase—the Customs inspector called it my shit box—was on the bottom of the river. I did not care about any of its contents except my university reports cards and our photos together.

"Before taking the bus to Athens, I visited my brother Alkis at the boarding school in Thessalonica for a couple of days. I arrived in Athens with a few dollars in my pocket."

He looked at his watch. "We got a couple of more hours, Süheylā. After that I need to tend to my daughter."

"When can I meet your daughter?" asked Süheylā, looking at Costa intensely.

"Is there anybody in Turkey who does not know about my daughter?" smiled Costa, knowing full well, that Süheylā knew more about Nilüfer than anybody.

"Just like everybody else; I had followed the news media, Costa," replied Süheylā coyly.

He wanted to ask her a couple of questions, but he would wait for the right momenet. "Why don't you order us lunch; I will call Kadife."

"Kadife?"

"She is Nilüfer's governess, helping me transition her into my life.""Okay," she said, looking elated. "I will order us lunch."

Chapter 46: A New Life

Room service delivered their lunch. They ate in silence, trying to grasp the drama unfolding.

"Please go on, Costa," begged Süheylā. "I need to hear your story before I tell you mine."

"After arriving in Athens, I called my cousin in Congo, Africa. When he told me that Congo might be experiencing civil unrest, I lost my appetite. I did not want to go into another hornet's nest. If I could make it into the United States, it would be a better option."

"Now I know," interjected Süheylā. "I never thought of the United States. I spent two years searching for you in Africa. I did not even know where to look. You told me that your cousin was in Congo, but you never told me which one—the French or the Belgian—or what city."

"I never thought I would lose you so suddenly, Süheylā; I didn't have time to sort things out."

"Please go on, Costa."

"In all my turmoil and my haste, I realized that I'd been wearing the same clothes for several days. I took off my worn-out pants, my shirt and my stinking underwear and threw them in the sink. Before I soaked them, I searched the pockets, just in case I forgot anything. My hand came out with two pieces of paper: my arrest warrant and the address and phone number of the lady I had assisted at the border. *Maybe this poor woman would be willing to give me shelter for a couple of days.* I took a chance and called her; she remembered me. 'Come by,' she said. 'I want to thank you personally.'

"I took the Athens Metro to her address. I saw the villa and blinked. *No, this raggedy old woman could not be living in a villa like this,* I thought. I knocked on the door anyway. A housekeeper opened it. 'I must have the wrong address,' I mumbled, and started to leave.

" 'You have the right address, young man. Come in. Mrs. Karayiannis is expecting you.' She led me into the living room. Standing in the middle was the old lady from the border crossing.

" 'I am Mrs. Karayiannis,' she said warmly. 'I did not have the chance to introduce myself at the border. What is your name?'

" 'Costa Rigas,' I said and shook her hand.

" 'You are the bravest young man I have ever met. Do you want to see the icon?'

"I followed her into a side room; it was her private chapel.

" 'There she is, the Virgin Mary,' she said proudly; 'the icon that awful inspector wanted to take away from me. If it were not for you, I would have lost it. Do you know how old it is?'

"I shrugged my shoulders.

" 'It is over five-hundred years old,' she said, reverently as she crossed herself. 'It is priceless. You cannot put a value on an item like this!'

"As I followed her around, I marveled at the opulence of her villa. She took me into her dining room and asked her housekeeper to bring me something to eat.

" 'I assume you are hungry,' she asked kindly.

"I smiled back. 'I've heard your name before,' I managed. 'Aren't you the matriarch of the Karayiannis family?'

" 'Yes, I am. My family was one of the oldest Byzantine families of Istanbul. Although my children left Turkey long ago, I did not want to. I loved the queen city. Parting from her was unthinkable, but I could not stand it anymore. I spent months trying to figure a way out of Turkey. I finally made up my mind. Dress as drably as I could and take the bus out of the country. I was terrified of flying. I stuffed my suitcase with some worn-out clothes and hid my precious icon in the middle. As it turned out the inspector found it and if it were not for you, I would have lost it forever.'

"She watched me eat in silence. I had not eaten well for days.

" 'Where are you staying?' she asked.

"When I told her the area, she cringed. She called her housekeeper over.

" 'Take Costa to the guest house and make him comfortable' she instructed. She looked at me kindly. 'What are you doing in Athens anyway?'

" 'I am trying to get to the States, Mrs. Karayiannis. I am hoping my aunt will sponsor me.'

"She excused herself and came back in a few minutes. 'Here is something for you,' she said, and handed me an envelope.

"I hesitated. 'I couldn't, Mrs. Karayiannis. I already have a job lined up in one of the restaurants in Plaka[87] next week.'

"She handed the envelope back to me. 'Please take it; stay here as long as you like. I will be delighted to see you off to the States."

"I kissed her hand and followed the housekeeper into the guesthouse. I lay in bed clutching the envelope in my hands. I finally mastered the courage and opened it. After counting five hundred dollars, I was speechless. I wanted to jump up and scream with joy.

"The next day I translated my high school diploma and applied for college. My first year's tuition required payment in advance. I called my aunt and she agreed to lend me the money. While waiting for my college papers, I worked as a waiter and saved every penny. When the documents came, I went to the U.S. Embassy in Athens and processed my visa. My Turkish passport was valid for two years. I had time on my side. Finally, I bade Mrs.

---

87. The entertainment district of Athens, located at the foot of the Acropolis.

Karayiannis goodbye and took the next flight to New York.

"I arrived in the States with very little money. The school year was around the corner. Since I had no college transcripts, I started from scratch, hoping that I would be able to write to the University of Istanbul for a copy."

"Did you?"

"Yes I did. The university was prompt and efficient as though it weren't even part of Turkey. My transcripts got me twelve credit hours against my major."

"What did you major in?"

"International Relations and Arabic."

"Why Arabic?"

"I saw Middle East as a coming challenge for USA; I thought it would be an opportunity."

"You have me intrigued. How did you manage all that?"

"It wasn't easy. As soon as I enrolled in college, I took a job at a restaurant working as a waiter. The owner liked me so much, he let me make my own schedule. Still, full-time college and a job was very difficult. Thankfully, my aunt gave me free room and board. By the second year, I took a part-time job in the United Nations as a translator for Greek and Turkish documents. By my third year in college, I was beginning to translate Arabic."

"Did you have time for anything else?"

"No, I did not. I either push forward or give up and die. My passport was expiring soon, and I was not about to be sent back to Turkey. I feared she would lock me up; I dreaded that serious charge of treason."

"That was a fabricated charge, Costa. It was all contrived by my father."

Costa got up from the couch and began to pace like a caged animal. "How do you know that?" he asked, feeling his blood rushing to his head. "Please tell me; I need to know."

"When you were in Imvros, several Kurdish people from Diyarbakir came to visit. They were looking for extra space, and I agreed to let them sleep in your apartment. Unbeknownst to me, these Kurds were really anarchists. They were here to recruit other students to their cause."

"Let me guess; they used my phone, which was tapped, is that it?"

"That is it. The Turkish secret police tapped your phone right from the start. The Interior Ministry was looking for ways to snoop into the dealings of its minorities—finding any excuse to either lock them up or deport them."

Costa finally remembered Orhan Akduman's warning, something that he never mentioned to Süheylā. "Watch yourself, Costa, and tell that girlfriend of yours to be careful." Costa did not put things together then, but now it was all clear. "I had no influence with anybody, Süheylā?"

"You knew the Gregorys, who were wealthy and influential, and some of the Greek community leaders of Istanbul. Anybody you conversed with on your phone, they were listening on the other end."

"You are making my head spin."

"As you know, my father was given a high position within the Ministry of Interior Department in Ankara. When the terrorist used your phone, the Turkish Secret Service intercepted all those conversations. Guess who was in charge of those documents at the Ministry of Interior?"

"Your father?"

"Yes. Once my father found out that you and I were serious, he was looking for any way to force me to end our relationship. As you recall, about a month before my fateful farewell letter to you I began acting strange and aloof. It was because my father had given me an ultimatum. Either I stop seeing you or he was going to do

329

something about it. He was going to lock you up in the jail of no return."

Costa squeezed his head with his hands. This was unbelievable.

Süheylā got up from the couch. She grabbed him by the arm. "Stop pacing, Costa," she implored. "Please sit down for this.

"I told my father that there was nothing he could do. Either he left me alone, or I was going to elope with you. That is where things got nasty. Within days, he had the Ministry of Interior issue a warrant for your arrest. As a matter of fact, to convince me that he meant business, he showed it to me."

By the order of the Turkish State, Costa Rigas is to be arrested immediately for the following charges:

A: Consorting with terrorists

B: Engaging in Anti-State Propaganda

The Department of Interior / Chief of Investigations / Mustafa Beylerbey

"I was shocked. I begged him to no end; my mother tried, too."

"Wait a minute. Did you say your mother tried to stop him?"

"Yes, she did, Costa, but at the end she lost her nerve."

"I am surprised about that. I thought she did not want any part of me."

"You are wrong. Once she knew I was not going to give you up, my mother came to her senses; I cried on her shoulder many a night."

"So it was your father all the way."

"I even threatened him with suicide, to which end he replied, 'that would be more honorable, considering you had sex with him.'

"I panicked. The possibility of a virginity test left me horrified. How did he know, Costa?"

"I think I know. Do you remember our night in Kilyos?"

"How can I forget?"

"I think your father had someone tail us."

"Why didn't you tell me?"

"I did not want to alarm you. By the time I knew, we were past the point of no return."

"He left me with a single choice, Costa. He would have ruined your life.

"Time and time again I asked him why he was so cruel. His reply was always the same. 'I am not going to be dishonored.' He wanted to see me married to some wealthy Turk, not to some lowly Greek. He was not going to tolerate my relationship with a 'giaour'. I remember his words to this very day—they never left me.

"Hoping to stall for time, I agreed. Once you were out of the country, I would find a way to get in touch with you, but what happened next is unreal. Overnight he moved us to Ankara and placed me under house arrest. I could not see anybody, go anywhere or write to anyone. He stationed a guard outside our apartment twenty-four hours a day. For good measure, he even removed the telephone. For six months, I was a prisoner inside our own apartment. Just to make sure that I did not attempt to communicate with anyone, he threatened me with a virginity test. Being subjected to such a humiliation meant that my life was finished."

She started to cry. Despite Costa's efforts, she was inconsolable.

"I had no choice, Costa, no choice at all. I either renounced you and set you free, or refused and sent you to the jail of no return. I knew my father could do great harm to you.

"My God," she wailed, "what could I have done? I have been asking that question all my life!"

Feeling her sheer torment, Costa became numb. He gathered her into his arms and cuddled her with all his might. He knew pain. The loss of his wife Lale, the abduction of his daughter Nilüfer, and the death of his parents; this one was just as cruel.

"I hated my father then, and I hate him now. I have not spoken to him in years. I have waited all my life to tell you, Costa."

"Stop, Süheylā. You are killing yourself." He took a deep breath.

"And I thought what I was going to tell you were heavy stuff. In comparison to what you went through, my travails are a picnic."

She smiled. "Yours are more hellish than mine." She ran her palm up and down his chest and looked into his eyes intently. "Let's go to bed, Costa; I missed you so much."

Costa, feeling happily spent, said, "Süheylā, can we stop?"

"For now," she replied tempestuously. Her innocent personality disappeared long ago. She was a full-blooded tigress now.

He looked at her and exhaled. "I always wanted to tell you this, Süheylā, but never got around to it."

"Tell me what?" she smirked, snuggling closer.

He made a dismissive motion. "Nothing important."

"I want to know."

"Will you promise not to laugh?"

"I promise."

"When I sailed into Troy I fantasized I would meet Helen, the first liberated female of mankind."

"And did you find her?"

"Yes, I did." He paused for a while.

She got impatient. "Who was she, then?"

"It was you, Süheylā. It was you."

She laughed aloud with he throaty voice.

"But you promised you wouldn't laugh," Costa protested.

"I laughed because I did not want to cry. How is it that I compare to Helen of Troy?"

"You had foresworn race, religion, taboos, customs, family and country to love me. You will always be my Helen of Troy."

When she pressed her face to his chest, he asked if she was ready for the sequel.

"What sequel?" she questioned.

"There is something more. What I really want to call you is 'The Muslim Madonna,' a fire-breathing Turkish woman."

"Costa, that is a beautiful compliment; I am speechless."

"I mean all of it."

With tears in her eyes, she wrapped herself around him. "Costa, I never stopped longing for you. You are the only man I ever loved."

Costa was touched. He never thought that in a single day he would be so much in love. "I love you, Süheylā, with all that I am."

She sank her fingers into his hair. "After you compared me to Helen of Troy, I was thinking of a fitting name for you."

"And?"

"I think I got it. You are my Hector," she said teasingly.

"How so?"

"Unlike the murderous Achilles, who came for revenge, pillage and plunder, Hector fought for the love of wife, child and country."

Costa was flattered beyond measure but he pretended not to hear. "I continued to work for that restaurant and go to college full time. The owner liked me a lot and he co-signed for a student loan. It took me six years to graduate."

"What a coincidence," Süheylā said. "After my father pulled me out of the University of Istanbul, I was so despondent I spent a year looking for you. I became depressed and suicidal. Finally, I mustered my courage and enrolled at the University of Ankara. It took me five years to graduate."

"You wanted to be a lawyer ever since we met. You did the right thing."

"I saw an opportunity for the women in Turkey and went for it. For a few years, I worked in Ankara as a freelance lawyer. After that I decided to open my own practice. My specialty was international law. Turkey's economy was in the upswing, and there was a great deal of international business activity involving the government. Within five years I opened another office in Istanbul and most recently another one in Izmir; I have done well in the law business."

"I am not surprised."

"As I said, Costa, once you are done with your story, I will reward you," she teased with a loving kiss.

Costa continued, "My main worry was my resident status in USA. With an expired passport, I would be subject to deportation. Finding a legal way to stay in USA became my priority. By sheer luck, the restaurant owner's brother was an immigration lawyer, who guided me to apply for political asylum. This was a huge matter, and I had to have proof that I was a political refugee. That is when I remembered I had stashed away my arrest warrant with some old books in my room. Believe it or not, that document, along with the various newspaper clippings I produced about the persecution of Greeks and Imvrians by Turkey, was enough to convince the US Immigration service to grant me a temporary stay—as long as I continued to go to college."

"So what happened after you graduated?"

"The quickest path to U.S. citizenship was through the U.S. Army. The minute I graduated, I enlisted. With Israel and Middle East in a perpetual turmoil, my fluency in Arabic and Turkish gave me an advantage. I joined the Army's intelligence unit and did mid-level analysis of the Middle East. It was at the height of the Kurdish agitation. USA was looking for ways to solve this problem between the warring factions. My unit was sent to Qatar for hands-on operations. I continued to rise through the ranks. I am now a Lieutenant Colonel in the US Army. Anyway, at the end of three years in the Army I applied for U.S. citizenship."

"So what do you call yourself now?"

"I call myself an American and am proud of it; no other country comes close!"

"I am proud of you, Costa; didn't you miss your home, your country?"

"Of course I did, but the news from home continued to get worse. After thousands of years, the only natives remaining were a few elderly and people in between like my parents. Ankara started to relocate displaced Kurds from southeast Turkey. If you can imagine, the government was giving them monetary incentives to relocate on our homes. The Turkish government was building new villages in the confiscated lands of the natives. To add insult to injury, I received news that as a punishment for my failure to complete my military duties, Turkey had revoked my citizenship. This was published in the government's official newspaper in Ankara. Turkey's avowed policy to purge any remaining giaours from their homes was becoming a reality."

"I know, Costa; I am really sorry."

"During my first ten years in USA I thought of Turkey as a nightmare, nothing less. On a silly whim, the day I became an American citizen, I bundled my expired passport and any Turkish documentation I had and mailed them back to the embassy of Turkey in Washington. That was mean-spirited on my part, but considering what Turkey had done to us Greeks, it was a symbolic retribution. I was an officer of the U.S. Army and an American Citizen. I did not give a damn about Turkey."

"Do you still hate Turkey?"

"When I look back, my life in Turkey was a love-hate relationship. Any time I thought I loved her, she would give me a reason to hate her. I no longer think this way. It was not the fault of the Turkish people. It was misguided leadership."

"So you have forgiven Turkey?"

"I am not at that stage, yet; but, I no longer hate her. Hate consumes too much energy. Now that I am back, I really feel sad for all the culture I missed. I knew that my future was elsewhere, but I never wanted to leave Turkey under those conditions."

"I am sad too, Costa. My heart breaks."

"Just so that you know, Süheylā, during the first several years, I wrote to every university in Turkey inquiring of you. They never answered back. Finally, I found your home address and wrote you several letters; I never received an answer."

Süheylā looked apoplectic, "I never saw them, Costa," she lamented. "In all probability, your letters were intercepted."

Costa gulped for air. All this was suffocating.

"Some years ago, I ran into Colonel Ersoy—now General Ersoy of the Turkish army—at the U.S. Army's Staff and Command College in Ft. Leavenworth, Kansas. When he told me you were married, my world crumbled. My last connection with Turkey, my motherland, was over. I never hated Turkey as much as at that moment. Your marriage did not surprise me, but I still took it hard."

"I wish I'd known, Costa. Did you date anyone?" Süheylā asked, searching his face.

"I dated several nice girls, but had no heart for marriage."

"You did not like even one?"

"I tried; your shadow was always in between."

"You are breaking my heart."

"I kept on looking for someone who could measure up, but there were no girls around like you, Süheylā."

"You are a snob, Costa."

"You have spoiled me, Süheylā."

"So how did you spend your free time?"

"As you well know, I loved sailing. While stationed in the Middle East, as consolation for your loss, I bought a sailboat in Greece and named it 'Süheylā.' "

"You are killing me."

"You said you wanted to hear my story."

"Of course I do."

"Anyway, my sailboat was my escape from reality. I sailed the Greek Isles into the sunset many times hoping that the winds would blow you my way. I kept sniffing the air for your scent, longing to touch you, but you were nowhere near. I could never erase your memory."

"I told you this many times before. You were always a hopeless romantic."

"I admit it. Anyway, at the age of thirty-seven, I met Lale. In so many ways, she resembled you. She fit your style, and she was very bright."

"Where did you meet her?"

"In Kuwait. She had a hospitality degree from Cornell University; she was the assistant G.M. for Sheraton Kuwait."

"Was she a Muslim girl?"

"She was, but just like you, she understood the limitations of religion, although she subscribed to family tradition."

"Which was . . ."

"Kurdish; her parents lived in Kirkuk, Kurdistan."

"Am I detecting a connection to me?" she asked, looking rather sad.

"Without a doubt; as you said, I am a hopeless romantic."

"Did you date very long?"

"We got married within a year and had Nilüfer."

"Who came up with that name?"

"We both loved that Turkish name. In a way, this was a subconscious effort on my part to keep a cultural connection to my ex-homeland."

"I love Lale already."

"Thank you for that; she was your kin."

"It seems to me that Turkey has never left you, Costa!"

"Maybe I never left her either."

Costa looked at Süheylā and saw her watery eyes. "Are you sure you want me to continue with this story?"

She wrapped her arms tightly around him. "Yes I do, even if it leads to the gates of Hell!"

"Just about three months before Nilüfer's second birthday, the Gulf War broke out. I was sent to Kurdistan for reconnaissance and intelligence. I escaped death a couple of times, but some of my men were not as fortunate.

"At the end, a peace treaty was signed between Saddam Hussein and the allies. We thought the war was over, but soon after that, Saddam went after the Kurds.

"The humanitarian crisis that followed in Kurdistan had consequences. Lale's father was a prominent Kurd in Kirkuk; she was worried that Saddam Hussein would go after him. My unit was stationed at Incirlik, Turkey, but I was in the Gulf, assisting the Kuwaitis with military logistics.

"Lale was worried sick about her parents. In her desperation, she flew to Diyarbakir to see my friend, General Ersoy; he was the commander of the Southeast Turkish Army. She knew General Ersoy well through me and claimed that she spoke on my behalf.

"It was the worst mistake of General Ersoy's army career. He authorized a helicopter lift out of Kurdistan just for her family. Foolishly Lale insisted on going along; even worse, she took Nilüfer along. You know the rest. The helicopter was shot down by mistake by Turkish forces across the border. Lale, her parents, a couple of relatives and the pilots were killed. Satellite pictures confirmed the wreck."

"How did you handle all that?"

"I learned about the accident two days later. I nearly lost my mind. I wanted to fly to Kurdistan and retrieve Lale's body and my daughter's, but it was against military procedures. After some lengthy haggling with the Turkish military, they agreed to send a commando unit across the border. They came back with a body missing—Nilüfer's. She had disappeared."

"I am numb, Costa."

"The effort to find Nilüfer was exhausting; it took three years to track her down amidst a labyrinth of refugee camps."

"I had no idea she was your daughter, Costa. I only found that out a week before they located her at the refugee camp."

"Well, not that many people knew, except General Ersoy. How did you find out?"

Süheylā bit her lip. She had made a slip of the tongue. It was obvious she did not want to volunteer this information. "Can I tell you another time, Costa?" she begged.

"Promise," he admonished. Süheylā looked relieved and continued.

"I wanted to get in touch with you right then, but for some reason, I held back. I had no idea why. Probably I was afraid to face you, Costa. When I learned of Nilüfer's abduction, I lost my mind. I planted myself in front of the TV anxiously waiting for news, and when I saw your face after twenty years, my heart exploded for the second time."

"And when was that first time, may I ask?"

She took a deep breath and stared at him with her enormous eyes, "I told you that before. It was the very day when we locked eyes in Troy!"

"*Now* who is the hopeless romantic, Süheylā?"

"I am afraid we both are. Anyway, my living memories of our times together were swirling in my mind day and night. I got very depressed. Hoping for good news, I stayed home, glued to the TV. At first, we all thought that the militants were determined to kill her as a vendetta against America—we were all misled."

"It is probably a good thing you did not track me down then. I would have lost it completely."

"I finally could not stand the agony and called General Ersoy. The general was receptive and friendly, but the only thing he told me was about your wife's tragedy. Basically, he blew me off."

"So General Ersoy blew you off?" Costa wondered aloud, but Süheylā brushed him off again with a smile.

"I hung up the phone, hoping for Nilüfer's safe return. When I heard of her rescue, I cried a river. I wanted to give you a call right then but held back, again. Nilüfer and you needed time."

How did she make contact with the terrorists and pay off the ransom? Nilüfer's abductors were a splinter guerrilla group, and no one knew of them except General Ersoy. Costa knew right there that it was more than a casual conversation she'd with General Ersoy, but he let it go—for now.

"In all my life, Süheylā, I never thought I would be in such a tight spot. I tried to keep the negotiations secret while raising all that cash on my own. Just in time and unexpectedly, somebody stepped forward and paid the ransom. Overnight, Nilüfer's ordeal was over. I am dying to find out who that benevolent individual is."

"I didn't know the ransom was paid by someone anonymously," said Süheylā with feigned indifference. "We thought it was paid by the American military."

"I hope to run into that individual some day," said Costa. "I would love to get down on my knees and offer my thanks."

"I hope you do, Costa. I hope you do."

"I have a few questions for you, Süheylā," said Costa seriously. She lifted her eyebrows.

"How did you ever decide to give up your revolutionary zeal about a free Kurdistan?"

Looking pensive, she collected her thoughts. "As time went on, I began to see the futility of an armed struggle, although I am still hoping for a semi-autonomous Kurdistan. The majority of the Kurds within the Turkish border were beginning to homogenize and the two cultures were becoming indistinguishable. It would have been impossible to separate the two races without mass upheaval. I had no appetite for violence. I began to look at things for the long run. In time, Turkey, like the rest of the world, would change. Eventually the intermingling cultures and language will blur the borders and facilitate racial coexistence."

"Turkey does not feel secure enough to allow such a thing, yet; she has way to go."

She raised her eyebrows. "How did you determine that?"

"I think modern Turkey is still trying to recover from the collapse of the Ottoman Empire after the end of WW1. When the Turks saw their huge empire disintegrate within such a short time, they panicked. Every minority—maybe with some justification—became their enemy. They couldn't trust anyone; they still don't."

"Why did they have to go to such extremes, Costa?"

As, I said, they panicked. The powers-to-be at that time wanted to tear her to shreds; modern Turkey has yet to recover from that shock."

"I never looked at Turkey this way before, Costa."

"Neither did I. Not until I began to study the lessons of the last two major wars and especially the collapse of the Ottoman Empire."

"So you think I did the right thing."

"Of course you did, Süheylā. As I told you many times before, you are ahead of your time."

"Thank you, Costa."

Costa took a deep breath and looked straight into her eyes.

She blinked. "What is it," she asked. "You look so serious."

"How did you reconcile with your father?"

"I didn't. I hated him for what he did to us, but I was not about to do anything to cost him his job and ruin my family's life. He was moving up the ladder. Finally, he was getting along with my mom. He allowed her to travel to Austria frequently, and she was very happy. She even began to paint more and hold exhibitions. As you may recall, she loved to design clothes. Somehow, she came up with the idea to open an Islamic clothing boutique that featured her own designs. It is now a chain all over Turkey."

"If her clothes were as good as the Islamic head covers she designed for you, no wonder."

"Thank you, Costa. Unfortunately, she did not live long to enjoy her success."

"What happened to the clothing chain?"

"We sold it years ago. My sister and I did not want to deal with it and neither did my father."

"Is he still very devout?"

"I call him a righteous Muslim. His passions are Islamic Reform, secularism and women's causes."

"That says a lot about your father. He sounds like an intellectual."

"I agree, but still I cannot find a way to approach him."

Costa took a sip from his drink. "You must, Süheylā. Don't let it consume so much of your energy." He ran his palm up to her cheek and tried to say something, but stopped short.

"Come on, Costa, what is your second question?"

"How did you decide to get married?" he asked slowly.

She was expecting it. "He was the best substitute for you, Costa. He looked and thought like you."

"That's all?"

"I married him because I was lonely. It was a mistake. I knew it right from the beginning."

"How long have you been a widow?"

"Eight years. His death was a blessing. He was paralyzed from his waist down and had partial use of his right hand. I had left him to go Izmir for a seminar. His nurse found him dead; he'd shot himself."

"What a tragedy; I am really sorry."

"Even if he'd stayed healthy, I would have divorced him. Your ghost kept following me all my life, Costa. Whenever he made love to me, I fantasized it was you. During one occasion, I got angry and called your name. He only looked at me with a pained expression, and said, 'I know all about Costa, Süheylā. I wish I could be him. I am sorry.'

"I cried for days. I had just realized that this man really loved me, and became even sadder. I woke up every morning hoping to see you pop around my bedroom door while on the other hand trying to co-exist with my husband.

"Just as we started to build a relationship, he got wounded; that was the end of that. Between you and him, I became a grieving widow, twice. I had lost my first prize and now I had lost my second. I could not stand living with any with anybody else." Then she started to cry, so Costa pulled her into his arms.

"I don't usually cry, Costa. The last few days have opened my flood gates."

He wiped away her tears with his hands. They finished their drinks and dressed up. "I will have to leave you for now," apologized Costa. "Nilüfer is waiting."

"When can I meet her?" she asked, pulling him close.

"Tomorrow; would that be all right?"

"I cannot wait."

He did not want to leave Süheylā alone, but his daughter was waiting.

Chapter 48: Old Icons Never Fade

The minute Costa arrived at the hotel, the concierge informed him that there was a man in the coffee shop waiting to see him.

"Did he give you his name?"

"No, Colonel, he didn't."

"How does he look?"

"He is dressed in a black suit. I think he might be a priest."

"Thank you." When Costa entered the coffee shop, his friend Bishop Nicolas spotted him and waved.

"Sorry for the surprise visit, Costa. I tried calling you earlier, but your daughter's governess told me you were out; I took a chance."

"Have you been waiting long?"

"Less than half an hour."

"Okay. What are you up to?"

"I have some interesting news—I am wondering whether you can shed any light."

"What kind of news?"

"Please bear with me. A couple of days ago I received this box. It was tightly packaged and labeled 'PRIVATE.' I looked for a sender's address, but there was none. Curious, I opened it. Meticulously wrapped with old newspapers were six icons. One look at them and my jaw dropped. As I have told you, I am an expert of precious icons and other artifacts like that; I knew immediately that these icons were very old. We are having them evaluated as we speak; we think they are very valuable."

"I am happy to hear all that, but what do these icons have to do with me?"

Bishop Nicolas cleared his throat. "I took my time and examined the contents for any trace of the sender."

"And?"

"I scanned the back of the icons carefully, Costa. Unfortunately, the names of the owner or owners were filed away by either sandpaper or some other erasure technique, almost invisible to the naked eye. I used my high-powered magnifier and traced some partial names."

Costa's mind began to do a fast-forward. He was beginning to see what was coming next. "And whose names were they, Nicolas?"

The Bishop looked Costa in the eye. "The first name has only the initial 'S' followed by the letters 'Gulp'. The second name is more visible. 'C. Rigas.' "

Süheylā must have marked these icons, Costa surmised. He pretended to be surprised. "Nicolas, do you really think that these initials are mine?"

"That is what I think, my friend."

Costa laughed. "You have a great imagination, Nicolas. There must be a dozen individuals with those initials."

"I know that, but hardly anybody's name can be associated with a name like S. Gulp."

"What are you implying?"

"Who in the world but you had an association with a Turkish girl, Süheylā Gülpinar?"

"And how did you know about Süheylā Gülpinar?"

"Your mother told me when I visited her before you brought her to the States for treatment."

"Okay, Nicolas, that might be true, but these icons have nothing to do with me."

"Can you swear?"

"I have only sworn to uphold the Constitution of the United States of America."

"Okay, Costa, I am sorry to have bothered you."

The bishop pretended to rise from his chair. "Oh, I forgot. Remember the story I told you about the lady who sold me that cross?"

"Yes, what of it?"

"As I have told you, that lady was so clever she had taped our conversation."

"And?"

"The next time she visited me, I was prepared. I know what I'm about to tell you was unethical, but I did it anyway!"

"What did you do?"

The bishop reached into his pocket, took out a small tape recorder, and placed it on the table. "I taped her," he said, smiling. He turned on the tape recorder. The two men listened for a minute or so.

"The voice sounds so very garbled," remarked Costa.

Nicolas exhaled in frustration. "I thought I had measured up to that lady," he repeated, "but she was too clever."

"How so?"

"She knew I was recording her. Probably, she was carrying an electronic voice scrambler in her pocket." Finally, Bishop Nicolas shut it off.

"Do you recognize that voice?" he asked Costa, hoping for an answer.

Costa was prepared. "I have no idea, Nicolas. How can anyone recognize such a garbled voice?"

"I am sorry I bothered you. You say you are not a Christian; frankly, you are better than that, I know. You are the truest patriot I have ever met. I will be praying for you."

Bishop Nicolas stood up to shake Costa's hand. "One more question, Costa. Did you find her?"

Costa smiled, "yes, Nicolas, I found her."

"I am really happy for you. Good luck, my friend. God be with you."

Chapter 49: Judge Gülpinar

It was a beautiful Sunday morning and Khadife was getting Nilüfer ready for the day when the phone rang. It was Metin, the concierge. "Colonel, there is a gentleman in the lobby who wants to see you."

Costa was intrigued. *Who could that be?* "Ask him to wait a few minutes." He took the elevator down and asked Metin where the man was.

"Over by that couch, Colonel," he pointed.

The man was sitting facing out. All he could see was a man's full head of gray hair. As he made his way to the couch, the man spotted him and rose to his feet. Costa racked his memory.

"Excuse the intrusion, Colonel," the man apologized.

"And you are?"

The man gulped for air. "I am Judge Mehmet Gülpinar," he said in a low tone. "I am Süheylā's father."

Costa felt his jaw drop; he could not believe it. This judge was the main reason that he'd had to endure the loss of Süheylā; he would gladly wring his neck. "What brings you here, Judge Gülpinar?" asked Costa halfway-politely.

Judge Gülpinar cleared his throat. "Is there a quiet place we can talk, Colonel Rigas?"

Costa was surprised even more. *What did he want?* He asked Metin if there was a private room available nearby.

"Yes, Colonel; you can have that conference area behind the front desk."

"Thank you, Metin."

Costa let the judge in and closed the door behind him. He pointed to a seat. The judge sat, looking somewhat uncomfortable.

"Your presence here is a big surprise, Judge Gülpinar," said Costa, trying to guess the judge's intentions.

"I can imagine, Colonel Rigas." The judge looked at Costa kindly. "I am really happy you have found your daughter."

"Thank you, Judge" replied Costa curtly; "but seriously, you are not here to talk to me about my daughter, are you?"

"You are right, Colonel. At least that is not the main reason." The judge cleared his throat as if dreading what he was about to say. "I am here to apologize for all the hardships I have caused you."

Costa could not believe his ears. This was impossible. No Turk ever apologized for anything. "You mean about engineering that phony warrant for my arrest?"

"Yes, but there is more."

Costa had an idea what was coming. "What is more?" he asked.

"For messing up your and Süheylā's lives. I sincerely beg your forgiveness."

Costa could not help but notice a slight quiver in the judge's voice. It takes courage to do a thing like that. It takes a great human being to admit guilt. With all his dignity, his power, his prestige, this man was the bravest Turk he had ever met. Suddenly, if there was any remaining hatred toward Judge Gülpinar, and even Turkey, it flew right off his chest.

"It takes great courage to say something like that, Judge Gülpinar. You did what you thought was best for Süheylā and your family—I wish you hadn't. You are a noble man. I accept your apology."

Judge Gülpinar looked like he was in shock. He rose to his feet, took Costa's hand, and shook it gracefully. "You are a man of honor, Colonel. The U.S. Army is lucky to have you. Turkey is poorer for having evicted you."

"We cannot turn back the clock, can we, Judge?"

"No, we cannot, but we can correct things as we go forward. What makes a country great is what makes it human; we are trying."

Costa felt pensive and even sympathetic. "Do you want some coffee, Judge," he asked, trying to make him feel more at ease. The humane capacity of this Turk was unlike anyone he ever imagined.

"If you have the time, Colonel," replied the judge humbly.

Costa opened the door and called out to the concierge, "Metin, two coffees and water please."

"My daughter Süheylā has not spoken to me since the day I removed her from our apartment by force," said the judge dejectedly, as if he did not even hear Costa calling Metin. "Why?" asked Costa feigning surprise. "I don't understand."

The judge made a pained grimace. "She has forgotten me, Colonel Rigas, purposely, I think. She didn't even invite me to her wedding."

"That is bizarre, Judge. I am sorry."

"Thank you, Colonel Rigas. Süheylā is a very successful lawyer, but she has treated me very unkindly."

Costa remained pensive for a few minutes. Although he understood Süheylā's frustration with her father, he did not think she would go to this extent.

"Time bends people's hearts, Judge. Maybe Süheylā needs more time."

"We all need more time, Colonel Rigas, but I have not much of it left. Even my daughter Gülēngül treats me like a leper. I follow her through her television appearances and listen to her music at my home. Occasionally, I talk to her husband Errol. That's about it."

"Loneliness is a killer, Judge. You do not deserve that."

"Well, my daughters must think otherwise. I hardly see them since my wife passed away. I retired a few years ago, but my life has been hell. I cannot stand it without my daughters."

"I sympathize with that, Judge," said Costa sincerely."

The judge looked like he was ready to cry; Costa had to change the subject.

"Where do you live, Judge?"

"I live in Ankara. I would love to live in Istanbul, closer to my daughters, but they are constantly on the go with their careers. They have no time for me."

Metin knocked on the door and brought in their coffee. The judge took a sip and looked at Costa with humility.

"How are things going between you and Nilüfer?"

"Really well, Judge; we both need time to adjust."

The judge looked at Costa with much kindness. "Thank you for your hospitality, Colonel; may I ask you one more question before I go?"

"Okay, Judge Gülpinar, ask it."

The judge gulped for air. "Do you have any plans to see my Süheylā?"

Costa did not expect this question; like the judge, he too gulped for air. "I have already seen her, Judge. I saw her yesterday."

Costa thought that the judge was going to faint, but he collected himself.

"Thank you, Colonel." He shook Costa's hand and headed for the door. Just before he exited, he turned around. "Turkey is moving forward, Colonel; I am optimistic."

"I know, Judge. Time heals most things."

"Good luck to you, Colonel Rigas. Good luck with your daughter Nilüfer, too. I hope to see you again soon."

"Me too, Judge Gülpinar."

Chapter 50: Time Marches On

Costa escorted the judge to the hotel's exit and took the elevator up to his suite. Kadife had already prepared Nilüfer for the day.

"Thank you, Kadife. Nilüfer and I will be visiting friends today. Take the rest of the day off."

"But, Colonel Rigas!"

"I will see you tomorrow—whenever you get here."

"Bye," said Nilüfer to Kadife, waving.

Costa gave his daughter a kiss. "You are learning fast, my little one!" He dialed Hilton's Presidential Suite. Gülēngül answered. "Good morning, Gülēngül."

"Oh Costa, Costa," she exclaimed. "How are you?"

"Any day with Nilüfer is a new experience," he laughed; she is wearing me out."

"How fun can that be? I'll give you Süheylā."

He waited for a few seconds.

"I missed you last night, Costa," whirled Süheylā with her Melina Merkouri impersonation. The temptress was always at the ready. "I am sorry, but Nilüfer was a better offer," Costa joked.

"How can I compete with Nilüfer. What did you do?"

"We did some shopping and had a leisurely evening. How was your night?"

"I did some shopping, too, but that is all. I ordered in last night. I did not feel like joining my sister at her concert; frankly, nothing could top yesterday. "

Costa paused for a few seconds. "Are you ready to meet Nilüfer?"

"We are sitting around here dying to see her. Do you want to meet us for brunch at the main restaurant?"

Costa thought for a few seconds. "Why don't we meet up in your suite? We might need some privacy."

"Okay, Costa; "what do you have up your sleeve?"" She never missed anything.

"I'll tell you when I see you. Nilüfer and I will be over there in ten minutes."

The three of them were at the door waiting. When Süheylā saw Nilüfer holding Costa by the hand, she nearly fainted from joy. Gülēngül and Errol were ecstatic. Süheylā could not resist giving Nilüfer a quick peck on her cheek.

They sat around the huge coffee table. Nilüfer sat on Costa's lap and Süheylā next to Costa. Süheylā could not keep her eyes off Nilüfer—and vice versa. Nilüfer was fascinated with Süheylā's blonde hair. She suddenly leaned away from Costa and pulled on Süheylā's hair playfully.

Süheylā let out a laugh, Errol clapped and so did Gülēngül. Süheylā reached out and took Nilüfer by the hand. "Come with me, Nilüfer," she beckoned in Kurdish. "I have something for you."

Nilüfer looked at her dad, unsure what to do. "Go on, Nilüfer," urged Costa. "It is okay."

She led Nilüfer into her bedroom. They returned with Nilüfer holding a gift box. She walked to her dad and deposited it on his lap.

"Aren't you going to open it?" Costa asked; she scrunched her face.

"Here, Nilüfer," offered Süheylā, "I will help you." Süheylā lifted the bow and assisted Nilüfer in opening the box. When Nilüfer finally pulled the tissue cover away, her eyes got so big she clapped her hands and jumped up and down from joy. It was her cute habit to clap and jump any time she was happy about something. In the box was a Raggedy Anne doll. Nilüfer lifted the doll and hugged her with gusto.

"Is that what you went shopping for, Süheylā?"

"That was it, Costa. It was the first gift I ever bought for a little girl. It was so much fun." Just as she said it,

Nilüfer opened her arms and gave Süheylā a big hug, still holding her doll. Süheylā lifted her in her lap, beaming from ear to ear.

The hotel's room service brought brunch. The conversation could not have been more jovial. They took their coffee on the veranda. Fascinated with all the marine activity of Bosporus, Nilüfer was darting around, keeping Süheylā occupied. With Süheylā speaking to Nilüfer in Kurdish, it was leading to a fast friendship.

After some roundabout discussion, the phone rang. Errol picked it up; it was Mrs. Sariyer.

"Nothing serious I hope?" asked Gülēngül after Errol hung up the phone.

"Nothing," replied Errol, patting Gülēngül on the cheek.

"You can tell me, my darling!"

"I told my mother that we would be meeting Nilüfer today, and she was eager to know how it is going. Since my father passed away, she is looking for anything that will brighten her day."

Costa, who was looking for an opportunity to say something about fatherhood, knew this was the time. "Speaking of fathers, Gülēngül, how is your father doing?"

"Errol talks to him occasionally; I am very busy. When I branched into pop, I do not think he approved of my career move. Now that I have veered back into traditional Turkish music, he is more receptive. You never know about my father. He is a difficult man."

Costa looked toward Süheylā. "I saw him only three times during the last twenty years." That was on my college graduation, my mother's funeral, and Gülēngül's wedding. I did not invite him to my wedding."

Costa cleared his throat. "Isn't that a bit harsh?"

"It is what it is. I wished things had been better, but as time rolled on, I had no stomach to seek him out."

"I have something to tell you," said Costa seriously. "I had a very important visitor this morning."

"Who?" asked the sisters.

"Your father," added Costa with gravity.

It may as well have been a bomb. Gülēngül choked and Süheylā nearly went into shock; Errol shook his head in disbelief. Before Costa could add anything, Süheylā railed.

"My father has a lot of nerve. I had never expected this," she quivered, looking angry. On the other hand, Gülēngül was animated.

"What did he tell you, Costa?"

"In due time; I think you are being a little too hard on your father."

The sisters looked at one another. "So what do you suggest?" asked Gülēngül.

"Call him!" advised Costa seriously

Where is he staying, Costa?"

"Gülēngül, he didn't tell me where, and I did not ask."

"I think I know where," said Errol. "At the Çiragan Palace; it is his favorite hotel."

"The only thing I can tell you, Süheylā, is that he apologized for having ruined our lives—yours and mine."

This hit Süheylā hard. She started to cry, as did Gülēngül. The two sisters looked bewildered.

Costa excused himself to take Nilüfer for some air. This was a family matter and he did not want to meddle. After half an hour or so Süheylā came down and found them.

"Gülēngül and Errol would like to take Nilüfer for a couple of hours. Will you let them?"

"I will have to ask her," he said jokingly. He pulled Nilüfer by the hand and the three of them walked back to the suite.

"Nilüfer, Gülēngül and Errol would like to take you for a walk; do you want to go?" asked Süheylā, in Kurdish.

Nilüfer jumped with joy and clapped her hands again. Gülēngül and Errol were delighted. They took Nilüfer by the hand, and she waved goodbye.

Süheylā was still in shock about her father. When Costa told her that he was miserable without his daughters, she became teary-eyed and pensive.

"Many times over the past several years I have searched for a way to break this impasse, but I could not think of one," she murmured. "Maybe I didn't want to."

"That is a long time, Süheylā."

"Time marches on, Costa, and leaves all of us in the dust." She looked at him with loving eyes. "I want to take you to a place. It is not far."

"What about Nilüfer?"

"She is with Gülēngül and Errol. We will leave them a note."

"Okay. Let's go."

Chapter 51: The Tigress of Bosporus

They freshened up and took the elevator down to the lobby. The concierge asked if they needed a taxi, but Süheylā waved him off and slipped under Costa's arm.

She led him down Hilton's driveway all the way to Istiklal Caddesi[88] and took a left. Costa searched her face for any clues, but she gave him none. After two blocks, they turned into a large courtyard that separated two very impressive apartment dwellings about ten stories high. She guided him to the one on the right. The doorkeeper recognized her immediately.

Costa followed her straight to the elevator. She pushed the top button, number ten. When the elevator stopped, she directed him to the only door on the floor. She took a key from her purse, opened the heavy door and flipped the light switch.

"Excuse me, love." She walked through the huge salon and pulled the heavy drapes open, one by one. In front of his eyes popped the entire Bosporus; the view was indescribable. A quick glance to the sidewalls left him gasping. At the center of each wall was a large replica of Eugene Delacroix's masterpieces. To the right was 'La Liberté, Leading the People,' and to the left, 'Jacob wrestling with the Angel[89].' He was transfixed; Eugene Delacroix was his favorite painter.

She woke him up from his dream. "Do you want a drink, love?"

"Yes, thank you."

---

88. Independence Avenue.

89. 'Lute de Jacob avec L'Ange". Another masterpiece by Eugene Delacroix.

"Please sit." She returned with two giant glasses of gin and tonic. "Welcome to my flat, Costa; here's to life."

"To you, Süheylā; you overwhelm me."

"And to you, love. I still can't believe we are together."

"Neither can I. This is an incredible place—the Delacroixs are amazing."

"I have you to thank for that. You introduced me to him."

" 'La Liberté,' is you, Süheylā."

"Thank you, Costa. When I first saw this flat, I bought it on the spot, solely for the view and those two walls. I knew what I wanted to do with them. I flew to Paris to visit the museum of Delacroix. Since the actual pieces are priceless, I did the next-best thing. I commissioned one of their artists to paint these replicas in proportionality to the dimensions of these walls. This salon is my escape. This is where I spend most of my free time."

"Your taste was always impeccable," he said, trying to read her trademark foxy smirk.

"Thank you. Would you like another drink?"

"Yes, please."

She went back to the bar while Costa occupied himself gazing at the breathtaking view. She came back and sat by his side, giving him a quick kiss. "Here is your drink, love."

He caught her devilish smirk. "This place is very seductive," Costa continued. *She was up to something.*

"I remember that word 'seduction' from so many years ago."

"I remember, too; especially when you told me that we can seduce each other."

"We were so innocent, so naïve. Where did all the time go?" she sighed and stood up.

"Excuse me, Costa. I will be back in a few minutes. A couple of maintenance people will be knocking on the door. They are taking this oriental rug for cleaning; please let them in. She gave him a wink and disappeared behind a door at the far end of the flat.

Costa sipped his drink, still marveling at the apartment. Her taste was exquisite. Within a few minutes, he heard the knock at the door and opened it. Three men dressed in uniforms walked in, moved the pedestal table by the window, rolled up the oriental rug and dusted off the parquet floor. They lifted the heavy rug on their shoulders and left.

Just about at that time Gülēngül's mellifluous voice filled the penthouse. The surround sound was like a chorus of a thousand angels singing in Heaven. It was the waltz tune, "I heard that you forgot the color of my eyes[90]," one of their favorite Ottoman classics of the olden days.

When he saw her walk into the middle of the penthouse, his heart started to flutter. Washed in the light of Bosporus was Süheylā, dressed in the most sensual harem's outfit; she was covered in translucent silk—the colors of pink, white, and red. Boring through the white veil her fiery eyes sparkled in a sea of blue. Feeling hypnotized, he rose from his chair and took a few steps toward her.

She looked at him with her enormous eyes, and offered him her hand. "Costa, please, I want to waltz. This is our song; you remember?"

"How can I forget?" Twenty years ago, they'd promised to marry each other and spend their honeymoon waltzing in the halls of Vienna.

He led her by the pedestal table, pulled out a rose from the vase, and tucked it behind her ear. She settled into his arms, and they began to whirl around the huge floor. Finally, when the song ended, Costa led her to the

---

90. Duydum ki unutmuşsun gözlerimin rengini.

window and lifted her veil. They kissed as if it were their first time.

"Come, love," she whispered, taking his hand.

She led him into her bedroom. What he saw next made his heart leap out of his chest. Covering the wall were two pieces of artwork of immense size. Off to the right, in chiaroscuro, was a huge nude of Süheylā, standing. Her face and head—except for her eyes—were covered in a tigreeseque silk scarf, which fell partially over her breasts. With her left arm partially covering her love-nest, her profile was turned to the right, while her right arm was extended in the sign of beckoning at a sketch of a young man in his early twenties. Costa knew immediately. It was the same sketch Süheylā had drawn of him in her studio some twenty-one years ago. In an instant the memories of those moments set his loins on fire.

He lifted her in his arms and placed her gently on the huge bed. Her shimmering eyes sparkled behind her veil like a tigress on the prowl.

"Madam, I am going to punish you for setting me up." He pulled off her veil slowly along with her golden head bandana, spilling her hair over the silk pillow.

She pulled him tightly, whispering, "grab hold of me, love; please make love to me." In her delirium, she grabbed his hair, locked her lips onto his, whispering softly, "my dear Costa, oh honey."

Her long legs wrapped around him felt like the sweetest vice while her tight walls were lifting him up to Heaven. Wrapped in each other's arms they lost themselves. Just before they exploded, they screamed their love for one another in breathless delirium. Exhausted and spent, Costa collapsed on Süheylā, swallowing her breath in total contentment.

"You really took me up into the white clouds as if it were yesterday," she whispered, sticking her tongue in his ear.

"If you are not careful, there might be more of these."

"You promise?"

"With all my heart," he assured her.

She smiled, and bit him on the lip.

"Ouch, he protested, feeling his lip. "I am glad you did not bleed me this time."

She giggled. "Do you still remember that?"

"How can I forget?"

"Don't worry; in due time we will have to renew our blood kinship."

That memory flushed on Costa's mind as though it were yesterday. Some twenty years ago, they fused together in actual blood. He looked up at her portrait again.

"This portrait of yours is a sensual piece of artwork. Whoever drew it is a great artist."

"He is the same one I commissioned for the other two pieces. Partly I posed and in part we used the picture you took in your apartment, after we came from visiting that church; do you remember that day?"

"How can I forget, Süheylā? It articulates who you really are."

"Flattery will always get you . . . me!"

Costa looked at her for a few moments, trying to find the right words. Süheylā stared back at him. "Do you want to ask me something, Costa?"

"How did you come about these art pieces, Süheylā?"

"I bought this apartment right after my husband died. After that, I did not want to have another man in my life. I could not forget the past, and my past was you love."

"You are an indescribable woman!"

"You keep talking like that and I am going to bite you, harder this time," she threatened teasingly

"I always loved your bites, Süheylā. You bit me when we made love and you bit me when you kissed me."

"And you, love, bit my nipples; I loved it!"

"I could not help it—erect and so tall—they reminded me of the Minarets of Santa Sophia."

Süheylā let out that cascading, husky laugh of hers, cupped Costa's face, and kissed him.

"You are the complete package, Süheylā."

"Oh, stop it! You are making me all wet again," she teased tempestuously.

He gave her a kiss and looked at his sketch. "What about him; who is he?"

She stuck her tongue out.

"Did I really look that good?"

"You look even better now, Costa!"

"You are charming me all the way to Heaven."

"I have a confession, Costa," she said, squeezing her lips.

He raised his eyebrows. *Oh no, what now?*

"Every time I gaze into your sketch, I get wet and make love to myself."

He wrapped her in his arms with all the love he could muster.

"When you came into the salon wearing the harem's outfit, the memory of our first waltz by the beach shook me to pieces. I never wanted that evening to end."

"You are such a romantic, Costa; I fell in love with you, way before then!"

"I never imagined life without you, Süheylā."

She took a deep sigh and trawled her palm on his cheek. "Life is an enigma, Costa. Having you in my bed again is the surprise of my life."

"Mine too, love; can I go get us a towel?"

"That sounds familiar; I still remember our first time."

He came back, sponged her off, and lay beside her.

"Thank you, Costa; I'll get us a couple of robes."

They walked out onto the small veranda. Süheylā took a seat next to him and straddled her leg over his thighs. He never remembered sitting anywhere without Süheylā touching some part of his body, and he always loved it.

She had a magnetic ability to make him feel much loved. It was one of her endearing traits.

She bore her eyes into his face for a few seconds, looking uncertain. "Let's talk about Nilüfer, Costa; what are your plans for her?"

Her question did not surprise him. It was her anxiety that tore into his heart. "My priority is to settle her into a permanent home," he replied, pulling her close.

"I fell in love with Nilüfer before I even saw her. When I heard of her rescue, I was ecstatic, but when I found out she was your daughter, I nearly lost my mind. Who would have thought?"

"Who would have thought?" echoed Costa, squeezing her tighter.

"How I wish she could have been mine, Costa," she muttered, looking into his eyes achingly. "She could have been mine," she repeated many times over as if she were in a trance. Suddenly, she sank her fingernails into his shoulders and growled. "She could have been mine, Costa; she could have been ours," she bellowed. "Why did it have to be this way?"

Costa cupped her cheeks and looked into her teary eyes, "She can be, Süheylā, she can be."

She tensed. "What are you saying?"

He raced into her bedroom, searched his pocket, found the tiny box, ran back and took her in his arms.

"Before I you give this, Süheylā, I want to tell you that I would be the happiest man if I died in your arms."

She gave him a hollow look and with trembling hands took the box. When she pulled out the diamond ring, her mouth opened wide.

Costa sunk to his knees, "Süheylā, will you marry me?"

She flew into his arms, "yes, yes, yes, love, today, tomorrow any time. After twenty years, time no longer matters," she stammered as Costa slipped the ring onto her finger.

He buried his nose in her hair and inhaled deeply. Her smell of basil, mint and Ottoman roses was the only narcotic he'd ever craved.

"Oh love, you have cured my aching heart, filled my arms, and most of all, you have seeded my empty womb by giving me Nilüfer." Within seconds her contemplative mood began to change. She now looked like the menacing seductress of old. She loosened his robe, sank her fingernails into his ribs, and dragged him back into her bedroom. The Tigress of Bosporus was famished, and her prey did not stand a chance.

Chapter 52: Miracles Do Happen

They lay in bed staring at the ceiling.

"Costa?" she asked playing with the ring in her finger.

"Yes, love."

"This ring looks like nothing I have seen around. I can't believe that have bought it last night!"

"I didn't," replied Costa, giving her a kiss.

She looked surprised. "When did you get it then?"

He looked pensive for a few seconds, "I bought it twenty years ago, Süheylā. This was the ring I had planned to propose to you before I left for Congo."

She let out this piercing cry as if someone just stubbed her though the heart. "I am sorry, I am sorry," she kept on repeating nonstop.

Costa shook her gently. "Let us not blame ourselves Süheylā. We are together now; I love you." Gradually, his soothing voice calmed her down.

"I will wear this ring to my grave Costa," she said and squeezed tighter. Slowly, she regained her old self again. "I have an idea," she said, kissing him passionately.

"Just one?"

"For now," she lilted, as if to reserve the rest for later.

"What is it?"

"I'd like to bring the same artist from Paris to overlay my sketch with your full portrait."

"Wow!"

"That is not all," she replied, looking serious.

"You are an endless surprise, Süheylā. I am not even going to try!"

"As you noticed, I have purposely left a large space between those two pieces of artwork. I was hoping to put the portrait of my child there some day. I now have one; it is Nilüfer."

He gave her a kiss. "You are an amazing woman."

"It is settled then. Nilüfer will be between our two portraits; I love it." She started to tear up again.

Costa smothered her with kisses. "Süheylā, your imagination is infinite, but your heart is deeper than the ocean. Nilüfer and I are the luckiest people on earth. I will love you forever."

"Thank you, love. I have one more thing to ask you."

"You mean tell me," he teased.

She grinned. "I would like to let my sister in on our secret."

He pretended to be surprised. "That soon?"

"She is my best friend; I never surprise her."

"Why don't we make an announcement over dinner tonight?"

"That sounds perfect."

"It will have to be a private dinner—Gülēngül, Errol and the three of us."

"I love it."

"About the private dinner?"

"About the three of us . . . you, me and Nilüfer. I cannot wait to have Nilüfer in my life, Costa. Who says miracles don't happen?"

"Shall we say seven-thirty?"

She beamed, "I wish it were now."

"Nilüfer will be looking for us; can we dress up, love?"

She glinted. "I thought we could make love one more time to celebrate our engagement, fiancé."

"Fiancé? That is what you called me the night we went to Melek Theater to see Fatma Girik."

"And you remember that?"

"How can I forget? We rushed out in in the middle of the film to go to my apartment because you wanted to kiss!"

"That's all?"

"Well, there was more! You were insatiable then. You are a tigress now!" Costa said teasingly.

"For you; do you remember our wild night in your apartment after we came back from Kilyos?"

"Not really," he smiled slyly.

"Liar; you don't want to admit it, do you?"

He pretended ignorance. "Admit what?"

"For deflowering an innocent Muslim girl like me!" she stated in protest.

"Are you still mad about that?"

"Of course I am; you have deprived me of your intimacy for twenty years!"

"I am sorry, love. You know I am."

"Yes I know, but just for that I am going to punish you many times over," she cackled, letting her voice echo around the bedroom.

"I can hardly wait to start our lives together, Süheylā."

She pursed her lips and trailed her palm across his chest. "Let's take a shower, love; you can wash my hair."

There she goes again. "We don't have time for another game, Süheylā. Nilüfer is waiting, and don't forget my appointment with General Ersoy."

"I forgot about that. In that case, use the other shower in the next room. I will be out shortly."

Costa gathered his clothes slowly and his wits even more so. He never felt happier. He found the other bathroom, took a quick shower, and dressed up to wait for Süheylā. She was out in less than fifteen minutes. She never needed any makeup.

"Here I am, love, let's go."

"Before we go, you need to take off that ring until tonight."

She glowered. "Never; I will get a pair of gloves." She hurried into her bedroom and swaggered back, with white gloves on her hands. "Are you happy now?"

"Yes, thank you." Costa thought that now might be the right time to ask that question.

"Süheylā, do you know Bishop Nicolas?"

She did not even flinch. "I have never heard of him."

369

He tried to say something, but she sealed his mouth with her tongue. He gave up all further questions.

They hurried down the elevator and out into the street. The Hilton was around the corner. Standing in the middle of the lobby was Errol and Gülēngül holding Nilüfer.

"Where have you been?" lilted Gülēngül, staring at her sister's hands.

"We have visited my flat, little sister," winked Süheylā innocently. She reached for Nilüfer, who jumped into her arms immediately.

"I missed you, my baby," she whispered, cuddling the little girl lovingly. Nilüfer wrapped her arms around her neck and squeezed tightly.

Süheylā looked at Costa and winked. Holding that child in her arms, she looked thrilled.

"Costa, can I keep Nilüfer with me for the afternoon, please?"

She was already claiming Nilüfer as her own.

Costa looked at his daughter, who was not about to leave Süheylā's arms. "Would you like to stay with Süheylā for the afternoon?"

"Evet Baba[91]," she replied, clapping her hands. Süheylā beamed from ear to ear.

"I guess so, but she will need a nap."

"I will take care of that, Costa." She leaned close to his ear. "You are moving into my flat tonight. I want you in my bed. Nilüfer will have the room next to us. I could not stand a single night away from the two of you."

"Okay, Süheylā, I have to go now."

She fixed her eyes on his face. "You are a free man until seven-thirty tonight. After that, you shall be my prisoner," she whispered possessively.

"I have always been, Süheylā."

---

91. "Yes, Daddy."

Gülēngül and Errol were trying to follow with heightened interest.

Nilüfer staying with Süheylā for the afternoon? What is going on?

Süheylā looked at her sister and Errol, "Costa and I would like to invite you to a private dinner at his hotel tonight."

Gülēngül opened her mouth to say something, but Errol was quicker. "Gladly," he replied. He too, like Gülēngül, was looking at Süheylā's gloved hands with curiosity.

Before Errol could ask a question, Süheylā pulled him off to the side. After speaking to him for a few moments, she reached into her pocketbook, pulled out a note, and handed it to him.

Errol looked at Gülēngül. "Excuse me, love, I will have to leave you for a while." He gave her a kiss and waved to Costa. "I will see you this evening."

Costa stared at Süheylā, but she gave him that evasive languid, "mind-your-own-business-love" look.

"Thank you for letting me keep Nilüfer, Costa," she grinned, giving him a quick kiss. "Now go, before you are late for your appointment with the general."

Chapter 53: General Ersoy

General Ersoy, accompanied by a couple of his staff members, was in the lobby when Costa walked in.

"I am sorry, General Ersoy. I hope you did not wait too long."

"We just got here, Colonel Rigas. Is there a private room where we can talk?"

"Yes, it has been arranged."

Metin, the concierge, ushered them into the private conference room. General Ersoy and his attendants took their seats. Water and coffee was already set. A server brought a tray of sandwiches, placed them on the conference table, and left the room.

"Where are we, Colonel Rigas? I hear you and your daughter are doing well."

"Yes, thank you for your help, General Ersoy. I will always be grateful."

"Let's discuss our mutual subject first and we can talk about Nilüfer later, shall we?"

"Yes, absolutely."

"Colonels Akdeniz and Karaduman will serve as my adjutants. Since this is an exploratory meeting, no notes will be taken; you agree?"

"Yes, of course."

The discussion was on military intelligence in the Middle East, primarily in the field of logistics. The meeting lasted more than two hours, at the end of which General Ersoy dismissed his aides and asked them to wait in the lobby.

Finally, General Ersoy cracked a smile. "Do you mind if I put my feet up, Colonel Rigas? I have been on the go for the last forty-eight hours."

Costa smiled. "As a general you can do anything you want!"

"Thank you, Colonel Rigas; how are things going with Nilüfer?"

"Right now she is with Süheylā."

"So you found each other; I am delighted to hear it!"

"I think you had something to do with that."

The General pretended slight ignorance "Just a minor role, Colonel Rigas."

"I don't think I will ever be able to thank you enough. I owe you my daughter's life."

"We did what we had to do. You would have done the same."

"What you did General Ersoy was above and beyond the call of duty. You are a true humanitarian."

General Ersoy made an abstract motion. "When your wife died in that helicopter disaster, it was my worst nightmare. Not knowing what happened to your child for those three years became my obsession."

"I know, General Ersoy. As I said, I will always be grateful."

"Nilüfer's abduction was a horror, Colonel. The news media, which never blames the Turkish military for anything, this time found a target—and that was me. Amidst all that, I was surprised when I got a call from Süheylā claiming that she could raise the cash. I told her that it would be helpful, but I had no way of influencing established policy of the Turkish government 'not to negotiate with terrorists.' She became pushy, even aggressive."

" 'What about my father?' she asked.

" 'I don't think your father can pull any more weight, Süheylā. He is retired now,' I replied.

" 'You are my only hope then, General Ersoy' she stated in protest, 'If not my father and not you, who else?' "

"I had no idea, General Ersoy," said Costa, feeling surprised.

"There is more to this, Colonel Rigas. I picked up the phone and dialed Judge Mehmet Gülpinar. I had not talked to him in years. I told him that he needed to fly to my base. He flew in the next morning. I got right down to business.

" 'Judge Gülpinar, the military is in a jam, but there is nothing we can do. We need the government to free some terrorists for humanitarian reasons.'

" 'Where do I fit in all of this, General Ersoy? he asked, looking surprised.

" ' I told him where; he knew the politicians who could make such a decision.'

" 'I have been out of the government business for three years. What makes you think I can influence anybody?'

" 'With your position in the Interior Department, you had the goods on some of these politicians. If anybody can, you are the one.'

"He rose from his chair. He told me there was no way he could pull off a thing like that.

"He was almost at the door. 'If you ever want to get Süheylā back, this is your opportunity, Judge Gülpinar.'

He turned around and looking pained, he stared at me. 'I don't think that will ever happen; she hates me.'

" 'I don't know about that, but here is an additional incentive for you. Do you remember Costa Rigas?' I saw him flinch.

" 'The girl that has been abducted is his daughter,' I continued. I let my words sink in and watched his face twitch. I told him the whole story about your wife Lale, how your daughter was lost for three years, and her subsequent abduction.

" 'I had no idea, General Ersoy. I read some bits and pieces in the newspaper but did not follow the news that closely. What a calamity.' He put his head down and paced around my office for a while. Finally, he looked straight at me. 'I will do my best, General,' he said, and flew back to Ankara."

"I am amazed that he would even try."

"Try? Judge Gülpinar was relentless. He finally managed to persuade the government to release three terrorists in good faith before the ransom was paid, with an additional three after that. It was all part of the deal; otherwise there would be no release, even if your daughter's life was in danger."

"So that's why her abductors gave up their demand for her release?"

"Yes. Judge Mehmet Gülpinar orchestrated the whole thing!"

"This is incredible, General Ersoy; I would never have known."

The general smiled. "I am so happy you have reconnected with your lost love."

"We plan to marry; will you come to our wedding?"

"Mrs. Ersoy and I would love to attend."

"I think Süheylā would love to see you, General."

He got up from his chair. "I must be going, Colonel Rigas. My staff and I are flying back to Diyarbakir tonight. I'll see you in a couple of months at the base."

"Thank you, General Ersoy, for all you have done. Go with God," said Costa and opened the door to let the general out.

Costa hurried up to his suite to get ready for the night.

Chapter 54: The Madonna

Costa was still in his suite when Süheylā rang.

"Excuse me, love. We have two more guests."

"Great! May I ask who they are?"

"They are a surprise."

"Okay; anything else?"

"One more thing!"

"Well hurry up, we are running out of time, Süheylā."

"I want you dressed in your uniform tonight; please indulge me."

"Ok, Süheylā."

She laughed, "and how do you want me dressed?"

He coughed, "ready for the bedroom!"

"Costa, I love you so much if I were near, I would do bad things to you!"

"You have to contain yourself …for a few hours, Süheylā."

"That long?" she sighed. "I will be in with Nilüfer a bit early to welcome our guests."

His mind began to wonder about the surprise guests. He called Mahmood, the catering manager, and asked him to add two more settings. He dressed in his uniform and took the elevator to the banquet hall. The private room looked great, and the table was perfect.

At seven-fifteen Süheylā walked into the room holding Nilüfer by the hand.

Seeing his daughter holding on Süheylā' hand, his heart skipped.

"Hello, my baby girl. Did you miss me?" he asked, lifting his daughter in his arms.

"Nilüfer squeezed her dad in return but almost immediately she begged for Süheylā.

"I give you my daughter for one afternoon and you steal her from me," Costa grumbled to Süheylā, who was sniggering.

She was dressed in soft white silk from head to toe; fluffy pantaloons furrowed above her ankles with golden straps, a low-cut shirt over the collar of a flowing body-length-maxi-coat with side cuts. Standing tall on her high heels, she was the angel of temptation. True to her promise, she slipped on a pair of white gloves.

Costa feasted his eyes. "Süheylā; you are truly a Madonna."

She placed her palm over her heart. "Oh Costa, I love that name more than anything else."

"I mean it; you are a Madonna in every way."

She eyed him seductively, "and you, love, are the handsomest prince."

He raised his eyebrows. "You mean colonel?"

"No, I mean prince. You are my Turkish, Greek, Kurdish and my American prince—all in one. And tonight love, I am going to peel off that uniform of yours and torment you," she smirked.

He gave her a kiss, "I will hold you to that, Madam… later."

Exactly at seven-thirty, the concierge ushered Gülēngül and Errol into the room. The two sisters hugged and kissed, giggling endlessly; Costa and Errol shook hands jovially.

"We should have a drink, Errol," suggested Costa.

"The way these sisters are acting tonight, we might need more than one. Do you know what they are up to, Costa?"

Pretending ignorance, Costa smiled, "I have no idea, Errol!"

The catering manager was standing nearby. "Mr. Mahmood, champagne for the ladies, orange juice for Nilüfer, and two double gin and tonics, please." He wanted to ask Süheylā what happened to the surprise guests, but the door opened and in walked Mrs. Sariyer.

"Mom, what a pleasant surprise," exclaimed Errol, casting an accusatory look toward Gülēngül.

"Sorry, darling," Gülēngül lilted as she rolled her tongue around her lips, looking at Errol seductively.

God help us, there goes another Süheylā; lucky Errol!

Mrs. Sariyer hugged her daughter-in-law and thanked her for the invitation. She gave Süheylā a big hug, too. Costa greeted Mrs. Sariyer with the Turkish customary kiss on both cheeks. Noticing Nilüfer tugging at Süheylā, Mrs. Sariyer shook took the little girl's hand. "What is your name," she asked, squeezing her cheek.

"Nilüfer," she replied, wrapping her arm around Süheylā's thigh.

"I am happy to meet you, Nilüfer. Do you like Istanbul?"

Nilüfer smiled and clapped her hands. Mrs. Sariyer put her palm on Nilüfer's face, gave the little girl a kiss, and turned to Errol. "It is about time you and Gülēngül got busy, my son," she scolded him lovingly. "I want a grandchild like Nilüfer; I am running out of time."

"It is up to Gülēngül, Mom," Errol apologized playfully.

"Just get busy, my son, please."

"Okay, Mom, you have our word," smiled Errol looking at Gülēngül, who curtsied suggestively.

Costa looked toward Süheylā and gave her a wink. *What is with you Turkish women? Can you get any sexier?*

"We have one more guest, Costa," winked Süheylā; he should be here any minute."

He had a hunch as to who it might be, but he asked anyway. "Anybody I know, Süheylā?"

Just at that point, Metin, the concierge, ushered in Judge Gülpinar. With the most surprised look on their faces, Costa and Errol stared at one another. The two sisters however rushed to their father and started to embrace him madly. Amidst tears, sobs, hugs and kisses, they were squeezing the man to death.

Finally, Süheylā let go of her father. "Costa love, although the two of you met this morning, this is my father, Judge Mehmet Gülpinar."

Costa shook the judge's hand for the second time today. "Süheylā had informed me she had a surprise guest, but I did not connect the dots. I am delighted to see you again, Judge Gülpinar."

"Thank you, Colonel Rigas; this is a very happy day in my life."

The judge was also delighted to see Mrs. Sariyer. "What a pleasure, Cihan," he smiled kindly, kissing her on both cheeks.

Mrs. Sariyer was delighted too. "I am happy to see you again, Mehmet. How many years has it been?"

He scratched his temple. "More than six; I think."

"Let's plan to see each other more often, Judge. Life is too short."

The judge turned around to hug his son-in-law, Errol. "Where is my grandchild?" he grumbled. "How long do I have to wait?"

"Not again, Judge. Mom just asked me the same thing a minute ago!"

During all this commotion, Nilüfer was eyeing the judge with curiosity. Judge Gülpinar was a distinguished patrician. In his mid-sixties, he cut an imposing figure. With a square jaw and a full set of grey hair, he looked like a seasoned movie star than a bureaucrat. When the judge noticed the little girl looking at him, he took a couple of steps toward her.

"Hello, Nilüfer," he smiled kindly. "I am her father," he said, pointing at Süheylā.

Nilüfer sized him up for a few seconds and noticing his friendly smile, extended her hand. With a surprised look, the judge took the little girl's hand warmly; he was touched. He leaned down, picked Nilüfer up in his arms, and gave her a hug. Nilüfer wrapped her arms around his neck and gave the judge a big squeeze in return. The judge looked as though he might melt. If there was any tension in the room, it disappeared quickly.

Holding Nilüfer, he turned toward Costa. "I am so glad you found your daughter, Colonel. I could not be any happier for you."

"Thank you, Judge. It looks like both of us have found our daughters."

The judge handed Nilüfer back to Costa to take his handkerchief to wipe his watery eyes. "Sorry, Colonel Rigas, I cannot help but be so emotional today."

Süheylā, who was standing nearby, "Dad, please don't cry; I love you."

That was what the judge Gülpinar needed to hear. He enfolded Süheylā in his arms and reached out for Gülēngül. The three of them were crying, again.

After a minute or so, the judge found his composure and begged for everybody's attention. "I am sorry for being such an emotional wreck," he apologized. "As I was on my way to the airport, the concierge informed me that there was a lady on the phone who wanted to talk to me urgently. When I heard Süheylā's voice, I nearly passed out. If that were not enough of a surprise, Gülēngül got on the other phone. The three of us talked for a long time. I checked back into my hotel and counted the minutes until I could not stand it any longer; I am so happy to be here."

Costa in the meantime was looking for a way to talk to the judge privately. The opportunity came when the judge left for the bathroom. Tactfully, Costa followed behind and stopped the judge in the hallway.

"Excuse me, Judge Gülpinar. Can I talk to you for a minute?" asked Costa politely.

The Judge looked at Costa, wondering.

"Judge Gülpinar, I want to thank you for saving my daughter's life," said Costa somberly.

The judge put his head down to think. "If you talked to General Ersoy, don't believe everything he says, Colonel. I am glad your daughter is with you; I am really happy."

"Thank you again, Judge Gülpinar, with all my heart."

"As I said, Colonel, I am really happy you have found your daughter. I am equally indebted to you for giving me my daughters back; I am the one who owes you thanks."

Costa was touched. "You are a noble man, Judge. I'll always be grateful."

"Thank you Colonel Rigas. Please get back to Süheylā before she gets suspicious."

"You secret is safe with me Judge; although someday I am going have to tell her."

"She will figure things on her own Colonel Rigas. Nothing gets by that girl. You know that."

"Yes, I do," replied Costa, and went back into the room.

The minute he entered, he saw Süheylā's inquisitive face and scrambled for something to say. Luckily, Mahmood came to his rescue.

"The chef advises that dinner will be ready in ten minutes, Colonel. Here are the place cards."

"Thank you Mahmood," replied Costa, winking at Süheylā.

She winked back, "are you going to tell me, Costa?"

"I will love, but not tonight. Let me arrange these place cards."

Nilüfer was to his left, Süheylā to his right, Judge Gülpinar between his two daughters, followed by Errol and Mrs. Sariyer. Finally, when everyone settled down, Costa looked at Süheylā, who chimed her glass.

"Süheylā and I want to thank you for coming," Costa spoke humbly. "It is an honor to have all of you here. Please, enjoy dinner."

Divan Hotel had a reputation for great food. The dinner was excellent, and the conversation was even better. Judge Gülpinar and his daughters were talking nonstop; they had a lot to catch on.

The different Turkish wines were excellent, but Judge Gülpinar chose to drink raki, the Turkish national spirit. In spite of his jovial mood, he drank moderately. He had the manners of a prince.

At mid-point through dessert, Süheylā chimed her glass again to get everybody's attention. She planted a kiss on Costa and stood up.

"Costa and I have an announcement to make," she said slowly. "As all of you know, Costa and I fell in love long ago. After we lost one another—twenty years ago to be exact—our separate lives took so many turns, it is too painful to think about it. When I saw him two days ago, I feared my heart was going to burst." She paused to take a sip of water, trying to hold back her tears.

"Just a few hours ago Costa asked me to marry him."

Up to this point, she was wearing her gloves. Now she took them off. Lifting her hand, she exposed the diamond ring for all to see. "This ring on my finger, Costa bought it when he planned to propose to me some twenty years ago, but he never got the chance. He proposed today, and I have accepted." She turned to Costa, and they kissed to thunderous applause and well wishes.

Süheylā disappeared into her father's arms as tears of joy ran down their faces. Reluctantly the judge let go of his daughter, and reached out to shake Costa's hand.

"I will be honored to be your father-in-law, Colonel Rigas. You are the only man she ever loved. You have delivered my daughter back to me, and I thank you."

Costa was at a loss for words. Thankfully, Errol jostled behind the judge to offer his congratulations. With Gülēngül and Mrs. Sariyer in line, it took several minutes for things to subside. Finally, Costa found his voice.

"I want to apologize to Süheylā for making her wait so long. It was a most trying time."

He bent down and lifted Nilüfer in his arms. "When I recovered my daughter, it was one of the happiest days of my life." He pecked Nilüfer on the cheek and looked at Süheylā, lovingly. "Finding Süheylā is my dream-come-true."

Everyone clapped except Judge Gülpinar, who was now in shreds. Gülēngül wrapped her arms around him tenderly. The judge patted her on the cheek and stood up, smiling.

This time he beckoned Costa and Süheylā into his arms and kissed them. Finally, he sat down, looking happily spent.

Nilüfer, who was trying to grasp all the fuss, tugged on her father's arm.

"This is your mom, Nilüfer," said Costa, pointing to Süheylā.

Nilüfer scrunched up her face and begged into Süheylā's arms, squeezing her hard.

"I am not through yet," smiled Süheylā," as she stood Nilüfer onto her chair. She reached into her purse to take out a small box. "Before I hand my special gift to Costa, I want to thank Errol for spending his afternoon to expedite it." She blew Errol a kiss and handed Costa the box. "For you, my love."

Costa took the box, pulled off the ribbon, and opened it. Hanging on a chain was a golden medallion of Santa Sophia with the four minarets. Etched in the back was Süheylā's silhouette with this inscription:

To Costa.
The love of my life.
Süheylā.

The medallion was an exact replica of the one the customs inspector had confiscated from Costa some twenty years earlier. With tears of joy, he opened his arms and swamped her. Their embrace was long and tender as

384

both sobbed. There was not a dry eye around, except Nilüfer, who was clapping wildly.

Finally things subsided, and the judge, ever so tactful, said, "your love for one another leaves me speechless." For one more time, his handkerchief came in handy as he managed a happy smile. "As I told you before, I am a total wreck, but now I am anxious; when is the wedding?"

Costa looked at Süheylā for help.

"Dad, we have not set a date yet. Costa asked me to marry him just a few hours ago."

"Your Honor," smiled Costa. "We've waited more than twenty years. I can assure you it will not take that long."

Everybody laughed, but the judge had another question. "Can I ask a favor?"

"Anything, Dad," replied Süheylā, giving him a kiss.

The judge cleared his throat, "it would be my fondest wish that the wedding take place in Turkey."

Süheylā searched Costa's face.

Costa wrapped his arm around her waist. "We could not think of a better place, Judge; don't you think, love?"

"That is perfect," she whispered.

"USA is my adopted country, but Turkey is still my homeland," said Costa nostalgically. His old country was clawing back into his heart.

The judge clapped his hands enthusiastically. "Bravo. Bravo."

"Süheylā and I would not want to marry anywhere else, but Istanbul," Costa continued. "With Süheylā's permission we will let you choose the place for the reception, Judge," Costa offered, looking at Süheylā, who nodded in agreement.

The judge was elated. Once more, he raised his glass. "To Süheylā and Costa; I salute you and wish you all the best."

"As Süheylā said, we have not set a date yet, but I know where we would like to have our wedding ceremony; I am sure Süheylā will agree," beamed Costa looking at Süheylā, adoringly.

Süheylā raised her eyebrows.

"There is a place by a beach," continued Costa. "It is the very spot where Süheylā and I promised to marry each other. It is the beach of Kilyos," he added, looking deeply into Süheylā's eyes.

"That is the greatest place I could ever think of, love," she quivered and fell into his arms, whispering,

"Welcome home, Costa, I love you."

Paralogue

An Ottoman Firman:

In the name of our Esteemed Sultan Suleiman, I challenge the island of Imvros to produce their strongest man to wrestle my champion. If my champion wins, the island will have to offer six virgins (one from every village) for the Sultan's harem; and if he loses, the local champion will be entitled to wed any local virgin he chooses, while I would be providing the dowry. If the island does not agree, my fleet will sack the island for three days."

Hayreddin Barbarossa / the Admiral of the Ottoman Empire.

With an epidemic raging through his fleet, the admiral, fearing the spread of the disease, did not want to return to Istanbul. Instead, he decided to winter over on the island of Imvros. Aware of the mythical reputation of the beautiful women of the island and its strong men, a wrestling match would be a great opportunity to entertain his troops. The admiral was speaking on behalf of the Buyük Effendi[92]; disregard of his firman meant severe punishment, even death.

This was a calamity. The island of Imvros was now under Ottoman occupation, and worse, their daughters were slated to become concubines in the sultan's harem.

Town criers set out to the villages to announce the firman. In the village of Agridia[93], someone suggested Eurelaos, the stonemason, a young man of mythical strength. Last fall, Eurelaos had carried a loaded jackass on his shoulders all the way up a hill. Apparently, the pack animal, laden with hewn stones, got stuck in the

---

92. The big boss.
93. Little fields.

mud. A delegation went out to beg Eurelaos to accept the challenge, but he refused. When they told him that Penelope, the mayor's daughter, was one of the virgins slated for the Sultan's harem, he immediately changed his mind; he and Penelope were in love. In the mind of Eurelaos, it would a shame not to defend the honor of his beloved. Now this stonemason was a powerful young man, but he was no wrestler; the chance that he would defeat the admiral's champion was nil, but with Penelope in peril, he had no choice. By the third day, as the Admiral had demanded, the match was set. With much consternation, the people of the island descended to the shore to witness this ominous event. If Eurelaos lost, their daughters would be carted off for the sultan's harem in Istanbul, never to be seen again. After some preliminary events, such as monkey jumping, bear dancing and a magic show, it was time for the main event.

With huge thighs and muscular biceps, the powerful giant champion wrestler walked into the ring first. With long handlebars of a mustache, a shaved head and large bulging eyes, he looked like a monster. When he saw Eurelaos enter the ring at the opposite end, the giant let out an ear-splitting jeer, frightening everybody to death.

Eurelaos waddled into the ring like a duck. His arms aimlessly hung about his shoulders while his large hands looked like stiff claws. Although shorter and stockier than the wrestler, his barrel chest glistening with oil made him look like a clown, eliciting more jeers from the giant. Unsure and clumsy, Eurelaos stared back at the giant innocently, and even smiled.

The trumpet sounded for the Admiral's entry. No contest would ever start without *His Presence*. Dressed in flowing robes and followed by an entourage of several lieutenants, the Admiral entered the huge tent, looking magnificent. As he sat, the champion wrestler made a protracted genuflection toward his patron, the Admiral; Eurelaos' imitation of the giant's move was so comical, it elicited giggles from the crowd and a smile from the Admiral.

For the second time, the trumpeter sounded for the start of the match. Within a blink of an eye, the giant took a couple of steps toward Eurelaos, spun on his heels and leveled a hard elbow to his chest. Eurelaos doubled up, gasping for air. A ferocious kick in the middle of the stomach sent Eurelaos sprawling on the ground several feet away. Flexing his biceps, the giant bowed to the Admiral who waved back in admiration. Just as the giant turned around, Eurelaos charged. The experienced giant took a side step and belted Eurelaos square in his face, dispatching him to the dirt once more. The crowd recoiled in horror.

The giant leaped toward the helpless Eurelaos, but adeptly, Eurelaos rolled off to his side and the giant hit the dirt. Surprised, the giant sprung to his feet staring at Eurelaos with contempt. Although bleeding from his nose, Eurelaos dusted himself off and made an obscene gesture. Never expecting such an insult, especially in the presence of the Admiral, the giant charged like a mad bull. Eurelaos sidestepped and leveled a hard blow on the giant's neck, which sent him tumbling out of the ring. The Admiral leaped to his feet in amazement.

Finding himself out of the ring was an embarrassment. The giant jumped back into the ring and shook his fist at Eurelaos menacingly. Cunningly, he grabbed a handful of dirt and flung it into the eyes of Eurelaos. The crowd held their breath as Eurelaos stumbled about the ring half-blind; this was not in the rules and the only one that could enforce them was the Admiral, but he remained impassive. Quick as lightning, the giant snuck behind Eurelaos and put him in chokehold.

Even though Eurelaos was half-blind, at least he now knew where his opponent was. The more the giant pressed, the more Eurelaos endured and fought back. His strength was Herculean; the giant was having a hard time breaking him. Perspiration began to trickle down the giant's face. In a cat-like move, Eurelaos bent forward and heaved the giant over his head and onto the ground. The crowd roared in excitement, but Eurelaos still dazed from the chokehold was gasping for air. This gave the giant a bit of a time to get back to his feet again. With eyes bulging with rage, he charged again, but Eurelaos sidestepped and leveled a ferocious kick into the giant's middle. This sent the giant tumbling to the ground once more. The crowd held their breath.

Frothing with rage, the giant leaped to his feet like a gorilla and lunged at Eurelaos, scowling. Eurelaos met his charge and, thrusting his hand forward with force, he sank his powerful fingers into the giant's belly; it was as though an eagle had grabbed its prey with its talons. Blinking in terror, the giant let out a mournful yelp as Eurelaos started to pull him around the ring from his huge belly like a puppet. The more they moved, the more the giant tried to free himself anyway he could, but Eurelaos' claw was unbendable.

The two wrestlers danced around the ring for a while; Eurelaos pulling the giant from his stomach and the giant desperately trying to free himself from this death grasp. Blood began to spurt out of the giant's belly. In desperation, he attempted to trip Eurelaos, but he lost his balance and fell backward. His belly, still hooked by Eurelaos' claw, suddenly ripped open, spilling the giant's intestines all over. The giant let out thunderous cry. With eyes glazed with fear, he knelt on the ground and valiantly attempted to stuff his intestines back into his stomach.

The Admiral, shaken, leaped to his feet once more in utter astonishment. The crowed smelled blood and let out a tremendous roar. In their frenzy, they extolled Eurelaos to finish the giant off, but Eurelaos did not even hear them; he stood in the middle of the tent and stared at the giant in horror. Finally and clumsily, he bowed to the

Admiral and started to walk away, but the Admiral stopped him. Dispatching one of his lieutenants to hand him a scimitar, he ordered Eurelaos to finish off his champion wrestler.

Eurelaos was aghast. He had never killed anyone before. With outstretched arms, he begged the Admiral to spare him the horror. Looking annoyed, the Admiral stepped into ring, unsheathed his own scimitar, and with one chop, hacked off the giant's head. He then ordered Eurelaos to parade the severed head around the tent.

Eurelaos heard the delirium of the crowd and took heart. Reluctantly, he picked up the giant's head, raised it above his shoulders, and walked around in triumph, looking like Cerberus[94].

The crowd went wild with joy; they had just realized that their island might be safe and that their daughters would remain unmolested. After a few minutes of this macabre scene, the Admiral stood up and raised his hand in a motion of silence.

"I congratulate the people of Imvros for producing such a man as Eurelaos. I am putting the island under my protection. Eurelaos is free to marry whom he pleases. In the name of our Illustrious Sultan, I am providing the dowry. I also entrust my friend Galib[95] to the care of the island."

Admiral Barbarossa returned the following year to collect his ailing lover, Galib. Unfortunately, Galib succumbed to the epidemic. Nonetheless, Barbarossa was appreciative of the hospitality shown to him and his fleet

---

94. The two-headed dog that guarded the gates of Hades.

95. He was the admiral's lover. During those times, for superstitious reasons women were not permitted to travel in any war vessel, as they were considered bad luck. It was the practice of Eastern rulers to have male lovers who were primarily eunuchs. Galib was Barbarossa's lover. The handsome eunuch was ailing from the same epidemic that afflicted the Otoman fleet.

by the people of Imvros. In gratitude and in the name of Sultan Suleiman the Magnificent, he decreed the island exempt from all taxation. He also built a monument in honor of Galib, which still stands today. The Imvrians, ever so grateful for the Admiral's generosity, honored Galib by building a small chapel and because of their Christian sensibilities, they named it Santa Calliope, the closest female Greek synonym to "Galib." This synophonic[96] name somehow couched the fact that Barbarossa's lover was a male.

Such was the legend of Eurelaos, the stonemason, who, for his love for Penelope, tackled the impossible. After five-hundred-fifty years, the legend of Admiral Barbarossa still lives in the hearts and minds of the few remaining Greek natives of Imvros.

The name "Imvros' was given to the island by its first known king, Imvranos. During the Trojan War between the Greeks and the Trojans, the island was an ally of the Trojans. By the fifth century B.C., Imvros was a colony of the ancient city-state of Athens. Like most of its sister islands of the Aegean, Imvros suffered invasions from the Persians, the Romans, the Avars, the Slavs and the Venetians, but none as enduring as that of the Ottoman Turks, whose occupation lasted more than six centuries. Imvros today is a permanent territory of Turkey, the successor to the Ottoman Empire.

Located about 25 miles southwest of the Dardanelles (Çanakkale), the island of Imvros officially was renamed Gökçeada on July 29, 1970. It is the largest island of Turkey. It is located in the Aegean Sea at the entrance of Saros Bay; it is the westernmost point of Turkey. Imvros has an area of 279km^2 (108 sq. mi).

For a brief period between November 1912 and September 1923, Imvros, together with Tenedos, were

---

96. Having the same sound.

under Greek administration. Both islands were overwhelmingly Greek, and in the case of Imvros, the population was Greek. After the Greco-Turkish War ended in Greek defeat in Anatolia, under the Treaty of Lausanne, Greece ceded back the island to Turkey with the guarantee of a special autonomous, administrative status.

However, shortly after the legislation of "Civil Law" on 26 June 1927 (Mahalli Idareler Kanunu), the rights accorded to the Greek population of Imvros and Tenedos were revoked, in violation of the Lausanne Treaty. Thus, the island was demoted from an administrative district to a sub district, which resulted in the island being stripped of its local tribunals. Moreover, the candidates for the local council were obliged to have adequate knowledge of the Turkish language, which meant that the vast majority of the islanders were excluded. Furthermore, according to this law, the Turkish government retained the right to dissolve this council, and in certain circumstances, to introduce police force and other officials that were non-islanders. This law also violated the educational rights of the local community and imposed an educational system similar to that followed by ordinary Turkish schools.

The first concrete sign of Turkification policy occurred in 1946, when the Turkish authorities installed the first wave of Turkish settlers from the Black Sea region. Mass-scale persecution of the local Greek element started in 1961 as part of the *Eritme Programmi* operation, which aimed at the elimination of Greek education and the enforcement of economic, psychological pressure and violence. Under these conditions, the Turkish government approved the appropriation of the 90% of the cultivated areas of the island and the settlement of additional 6,000 ethnic Turks from mainland Turkey. In addition, Turkey began using the island as a heavy penitentiary with the ulterior motive to intimidate the Imvrians into abandoning their homes. Hard-core criminals were allowed to roam free. Murders and robberies became routine, and the islanders were defenseless. The body of a shopkeeper—missing for months—was discovered dumped in a well. He had been sexually assaulted and his head was partially severed. Several women were raped, and two of the husbands committed suicide. Intimidation, confiscation of property, systemic terror and violent criminal acts by Turkish hoodlums became the norm.

Additional population settlements from Anatolia occurred in 1973, 1984 and 2000. The state provided special credit opportunities and agricultural aid to those who elected to settle in the island. The indigenous Greek population, finding itself deprived of its means of production and facing hostile behavior from the Turkish government and the newly arrived settlers, left in droves. The peak of this exodus was in 1974. Within a span of fifteen years, the population dropped from 10,000 Greeks to only 300 on the entire island. It has been repopulated by about ten-thousand Turks.

The author of this novel is an expatriate of Imvros, who, like some of his fellow Imvrians, has found a home in the USA. Spanning the course of two and a half decades, this a para-historical novel, centered on the quadrangle of Imvros (Gokceada), Troy, the city of Istanbul and the USA. In spite of its many trials and drama, it aims to tame human cruelty, keeping love as the ultimate shield against human excess.

In the opinion to this author, all sins are forgivable as long as the offender shows an ounce of contrition, but so far, Turkey has failed miserably in this regard. Forcing people to abandon their lands and homes, and then claiming ownership on legal grounds, is contrived evil. Refusing to let them speak their own language is a depraved human behavior. Nonetheless, the perpetuation of hatred and the pursuit of revenge are futile traits of human weakness, while redress of past injustices is cathartic. In addition, ethnic hatred, national purity, territorial expansion, jingoism, economic group affiliations, vengeance and religious beliefs are all liabilities that hinder human progress. Foreswearing allegiance to one's own race, religion, culture, and homeland, and the determination to seek the truth might be the ultimate sacrifice for global peace.

The author advocates justice, urging Turkey to compensate all Imvrians for infliction of pain, displacement and restore all their property rights, regardless of fabricated legalities. In addition, Turkey should restore the full Turkish citizenship of all Imvrians and Tenedians. This author not only remains optimistic, but he also thankful that under the leadership of the current Prime Minister Tayyib Erdoğan, Turkey's militant stance against all minorities has softened and made more progress than any other Turkish government since 1921. However not all these changes are adequate or fast enough. The complete restoration of the rights of these minorities would be Turkey's finest hour.